Dream Whisperer

By

Daniel Draym

ISBN: 9798631583740
Imprint: Independently published

PART 1

Prologue

Compared to Vienna, Sarajevo was a hole in the ground. Its Kafe Zemljak was modelled after Café Landtmann, next to the Burgtheater in the Habsburg capital. It was a tad less grand but not for want of trying. Kafe Zemljak had high ceilings and dark wood panelling. The place was famous for its thick, strong Bosnian coffee served in a copper can, accompanied by rosewater-flavoured *lokum*. Its haughty waiters in black tie observed the scarce clientele's every move. It was a slow evening. The real action took place in the back room. Despite its sedate outlook, the café provided a meeting space for seditious Bosnian Serbs. The insurrectionists agitated against the Kaiserliche und Königliche Doppelmonarchie — the Austro-Hungarian Empire and its Habsburg rulers — which occupied their country since the Congress of Berlin in 1878. The room's two exits into the warren of streets behind the café were an asset in a city where police raids were both frequent and brutal.

The man on the podium was a greying seventy-year-old. He wore a black *šajkača* cap — a nationalist symbol named after the Serb troops that had fought off the Ottomans on the banks of the Danube and the Sava River to safeguard the Austrian Empire two centuries ago. The cap was a reminder to the Austrian authorities of how poorly the Empire had rewarded the Bosnian Serbs for their loyal services.

The speaker was an hour into his speech and getting tired. Not that it mattered much. There was no need to convince his audience. They all felt the Empire treated Bosnian Serbs as second-rate citizens.

The Hungarians had obtained self-rule half a century ago. If the emperor wanted their support on any matter, he needed explicit approval by the Hungarian parliament and government. No such courtesy had ever been extended to the Bosnian Serbs, regardless of their merits in defending the realm. They expected nothing from Emperor Franz Joseph. The old goat had been in power for sixty-six years and was stone deaf to their legitimate demands for more autonomy. His fat nephew Archduke Franz Ferdinand, who also happened to be the heir presumptive, appeared to show more understanding for their grievances. But could they expect *any* scion of the House of Habsburg to yield to their demands? The question was ridiculous. Ever since the Napoleonic wars, the Habsburgs' reign had been in steady decline. That only made them hold on to power even more stubbornly. No, the Bosnian Serbs' future didn't lie within the confines of the Habsburg Empire. Outside help was required. The Kingdoms of Serbia and Bulgaria were natural Slavic allies. The Russian Tsar also appeared eager for an opportunity to take a bite out of the Doppelmonarchie's flank and — as an additional bonus — to push the Ottomans back to Constantinople.

The silent audience, which filled the room to half capacity, listened politely. About eighty men were present. Some dressed in traditional gear like the speaker. The majority wore cheap, dark suits. Most of their clothes were the worse for wear. Times were hard.

There was *one* woman in the room. She was sitting front centre. No one seemed to notice her, although she was conspicuously out of place. She had outspoken Aryan features — not a drop of Slavic blood in *her* veins — and dressed expensively in the latest Viennese fashion. Her chequered, black and white silk dress was designed by Emilie Flöge. The matching hat was an equally exquisite creation — a broad-rimmed *canotier* of black crinoline braid from the trendy Mühlbauer Hutmanufaktur. Her outfit cost more than the combined monthly wages of all the men present in the room.

She was looking at the speaker with a vacant expression. Her eyes were deep blue, sometimes changing inexplicably towards violet tinged with red. The orator was sweating. The limited eloquence he'd mustered at the beginning of his speech had declined into a breathless mumble. Though the woman focused all her attention on him, she had no use for the man. He'd be dead in less than five months. A fledgling cancerous tumour nested in the lower half of his left lung, she knew. Pea-sized now, it would develop in the coming weeks at an alarming rate into sprawling carcinoma. Then it would start spreading to other parts of the body — the right lung, the liver, the kidneys, the brain. In its final stage, it would transform into bone cancer. Its victim's last weeks would be a living hell of ceaseless pain.

The young man sitting to her left was the real reason for her presence. He'd never met her. Even though the room was almost empty upon his arrival, he'd chosen the chair next to hers without hesitation. He hadn't nodded or looked at her. They'd been sitting next to each other for twenty minutes in complete silence before the speaker started his introduction.

The man wasn't much to look at. He was short and narrow-shouldered. His eyes were deep-set and had dark circles; his nose was too big for the thin face with jutting cheekbones. He tried to dress like a dandy but lacked the means to pull it off. His most distinctive feature was a pencil-thin moustache, which contrasted sharply with the bushy extravaganzas sported by the other men.

The tiring speaker paused to pour himself a glass of water when a young man came barging into the room, yelling, 'Get out! The coppers are coming!'

The youngster had been loitering across the street, acting as a lookout. He'd seen a group of twelve uniformed policemen turning the corner, marching in the direction of Kafe Zemljak, truncheons at the ready.

The men in the room bolted in a panic towards the two back exits, left and right of the podium. In the melee, the younger men shoved aside the elderly. The doorways were too narrow to facilitate a speedy escape. Most of the attendees were struggling to get to the doors as the police rushed in.

The short man took advantage of his front-row seat to reach the left exit as one of the first, only to be elbowed aside by somebody much larger than he. A blow to the throat left him momentarily breathless before he tried to push through the door again. He put his hand in his trouser pocket to retrieve his knuckle duster and punched the man in front of him in the kidneys.

Constables were clubbing down the laggards in the room and moved towards the crowd near the exits. Fifteen men had escaped; the rest were engaged in a chaotic hand-to-hand scuffle with the law. Several men lay cowering on the floor, bleeding from head injuries. The woman was nowhere to be seen.

When a police officer grabbed the person in front of him by the scruff and yanked him backwards, the short man saw his chance. He ducked and weaved his way through the doorway. Disoriented, he hesitated briefly before running away, turning left and right to throw the police off his trail. The cop whistles came from everywhere;

the sound of hobnailed boots pounding the pavement closed in on him quickly. The fugitive risked a look over his shoulder and saw a huge brute barely thirty feet behind him. He was no match for this colossus — there was no way he could outrun or outfight him. Panic dug its sharp claws into his brain, but fear didn't give him wings. Fatigue was getting hold of him. His legs felt like flannel, and his laboured breathing scorched his windpipe. Five steps after he'd turned the next corner, he was pulled off the street inside a house.

The front door remained partially open. When the policeman reached the spot, he stopped and peered into the semidarkness of the hallway, looking straight at the short man. Then he turned on his heels and ran on.

The chased man couldn't believe his eyes. What had just happened? Panting, he turned to see who'd pulled him inside. It was the woman he'd been sitting next to during the meeting. He looked at her, confused, not recognising her. She was almost a head taller than he and dressed like nobody he'd ever met. She looked composed. There was no indication she'd ran a four-hundred-yard dash in high heels. And how could she have been strong enough to pull a running man — even a lightweight like him — into the house?

She stared down at him with a mocking smile.

'Don't you think you should stop wasting your time listening to old men's speeches?' she asked him in accentless Serbian.

The woman was a total stranger. Her opinion shouldn't have mattered to him, but her remark cut him to the bone. She made him feel like he somehow needed to justify himself. He wanted to tell her he'd tried damned hard to be a soldier. He'd attempted several times to get accepted by the Black Hand in Belgrade — the secret military organisation that aimed to unite all South Slavic territories. Each time, they had rejected him because of his diminutive stature. He'd been able to join the Srpska Revolu-cionarna Organizacija and had trained with them in hand-to-hand combat, learnt to use firearms, and how to make bombs, and then: nothing. Nothing had ever happened. Not once had they called him into action. He'd been to more secret meetings than he cared to count, and it was all talk, talk, nothing but talk. It was frustrating. Though he yearned to make his mark on history, he'd found himself forever relegated to the sidelines — always an observer, never a player. He was nineteen, and his time was already running out. Each morning, he coughed up phlegm laced with blood. He knew he suffered from consumption; he didn't have long to live.

He looked into her eyes and knew she understood. She felt his anger, his hatred, his impotence. He wanted her to like him; he wanted to make her proud. In the doorway's feeble light, he fell under her spell. He was her slave. Her mesmerising eyes of ever-changing colours looked right into his tormented soul.

He closed his eyes and let himself be carried by her musky perfume. She smelt of the Nordic snowy pine forests. He sensed the hungry wolves marauding among the trees and their prey's feverish heartbeat, the smell of blood coursing right beneath the skin. He felt another pres-ence, older than the trees or even the snow on the moun-taintops, powerful and oppressive. The scent deepened. It turned resinous, flavoured with southern aromas — myrrh, cinnamon, and undertones of cardamom. The landscape changed: a blistering sun, vast expanses of sand, utter emp-tiness devoid of life, except for the occasional slithering beast. Through the radiating heat, he saw a dark presence shimmering in and out of existence — like a fata morgana, a wordless enchantment made of hot air. It was unbear-able, and it felt like home.

Opening his eyes again, he was flustered and soaked in sweat.

'Gavrilo, be the change you want to see in the world,' she whispered.

She touched his cheek with her gloved right hand and pressed a light kiss on his lips, a sweet promise of more to come.

Sarajevo

Sunday, 28 June 1914

Ever since his meeting with the mysterious lady, Gavrilo Princip had the weirdest nightmares that woke him up screaming in the middle of the night. Sitting up in bed — gasping for air, eyes wide open in the dark — eerie images still haunted his memories. Even walking the streets of Sarajevo, he felt there was always something watching him — a dark shadow hovering at the edges of his perception.

He tried to convince himself he was being paranoid. After his flight from Kafe Zemljak, he took matters into his own hands. He contacted a couple of fellow Bosnian Serbs he knew from earlier secret meetings, and who were more or less his age.

Trifko Grabež was a hothead who'd been expelled from school after striking a teacher. He quickly radicalised, and the Black Hand accepted him as a member. Still, he too was champing at the bit, as impatient and frustrated as Princip.

Nedeljko Čabrinović had run away from home and dropped out of school because of his abusive father. He couldn't hold a job for long, and his work in the printing industry paid poorly. Čabrinović was more of a thinker than the other two and avidly read Marxist literature. As he always felt exploited, the youth was fertile soil for incendiary, left-wing ideas. He loathed the Austrians and had been a natural recruit for the Black Hand.

The three of them were teenage rebels with a cause, aching for action.

When the newspapers announced Archduke Franz Ferdinand's visit to Sarajevo, it took them little discussion to decide they'd kill him. They needed explosives and guns. Princip spoke of their plans to a local man who was well-connected with the Black Hand's higher echelons. To their surprise, Major Vojislav Tankosić himself came through. He was the right-hand man of the head of the Black Hand — Colonel Dragutin Dimitrijević of the Serbian army, who hid behind the codename Apis.

Tankosić had been involved in several violent operations. Famously, he was one of the army officers who'd participated in the May Coup in 1903, which ended the reign of the unpopular Serbian King Alexander. The royal couple were murdered in their palace and then tossed out of a window on a manure pile. Tankosić himself executed the queen's two brothers. Moreover, he'd become a spymaster. He'd established a network of thousands of Bosnian Serbs after the Austrian-Hungarian Empire annexed Bosnia-Herzegovina in 1908.

Princip and his two friends were awestruck in his presence. Tankosić was a sharp dresser and sported a fierce handlebar moustache. Even in civilian clothes, his ramrod demeanour, brusque manners, and authoritative speech gave him away as an army officer. He had the cold look of a fanatic. Tankosić had also been plotting an assassination attempt on the archduke with four other Bosnian Serbs, and he embraced the opportunity to enlarge his team.

The three would-be assassins were called to Belgrade for firearms training. The first morning, Tankosić put apples on their heads. He ordered them to stand still, and then — cocksure, at a twenty-pace distance — shot the apples clean off, barely taking the time to aim. Grabež pissed his pants, and Čabrinović threw up. Princip thought he'd faint, but he stayed on his feet, looking more composed than he felt.

• 'Never think while pulling the trigger,' Tankosić told them. 'A man who thinks is a worthless killer. Your mind needs to be a complete blank. You mustn't even be aware there's a gun in your hand. The gun is part of your body; it'll fire at whatever you focus your eyes on. There's only you and the target. The rest of the world doesn't exist.'

Tankosić was a harsh taskmaster. The training was relentless. After three days, Princip proved to be a reasonably accurate shot. He was able to hit a moving target while running. The major grabbed him by the shoulders and looked him straight in the eye.

'You'll do fine,' he said. 'Just fine.'

Tankosić provided the assassination team with six hand grenades and four Browning FN Model 1910 pistols with .380 ACP rounds. In case they were captured, he handed them suicide pills. A map of Sarajevo showed the archduke's planned route and the spots where policemen would stand guard. Franz Ferdinand would use an open motorcar. That made him a sitting duck for anybody with the nerve to throw a bomb or pull a trigger. The assassins planned a gauntlet of successive attacks — if the first one didn't succeed, the next one would. It was a foregone conclusion that the operation would be a success.

Princip was over the moon. This was what he was born to do.

The morning of the long-awaited day turned into a terrible disillusion.

It was a bright and cloudless Sunday. Throngs of excited spectators lined the road from an early hour. After the archduke and his party arrived in Sarajevo by train, officials immediately led them to their respective automobiles.

Franz Ferdinand and his wife, Duchess Sophie von Chotkow und Wognin, shared the third car in the motorcade — a large, dark-green convertible Gräf & Stift 28/32 PS Double Phaeton — with Governor Oskar Potiorek and Lieutenant Colonel Count Franz von Harrach. Security was a shambles. The local military commander had pleaded to line the route with soldiers, but the city councillors refused to go along with this scheme. They feared the citizens would consider such draconian measures an affront to their loyalty to the Crown. At long last, the council decided not to deploy the army at all and put local police in charge of security. The policemen were inadequate for the task. They neither had the training nor the manpower to guarantee the archduke's safety.

The motorcade slowly drove down the Appel Quay bordering the Miljacka River. When it passed the first two assassins — one armed with a bomb and the other with a gun — both men lost their nerve and failed to act. Čabrinović — armed with a bomb — was the third assassin in the gauntlet. Nervously, he pulled the pin on the grenade and then fumbled his throw. The bomb bounced off the Gräf & Stift's retracted soft top and rolled under the next car where it detonated. The explosion tore the car apart, wounding two officers. A hail of shrapnel cut into the onlookers alongside the road.

A large woman standing next to Čabrinović received a glancing blow to the forehead from a random piece of metal. She sagged in her husband's arms, bleeding from a deep cut right below the hairline. By now, two men were tugging at Čabrinović's coat, calling to others for help. He struck one of the men on the jaw with a wild swing and tore himself free. He pushed two others out of the way, swallowed his suicide pill, and jumped into the river. Čabrinović landed hard. The water was only four inches deep. He crawled back to his feet, retching, nauseous, and dizzy. Pain shot up from his left ankle. He went back down on one knee, bile dripping from his mouth. Two policemen and some other bystanders jumped in the river and pinned him down in the shallow water. He was dry-heaving; his vision became blurred. He didn't die. The poison pill was so far past its sell-by-date that the cyanide failed to work.

In the meantime, the archduke's chauffeur had floored the gas pedal. He sped down the quay in the direction of the city hall. The governor had jumped up from his seat and acted as a human shield for his guests. Shoved back and forth in the swirling crowd, none of the other assassins were able to make another attempt on the archduke's life. Franz Ferdinand looked over his shoulder at the exploded car's smouldering wreck. He held his wife's hand tight; the duchess blankly stared ahead, in shocked silence.

The chaos was deafening. The grenade had injured over twenty people. Constables milled about in total panic, shouting out orders heeded by no one. Bystanders tried to get away from the place of the explosion while others wanted to get closer to have a better view of the carnage. They spilt from the pavement onto the street, trampling one another and preventing any medical services from reaching the victims.

Princip, who was the second-to-last assassin of the set-up, had taken up a position near the Lateiner Bridge. He'd lost sight of his companions in the melee and was cursing his bad luck. He'd seen Čabrinović apprehended in the river. The police didn't make any efforts to determine whether there were still other would-be assassins in the crowd. A few clueless coppers were trying to clear the street to little avail. Princip's head was buzzing. He knew that, after the ceremony in the city hall, the archduke was scheduled to head back down Appel Quay and then make a right turn into Franz Joseph Street, right where Princip was standing now. No doubt the botched attack had messed up the official planning. It was impossible to know whether the archduke would come back and if so, when and via which route.

A coughing spasm shook his frail frame. Princip wiped his mouth and noticed traces of blood on his hand. He spat on the pavement. The world slowed down. His vision clouded, and the street noises receded until they were but a dim buzz. All he heard was the dull, deafening thud of his irregular heartbeat. His mind went blank, and then he found himself standing on a vast, empty square. A blinding, white sun bore down on him. The temperature was blistering. He felt his skin tightening, and the scorching air seared his lungs with every gasping breath. It felt as if each gulp of oxygen cauterised the micro-lacerations deep in his pulmonary tissue. In front of him hovered an indefinable presence — an obsidian hole of sheer nothingness, deep as space. Carmine eyes peered out at him.

'Cross the street and wait there,' a soothing woman's voice whispered.

When he opened his eyes again, a concerned elderly man stood over him.

'Are you all right, my boy?' the pensioner asked.

'Yes..., yes, I'm fine,' Princip assured him, blinking. 'My blood pressure's probably a bit low. I think I've been standing too long in the sun. Thanks for your concern; I'm quite all right now.'

'You need to drink some water, son. You look parched. And eat! Put some meat on those bones,' the man advised and stretched out his hand to help the youngster stand up.

Princip thanked him once more and crossed the road. He felt whether he still had his gun in his pocket. It was there, a silent reminder of what he'd set out to do on this Sunday morning. On the corner of Appel Quay and Franz Joseph Street stood Moritz Schiller's Delicatessen. Princip hesitated. He could use a drink and a bite. Then he thought better of it and posted himself right in front of the café.

Schiller's was bustling with people. A line of customers was waiting to get in. Princip hoped nobody would show up and distract him from his purpose. Unfortunately, it took only a few moments before Mihajlo Pušara turned up and clapped him too hard on the back. Pušara brought back jarring memories. He was an old school friend who shared Princip's aversion to the Austrian regime. They'd been in a few demonstrations together and in a couple of scraps. After Princip had decided he wanted to join the Black Hand, he found himself in a waiting room in Belgrade along with his old comrade. They had the same idea at the same time. The interview went badly for Princip. The recruiter took one look at his skinny figure and told Princip he had no use for him. He needed men, he said, not scarecrows. Princip tried in vain to plead his case. The interviewer turned to his papers and waved him out without another look. When he next met Pušara, the man's smug look told Princip all he didn't want to know. He'd avoided his friend ever since. Look at him now! Princip thought. Who carries a gun in his pocket? Who did the Black Hand select for this vital mission? Well, it wasn't Mihajlo bloody Pušara!

After what seemed an endless exchange of banalities, Pušara was called away by his lover, who had secured seats in the Delicatessen. She was a pretty wisp of a girl with striking, full lips — far better-looking than the jerk deserved. Princip wiped his brow. He was sweating like a pig. His shirt clung uncomfortably to his back, and the stains under his armpits kept growing. Missing breakfast had not been a smart idea; hunger pangs gnawed at his intestines. Nerves had knotted his stomach after a sleepless night. He'd tried a little cold *burek* — a leftover from the day before — with some yoghurt but had given up after a few bites.

Before he could make up his mind to quickly enter Schiller's and buy some food to eat on the go, he was amazed to see the green Gräf & Stift rounding the corner, turning into Franz Joseph Street. One of the passengers yelled angrily and hit the driver on the shoulder. Princip could make out that the car should have continued its way along the Appel Quay and that turning into Franz Joseph Street had been a mistake. The chauffeur turned purple. He slammed the brakes and stalled the engine by clumsily putting the gears in reverse. They were less than fifteen feet away from where Princip was standing. Princip didn't have an ounce of religion, but this — there was no other word for it — this was a gift from the gods.

He stepped off the pavement onto the street, taking quick, long strides. He pulled his gun. The rest of the world ceased to exist. Duchess Sophie saw him first and looked straight at him. Although a light veil covered her face, Princip couldn't help but notice she had sad eyes.

After a brief ceremony at the city hall, *Freiherr* Morsey had argued she should not accompany her husband during his visit to the hospital. The archduke wanted to comfort the victims wounded in the failed attempt on his life. The duchess firmly declined. On too many occasions, she'd been refused to sit at her husband's side. The emperor's court never passed on an opportunity to remind her she wasn't a suitable consort for the heir presumptive to the Habsburg throne. Her parents were counts of ancient stock, but they didn't belong to any of Europe's reigning dynasties. First, it took the emperor absurdly long to approve Franz Ferdinand's marriage proposal to her. Then he made sure her children could never succeed to the throne. As a final insult, all of the archduchesses, princesses, and countesses of the Empire continued to take precedence before her — even though she now held the rank of duchess. Thus, protocol prevented her from *ever* taking a seat next to her husband at official events.

Princip was five feet away from the car when he pulled the trigger once. He aimed for the body. During his training in Belgrade, Major Tankosić repeatedly told him never to aim for the head. 'Always the body,' the major had kept saying. 'Aim for the head, and you'll miss. You'll never get a second chance. Aim for the body and put in three or four slugs.'

The duchess moved in front of her husband to protect him when the shot rang. A crimson flower bloomed on her white dress. He'd shot her in the abdomen. Whatever happened, she wouldn't live; she'd bleed out slowly.

The archduke anxiously turned to his wife, which put Princip off his aim. He shot again. Instead of hitting the large man in the chest or belly, the bullet went wide and nicked Franz Ferdinand's jugular vein. Blood spattered from his neck and stained his sky-blue cavalry officer tunic. The dying heir to the Austro-Hungarian throne held on to his spouse and whispered something Princip didn't understand. Before he could take another shot, policemen and civilians jumped him and wrested the gun away.

It was done. His life was forfeit, and it had been worth it. History books would forever remember his name. The filthy disease eating his lungs away had failed to prevent him from achieving greatness. The tyrant was dead, and thus he'd brought the Bosnian Serbs one step closer to freedom. Somebody hit him behind the right ear with the pommel of a sabre. Everything went dark.

From an open window of the second-floor flat in the building across the street from Schiller's, a splendidly attired couple had witnessed the double assassination and subsequent capture of the assassin. The man wore a dark suit with a colourful double-breasted silk waistcoat and matching tie on a white shirt with a round club collar. He was in his late forties. His hair and ducktail beard were greying elegantly, and his hairline receded at the temples.

His build had once been athletic. Now, a slight paunch was showing. A duelling scar marked his left cheekbone, a reminder of his days as a member of a fencing fraternity. He was looking admiringly at his partner. The woman who had approached Princip months earlier was — once again — a fashion plate. She was wearing a high-necked dress with bold patterns, similar to those Gustav Klimt used in his first portrait of Adèle Bloch-Bauer.

'Someday, *Frau Gräfin*, you'll have to tell me how you knew, three months ago, this exact window would offer us such an entertaining spectacle today,' the man complimented her.

She smiled and raised her glass of sparkling *Burgunder Sekt* in a toast.

'To the end of the world as we know it, *Freiherr*, *zum Wohl*!'

They clinked glasses and laughed.

'You don't expect *der Alte* to declare war on Bosnia for *this*, do you, my dear? Not because of the murder of an heir to the throne he thoroughly despised, nor for the death of a cow whose children he never wanted to see on the throne. He's probably dancing a merry polka with Miss Schratt in Schönbrunn by now, don't you think?' the *Freiherr* supposed and winked mischievously.

'Honour is a fickle thing,' the countess replied. 'It makes one do things common sense dictates to avoid at all costs. The emperor will be forced to make a move, and *any* move is fine by me. Do you play billiards, *Freiherr*?'

'Yes, of course, but I don't see — '

'Europe is a billiards table full of shiny balls,' she cut him off. 'Take a cue and hit a random ball on the table hard enough in whatever direction, and *not one* of the balls will remain in its original place. Today, the balls started rolling.'

In a flat across the street, carefully hidden behind heavy curtains, another individual was observing the countess and the baron through binoculars. He paid no heed to the chaos below, intent as he was on trying to lip-read the conversation. After a short while, he put his binoculars away and reached behind him to take a small Simplex camera. Unlike most contemporary photo equipment, it wasn't a folding camera. It looked like an oblong box with rounded corners, covered in black leather. It was tiny by comparison to other cameras on the market, barely the size of a cigar etui. The man raised the viewer to his right eye and snapped a film roll's worth of pictures.

1

Zoetevoorde, Flanders

Thursday, 12 October 1916

When France called its citizens to arms in August 1914 in response to the mobilisation of German conscripts, farmers' sons expected to be back from the war in time for the harvest. Nothing had prepared them for a war of attrition that would last for years.

On 3 August, King Albert I of Belgium refused the German army free passage through his country. The *Kaiser* had planned to avoid the French fortifications lining the German-French border by making a quick, circumventing troop movement through Belgium. He wanted to take the French by surprise from the north, capturing Paris before France could organise its defences. The Belgian king's refusal was a first disappointment for the Germans. What made matters worse: The weak Belgian army held off the German onslaught for about a month — against all expectations. Belgium's resistance sent the Germans into a frenzy. They murdered civilians and burnt entire towns to the ground. The Germans captured the fortresses of Liège and Namur by shelling them with two of Krupp's monstrous Big Bertha howitzers. They then chased the fleeing Belgian troops from Antwerp and raced to the North Sea coast, only to be frustrated once again. The Germans were stalemated when, after about half a month of heavy fighting near the

Belgian coast, the Belgians decided to open the sluices at Nieuport and inundate the Yser Plain from Nieuport to Dixmude on the evening of 28 October. It stopped German progress in its tracks and signified the end of open warfare in that region. The Germans held the coast from Zeebrugge to Nieuport and captured inland Dixmude. Then the war shifted to Ypres. On both sides of the flooded Yser Plain, Belgian, French, British, and German troops dug themselves in. Trench warfare had begun.

Two years later, nothing much had changed. Continuous shelling and heavy rains had transformed Flanders' green fields into long stretches of nightmarish mud pools. It was a no man's land marked with splintered tree stumps, sinister curls of barbed wire, unexploded shells, and rotting corpses nobody cared to collect. Living conditions were infernal. The trenches regularly filled up with water. Exhausted soldiers were forced to stand knee-deep in a slimy, brownish soup for days on end — their boots stuck in the heavy, waterlogged Flemish clay. Rats had a field day. They swamped the trenches, stealing food and taking the occasional bite out of a sleeping *Poilu* or Tommy.

Zoetevoorde was an insignificant village a few miles north of Dixmude on the bank of the Yser Plain. When the Germans captured it, a couple of days before entering Dixmude, a civilian sniper killed four of their soldiers with a hunting rifle from the St.Andreas church tower. In retaliation, *Oberstleutnant* von Stück gathered the village's entire population on the church square and had everybody shot. Then he proceeded to burn down all of the houses. Finally, for good measure, he ordered a nearby artillery unit to use the church for target practice. Zoetevoorde was now nothing but a ghost town. Its remaining houses were burnt-out, empty shells. The church nave was destroyed. Its west wall and the tower were left partially standing, whereas the north transept and the apse also survived. The ruins offered a chilling sight on cloudless nights when there was a full moon.

On the night of 12 October 1916, an icy wind howled through the derelict streets of what had once been Zoetevoorde. It had been raining incessantly during the day; large puddles had formed everywhere. Two crows had found a refuge in the remaining transept, and that was all the life for miles around. Until a black Mercedes 80/90 HP stopped in front of the church. Its headlights were taped off, allowing the light beams to pass through narrow slits. Only the bass-heavy rumble of the powerful six-cylinder engine could have given it away if anybody had been around to care. Four people clad in long fur coats and caps with goggles descended from the car and walked in silence towards the church ruins. Each one carried a wooden, battery-operated trench torch with a large bull's eye lens.

They avoided the fissured west wall and entered the building via the nave. The floor was covered with debris, making their progress slow. The leader was a woman; she picked the path to follow. The four torch lights projected whimsical shadows on the pocked church interior — it looked as if giant, hairy creatures from another world were roaming through the ruins. One man slipped in a puddle and hurt his elbow. He loudly cursed in German and was immediately hushed by the others. A stone pulpit jutted above the hundreds of limestone roof fragments scattered all over the floor. Its ancient carvings of wild beasts and devils acquired a life of their own in the torches' erratic light beams. Without another mishap, the little group reached the transept. They were startled by the flapping noises and cawing of the two crows flying away from their perches. Carefully, they continued in the direction of the apse. The back of the church was relatively free of rubble. They quickly cleared away the few chunks of masonry that littered the floor.

The four huddled together, and the woman said, 'This is it. Look for the signs on the floor.'

The apse floor consisted of a mix of small and medium-sized limestone flagstones. The three men scattered and shone their light beams at the floor, shuffling the dust away with their boots.

'I found one!' one of the men shouted after a couple of minutes.

He pointed at a smaller flagstone. Eight centuries of wear had almost erased the image carved into the stone. Superficially, it looked like a curly, vegetal design. On closer inspection, one could distinguish something resembling tentacles. The other three found similar images on other flagstones. The four spots formed a trapezoid, with its larger base to the back of the apse's wall.

'On my mark,' commanded the woman.

All four were standing next to the flagstones they'd discovered.

'Now.'

They each stepped on their marked stones. For a while, all was silent; only the wind could be heard lashing against the ruined walls. It began to drizzle again. Their weight pushed down the stones, ever so slowly. After about five minutes, they had sunk two inches. The intruders heard faint clicking and grating noises. A rectangular surface within the trapezoid sank as well. Its descent stopped after ten inches, and then — no doubt managed by a sophisticated system of pulleys and weights — the rectangle split lengthwise. Both halves slid left and right under the flagstones of the apse's floor. A dark hole opened, exuding a stale, fungal smell.

The four stepped to the rim and shone their torches in the opening. A stone staircase led straight down. As the torch lights played over the staircase's sidewalls, they noticed that, about thirty feet beneath the church's foundations, black stone slabs covered the walls.

They climbed down the thirty-inch-high steps with difficulty. When they reached the black slabs, these appeared to be neither granite nor marble. The slightly diaphanous material had a crystalline structure. Mineralogists could have identified it as alabandite — a sulphide mineral found in meteorites. There are no alabandite quarries on Earth. The mineral only occurs in the form of small crystals and tumble stones the size of pebbles. Here, the alabandite slabs extended over *thousands* of square feet.

They were covered in bas-reliefs reminiscent of Mayan art found about seventy years earlier in Quirigua in Guatemala. The reliefs represented bizarre creatures far beyond even the most spine-chilling imaginings of the old Mayans. At least, the Mayan gods and monsters remained anthropomorphic or shared traits with animals that roamed the jungles surrounding the Mayan cities. The creatures depicted here were so alien the human mind could barely hold their images. No doubt the reliefs told a story that, given time, could be deciphered. That wasn't the team's purpose. They continued their descent in silence.

The four reached the bottom of the stairs an hour later. During the descent, the temperature had steadily declined, and the cold condensed their breath into wispy fog plumes. A monumental corridor led from the stairwell into an immense, oval chamber. The three men gasped in disbelief as they were met by a green, spectral glow generated by phosphorescent lichen. They warily brushed their fingers against the walls, which consisted of rough stone, and admired the seven massive pillars supporting the fan vault. The same type of terrible carvings they'd seen in the staircase covered the walls and pillars. The centre of the chamber held a pedestal or altar with a large ovoid on top. In the torches' beams, the shape revealed itself as organic. Skin folds curled from one end to another; veins ran close beneath the seaweed-green dermis. Its surface was irregular and made the whole look asymmetrical.

'The chamber is intact. I have no further need for you,' the leader declared.

Noticing the others were about to protest, she snapped, 'Go back to the surface at once! You have one hour. Drive to the agreed spot and wait there. I'll give you a sign when to return to the church.'

She patted the holster to her side, under her fur coat. It contained a flare gun.

'Now, hurry.'

The others turned on their heels, back to the staircase.

The woman watched them go. When they were well on their way, she looked back at the thing on the altar and switched off her torch. The phosphorescent lichen provided just about enough light to make out the shapes in the room. Disregarding the cold, she slipped out of her fur overcoat. Underneath, she wore a woollen pullover, a pair of mountaineering trousers, and sturdy, knee-length boots. She folded the thick coat, sat down on it, crossed her legs, and lit a cigarette. As soon as she'd finished smoking it, she flicked the butt at the ovoid and lit another one.

An hour had passed when the woman got up and languorously stretched her back. She stopped to study a carving on one of the pillars. It represented a snake-like creature consisting entirely of sharp corners and hooks, with eyes along the sides of its body and a vertical, toothy maw that opened in its belly. She grinned and ran her fingers along its shape. Then she turned her attention back to the thing on the altar. Standing fifteen feet away from it, she began chanting in a deep baritone. The song's words were guttural — no human speech could emulate these sounds. The incantation was slow at first. Then the rhythm, punctuated by throaty grunts, picked up speed until, after about ten minutes, the singing turned wild and frenzied. Her voice covered six octaves and reverberated throughout the chamber. The woman remained motionless with her arms spread as if crucified.

The shape on the altar unfolded. The skin folds belonged to bat-like wings that enclosed and hid the awakening creature's body. Opening, they revealed the being they'd enfolded for countless years. The grooves on the ovoid's bottom also came alive in a squirming movement as a mass of tentacles uncoiled. They slithered over the floor and waved in the air as if tasting their surroundings. While the monster further uncurled, it produced a long, booming howl. The air crackled with sudden energy. The newborn began to glow and eventually filled the room with blinding light.

On the other side of the flooded plain, the Belgian, French, and British soldiers became aware of a deep sound travelling over the water. Risking a peek over the rim of their trenches, they saw, in a flash, a yellow-green light beam shooting up from the ruined Zoetevoorde church. Then darkness returned. The howling noise stopped. For half an hour, all was normal again.

Some soldiers doubted their eyes; others believed it was a sign from God and prayed. There was talk in the trenches about the Germans testing a new weapon. Fear took hold of those soldiers who had escaped the test attacks with chlorine gas in Langemarck-Poelcapelle, about a year and a half ago. They remembered with horror the grey-green clouds drifting in their direction for the first time, and their comrades dying in excruciating pain from asphyxiation as the chlorine burnt their throats and lungs. Maybe this was a new type of gas attack. They put on their gas masks and ran to wake their sleeping mates so that they could take their precautions as well.

Nothing could have prepared them for what followed.

2

Gravelines, France

Wednesday, 3 January 1917

Gravelines had been in many sieges and wars but not in this one. It was safely ensconced within French territory, twenty miles from the Belgian border, on the North Sea coast. Gravelines was once again a simple fishermen's town without military importance. Its star-shaped ramparts, built to withstand the onslaughts of wars of another age, were long since outclassed by developments in modern heavy artillery. Its most recent reinforcements dated from the end of the seventeenth century. They were added by Vauban, the foremost military engineer of his time, who had transformed many French cities into angular citadels.

Today, the declassified military stronghold hosted a meeting of several remarkable personalities. In the largest room of its town hall, five gentlemen were sitting at a long table. Three of them were in military attire; two wore civilian dress.

Two of the uniformed men were among this war's most powerful military commanders. Field Marshall Douglas Haig had been, from the start of the British involvement in the war, the commander of the British Expeditionary Force. The other one was a far more recent appointment as

Commander-in-Chief of the French armies on the Western front. General Robert Nivelle had impressed the French prime minister, Aristide Briand, by his successes in the battle of Verdun last October. He was promoted last December, replacing General Joffre. Both Haig and Nivelle were soldiers seasoned in several colonial wars. They had a reputation for squandering ordinary soldiers' lives in meaningless attacks and were widely unpopular with their troops.

The other man in uniform was Albert I, King of Belgium. He'd declined to follow his government's ministers in their exile to Le Havre. He was a man of strong principles, which had led him to refuse the Germans safe passage through Belgian territory. The king felt that, in this hour of need, his place was among his soldiers. He was frequently visiting the trenches, encouraging and comforting his men, which greatly contributed to his popularity. Contrary to Haig and Nivelle, he'd vetoed the participation of Belgian troops in attacks he deemed both dangerous and useless, saving numerous lives in the process. His spouse, Queen Elisabeth, often visited the field hospital 'L'Ambulance de l'Océan' in De Panne. She talked to the wounded and occasionally acted as a nurse. She was a duchess of Bavaria, and *Kaiser* Wilhelm II had spitefully seen to it that all of her German relatives were deployed in regiments fighting in Flanders.

France's prime minister was also present, although he was pressed for time. He was expected in Rome in a couple of days. The Allies intended to discuss how to turn the recent Greek putsch to their advantage and make Greece join their side in the war. Aristide Briand was a socialist career politician. He'd started out as a radical leftist and steadily moved to a more centrist point of view. His sudden reversals in policy had dismayed his former supporters on several occasions. A skilful survivor in the hyper-volatile environment of French politics, he was *prési-*

dent du conseil — which is what the French call their prime minister — for the sixth time since July 1909.

The most enigmatic presence in the room was also the person who had called the meeting. His letterhead said, 'Mycroft Holmes, 1st Earl Holmes, GCVO, GCB, ISO, in the Service of His Majesty the King'. Nobody knew exactly what he did. It was whispered he *was* the British government. Even Prime Minister Lloyd George was said to defer to him. His signature — always in green ink — was one letter: *M*. Officially, he was addressed as Lord Holmes, but his subordinates usually called him M. Mycroft Holmes was an imposing, heavyset figure, easily half a head taller than the tallest person in the room. He was groomed to perfection. His black hair — fastidiously coloured every week — was combed backwards over his balding scalp, and his delicate moustache was waxed into an elegant curl. His eyes shone with keen intelligence and could, with one glance, quickly silence an assembly of people — even one as exalted as the present one.

'Thank you all, Your Majesty, Your Excellency, and Commanders-in-Chief, for coming to this hearing. I appreciate that making time in your busy schedules has been difficult,' M began in a soft-spoken manner while the others leaned in to better understand him.

Out of respect for the majority of native French speakers in the meeting, M spoke French, even though he knew their English to be excellent. His French was flawless, indistinguishable from a native speaker's, even if it was only one of twelve languages he spoke fluently. French held a fond place in his heart. He thought the French army had been useless ever since Napoleon I's defeat at Waterloo. Also, the French's chaotic behaviour in meetings and their verbose interventions often exasperated him. But they had such brilliant philosophers and writers! M's favourite author was Michel de Montaigne. Montaigne's essays were always on his nightstand. There were few nights he didn't read at least one of them before going to sleep.

'We were all shocked by the events of 12 October last, which cost the lives of several thousands of our soldiers,' he went on. 'Unfortunately, this war has confronted us with a death toll on a scale not many among us had foreseen. The battles of the Marne, the Chemin des Dames, and Verdun have all resulted in shocking numbers of casualties on both sides. These losses could have made us insensitive to the tragedy in the Yser Plain a few months ago.'

Both Haig and Nivelle frowned but kept their silence. Lord Holmes's introduction could be construed as a not-so-veiled criticism of the way they'd managed the war — as if ending the conflict sooner and with fewer casualties had ever been an option! Better let their host continue and get to the heart of the matter of this meeting, instead of trying to debunk his naive, civilian perception of the war. There were plenty of armchair strategists around. They'd never seen a battlefield and were nonetheless convinced they could outthink the professionals.

'Compared to the major battles, this one represents but a minor skirmish,' M pointed out. 'However, the peculiar nature of the event was alarming. It was unlike anything we'd ever experienced in any other confrontation with the enemy. The notion that the Germans might have developed a new doomsday weapon couldn't be discarded out of hand. Our three governments have wisely decided the matter was sufficiently grave as to require further investigation. This work is finalised, and we want to present you with its conclusions today. If you allow me, I'll now call in Commander Fleming. He's been leading the effort and is the most qualified person to report its findings to you.'

The other four agreed, and M rang the large hotel reception bell in front of him. A handsome man in his mid-thirties, wearing a dark blue uniform and carrying a large cardboard box, entered the room. He walked to the table and put his box on the floor.

Haig was looking sharply at him and couldn't keep the irritation from his voice asking, 'Commander, I don't recognise your uniform. Would you mind telling us what regiment you belong to?'

'The commander belongs to His Majesty's Secret Service Bureau and, as such, isn't part of any regiment,' M answered while staring down Haig.

Fleming looked at M for permission to speak, which he gave by an almost imperceptible nod.

'Your Majesty, Your Excellency, Field-Marshal, and General, thank you for taking the time to hear my report. I'll try to use your precious time sparingly and be as succinct as possible. Feel free to interrupt me if you have questions. I must warn you that our findings will be hard to accept or believe. We did not, however, come to these conclusions lightly,' Fleming began.

He lifted a thick folder from the box, took out a series of photos, and passed them around.

'These pictures were taken in the aftermath of the attack. They show the situation in our trenches.'

Even Haig and Nivelle had to swallow looking at the carnage in the pictures. The trenches were littered with mauled corpses. The bodies were atrociously disfigured. Some of them showed gaping holes as if they'd been impaled or shot with hollow-point bullets. Other soldiers were ripped apart, their body parts strewn all over the place. Still others were crushed to a pulp, every bone in their bodies broken. Only a wrecking ball or a fall from a great height could have wrought such horrific damage. The trenches themselves were completely ruined as if herds of wild elephants had been driven through them.

'This is what happened in most trenches, from Caeskerke all the way to Ramscapelle, along the banks of the flooded Ypres Plain,' Fleming explained and then handed out another set of pictures.

'This gave us a first clue to what we might be dealing with,' he added.

The pictures were close-ups of body parts. The faces and the naked arms, legs, and torsos had one thing in common: They all showed double rows of dark, round blotches. The diameter of the bruises varied from two to eight inches.

'It set us thinking. If what attacked our soldiers made these marks, we might look for traces outside of the trenches as well, to give us a better understanding of what the attacker looked like,' Fleming explained. 'And then we were helped by these.'

He handed out yet another set of pictures. They were large blow-ups of aerial photographs showing in minute detail the trenches on both sides of the Ypres Plain.

'The French made these the morning after the attack. They gracefully showed them to us, and we learnt a lot from them,' Fleming said with a grateful nod to Nivelle and Briand.

'First, we looked for traces where the attacker had made landfall. As you can see *here*,' Fleming continued, pointing at one of the photographs, 'it happened near the town of Pervyse. There are distinct traces of something climbing out of the water and then moving — or should I say "digging its way"? — towards the Allied trenches. Though the tracks are confusing, they don't belong to a mechanical device. So I can confirm that the Germans have *not* developed some sort of amphibious war machine. There are other, less clear tracks at other locations — here, here, and here — indicating the attacker moved out of the trenches on several occasions, back into the water, only to re-emerge at another spot to resume his carnage.'

Fleming let this sink in. There were no questions; his audience stared in silence at the photographs scattered in front of them.

'What surprised us most was the evidence that similar attacks ravaged the trenches on the German side. These pictures here show identical tracks on the east side of the Ypres Plain. There are obvious signs of the destruction of German trenches near the towns of Beerst, Stuyvekenskerke, Schoore, and Mannekensveere. They must have suffered similar losses. The conclusion to be drawn from our evidence is that the attacker is unlikely to be German as he doesn't distinguish between Allied and German troops.'

Both military leaders received this statement with incredulous huffing.

'If not the *Boches*, then who could be responsible for such a bloodbath?' Nivelle asked.

'Preposterous!' was all Haig had to add.

'Gentlemen, I propose we hear out Commander Fleming. Manifestly, he's studied the matter earnestly, and the photos look convincing,' King Albert I advised.

'Continue, Fleming,' M ordered.

'Knowing where to look for traces near the tideline, I sent in a team. This was a dangerous mission because it had to be carried out in the open field. For this reason, we decided to do it under cover of the evening dusk. The darkness and the waterlogged condition of the soil made it difficult to distinguish the tracks. Nevertheless, the team was able to find a few fine tracks in somewhat dryer areas and to make plaster casts of them.'

Fleming delved in his cardboard box again, retrieved two plaster casts, and put them on the table for inspection.

'Given the weather conditions, these casts are hardly perfect specimens, but they'll suffice to give you a first impression. The first one is a partial cast of the business side of a cephalopod's tentacle. One can clearly distinguish the two rows of suckers. The dimensions of these suckers are an exact match for the shape and size of the bruises found on the soldiers' bodies. The second cast gives us a part of a webbed foot and claw.'

'Are you telling us our men have been attacked by a giant octopus?' exclaimed Briand.

'And what of the footprint?' asked King Albert I. 'Squids don't have feet, or do they?'

'An army of monsters from the deep getting involved in a war among humans,' mumbled a perplexed Haig.

'As to the nature of the assailant, much is yet unclear. If you allow me, I'll return to that matter shortly,' Fleming replied evasively. 'After these discoveries, we studied the aerial photographs again. Our attention was drawn to Zoetevoorde. It's a small village near Dixmude, which was destroyed by the Germans early in the war. We looked at that area because several survivors of the attack reported they'd seen something peculiar over there, right before the massacre.'

Fleming waved three sheets about with the reports he was referring to and put them on the table.

'They heard a howling noise, and then a green light beam shot up into the sky from the church ruins. The first attack started half an hour later. Studying the aerial photograph of the church in Zoetevoorde and comparing it to pictures taken earlier, it was evident something had happened there. Rubble shown on the church floor in the older pictures was scattered outside in the recent photograph. One report mentioned a red flare over the church about an hour after the light beam. It set us thinking that something might have been released from that church by human intervention. We decided to investigate. A team was sent in, under cover of night, to cross the Ypres Plain and infiltrate behind enemy lines. The team managed to enter the church and take pictures.'

Again, Fleming put a sheaf of photographs on the table. They showed the ruined church interior.

'As can be seen, *something* moved from the apse through the church and left via the ruined nave on the south side. It cleared a path through the rubble and pushed stone fragments into the street. Based on this path's width, we can make an educated guess about the size of the creature that escaped from the church. It must be about nine feet wide. Its length is more difficult to estimate. In our opinion, twenty-four to thirty feet wouldn't be far off the mark. In the dust on the church floor, we found footprints that match the cast I've shown you. You can see them on these pictures here.'

Fleming pointed at five pictures on the table.

'We found traces of a crypt in the apse. There was evidence of a large staircase leading down. Unfortunately, the stair hall had collapsed, which prevented further investigation. A few depressed flagstones in the apse near the staircase caught our attention. They were the only flagstones in the apse we could find marked with an image. Here are the pictures of the three we've found.'

The audience studied the pictures of the flagstones.

'This carving looks like an octopus,' Neville commented.

'Very true, General,' Fleming replied. 'That was our conclusion too. Which brings me to my next point. Scholars have assured me early medieval depictions or carvings of large cephalopods are unheard of in Flanders. These images are atypical. This led us to investigate whether we could find similar ones elsewhere. With the help of the Bodleian Library, we came up with this.'

Fleming took an octavo-sized book in a green leather binding, wrapped in protective paper, from his box.

41

'This is a rare copy of a German book titled *Unaussprechliche Kulte*. Please turn to page eighty-three, Your Majesty,' Fleming said as he handed over the book to the Belgian king.

'Indeed,' the king confirmed, 'the illustration on this page is a near-perfect match for the carvings we've seen in the pictures.'

He handed the book to the French prime minister.

'The author of this book is Friedrich von Junzt,' Fleming explained. 'He was a German scholar, adventurer, and explorer, who travelled the entire globe for forty years, in search of obscure religious practices. He was obsessed with origin-of-the-world stories and apocalyptic myths. *Herr* von Junzt wrote several scientific articles on these topics. His bibliography includes books on the mythologies of pre-Columbian cultures in South America and on his travels through Africa, South East Asia, and Mongolia. These publications landed him a professorship at the Humboldt University in Berlin, where he taught Anthropology and Comparative Theology since 1836. Three years later, he published this book. It sent a shiver of indignation through the Berlin academia, and Von Junzt was hastily dismissed. The reason was his claim in *Unaussprechliche Kulte* that the primitive religions of a few obscure tribes keeping themselves far away from civilisation hold more truth than the Bible. He even went as far as to present some of their most outrageous beliefs as scientific facts. His colleagues considered him quite mad and couldn't get rid of him quickly enough to preserve the university's reputation. One year later, Von Junzt died in suspicious circumstances in his flat in Düsseldorf. His body was found in a room locked from the inside.'

Fleming almost quipped it could have been an excellent case for Sherlock Holmes but thought better of it.

'Most copies of his book were destroyed. Only a couple have escaped abroad, and one of them — the one you're now holding in your hands — made its way to Oxford. In this book, Von Junzt claims to have seen the image of the octopod in antediluvian buildings in Outer Mongolia, Borneo, and the jungles of Bolivia.'

'I'm puzzled,' confessed Briand. 'How did you make the connection between the image on a medieval flagstone and that crackpot's book? There are millions and millions of books! How did you know to pick this one?'

'Well, maybe Von Junzt wasn't such a crackpot after all, dear Prime Minister,' M replied.

'Oh, he *must* have been!' Briand cried out, making a dramatic gesture with both arms. 'Only a crackpot would confound religious beliefs with scientific facts! You know there are good reasons why religion is called "a belief". There's never any proof! It's all dogmas and hearsay! Stuff people tell themselves because they can't face life or death without protection by a caring God! Look how that's working out for them! God will have *a lot* of explaining to do after this war! So please don't tell me to take an author seriously who presents religious hocus-pocus as scientific fact because I'm not having any of it!'

'The reason why we ended up with Von Junzt is part of the next section of my report,' Fleming answered calmly.

He took another picture from his folder. It showed a well-dressed couple standing at an open window, toasting each other with sparkling wine.

'This, gentlemen, is the *Reichsgräfin* Mathilde von Corvey. She belongs to the German *Hochadel*. Her ancestry can be traced back to the eighth century, which makes her family one of the oldest in the country. She's extremely wealthy and influential. The man standing next to her is *Freiherr* Rudolph von Blaufels. He's also well-connected but lost a substantial part of his ancestors' fortunes in injudicious investments and gambling. The picture has been taken in Sarajevo, right after the archduke's murder. The window offered a splendid view of the event.'

'Well, she seems to think that was a right jolly business,' Haig muttered.

'Who took this picture and why?' Neville asked.

Fleming handed out more photographs of the countess. It showed her with personalities such as Bakunin, Trotsky, Lenin, Proudhon, Liebknecht, and Rosa Luxemburg.

'Our secret service has been keeping an eye on certain individuals on the continent for many years because they're deemed security risks. The countess has frequently been seen in the company of radicals, anarchists, socialist extremists, violent nationalists, and other members of our society's lunatic fringe. In the months preceding Archduke Franz Ferdinand's assassination, she was signalled with his future assassin. We even have good cause to believe *she* might have put the idea of murdering the archduke in Princip's head.'

Haig snorted derisively. The idea that a mere woman could have such a decisive impact on world events was too silly for words. He refrained, however, from voicing his opinion. The countess's presence at the crime scene was an unlikely coincidence, he had to admit.

'That's all very interesting, but I don't see the connection with what's happened last October,' King Albert I criticised.

'The countess, the baron, and two aides were seen in the neighbourhood of Zoetevoorde on the eve of the attack, Your Majesty,' Fleming replied. 'The night before, they stayed in Bruges, where they met with the Commander of the Fourth Army, *Generalfeldmarschall* Albrecht, Duke of Württemberg. According to our spies, they obtained a permit from him to visit the front line and then drove in a private car to Zoetevoorde at nightfall on the twelfth. There's no doubt whatsoever; they were present at the event. One of them fired the flare sometime after midnight. Later, they were seen driving to Ghent, where they spent the rest of the night in a hotel. They left for Germany the next day.'

'It's disturbing to hear that a person you associate with the assassination of the Austrian heir to the throne was also present at what happened in Zoetevoorde,' Briand admitted. 'But I still fail to see the link between the two events, and you've yet to explain the connection with that crackpot professor.'

'I'm afraid some issues are unresolved,' Fleming acknowledged. 'One of them has to do with the countess. As soon as she was put on the secret service's watch list, we compiled a substantial file about her. Our research shows she was the first female student ever at Humboldt University. We have no idea how she got into the university at that time because women in Prussia couldn't register as university students before 1908. She studied Anthropology under Professor von Junzt.'

'Wait, wait, this is ridiculous!' Haig erupted. 'You told us Von Junzt taught at the university in the 1830s! She can *never* have been a student of Von Junzt! In the pictures you showed us of the countess, she doesn't look a day over thirty-five!'

'I agree, Field Marshall,' Fleming answered with a smile, 'but neither does she in this daguerreotype, together with her mentor, Friedrich von Junzt. The picture dates from 1838.'

The men looked astounded at the old photograph.

'Commander Fleming, there must be some confusion. This lady in the picture must be the countess's great grandmother? It's not uncommon strong family resemblances are passed on via the maternal line,' Briand suggested.

'There's *no* confusion,' Fleming declared. 'The search of Von Junzt's flat after his mysterious demise found a box of letters written by the countess. We have compared the handwriting with letters the countess recently sent to Liebknecht and Trotsky. They were an exact match. Moreover, we have several other photographs of the countess in our possession, dating back to 1854, 1877, 1883, 1896, and 1901, and she looks *exactly* the same in all of them! We have looked for her birth certificate. The only one we could find dates from 1812. Ever since that date, no other females have been added to the Von Corvey family tree. She's now the last of her lineage.'

'What is she then? A vampire?' Haig grumbled, remembering a silly novel he'd tried to read almost twenty years ago. He'd never finished it; it was too ridiculous to spend one's time on.

'We don't know,' Fleming admitted. 'If the descriptions in *Unaussprechliche Kulte* are anything to go by, we may expect more creatures like the one in Zoetevoorde exist and will be set loose upon the world.'

The men behind the table were contemplating Fleming's last statement when M abruptly decided to wrap up the meeting. Fleming had gone into far more detail than he'd expected him to. His report might have raised more questions than it answered. M wanted to prevent the meeting from derailing into an uncontrollable avalanche of further enquiries. That would inevitably lead to the revelation of even more facts he needed to keep secret. The last thing he desired was blockheads like Haig wading into this delicate matter or scaring the French prime minister out of his mind.

'Gentlemen, this report has certainly given us a lot to think about. For our Commanders-in-Chief, the good news is the event was an unfortunate coincidence of circumstances, unrelated to the war. We can rest assured the Germans have *not* developed a doomsday weapon. Thus, we shouldn't burden our already overtaxed military with this issue. It remains, however, an unsettling occurrence. I assure you our secret service will look into it further. We'll try to identify other locations holding similar creatures and destroy them before the release of yet another abomination. In the meantime — I apologise for stating the obvious — this must remain of the highest possible confidentiality. Nobody, except those present, can know what has happened. All the photographic material from the trenches has already been put under embargo. A reassuring statement will be issued to the press forthwith. You'll all be provided with a copy.'

The other attendees were surprised at the sudden ending of the meeting but didn't make any objections. As they were rising from their seats, King Albert I asked, 'What about the "abomination", Commander? Do we know its current whereabouts? Is it still lurking in the waters of the Ypres Plain? We have moved new troops into the trenches that suffered from its attack, you know. It could happen again.'

'Excellent question, Your Majesty,' Fleming replied, 'I should have mentioned this earlier. We have evidence it left the Ypres Plain and reached the North Sea via the Yser. Our aeroplane pilots and Navy tasked with the surveillance of the Channel and the North Sea, have been instructed to keep an eye out for unusual appearances. Until now, none have been signalled.'

Before the French prime minister could leave the room, M took him aside.

'*Cher* Aristide,' he began, 'we need to keep in touch about this. My men will make short shrift of identifying likely locations for the hiding places of similar creatures. It's my expectation these will be scattered all over the world. We need to be able to intervene quickly, as time appears to be of the essence. France and Great Britain both command large territories, and we both have local troops that can be used effectively for search-and-destroy missions. We need to co-operate on this matter. I'd also like to propose to you that France detaches experts to Commander Fleming's team. That will guarantee you first-hand knowledge of the progress made and also provide the operation's HQ with world-class know-how.'

Briand appeared to be flustered at first.

Then he reassured M, 'The Rome Conference is now my priority. However, I guarantee you, my dear Mycroft, that, upon my return, I'll make sure to provide you with the best experts in France. And as far as actions in our overseas territories are concerned, you can rest assured France will provide all the necessary firepower to exterminate these creatures.'

They shook hands cordially, and Briand left the building with the others.

'Well done, Fleming,' M congratulated the commander.

'Thank you, M. I fear I got somewhat carried away in there. Maybe I should have been more careful with the revelations about our suspicions of the countess's supernatural qualities. I must confess, I was a tad surprised by some of the French prime minister's comments. He didn't seem to be aware of—, well, of the world order *we* know about,' Fleming confided.

'The French pride themselves on being a rational people,' M chuckled. 'They hold ghost and monster stories in contempt. The biggest monster they ever acknowledged and captured was an oversized wolf in the Gévaudan — one hundred and fifty years ago, you can imagine. You know the French Republic hasn't invested in services like the one you're leading for our Majesty the King. That's also why I advised you to hold back on the more sensitive information in your presentation.'

'Then they'll be in for a shock when they send their experts over to us,' Fleming remarked.

'What I need from the French is manpower in the field the instant we identify target locations in their territories,' M said. 'I don't want us to get into any avoidable international conflicts by infiltrating in French territories ourselves during search-and-destroy missions. Now is *not* the time to annoy the French. We'll have enough on our hands with Russia and South America. And as far as those French experts are concerned: Don't hold your breath. If they're forthcoming at all, my money would be on old, stubborn, useless university professors close to retirement age. Briand would want to vacate their chairs so he can appoint his cronies. You'll see. The prime minister has a way of taking care of *his* interests first. I had to ask him to get his approval on the other matter, though.'

3

Skjöldungen Fjord, Southeast Coast of Greenland

Friday, 12 January 1917

U-Boat U85 surfaced half a mile off the southeast coast of Greenland. It was one of the newest type U81 and had been launched at the Germaniawerft in Kiel six months ago. Only six vessels of this type had been commissioned. These sleek, diesel-powered ships were the killer sharks of the Kaiserliche Marine. They were the largest and fastest submarines in the German fleet, essential tools in its strategy of unrestricted naval warfare. U-Boats were involved in relentless hit-and-run attacks on merchant ships on all trade routes to Britain. They'd sunk thousands of civilian vessels since the beginning of the conflict. They tried to establish a naval blockade and cripple both the supply of raw goods to Britain's war industry and of food to its population. U-Boats were slow compared to large battleships but could act with great stealth. Once submerged, they were almost impossible to trace.

Kapitänleutnant Willy Petz and four warmly clad figures emerged from the conning tower. Three of them inflated a small rubber boat while the U85 coasted nearer to the shore and entered the fjord. Countess von Corvey used the captain's binoculars to peer at the jagged shoreline. She was satisfied to see how forbidding the rugged, snow-covered mountain scenery looked.

Skjöldungen was an uninhabited island in the shape of a thirty-mile-long, three-fingered paw with its 'claws' extending in the icy waters of the northern Atlantic Ocean. Strong katabatic gusts blew from the mountains into the sea while snow drifts clouded the view. As the U-Boat neared the tip of the middle 'claw', a party of Inuit with several dog sledges was revealed. They were impassively awaiting the countess's arrival in the biting cold on the pebble beach strewn with moraines.

'Willy, dear,' the countess whispered in the captain's ear, 'this won't take too long. Be a good boy and wait for us. Oh, and keep your men inside. They don't want to see what's about to happen.'

The captain didn't respond. He looked like a wax doll. His clear-blue eyes stared straight ahead without see-ing; his posture was unnaturally stiff. The frost was turning his face blue; ice crystals were forming in his eyebrows and on his eyelashes.

The countess squinted over her left shoulder. The rubber boat was fully inflated. The U-Boat was as near to the shore as it could come without foundering. She walked over to her acolytes and stepped into the rowboat. The three others pushed off and paddled furiously towards the shoreline. It took them a quarter of an hour, bobbing over choppy waters and battling against the fierce headwinds before they reached their destination.

As the countess stepped ashore, the Inuit bowed deeply. The short men were clad in heavy seal-fur coats. Like all Inuit, their faces had prominent cheekbones and deep-set, slanted eyes, but their noses were two small, ver-tical slits over too-wide mouths, and their skin looked scaly and hairless. The leader shuffled forwards and bowed again. His face had acquired a dark, leathery tan with age. The lack of teeth made him lisp when he welcomed the countess in a language that was only remotely related to the Tunumiisut spoken by the Inuit of eastern Greenland.

'Welcome, Dream Whisperer,' he said. 'We are honoured and proud to be chosen. We have faithfully carried out the responsibilities entrusted to us.'

'Your loyalty honours you, children of Dagon,' she solemnly replied in the same language. 'Now bring me to the Sleeper. The time of waiting and longing has passed. We shall presently fulfil age-old dreams.'

The countess and her companions stepped into the dog sledges, which carried them to the glacier's edge. The ice sheet was pushing its way to the sea between two craggy mountains, whose tops were obscured by snowdrifts. The howling wind was amplifying into a gale.

The worsening weather conditions concealed another ship's arrival. HMS Bellerophon had been chasing the U85 ever since the message of its departure from Kiel reached Captain Edward Bruen. He could have intercepted the submarine as early as the Faroe Islands if he hadn't received orders to stand down and pursue the German vessel without attacking. Under normal circumstances, that would have been an impossible task. This U-Boat, however, threw caution to the wind. In its haste, it refused to slow down by submerging. The vessel maintained its maximum speed of seventeen knots during the entire voyage. Oblivious to the Dreadnought in its wake, the U85 followed a straight course from the Faroe Islands to the south coast of Iceland, and then onwards to Greenland. When the HMS Bellerophon steamed eighty miles south of Reykjavik, a much smaller craft sailed alongside the battleship, and a man with the rank of commander came on board. There was a whiff of panic as the U85 submerged two hundred miles off the coast of Greenland. The HMS Bellerophon held a steady course and was rewarded when the submarine surfaced again near the Greenland coast without having veered off its original course.

Fleming had commandeered a small torpedo boat as soon as he learnt a U-Boat with the countess on board was sailing from Kiel via the Skagerrak to the North Sea in a north-westerly direction. It raced him at fifty knots from Glasgow to the Iceland coast, where he boarded the HMS Bellerophon.

Alfred Spencer was found in his hotel room in Kiel on 7 January, with severe burns to the forehead and a slit throat. His nose and lips had been cut off and were nowhere to be found. His lungs were draped around his shoulders while his entrails were heaped on the bed. The heart, liver, and kidneys were dumped in the bathtub. His genitals decorated the nightstand.

Spencer was part of the team that had been shadowing Mathilde von Corvey for the past eight years. He was the man who took the photographs of the countess and her helper in Sarajevo. Upon her return from Belgium to Germany, the countess appeared in no hurry. She attended several parties, concerts, and theatre performances in Berlin and visited friends in Potsdam and Brandenburg. She spent a couple of weeks alone in her villa in Oranienburg, before travelling to Binz, a posh sea resort on the island Rügen in the Baltic Sea. Binz was deserted in winter, which made it easy to rent a large summer residence on the seafront. The countess spent a lavish Christmas and New Year's Eve there with a group of friends. One of her friends was *Freiherr* von Blaufels. They left Rügen for Kiel with two others.

Spencer followed her there and was to be relieved by Henry Kidner, a teammate of his, when he was found murdered. Luckily, Kidner kept his wits about him and hunted down the countess before she and her companions boarded the U85. Aeroplanes detected the submarine as it rounded the top of Jutland and entered the Skagerrak. Then they tracked it to the Shetland Islands. In the meantime, the HMS Bellerophon was well on its way.

The 525-foot-long behemoth sat silently in the waters, half a mile from the submarine. Its 12-inch guns pointed at the shore where the countess had alighted; its 4-inch guns were directed at the U85. Captain Bruen and Commander Fleming stood on the aft deck, looking through their binoculars at what was happening on land.

Bruen turned to Fleming, sounding both confused and exasperated.

'I've *never* known a U-Boat captain to act so irresponsibly,' he said. 'He flouted even the most basic safety precautions. We've been tailing them for over two thousand miles, and not even once has he taken an evasive manoeuvre to shake us off. And now they're sitting ducks. We can blow them out of the water at any time. What's going on, Commander? I can't make heads or tails of this.'

'Let's wait and see, Captain,' Fleming said. 'My primary concern is with the landing party. We cannot engage the enemy before its purpose has become clear to us.'

The dog sledges had reached the glacier, and the party was walking on its treacherous surface. The Inuit led the way without hesitation. After a mile of laboured progress, they turned towards the mountain on the glacier's northern edge and started to climb it. Fleming scanned the steep mountainside and soon discerned the expedition's goal. A cavernous opening gaped in the rock flank, about two hundred yards above the glacier surface. The last part of the journey was particularly arduous. It took the party the better part of an hour to reach the cavern. Eventually, the countess and her acolytes disappeared into its shadows.

'Please aim your guns at that cavern, Captain, and tell your men to be ready to fire at your command,' Fleming advised.

Fleming and the captain left the aft deck and went inside to the bridge.

Inside the mountain, a roughly hewn staircase led down to an inner chamber of stupendous proportions. Its walls were lined with alabandite panels carved with complex entanglements of outlandish creatures, alternated with slabs inscribed with rows of pictograms. The room was strewn with elaborately decorated totemic pillars, which didn't quite reach the ceiling. At its centre stood an altar supporting a large ovoid. A bluish light was shining from icicles hanging from the vault.

The countess stepped up to the altar. She touched the ovoid with both hands and her forehead as a token of profound respect. Then she stepped back and intoned in a loud voice, clearly for the benefit of her companions, 'Greetings, Great Sleeper. Cthulhu, your time of awakening has come.'

The other members of her party had moved as far away as they could from the altar. They stood with their backs against the chamber walls. The countess solemnly raised her arms and chanted.

Captain Bruen was getting restless. Their targets had disappeared into the mountain half an hour ago, and the weather had considerably worsened. Visibility was further reduced. During the Battle of Jutland, he'd learnt to grasp opportunities as soon as they presented themselves. This waiting game didn't sit well with him. There was no reason not to sink the U-Boat right now. Bruen would have done it the very moment the landing party disappeared into the mountain. There was no telling when they'd re-emerge from the cavern. It was 2 p.m. The ephemeral daylight in these parts would give way to dusk in half an hour, making it more difficult to ascertain whether their targets had been destroyed. Also, Bruen didn't like taking orders from a lower-ranking officer — but his instructions were clear and had come directly from the First Sea Lord, Sir John Jellicoe, himself.

When the captain was about to insist again to Fleming they sink the U-Boat, there was an intense light flash. Something burst out of the cave opening in the mountain. Transfixed, Bruen gaped at it through his binoculars.

Long, wavy tentacles first probed the air before the creature fully emerged. The head appeared too big for its body and was teeming with agitated limbs of different lengths. From this distance, it was difficult to see how many eyes the monster had, but it most certainly had more than two. Underneath the swarming mass of tentacles, there was a circular maw filled with rows upon rows of sharp teeth. It had disproportionately large, claw-like hands at the end of its two muscular arms. Its scaly legs were short and crooked, ending in enormous, webbed feet. While the creature righted itself outside the cave opening, a pair of bat-like wings — too small to take flight with — unfolded from its back. It now stood at its full length of no less than twenty-five feet. Over the piercing howls of the brewing storm, a deafening bellow — eerie as the lowing of a foghorn — sounded through the fjord. As the creature gulped air for its next cry, its barrel chest doubled in size.

'Now would be a good time to open fire, Captain,' Fleming suggested to his awe-struck companion.

Four of the five twin Mk X gun turrets hurtled their 850-lb armour-piercing shells towards the mountain. The sharp smell of cordite penetrated the bridge, where Fleming and the captain stood. Through their binoculars, they anxiously observed whether the target had been hit.

The aim had been true right from the first blast. The eight guns were firing two rounds per minute each, pounding the mountain's flank non-stop for half an hour. After the smoke clouds lifted, Fleming could see that a large part of the mountain had been reduced to a quarry filled with rubble, which spilt over the glacier's edge. The glacier had cracked as well. Large ice chunks had tumbled on the shore and into the sea, and several sizeable icebergs stuck out of the shallow waters.

After the first salvo, the captain ordered a broadside torpedo to be fired at the U-Boat. The U85 hadn't moved and was hit amidships. It went up in a ball of fire. The remains sank without a trace, except for a large, burning oil mark on the waves.

The first gun burst hit the Cthulhu right in the chest and ripped it apart. The shock waves of the shells landing in the cave opening crushed the countess's companions against the rock walls. *Freiherr* von Blaufels was propelled from the top of the staircase back into the chamber. He fell hard on the floor and suffered from a head injury and a broken leg. His eardrums had split, and he was bleeding from his nose and ears.

Dazed, he was unsuccessfully trying to get up when he saw the countess standing — unscathed — with her back to the chamber's wall next to the staircase. Unlike her companion, she hadn't climbed up the stairs behind the released monster and had escaped the blast waves. Disregarding her partner, she ran across the room and pushed hard on one of the pictograms on the rear wall. A panel slid open sideways, and Mathilde von Corvey disappeared forever from the *Freiherr*'s life. The next rounds from the HMS Bellerophon brought down the chamber's roof, burying him alive.

Two hours later, the countess emerged from an aperture on the other side of the mountain. It was semi-dark. She beheld the wasteland ahead of her. The storm brewing for the last hours had turned into a full-strength gale and tugged at her clothes. Temperatures had dropped to minus 5°F. She crouched down in the opening and waited for the snowstorm to abate. After four hours, the weather calmed down slightly; the countess got up and marched down the slope in pitch-black darkness.

It's going to be a long walk, she thought.

'It's no use organising a landing party now,' Fleming told the captain once the ship's guns had ceased firing. 'Soon, it'll be dark, and the glacier has probably become unstable. It's too dangerous.'

The captain looked at him, inquiringly.

'Why should we send a landing party at all, Commander?' he asked. 'The target has been destroyed. It serves no purpose endangering men's lives by sending them up that glacier.'

'Normally, you'd be right, Captain,' Fleming agreed. 'However, I want to see if there's anything left of the monster. Take samples of its remains, if possible. I need pictures too. It isn't something we've ever encountered before; we must learn all we can about it.'

'Well, we learnt it can't take a shitload of 12-inch shells, pardon my French,' the captain answered and left the bridge.

The next morning at the crack of dawn — which was only around eight o'clock — heavily armed volunteers lowered six lifeboats into the water and rowed them to the shore, carefully avoiding the dozens of icebergs bobbing around between the Dreadnought and the coastline.

Fleming alighted first and took in the damage up close. In daylight, the mountainside's devastation was even more impressive. He hoped to find sufficient evidence of the creature's demise. A close inspection of the pebble beach didn't deliver any results. So Fleming was forced to take his crew on a perilous march over the glacier. They took a roundabout route to circumvent the crevasses, most of which had opened after the bombardment. The fissures glowed a mesmerising blue that could easily entice unsuspecting victims to venture too close to the rim. The wounded glacier moaned, hissed, shrieked, and crackled. Occasionally, the sailors were startled by a sound like thunder when yet another lorry-sized berg calved off from the ice sheet.

At the foot of the remaining mountain flank, Fleming distributed his search team for maximum effectiveness. It took them more than an hour to find a first body part. It felt like a piece of rubber, strong and elastic, impossible to tear by hand. There was no trace of blood on it. A bit of tentacle was next, and then one discovery quickly followed another. One hour later, they had found thirty fragments, both large and small.

Finally, a sailor called out from the far end of the search area. He'd found most of the rest of the creature's mangled corpse, covered by a mass of rubble and rocks. Given that it had sustained a direct hit from a 12-inch shell, it was surprisingly intact. The body had been ripped apart lengthwise. They discovered one leg twenty yards further away. The blast had torn off part of the tentacles attached to the lower part of its face. A viscous, fluorescent, green liquid was dripping from one of seven eye-sockets.

Fleming collected the liquid in a glass container. He ordered the men to clear away the stones covering the body and then had a photographer take as many pictures as possible of the corpse. He even asked a group of sailors to take hold of the flaps of mangled flesh along the rip in the creature's body and to pull them far apart, allowing the photographer to take pictures of the corpse's insides. It didn't have a skeletal structure. Inspecting the head, Fleming was surprised to find it was as malleable as a deflated rubber ball. He tried to cut open the head with a pocket knife to get a look at the structure inside. To no avail. A sailor's bayonet did the trick, with great effort. The head didn't contain a bone structure either, nor a brain for that matter. There was only a large amount of fluorescent green goo inside. Each eye had two oblong pupils. When Fleming scooped out an eye, he noted the absence of an optic nerve. The eyes floated untethered in their rubbery orbits, protected by several semi-transparent membranes, without any connection to inner organs — which, by the way, were also conspicuous in their absence.

As a feeble midday sun broke through the iron-grey clouds, Fleming noted the corpse emitted a pungent smell — the earthy odours of rotting wood and dank cellars, combined with the overpowering, foul stink of hydrogen sulphide or rotten eggs. Although it was freezing, the body was decomposing at an alarming rate.

Fleming had to rule out bringing the entire corpse over to the HMS Bellerophon. It was too large to carry, and it would take far too long to construct a couple of sledges big enough to move it over the glacier to the beach. Luckily, Fleming had the foresight to bring several containers of alcohol and formaldehyde with him. Not knowing what would work best, he ordered the sailors to slice off body parts that would fit in the glass preserving jars he'd also brought. Then he poured alcohol in one of the pots. The result was disastrous. The alcohol immediately dissolved the tissue sample. Next, he tried the formaldehyde. The result was less spectacularly bad at first. Nevertheless, after a couple of minutes, the tissue also reacted with the formaldehyde, and the decomposition process accelerated again.

Fleming sent six sailors back to the shore to fill canisters with seawater. Precious hours were lost in waiting. Fleming's crew covered the body with a tarpaulin in the hope of slowing down its decay. As soon as the sailors came back, Fleming used some of the water to dilute the formaldehyde and added baking soda, obtaining formalin. The result was no different from that with undiluted formaldehyde. Exasperated, Fleming poured pure seawater in a jar and was surprised to see the deterioration process appeared to be halted.

In the next two hours, they worked frantically to collect as many samples as possible from different parts of the creature's body while its stench amplified to nauseating levels. When they were done, they'd filled and labelled one hundred and fifty jars of various sizes.

4

SSB Special Branch HQ, Glasgow

Tuesday, 16 January 1917

'Yes, enter.'

Fleming looked up from his papers, expecting his secretary to shove even more paperwork his way. When the door opened, a slender figure stood in the opening. Fleming had to look twice. His first impression was that it was an androgynous sort of adolescent. On second thought, he decided it might be a woman. She was dressed as a man, with a tight-fitting black suit and a burgundy waistcoat over a white shirt. She wore black riding boots that almost reached her knees. Her hair gave her away, even though she wore it shorter than most women of her day.

'Who are you?' he asked.

'I wrote to you. My name is Doctor Rebecca Mumm,' she answered. She had a slight French accent, which gave her English a certain charm.

Pointing at the stack of unopened mail on his desk, Fleming said, 'I've been a bit busy lately; still need to catch up on my mail.'

'The French government sent me to assist you,' she said patiently.

Fleming hurriedly got up from his chair and waved her in.

'Glad you're here, Doctor Mumm,' he welcomed his guest. 'I apologise for the confusion. We can certainly use the help.'

'Please, tell me, what are your qualifications?' he asked her when they both sat down.

'I'm a doctor in marine biology and oceanography. An excellent one. I work as a researcher at the Museum of Natural History in Paris and have a significant list of published research papers to my name.'

It came out as a matter-of-fact statement. She wasn't trying to impress Fleming or convince him she was right for the job. It was understood the British were lucky to have her.

Fleming let that sink in.

'What did they tell you exactly?' he asked, suspecting that her superiors in France hadn't told her the full story.

'That you're hunting a new species of cephalopod,' she said. 'Huge and aggressive, maybe even a danger to smaller ships and submarines. Sounds interesting.'

'Right.'

Fleming scratched his chin in thought and then got up.

'Please, follow me, Doctor Mumm.'

They walked to the end of the hallway where they reached a heavy door. Fleming opened it, and then they were standing in a fully equipped, modern laboratory. Against the back wall, two giant electric refrigerators were humming — brand-new Kelvinators, imported from the USA. Fleming opened the door of one of them and pointed at the rows of glass containers inside.

'Recently, we found parts of a dead specimen of the creature we're hunting. We took samples for further research and preserve them here. You'd do me a great service by taking a closer look at them.'

'Of course,' Doctor Mumm agreed. 'I'll get started immediately.'

Half an hour later, she stood in Fleming's doorway again, looking furious.

'Is this a prank? Some sort of silly initiation ritual before I can join your secret fraternity? Do you think that, just because I'm a woman, you're allowed to make a fool out of me?' she shouted.

'I have no idea what you're going on about,' Fleming replied calmly, motioning her in. 'What did you discover that upset you so?'

'The samples you had me look at aren't of a cephalopod at all.'

'They aren't?'

'No, they aren't. It isn't even animal tissue. You must have thought I was a complete idiot!' Doctor Mumm said, seething.

'If it isn't animal tissue, then what is it?'

Fleming's relaxed demeanour irritated her unspeakably; she barely managed not to shout at him again.

'The texture is fibrous, like a plant or, more accurately, a fungus. It's tough and rubbery. I was almost unable to cut off a small sample for studying it under the microscope. I don't know what it is. It isn't a marine animal.'

She stared Fleming right in the eye.

'Are you planning to tell me what I've been wasting my time on or not?'

Fleming shoved a thick folder on his desk towards her.

'Please, have a look, Doctor Mumm. We took these pictures a couple of days ago.'

She undid the ribbon that tied the folder together and opened it. Inside, she found nearly one hundred pictures of the Greenland creature's carcass. They showed every detail of the monster, both inside and outside. She stared at them, one after the other, in silence. When she looked up, she'd calmed down.

'I've never seen anything like this,' she whispered almost inaudibly.

Fleming reached in the cupboard behind him and took out a bottle of Laphroaig and two shot glasses. He poured them both a stiff drink and told her what had happened in Flanders and Greenland.

'This isn't what I signed up for,' Doctor Mumm said in a toneless voice. 'I can never publish a scientific paper about this. You'll never go public with any of it, and if you did, it would make you — and me — the academic community's laughing stock. They'd all believe it was a hoax. And then to think I let the opportunity pass to be appointed assistant professor at the Sorbonne University for this. Damn Liard!'

'Who?', asked Fleming.

'Liard. Louis Liard. He's the Vice-Rector at the Sorbonne. Damned liar,' Doctor Mumm muttered. 'He buttered me up to accept this assignment. Told me it was "a project of great academic importance", a gateway to a quick appointment as a full professor. It appears it was only a scheme to get me out of the way, so he can appoint a protégé of his good friend Briand. Liard is a political animal. He's extremely well connected. Without his support, a career in academia in my country is almost unthinkable. He's been the Department of Higher Education's director for more than twenty years. He worked directly for the minister of education and served as a minister himself for a year in one of Briand's governments. I should have known he never had the intention to offer a professorship to a woman and a Jew to boot.'

'Mumm didn't strike me as a Jewish name,' was all Fleming found to reply.

Doctor Mumm finished her fourth shot of whisky.

'No, but Himmelfarb definitely is. That's my mother's name,' she said.

Fleming leaned back and looked at the crestfallen woman. He found he sympathised with her. He couldn't even begin to imagine the obstacles she must have overcome to make her way in the exclusively male world of French academia. And the Dreyfus Affair, which had rocked France for twelve years, could leave no one in doubt about the deep-rooted anti-Semitism that prevailed from the lowest to the highest ranks in French society.

'Maybe it's not what you signed up for,' he admitted, 'but it could be something much better. You could learn things here you never knew existed. There's an entire world out there that only a select inner circle knows about. If you stay with us, you will become one of the few initiated. Besides, what do you have to go back to, Doctor? A university that doesn't want you? You could do some great work here. We could use a good scientist, that's for certain.'

'What do you mean with "a world nobody knows about"? You sound mysterious. And vague. Vaguely mysterious or mysteriously vague. It's one or the other. You'll need to do better to convince me I'm not wasting my time here. Much, much better,' she sputtered, slightly slurring her words. 'And why would you even try to keep me? I'm French. There are plenty of British scientists who fit your needs just as well.'

'We asked the French prime minister to send over somebody to assist us and who could double as a liaison officer with the French government. If we want to fight this thing, we'd be better off with French support. That means we need your government's trust,' Fleming spelt out. 'If you go back to France, they'll send over someone else — someone I'll probably like less than you. So I'm asking you to think this over and stay.'

'I need more information,' she insisted. 'Fool me once, shame on you, fool me twice, — you know the rest.'

'All right, that's only fair,' Fleming said, getting up.

He knew he was taking a risk. M would have his head on a plate if he spilt all their secrets, and then Doctor Mumm still decided to abandon ship. He had a gut feeling, though, she could be convinced to stay — he'd been wrong before, though.

'I want to introduce you to a fellow academic. Please, follow me.'

He knocked on the door across the hall. After they'd both entered, Doctor Mumm saw a small, fat man with wild, white hair sitting behind a desk stacked with ancient tomes. The office had been transformed into a chaotic library. There wasn't a book on display that wasn't at least two centuries old.

'Isn't it a bit early for a pub crawl, Fleming?' the gnome behind the desk asked, sniffing the air for the Laphroaig's peaty smell.

Then he noticed Doctor Mumm.

'And why don't you introduce me to the charming young lady at your side, my boy? Where are your manners?'

He had a heavy Scandinavian accent and a smile that could melt icebergs.

'Professor, I want you to meet Doctor Rebecca Mumm. She's a researcher at the Museum of Natural History in Paris and a specialist in marine biology and oceanography,' Fleming obliged. 'Doctor Mumm, please meet Professor Ove Eliassen, Professor Emeritus at the History Department of the University of Uppsala in Sweden. The professor is specialised in ancient languages and religions, and also in esotericism.'

'It's a great pleasure to meet you,' the professor said, beaming at Doctor Mumm. 'How can I be of service?'

Fleming moved aside stacks of books from the chairs, so they could sit down.

'Doctor Mumm is considering joining our team. She requires more information about what we do before making her decision. I thought we could brief her together.'

Then he turned to Doctor Mumm.

'This Special Branch of His Majesty's Secret Service Bureau was already created under Good Queen Bess in 1567,' he began.

'That's Queen Elizabeth I,' the professor helpfully added, as he saw Doctor Mumm was puzzled at the mention of 'Good Queen Bess'.

'Right,' Fleming continued. 'She tasked her spymaster, Sir Francis Walsingham, and her cryptographer, alchemist, and mage, Doctor John Dee, with the establishment of a service that could keep track of the activities of non-human sentient beings on her territories. It was then a common belief that elves, pixies, goblins, leprechauns, and other creatures of myth truly existed and could meddle in human affairs. Naturally, the queen wished to be kept abreast of any scheming on these creatures' part that could affect her position.'

'You're pulling my leg!' Doctor Mumm exclaimed.

'I most certainly am not,' assured Fleming while the professor shook his head in confirmation. 'Although the English monarch was the first to establish such a service, she was by no means the only one. Gustav II, King of Sweden, created his in 1615. We've been working closely with the Swedes ever since a contingent of seventeen huge trolls landed in the town of Wick in Northern Scotland in 1722 and started a deadly rampage along the eastern Highland coast. Thanks to the information provided by our Swedish colleagues, we were able to stop them before they reached Invergordon. The Holy Roman Emperor Maximilian II ordered the creation of a similar specialist team in 1574, two years before his death. His successor, Rudolf II, built it into the best performing secret service on the continent. The visionary Tsar Peter the Great made sure Russia had one as of 1687. The Germans were much later. It was Frederick the Great, King of Prussia, who was the first to establish a team of esoteric investigators in 1751. Even France had its service for a brief while. Louis XVI created it in 1786. It didn't survive the French Revolution, and it was never resurrected.'

'This is such superstitious nonsense!' Doctor Mumm cried out, rolling her eyes. 'These things don't exist. They simply cannot! And I'll tell you why. There's no way all these fairy-tale creatures can be made to fit into Earth's Tree of Life, which, by the way, was established by your most eminent scientist, Charles Darwin. You know I'm a biologist. I can't be fooled like this. I have yet to see the first convincing evidence that refutes Darwin's theory of evolution, and I'm sure it won't be imps — or even trolls for that matter — that will change my mind.'

'Oh, Darwin was quite right,' Professor Eliassen agreed, 'and you're correct in assuming these creatures don't fit into Earth's Tree of Life, Doctor. They don't *need* to, as their origins do not lie on Earth.'

'Of course not, they all flew in from the moon,' Doctor Mumm snorted, and she made to stand up and leave the room. '*Quel cirque!* I'm done here.'

'Haven't you noticed anything peculiar about our Commander Fleming here, Doctor Mumm?' Professor Eliassen asked.

Doctor Mumm scrutinised Fleming. He had a triangular face with a strong jaw and a Roman nose, somewhat sad, grey-blue eyes, and dark-blond hair that could use a trimming, no beard nor moustache. He was good-looking but nothing exceptional.

'I can't say I have,' she concluded.

'Look closer. The ears,' Professor Eliassen insisted.

Doctor Mumm looked again. And then she saw it. Under the carefully combed hair covering the top of Fleming's ears, she distinguished a distinct sharpness of the helixes.

'So what? He has pointy ears. Does that make him a pixie maybe?' she jested.

'Heavens, no! I wouldn't dare to suggest anything outrageous like that,' Professor Eliassen conceded, adding with a mischievous smile, 'He's one-quarter elf and three-quarters human. His grandfather married an elf.'

She eyed Fleming again, expecting him to deny the preposterous claim. He did no such thing and looked back at her inscrutably.

'The reality, Doctor Mumm,' Professor Eliassen continued, 'is that almost all creatures from myth and legend — all the gods from all the different pantheons in the world — really exist or have existed at some point in time on our planet. And at the heart of that reality, known by only a few mortals, lies an even deeper, much darker secret.'

He stood up, walked to a blackboard covered in scribbles, and flipped it over on its horizontal axis. The other side was blank, and the professor drew a set of overlapping parallelograms on it.

'Our reality, our universe is only one of many. There are many, many parallel universes. Millions or even billions of them; we don't know for sure. Now, imagine a giant stack of thin wooden plates.'

He pointed at the parallelograms on the blackboard.

'Each plate represents a separate universe. Some universes are empty, devoid of life or even planets or stars. Others are teeming with life. The laws of nature may be extremely different from one universe to another. The beings in each universe live contained within their plate's confines. There appears to be no way they can know about the other plates in the stack. There also appears to be no way they can get from one plate to another. And yet, millions of years ago, *some* species in *some* universe that wasn't ours did exactly that. Let me use another figure of speech to make it clear to you what happened, and please keep in mind: This is only a metaphor. It's not what happened, but it'll help you to understand. It was as if that species in that faraway universe took a huge pickaxe and smashed it into the stack of plates.'

He drew a thick arrow through all the parallelograms on the blackboard.

'The pickaxe burst through an enormous number of plates in the stack, creating a gaping hole in each of them and forcing fragments from the upper plates into plates deeper in the stack. The hole now connects all of these previously hermetic universes. Moreover, all plates were cracked to some extent. This destroyed or at least weakened the boundaries between the different universes. Earth is the planet closest to the hole the pickaxe made in our universe, and there are lots of cracks radiating from that hole. Each universe lost its pristine integrity: Parts of other universes — splinters as it were — were mixed up with ours. The maze of cracks caused by the pickaxe hole are pathways leading from one universe to another. That's how life from thousands of other universes landed on Earth or indirectly obtained the means to reach our planet.'

'Where's the proof of all that? And who were the beings that wielded the "pickaxe"?' Doctor Mumm asked, far from convinced.

'Over the centuries, travellers, adventurers, and archaeologists have discovered artefacts and even edifices that are unimaginably ancient. They predate the earliest human societies by millions of years,' Fleming told her. 'In Britain, some of them are kept in a secret storage room and archive at the British Museum. We know the Humboldt University and the Kaiser Friedrich Museum in Berlin also have such archaeological oddities in their vaults. References to the beings that caused this disturbance of the universes can be found in many texts. The genesis myths in several cultures, such as the Mayan, the Aztec, and the

Hindu ones, vaguely hint at these terrifying beings. There are also more recent texts that let us believe that, throughout the ages, obscure cults have survived, which worship these creatures as gods who one day will return to Earth.'

'So they visited Earth, lived here for a while, and then packed up and left?' Doctor Mumm summarised.

'So it would seem, yes,' Professor Eliassen agreed.

'How would these "obscure cults" know anything reliable at all about these "gods" if they left Earth aeons before humankind came into existence? That doesn't make much sense now, does it?' Doctor Mumm challenged them.

'There were witnesses present at the moment of the cataclysm,' Fleming reminded her. 'Remember, many sentient species were displaced from other universes to ours and landed on our planet. Some of them have accounts of what happened because they wrote them down in their history books. I'll admit most of it isn't clear because they didn't know what exactly happened either. Nevertheless, if you piece together the accounts of several species, a fairly coherent view on what happened emerges.'

'You have books here written by goblins and fairies?' she blurted out in disbelief.

Professor Eliassen took a scroll from his library and partially unrolled it on his desk. On its parchment-like paper, Doctor Mumm could distinguish columns of alien squiggles written in purplish ink, which gave her an impression of great delicacy. The professor opened another tome, similar to a medieval grimoire, and its script consisted of a series of brush-painted square pictograms of varying sizes. Some of them covered an entire page; others were no larger than thumbnails. The last one he showed was a narrow, oblong gatefold book that contained something akin to cuneiform script. As in the Sumerian script, some characters looked like feathers while others resembled hooks, spiders, tree branches, or lightning flashes. Doctor Mumm passed her fingers over the pages in speechless wonder. The gatefold volume's pages didn't feel like either paper or parchment at all. They were razor-thin and hard and sleek as Bakelite. The characters were embossed on the surface.

'Can you read all this?' Doctor Mumm asked in awe.

'I'm reasonably fluent in about eight of these languages,' Professor Eliassen declared, 'and I have a rudimentary understanding of some twenty more. Quite a few of these scripts are no longer used or even understood by the peoples that created them. A surprising number of races never even developed a script. They keep their collective histories in hive minds or other types of information carriers that are difficult for humans to access. The majority of species that landed here originally are by now extinct anyway or have left Earth again, via the cracks I told you about.'

'Do these texts have anything helpful to say about what happened in Flanders or Greenland?' she wondered.

'As I already mentioned, most races were deeply confused when they were catapulted to Earth from their universes,' Professor Eliassen explained. 'Several describe the existence of a layered multiverse, though. We also have a few baffling descriptions of the powerful beings that landed them here. Most of them must have been so alien their looks couldn't be caught in words. It also seems they weren't a single species as we understand that concept. They appear to be a group of physically unrelated, individual entities of unimaginable power. That's why most texts call them "gods", although not in the sense of "creators of heaven and Earth". They came in from the outside and are mostly referred to as "Outer Gods".'

Ove Eliassen opened a luxuriously illustrated book and pointed at a picture of a dark and tentacled creature lifting its head above the water, dragging ships to the bottom of the sea, and tumbling mountains.

'The cephalopod species we recently encountered is described in several books. It even has a name: Catulou, Chootloo, or Cthulhu – depending on the source document. It's difficult to distinguish myth from actual information in these texts. They agree on several things, though. The Outer Gods left Earth well before the dawn of human civilisation. The reasons for their departure are unknown. A few documents describe the erection of temple-like structures in the centuries before they left. That indicates it was a carefully prepared move and not a head-over-heels flight. One text calls these edifices "*the Abodes of the Sleeping Gods*". Another reports one of those temples sinking to the bottom of the sea when the waves swallowed the antediluvian city of R'lyeh millennia later. Sometimes, Cthulhu is described as an individual being. However, several of the oldest texts refer to the cephalopod in the plural. They describe it as an incredibly powerful being, even if its powers and status don't seem to be on a par with those of the creatures who left Earth.'

The professor came to the core of his argument.

'A couple of primary sources hint at its purpose. Cthulhu is defined as a *gate opener* — sometimes singular, sometimes plural. This theme is, strangely enough, also found in a few obscure, apocalyptic, medieval and early Renaissance texts. They predict the end times will arrive "*when the stars are right*" and when "*He Who Whispers in Dreams*" awakens the Cthulhu. In an old Arabic text — of which I've found a partial copy in a Latin translation at the Bodleian — the Outer Gods' return is prophesied "*when the Five open the Gate*". This might mean five Cthulhus are needed to perform the ritual necessary to allow the Outer Gods to return.

'It doesn't take a whole lot of imagination to conclude that the gate openers' awakening has begun,' Fleming added. 'Countess von Corvey plays an important role in this process, and we've been following her for several years.

Unless other individuals are also involved, this would provide us with the certainty that she's awakened one Cthulhu and failed with a second one. As the Outer Gods have apparently hidden a large number of sites with dormant Cthulhus around the globe, we're now involved in a race against the countess to discover them first. If we fail, and the gates are opened to let the Outer Gods in again, there's no telling what would happen. I expect nothing good to come from it — to put it mildly. We may consider the current war against the Central Powers as the civilised world's Armageddon, whereas the true endgame might be played at an entirely different level altogether.'

Doctor Mumm nodded; her earlier scepticism had ebbed. This was indeed much bigger than the discovery of a new type of giant octopus, and she did want to be part of it. She still had difficulties believing everything she'd been told. The gravity with which both Fleming and Eliassen had explained their story was, however, compelling. And Fleming was right: What did she have to go back to?

5

SSB Special Branch HQ, Glasgow

Wednesday, 24 January 1917

The past week had been hectic. Fleming's team was scrambling for a meeting with M. Its outcome would decide on the priority level of the race against Countess von Corvey. Doctor Mumm spent day and night in her laboratory. Professor Eliassen barely left his library.

When M arrived late in the afternoon on a private train from London, they were all exhausted but felt well prepared. They sat down in a sparse meeting room. Over tea, Fleming introduced Doctor Mumm to M. Upon hearing Doctor Mumm had to give up on a Sorbonne lectureship to join this team, M gave Fleming a told-you-so look.

M had met Professor Eliassen before. Eliassen joined the team in the first year of the war, after his predecessor — a Professor Emeritus from Cambridge University — had died in an accident. A cable-car had upended his horse-drawn carriage in Chicago, where he'd been visiting his daughter. Fleming had tried to find a proper British substitute. One candidate categorically refused. Another proved to be inadequate. The only remaining alternative shot himself after being notified that both of his sons had fallen in the first battle of Ypres. Because of the Special Branch's close co-operation with the Swedish government, Fleming could secure Eliassen's candidature. The professor turned out to be a valuable asset.

Once the formalities were over, M opened the meeting by congratulating Fleming on his feat in Greenland.

'Thank you, M,' Fleming replied. 'We have Kidner's level-headedness to thank for this success. If he hadn't been able to pick up the countess's trace after the murder of poor Spencer, we could never have intervened in time.'

'I read the report on the Kiel murder,' M said. 'I'm sure you noticed the disturbing similarities with the murders of Catherine Eddowes and Mary Jane Kelly, Jack the Ripper's two last victims. Do you believe the murderer was trying to tell us something?'

'The Ripper murders date back almost thirty years. We know Countess von Corvey was already around at that time, so it's a distinct possibility,' Fleming agreed. 'It would, however, require a significant effort to trace her whereabouts in that period. I believe our resources can be put to better use. After all, it might only be a sick prank, messing with our minds to detract us from what really matters.'

'Then let's focus on what really matters,' M agreed. 'Tell me what you've found out.'

Fleming motioned Doctor Mumm to give her report.

'The creature is alien,' she began. 'At first sight, it looks like a chimera, a monster put together from body parts of different types of animals — bat wings, squid tentacles, amphibian webbed feet, fish scales, you name it. That's where the analogy ends, however.'

She opened a map and dug out several detailed anatomical drawings she'd made, based on the photographs Fleming had provided.

'As you can see, it has no skeletal structure whatsoever. No endoskeleton as can be found in vertebrates and no exoskeleton as in the arthropod phylum. That would put it in the mollusc phylum, of which cephalopods are a class. It's also entirely lacking in internal organs, though. No brains, lungs, heart, or digestive system. Nor could I detect reproductive or nervous systems. The eyes don't seem to be connected to anything. Its head contained a luminescent, viscous, green fluid, which was absent from other body parts. It's tempting to believe this fluid acts as some sort of brain, though I cannot support that with scientific facts. It might well be an energy source, like the yolk in an egg.'

She'd brought a glass jar half-filled with the mystery substance. It was still glowing. The intensity of its brightness varied over time. It went through a cycle that lasted about ten minutes from lowest to highest luminosity. The light pulse was steady over time and had a mesmerising effect on all present.

Doctor Mumm broke the spell by passing around a set of photographs and drawings of cell structures she'd observed under the microscope.

'I made these using the specimens Fleming brought in from Greenland. These cells are neither animal nor plant. The closest likeness I could find, are those of fungi. The cell walls are exceptionally rigid, which explains why the tissue is hard to slice through. One would expect polysaccharides in there as long-chain polymers like chitin are needed to strengthen the cell walls. I could, however, find no trace of glucose derivatives in any of the samples. Another, far stronger, substance must account for the toughness of the cell walls. Fleming has experienced that alcohol acts as a solvent on the creature's tissue. This indicates it isn't carbon-based. Alcohol dissolves the hydroxides in alkali metals, chlorides, and some metallic nitrates, whereas carbonates and sulphates are insoluble in alcohol. A further chemical analysis of tissue samples confirmed the presence of compounds containing tungsten, titanium, oxygen, phosphorus, and acidic hydrogen. It's well known to science that combinations of oxygen and certain metals can lead to highly complex and stable configurations, comparable to carbon-based organic compounds. What we have here is a non-carbon-based life form that mainly consists of fungi-like fibrous filaments. The presence of tough metals, like tungsten and titanium, render the cell walls, and thus the filaments, extremely robust. The filaments somehow bond together into solid structures that give the creature its outward appearance. Even though this being's precise organic chemistry largely eludes me, I think it's safe to say these cells may contain an extraordinary capacity for growth and further strengthening.'

'In other words: The creatures we've encountered thus far were in an early life stage. Given time, they'll grow much taller and be even more difficult to destroy,' M offered as a summary.

'Exactly,' affirmed Doctor Mumm. 'Think of a butterfly erupting from its chrysalid: It needs time to harden its wings in the air. This creature had just left its chrysalid — or whatever it was — when it was hit by a 12-inch armour-piercing shell. While it was indeed killed, its body remained largely intact. As it gets older, it's my understanding it'll become invulnerable to even our heaviest ordnance.'

'How big will it grow?' M asked.

'Difficult to say,' Doctor Mumm admitted. 'If you allow me to use the fungus analogy again: There's almost *no* limit to the growth of mycelium's hyphae. In the creature's case, I think gravity *will* impose limits on its growth. A final height of one hundred and fifty feet wouldn't surprise me at all. If its habitat is restricted to the oceans, it might even grow to a much larger size.'

They all considered this. A monster of those proportions could be a threat to mid-sized ships. As if U-Boats weren't a big enough problem already.

'There's one more thing I'd like to add,' Doctor Mumm said. 'This is a life form unlike any other found thus far on Earth. Its primary components are metal-oxides. Kicking off chemical reactions resulting in this type of complex molecular structures requires exceedingly high temperatures — in the range of several thousand degrees Centigrade. These temperatures only naturally occur in the planet's core. Moreover, natural evolution, which is the basis of all observable life on Earth, dictates a slow mutation process that leads from simple to ever more complex life forms. The evidence of evolution can be found in *every* being's anatomy. Part of every mammal's brain is reptilian; whale skeletons contain vestigial leg bones; our spine isn't designed for walking in an upright position. Except perhaps for the vestigial bat wings — which, by the way, may well grow into fully functional wings later in life and thus might *not* be vestigial at all — I couldn't find a single trace of evolution in the anatomy of this being. This creature is a sophisticated life form. It cannot have sprung, all at once, spontaneously, fully formed into existence in our Earth's core — or inside a star, for all I care.'

She emphatically concluded, 'As Leibniz said, and Darwin repeated after him, *"Natura non facit saltum"*. Nature doesn't make leaps. Therefore, it stands to reason this creature has been *designed* by other, highly evolved beings.'

M looked thoughtfully, first at Doctor Mumm and then at her colleagues.

'It doesn't come as a surprise that this is an extraterrestrial creature. Over the past centuries, we've discovered plenty of those. What concerns us is the nature and threat level of these monsters,' he pointed out. 'Are they "merely" an occasional danger to troops and sea traffic, or is there a different and far more threatening purpose to their existence? More specifically: Is there a connection between *this* species and the Outer Gods or not? And if so, is it their purpose to help the Outer Gods return to Earth? Do you have any answers to that?'

'I think it's safe to say this creature has to be linked to the Outer Gods,' Fleming said, confirming M's worst fears. 'Professor Eliassen has found sufficient references in his library to substantiate that conclusion.'

The Swedish professor confirmed, 'We're contending with two types of enemies: the monsters themselves and the one who unleashes them.'

'What do we know about the latter?' M asked.

'He's often mentioned in texts of varying ages,' Professor Eliassen replied. 'He's one of the Outer Gods and probably the only one left behind as all the others departed from Earth. In the most ancient texts, he's referred to by many names. The most common ones are the Faceless God, the Crawling Chaos, and also the Whisperer in Dreams. He's said to be the offspring of a being called Azathoth, apparently a primordial among the Outer Gods. Within their pantheon, Azathoth seems to hold the highest rank — if such a logic applies to them at all. The Faceless God is a disembodied entity, not so much a spirit as an absence of existence. A black, unfathomable void, ageless and deathless — easier to be defined by what he's *not*, than by what he truly is. In more recent texts, such as in the exceptionally rare Arabic *Necronomicon*, dating from the eighth century AD, he's called Nyarlathotep or the Black Pharaoh. As far as I can determine, this may be the name of an Upper Egyptian or Nubian pre-dynastic ruler, who lived well before the unified Old Kingdom's founding and the establishment of the first dynasty around 3,000 BC. The Outer God possessed this pharaoh's body and took his name. It's believed the Dream Whisperer can only interact with our world through physical beings he possesses. He first comes to them in their sleep. He appears in their dreams and entices them with promises of eternal youth, wealth, and great power.'

'Which explains the countess's youthful looks, despite her being over a century old,' Fleming added.

'Several authors establish links between the Faceless God and dark gods in various pantheons,' the professor continued, 'trickster gods, death gods, night gods, or chthonic deities. Many of them required human sacrifices or had cannibalistic cults that worshipped them. The list goes on forever. Just to give you an idea of what we might be dealing with: Kali in the Hindu pantheon, Loki among the Nordic gods, Eshu of the Yoruba, Huehuecoyotl or Mithlantecuhtli among the Aztecs, Erlik in Eurasia and Siberia, Mot in the Canaanite pantheon, and Hecate in the Greek one. And not to forget, the Christian, Jewish, and Muslim beliefs identify him as Satan.'

M sighed, 'So it seems our adversary is the Devil incarnate. I'd say the odds aren't stacked in our favour.'

'This is the worst we've ever had to deal with,' Fleming acknowledged. 'It makes Tunguska look like child's play.'

'Do we have a battle plan?' M asked.

'The Outer Gods left the Dream Whisperer behind for a reason, and that reason is linked to their return,' Fleming replied. 'Apparently, he's unable to open the gates — or portal, or whatever you want to call it — himself. He wakes up the beings the Outer Gods designed for this purpose. The good news is that a single Cthulhu cannot do the job either.'

'Yes, numerous texts indicate *five* of them are needed,' Professor Eliassen confirmed.

'The Outer Gods left Earth aeons ago,' Fleming continued. 'They knew that, even if they built fortified accommodations for their Sleepers, at least *some* of these dwellings would be lost before their residents were awakened. We can be sure that far more than five such sites exist.'

Professor Eliassen unfolded a large-scale world map dotted with several types of markings.

'I've tried to make an inventory of all known and potential Sleeper resting places. Mind you: This is a work in progress. Friedrich von Junzt, on his own, allegedly discovered three Sleeper sites during his travels, and there are many more. Once one knows how to look for them, references abound in occult texts — albeit often far too vague to pinpoint their exact spots. I also tracked down the locations of obscure cults that might indicate the presence of Sleepers. Some of the texts I consulted suggest such cults function as caretakers and protectors of the sites.'

Eliassen pointed at the map.

'I've distinguished between near-certainties and educated guesses. The former are marked with red crosses — there are only five of those — the latter with black ones. Note that neither Zoetevoorde nor Skjöldungen is among the locations on the map. I couldn't find a single reference to them in any of my books. So it's wise to assume there are plenty of other sites we don't know the first thing about. Then there are sites hinted at without exact specification of their geographical situation. For instance, there's often mention of an antediluvian city somewhere on Antarctica with a Sleeper's cradle at its heart. I have, however, *no* clue what the exact location of this city might be.'

'Confronting the Dream Whisperer directly, to prevent him from awakening any other Sleepers, would be suicidal. He's too powerful; we need to work *around* him,' Fleming continued. 'We'll go ahead as you announced in Gravelines, M. The plan would be to raid the locations marked with red crosses first. These targets have the highest probability of success. We should concentrate our resources on them first and then we'll focus on the black crosses. Our only chance is to destroy as many Sleepers as possible before the Dream Whisperer can get to them. If we kill enough of these monsters, the Dream Whisperer won't be able to awaken five Sleepers, and the portal will remain closed. To be effective, we'll need several teams working in parallel as the target sites are scattered all over the globe.'

'I agree. That's what I told the French president to get his support. I'll see to it that you get all the necessary British resources to organise these raids,' M said. 'But I

84

must tell you I'm far from convinced that we have a full picture of this Dream Whisperer's true intentions.'

M held up his hand as the professor began to protest.

'Consider this. He's had ages to prepare. He knows where all the caches are and which ones still contain viable Sleepers. He has a considerable advantage over us and could have proceeded on the quiet, without us knowing what he's up to. Awakening the Sleepers involves a lot of travel. Travelling is far easier — and less conspicuous — in peacetime. Nevertheless, with the murder of the Austrian archduke, he chose to set off the hostilities leading to the current world conflict. Of all Sleeper sites available to him, he picked one right in the middle of a heavily fought-over war zone. Then the creature went on a murderous rampage. It alerted everybody to its awakening and led us to the discovery of the Dream Whisperer.'

'Are you arguing the Dream Whisperer has made his task *deliberately* difficult, M?' Doctor Mumm suggested.

'His logic escapes me,' M conceded. 'Which leads me to conclude there's more to this than what we know.'

6

The Globe, Sauchiehall Street, Glasgow

Wednesday, 24 January 1917

After the meeting, M retired with Fleming to make some phone calls to secure the military's co-operation. Professor Eliassen and Doctor Mumm gathered their documents and walked back to their offices.

Professor Eliassen winked at his colleague, saying, 'What do you think, Mumm, are you up for drinks and dinner?'

He knew she loathed the local food in pubs and restaurants almost as much as cooking her own dinner. She contemplated his proposal without enthusiasm.

'Come on, Mumm, I found a nice place on Sauchiehall Street. It's called "The Globe".'

'And do they have a menu intelligible to a civilised person?' she replied tartly. 'I've had my fill of rumbledethumps, cock-a-leekie, mince 'n tatties, and haggis with clapshot.'

'They cook a mean steak. We can take the tramway,' Professor Eliassen said, wiggling his bushy eyebrows.

Doctor Mumm couldn't suppress a smile. The old man's eternal good humour had that effect on her.

The restaurant was crowded, and at first, it seemed they'd have to look elsewhere. Fortunately, the professor was a well-known patron. A helpful waiter ushered them to a quieter corner.

'I like coming here. The temperance mob hasn't sunk its claws in this place yet,' Professor Eliassen chuckled.

They'd barely sat down when the same waiter showed up with a cold pint of lager from Glasgow's Drygate Brewery and put it in front of the Swede while handing them the menus.

'I could use one of those as well,' Doctor Mumm told the waiter.

The waiter didn't blink, and a minute later she was sipping the ice-cold beer.

'So tell me Ove — and stop calling me Mumm; I'm not your mother; call me Rebecca — how did you get into the monster business?'

Ove put the menu aside and leaned towards his dinner partner.

'I was the runt of the litter,' he confessed. 'Father was a fur and lumber trader, and he owned a paper mill as well. My parents had six children, five boys and a girl. My four brothers were all eager to go into business. I had no head for it. I was doing well at school, though, and when I was sixteen, my headmaster entered an essay I'd written about the Edda and Nordic mythology in a national competition. In that essay, I wrote about how human — how much like us — the Nordic gods were, and how thin the line was between human heroes and the *Æsir*. I didn't win the competition, but a government official came knocking at our door a few weeks later. He proposed to let me study at the University of Uppsala at the government's expenses, provided that I agreed to specialise in old Nordic literature and history.'

The waiter returned to take their orders. Ove ordered steaks for both of them, without bothering to ask Rebecca whether that was all right with her.

'I was enthusiastic, and so was my father — because, frankly, he had no idea what to do with me,' Ove continued. 'After a year at the university, I was introduced to Laurentius Björklund. He was then heading the nation's secret service dealing with alien beings. He explained to me the *Æsir* and the other creatures of Nordic myths — like dwarves, kobolds, elves, giants, and trolls — were all real. The government needed people who could understand their languages and reason with them, he said, and he thought I was up to the task. I obtained my official degree at the university while I studied the more occult stuff on the side, under Björklund's tutelage. I've been working for the secret service ever since. I was also offered a professorship in old Norse and ancient Nordic literature at my university — which was great because I love teaching young people. After my retirement as a university professor in 1911, I stayed on at the secret service. Two and a half years ago, Fleming asked whether I'd be interested in joining his team. It was an unexpected but welcome challenge in my old age. With my superior's approval, I jumped at the opportunity.'

'Good for you. Wasn't it hard to leave your family behind in Sweden?'

Ove shrugged.

'What family? My brothers are all dead, and I never got on well with my sister. She's a religious fanatic; I can't talk to her without getting into an argument. I'm too old for that.'

'Lutheran reformed?' Rebecca asked.

'Yes, the worst. I could never bring myself to believe in God. It was always a bone of contention between my sister and me.'

'Isn't it strange being an atheist knowing gods actually exist?' Rebecca wondered.

'These beings are *not* gods!' Ove exclaimed. 'That's what a lot of people, even in our business, fail to understand. They didn't create the universe; they didn't create humankind, and they do not have our best interests at heart. Often, these creatures look at us with great disdain because they happen to be more powerful than we are. Some of them used this advantage over us to make our forefathers believe they were actual gods and worthy of worship and sacrifices. A lot of good it did them.'

'Why? Being venerated as gods doesn't strike me as too bad a deal.' Rebecca said, sipping her beer.

'Oh, well, you'd be surprised. This god business generated intense rivalry. They all wanted to be the most loved or most feared deity, preferably with the largest number of disciples. It all turned into some kind of competition. The result was spite, jealousy, and violence. There have been terrible fights between the so-called gods, and those petty quarrels led to their near-extinction. Only a few of the Old Gods are left.'

'How about the Christian and Jewish god?'

'Well, Nietzsche was right — at least, on that subject. God *is* dead,' Ove chuckled. 'He was a nasty piece of work. Originally, in the Bronze Age, Yahweh was an obscure, Bedouin nature deity, who didn't even have a place in the Canaanite pantheon. Through intrigue and murder, he supplanted El, the main god in the pantheon, and had himself proclaimed as the only true God, creator of heaven and Earth. His main competitor — Baal, a powerful fertility god — was recast as the Devil and ultimately killed off. Yahweh was a jealous, unjust, and interfering creature. That much is obvious from the Old Testament. He was responsible for a genocide among his equals, which left him as the last man standing. He lived to see the Roman Emperor Constantine the Great convert to Christianity and declare religious tol-

90

erance for Christians. Then he disappeared. Presumably, he died or left through one of the cracks to another universe. By then, the Christian church was well enough organised to establish itself as the Roman state religion and to propagate itself throughout the empire. You know the rest. All the schisms and feuds among Christians are of *their* making, not his.'

. 'And Christ?' Rebecca wanted to know, riveted by Ove's tale.

'A normal human being who never claimed to be a god, as far as I know. Saint Paul recast him — well after his death — as a divinity in his own right, and he also reformulated Christ's message to increase its appeal to gentile audiences. Saint Paul was quite a propaganda expert. Phineas T. Barnum had nothing on him.'

'My mother would love to hear this,' Rebecca laughed.

'She isn't a strict believer, then?' the professor presumed.

'Would she have married a *goy* if she was?' his table companion shot back with a big smile.

The waiter returned with a trolley carrying two plates of enormous Porterhouse steaks covered in whisky-sauce, a large bowl of baked potatoes, and another one with steaming greens.

'Who'll eat all that?' Rebecca exclaimed.

The professor didn't answer and knotted his napkin around his neck. For a while, it was silent at the table as they were digging into their mountains of food.

'Your turn,' Eliassen said between bites. 'What made you become a sea biologist?'

'*La mer est plus belle que les cathédrales*,' Rebecca answered.

'The sea is more beautiful than the cathedrals,' Eliassen repeated, tasting the words on his tongue, 'Nice. What does it mean?'

'It's a line by one of the sorriest beings who ever lived and also happened to be France's greatest poet: Paul Verlaine. I'm not a religious person, and I'm not entirely sure what Verlaine intended to say. To me, it means the divine can only be discovered in nature's splendour, in the oceans' awe-inspiring greatness, and not in the petty dogmas of the church. That line tells me not to bend down to any god man has fabricated, not to submit to any man-made institution that pretends to know what God expects of me, and to experience with all my senses nature's overwhelming beauty, which is the most marvellous gift bestowed on humanity.'

'That's more of a poetic than a scientific attitude if you ask me,' Ove commented.

'Why should one necessarily have to exclude the other?' Rebecca challenged him. 'Why couldn't we combine a sense of awe with a desire to understand how nature works? I don't see the contradiction. My father was a botanist, and he shared that same sense of wonder. The instant Darwin published his magnum opus in 1859, my father was smitten with the theory of evolution. He'd already written a few minor papers himself that went in that general direction. Darwin's work was an epiphany for my father. He wrote Darwin a supportive letter, and Darwin wrote back. It was the beginning of a warm long-distance friendship that was to last until Darwin's death. My father married late in life — he was already fifty when he met my mother, and I was their only child. He couldn't stop talking to me about the beauty of the plant and animal kingdoms, and about evolution as the guiding principle behind it all. So I was infected with these views from an early age. I'm attracted to the sea because it's our world's most mysterious habitat; it's the one we know the least about. The sea is where our origins lie; it's the mother who has disowned us. We're all like that little mermaid in Andersen's fairy tale. We were so curious about what dry land looks like, that we gave up on the home we were born in. My dearest childhood memories are those of the trips I took with my parents to the seashore when the summer season was already over — walking on the empty, windy beaches of the Côte d'Opale, Cap Gris Nez, Cap Blanc Nez, the cliffs at Étretat.'

She sighed, reminiscing about those happy, by-gone times.

Eliassen coughed, not entirely comfortable with where the conversation had taken them. He hadn't expected such mystical outpourings from somebody with a degree in science — then again, he'd never been able to figure out women.

'What did you want to achieve as a scientist?' he asked her, trying to get back to more solid grounds.

'Oh, I hoped to make a few long oceanic expeditions and use the material I'd gather on those voyages to write papers and books,' Rebecca said. 'I soon found out a female researcher could never raise the necessary funds. It's still a man's world out there. With my father's help, I was lucky enough to obtain a research position at the Museum of Natural History in Paris. They have a vast collection of marine specimens preserved in alcohol, which allowed me to write the papers that got me noticed in the field.'

Rebecca got through half of her steak and then gave up; Ove valiantly soldiered on.

'You said you didn't have any family to go back to in Sweden,' Rebecca mused, nursing her third pint of lager. 'Didn't you ever have the urge to start a family of your own?'

Ove grunted dismissively.

'Have you taken a good look at me? I look like a garden gnome. I never stood a chance in the mating rituals preceding matrimony. One glance at me sufficed to con-

93

vince every nubile female in Sweden their progeny should *not* have me as a father. I learnt to live with that fact from an early age. Aiming for the impossible is a sure-fire way of leading a miserable life, and I decided I didn't want to be miserable. I have several female friends, who appreciate me for my intelligence and wit, and whose husbands have understood I represent no threat to them whatsoever. So I content myself with the presence of their company and conversation. If I want more, I pay for it.'

He looked at her over his horn-rimmed glasses.

'I hope I didn't offend your sensibilities too much?' he said brusquely and stuck another chunk of medium-rare meat in his mouth.

Rebecca remained silent, regretting she'd broached the subject. It was a problem she was struggling with herself. More often than not, the answer kept eluding her. What was the price she was prepared to pay for leading the life she wanted?

Ove's next question drove the point home painfully.

'And what's *your* excuse for not being married? You're beautiful and intelligent. You could have any man you want. Why do you prefer to stay single and dress like a bloke?'

Ove was on his fourth pint, and he was openly annoyed at her.

'Marriage is a cage for a woman, even if the husband loves his wife,' Rebecca answered Ove's challenge calmly and with more conviction than she could often muster mulling over the issue on her own.

'Take my mother, for instance. She was a gifted painter and studied with Carolus-Duran and Jean-Léon Gérôme, the best teachers Paris had to offer. When she married my father, she had to give up on her artistic ambitions entirely. It's deemed unbecoming for a woman to pursue any interests or a career outside of marriage. It behoves the man to be the family's sole provider, and God forbid his wife should outshine him professionally. She's there to oversee the household, to birth children, to welcome guests at private functions, and to shine on her husband's arm at public occasions. Fashion sees to it that women cannot pursue active lives. Women's shoes are painfully uncomfortable; corsets constrain every movement and squeeze the air from our lungs, and if that wasn't enough to prevent us from getting around, the impractical long skirts and ridiculous hats will.'

Her tone became more vehement.

'I've seen intelligent women waste away in their homes from sheer boredom. Meanwhile, their husbands were leading full lives, spent their nights on the town, and indulged in affairs with other women. I vowed *never* to become a housewife or a kept woman. I want to be my own person. I don't intend to marry, and I don't want to dress up like a precious porcelain doll! Do you have a problem with that?'

'Cheers to that,' Ove answered, somehow heartened, and they clinked glasses.

7

SSB Special Branch HQ, Glasgow

Friday, 26 January 1917

The woman who walked into Fleming's office without bothering to knock was an elegantly dressed beauty, although her clothes were oddly out of fashion. She had an ageless, triangular face with a strong aquiline nose, thin lips, high cheekbones, and slightly slanted, emerald eyes. Her hair was silvery, which contrasted sharply with the rest of her youthful appearance.

'Good morning, Gorluin,' she greeted him in a deep, warm voice when he didn't immediately look up from his papers.

Recognising her, Fleming started and beamed. He jumped up from behind his desk, hugged her, and then offered her an armchair, seating himself in the opposite chair.

'Thank you for coming, dear grandmother,' he welcomed her.

'Your invitation sounded urgent,' she said, before switching to a different language, lilting and singsong. 'Does M know you've called for me?'

'He does not,' Fleming admitted in the same tongue.

'It must be serious.'

'It is. The prophecy is about to be fulfilled.'

'I see.'

'We've unmasked the Dream Whisperer,' Fleming announced. 'Although we foiled him once, he's preparing his masters' return, and he won't be stopped.'

'That's terrible news,' his grandmother acknowledged, adding, 'Not unexpected, though. We heard the rumblings already for many a year.'

'I'm afraid we're not up to the challenge,' Fleming confessed. 'The war has taken a terrible toll on our resources.'

'Yes, the human race is such a disappointment,' his guest replied. 'It's hell-bent on self-destruction and getting better at it every year. Humans don't need the Outer Gods to destroy their world; they're doing a fine job all by themselves.'

'You're judging harshly, grandmother.'

'No, I'm not,' she said. 'Even in times of peace, humankind is a cancer devouring Earth. Humans are yet to show any understanding at all of the environment they're living in. Despite our repeated warnings, they went down the path of mechanisation and industrialisation. Perpetual economic growth is their new god. Everything must give way to it, whatever the cost. This choice, combined with its innate rapacity and territorialism, will be humanity's undoing.'

'Humans are a young race,' Fleming pleaded. 'Faerie had aeons to learn the lessons they've tried to teach the humans.'

'It's a young race that has run out of time, unfortunately.'

'Dear grandmother, I've asked you to come because we need your people's help.'

'My dearest Gorluin, I have no more help to offer,' his visitor answered. 'I came to you not only because you asked me to. I too have something important to tell you. The Council has decided to set out on the Great Wandering.'

'What?' Fleming exclaimed.

'For hundreds of years, our race has been in decline as humans steadily encroached on our territories and destroyed our habitats,' his grandmother explained. 'Since the beginning of last century, the industrial revolution has accelerated this process to an unprecedented speed. And then came the madness of the Great War. The first of many, we fear. In Flanders and the north of France, almost all dryads, leimoniads, naiads, and little people have perished in the past three years. Our numbers dwindle at an alarming rate. This cannot go on: We have no future on Earth. With heavy hearts, we've decided to leave this planet and explore the pathways along the cracks. We don't know where that decision will lead us as we've never done this before. There was no need as Earth has long been close to paradise for us. But no more.'

She bent towards Fleming and took his hands in hers.

'I've come to ask you to join us. Nothing binds you to this world. Not anymore. You don't owe humans *anything*. This world has run its course — nobody can stop the Outer Gods from coming back. You're delusional if you think otherwise. It's hopeless. Come with us. With *me*. Please.'

Fleming was taken aback. Even though he was only a Halfling, the Faerie were also his people. They'd raised him, taught him everything he knew. This was heartbreaking. Losing them forever wasn't something he'd ever considered possible.

Nevertheless, he understood all too well why his grandmother's people had reached this decision. Though he was part human, his upbringing had taught him to look at the world in a non-human way. When he was still a young man, the London smog and the '*dark Satanic Mills*' spoiling city and countryside had convinced him humankind was doomed if it didn't soon change course. In earlier times, humans had been aware of their dependence on nature, and they accepted that, within the fabric of existence, everything was linked to everything else in one vast symbiotic continuum. That perception was now lost.

The Book of Genesis convinced the believers they stood above nature. All of God's creation was at their disposal to be used as *they* saw fit. The raw, short-sighted capitalism of the industrial revolution was the logical terminus of that train of thought.

The economy's purpose was no longer the fulfilment of the average man's reasonable needs, Fleming thought, and human greed was to blame. The maximisation of wealth for the elites had become the economy's foremost objective. Everything, including the planet's well-being, was sacrificed to an insane hunger for ever-increasing profits. Cities had become dreary, unhealthy places that housed the working poor in dismal hovels. Production processes left no room for personal satisfaction with a job well done. Cheap factory workers were reeled in from the countryside at a tender age, brutally exploited, and then discarded and replaced as soon as they were worn out — offerings on Mammon's altar, all of them. No future, indeed.

Fleming had shared these concerns with M some years earlier.

'Ha, yes, the Faerie have always been Luddites,' M had replied airily. 'Mind you, it works for them, I must admit. Mainly because they're a single nation governed by a Council of Elders. Their decisions are law, binding everyone.'

M had caught the doubtful look Fleming was giving him, and he took his time to offer a more convincing argument.

'Let me explain why their approach doesn't work for humans,' he said while settling himself more comfortably in his club's armchair. 'Imagine there are only two nations on Earth: Britain and Germany. Originally, they're both pastoral paradises. There is enough food to go around. Crafts-men produce all the other stuff that makes life tolerable: tools, pots and pans, textile, clothes, and so on. Everybody is happy. Nothing "needs" to change. I'm exaggerating, ob-viously, to make my point. This paradisiacal world has never existed; it's nothing but a romantic fiction. However, let's not go there and keep matters simple.'

Having set the scene, M went to the heart of his line of reasoning.

'Then somebody realises there are cheaper and more efficient ways to produce all the goods people need. The invention is called "industrialisation", and it forces both nations to reconsider their options. Of course, they could continue their old ways. Everybody was happy with that, so why change a good thing?'

M let the argument for doing nothing hang in the air for a moment and then rubbished it with his next question.

'What happens if one nation decides to leave things unchanged, and the other opts for industrialisation?' he asked and quickly provided the answer himself, 'The in-dustrialised nation would have the advantage that it could produce much more stuff than it did before and at a far lower cost. It could then export these cheap goods to the other country and put all their craftsmen out of a job.'

He poked his cigar at Fleming to emphasise his words.

'It's a winner-takes-all game. Cheap foreign pro-ducts flood the country that doesn't change. Its economy is wrecked; unemployment soars. Goodbye to bucolic bliss. The industrialised nation maintains full employment and gets rich exporting goods to the other nation — even if, admittedly, the new wealth is unevenly distributed. More-over, industrialisation gives it a military edge. It can pro-duce more, better, cheaper weapons than its Luddite rival. The logical consequence is that the industrialised country will invade and conquer the other one.'

Fleming wanted to object, but M cut him off.

'This isn't a fanciful theory, my dear Fleming. It's how the British Empire became what it is today. In our colonies, we outgunned and submitted the natives, who hadn't yet made the transition to an industrialised society.'

For M at least, the conclusion was crystal clear.

'In this example, Britain and Germany cannot rely on each other's willingness to leave things unchanged. Neither of them has any other option but to follow the path of industrialisation. For both, paradise is lost, alas, but the alternative would have been even worse. Needless to say, our reality is more complex still. There are many more nations in play, and none of them can be trusted *not* to choose for industrialisation. It's simple mathematics. I'm sure somebody will work it out someday and put it into a model.'

Fleming understood the logic of M's reasoning. That didn't prevent him from feeling miserable about it.

'We all decide to go from Eden to hell because we cannot trust the others *not* to choose for hell. What a sad bunch humans are,' he concluded.

'My dear Fleming, it isn't a black-or-white situation,' M replied. 'The initial transition from one economic model to another is always disruptive. The problems tend to be evened out later on. Labourers have already realised their work holds significant value for factory owners. They have united in trade unions to balance the scales of power. Their living conditions today are far superior to those of half a century ago. I'm sure, in the years to come, they'll obtain an increasing and fairer share of the added value our economy is producing. Your gloomy view on the common man's lot is outdated as we speak.'

The discussion with M was still vivid in his mind. It continued to leave an unsavoury aftertaste. The common man's lot might improve over time, indeed, but at what price? By making him complicit in the rape of nature perpetrated by the factory owners? Fleming believed M didn't see the full picture, despite his towering intelligence. He was all about short and medium-term compromises that would make the status quo last another day. With such an attitude, how was humankind to survive in a century, in a millennium? Fleming wondered.

His grandmother's offer was tempting, to say the least, though it was cruel on her part to point out that nothing bound him to human civilisation anymore. It re-opened wounds that had never truly healed — the loss of his parents, wife, and only child. Fleming's decision to join the Secret Service Bureau had been motivated both by a desire for revenge and a need for work to keep him from wallowing in self-pity. That and maybe — just maybe — a serious death wish.

Was he ready to turn his back on Earth and humanity? Right now, at the drop of a hat? He felt deep down in his bones he was not. A profound sadness overwhelmed him. Looking his grandmother in the eye, he didn't need to speak. She nodded regretfully and stood up. During their long embrace, Fleming relived the warm memories of his youth among the Faerie, entwined with a heart-rending feeling of loss.

'I'll never forget,' he said, choking on his emotions once they let go of each other.

'I know,' she answered.

After gently stroking his cheeks with the tips of her fingers, she left his office, crossing Rebecca in the hallway.

Rebecca looked at Fleming through the doorway and saw he was grief-stricken. She wanted to go to him and comfort him. He shook his head and closed the door.

8

Team A, Pulau Balambangan, Sarawak, Borneo

Saturday, 3 February 1917

Fleming wasn't terribly pleased with the shortlist of primary targets Professor Eliassen had drafted. At least, there were a couple within the British Empire's sphere of influence. Those shouldn't pose too much of a logistical problem or a diplomatic risk.

The Borneo target was one of them. The northern part of the island had been a British protectorate since 1888. Technically, Borneo remained an independent state. The British government didn't manage its administration. It was a dependency of the British Chartered North Borneo Company, which was entitled by Royal Charter to administer internal affairs, set up courts of justice, establish railways, and exploit the land. The BCNBC imported Sikh police officers from North India to maintain law and order. Cheap labour came from China and Japan as the local population was too small to tend all the plantations and man the timber business. The Company also imposed unheard-of taxes on the locals and propelled one in two local children into forced labour. In 1915 the Murut revolted against this brutal regime, and the Company sent in troops to restore order.

The adventurous Von Junzt visited the country in the 1820s and discovered an ancient, hidden temple on

Balambangan Island, off the most northern tip of Borneo. At first, Professor Eliassen was sceptical about this claim. The island was no stranger to the British. It happened to be the first location in the area where they'd set up a trading post. The sultan of Sulu granted occupation rights to the British East India Company as early as 1761; the settlement was established in 1773. It never became a commercial success, though, as it was constantly under attack by Sulu pirates, and the British moved their base to Kudat in 1805.

The professor scoured the Company's journals and those of its local employees without finding a reference to an ancient building on the island. He thought that was suspicious. After all, Balambangan was small. It was narrow and only fifteen miles long.

Von Junzt had been vague about the temple's exact location in his book *Unaussprechliche Kulte*, even if he'd included several interior sketches of sculptures related to the iconography left behind by the Outer Gods in other places. Eliassen had, however, obtained access to letters written by Von Junzt in that period. In two of them, the explorer was a bit more forthcoming about his findings on Balambangan.

It appeared he hadn't discovered the temple on the island surface but in one of many underground limestone caves. Rumour had it that pirates had used some of them as temporary storage for their loot. Until Von Junzt's exploits, Westerners hadn't explored any of them. In the second letter, he described how a local guide had him wade through a mangrove infested with saltwater crocodiles to reach the entrance to the cave. The mention of mangroves meant they could narrow down the search area significantly. Finally, Fleming gave the go-ahead for a search-and-destroy mission.

Everett Belknap was a retired colonel of the Duke of Wellington's Regiment. He'd served in the Second Boer War and spent the last years of his career on the Indian North-West Frontier. His brother-in-law, who was a high-ranking official in the BCNBC, had contacted him two years ago to lead the company army and subdue the Murut insurgence. He'd been happy to oblige and stayed on in Borneo ever since.

From the very moment Belknap received Fleming's cable asking him whether he was game for an expedition to Balambangan Island to blow up some stuff, he was all for it. Things had been too calm lately, and he was bored. As he got more detailed instructions, he grew even more enthusiastic. It took him less than a week to organise the expedition. Belknap brought together a team of ten mates, all with a military past. A ship from nearby Singapore delivered the explosives. He hired a guide and three small fishing boats, and they left from Limbuak on Banggi Island, less than ten miles from their destination. It was a sunny morning, and the temperature forecast was in the high eighties.

The crossing was quick and uneventful. The southern half of Balambangan Island was flat and covered in tropical forest while the other half consisted of limestone formations. The coastline was a mix of sheer cliffs, sandy beaches, and mangroves. They headed for the mangroves, near the middle of the island. When the water became too shallow for the fishing boats, they tied them to tree roots, shouldered their rifles and backpacks with explosives, and jumped in the knee-deep water. Their guide, Badin, led them through the mangrove. He was watching out for crocodiles — which were conspicuously absent, except for a single juvenile specimen, which quickly fled when it saw them coming. After a ten-minute wade, they reached dry higher ground. Badin picked a path through the forest until they reached a wide limestone cave. The brown-grey stalactites and stalagmites inside made it look like a smiling dragon maw, happy to welcome some juicy titbits.

As Belknap and his mates prepared to enter the cave, Badin made it clear this was the end of the road for him. Belknap tried to change his mind, but the guide wasn't having any of it. In the end, they agreed Badin would wait for them at the cave mouth. As the men entered, hundreds of bats flew out. The cavern was vast. As their eyes adapted to the semi-darkness, they noticed several tunnels converged in its first chamber. They lit their torches and let the lights play over the irregular stone formations.

'Which way, boss?' Fred Bellamy, Belknap's best friend, asked.

Belknap pointed towards the central tunnel.

'No use spelunking in the smaller tunnels,' he said. 'The thing we need to blow up is pretty big, so let's go for the widest one.'

The passage wound left and right, without significantly narrowing. Its steady decline brought the men deeper and deeper underground, and temperatures dropped as they progressed. After a half-hour descent, they noticed the first carvings on the tunnel walls. They were difficult to read. The moisture dripping from the limestone had erased most of the features. What they could discern was dark and disturbing. Their chummy banter first became forced and then ceased altogether when they reached a sizeable cavern with a central altar.

A large, egg-like object sat on the altar. Carvings and statues decorated the cavern. Millennia of water seepage and limestone deposits had obscured most of the details. The three sculptures positioned close to the walls looked like bizarre dripping candles. After a closer look, the men understood that the lack of recognisable features wasn't due to age-long erosion and layers of calcium carbonate deposits. The images with their tangles of strange body parts without discernable use had already looked alien from the very start.

'This place gives me the willies,' Belknap muttered, expressing what was on everyone's mind. 'I'll take some pictures while you guys rig the explosives and the timer. Let's concentrate on that thing's pedestal and blow it sky-high.'

It only took the men a short time to complete the job, although it felt like an eternity to them. Something was trying to distract them and make them stop what they were doing.

'I keep hearing and seeing things that aren't there, and I don't like it,' Bellamy panted, wiping the cold sweat from his brow. 'I can't wait to get out of this damned place.'

The others grunted in agreement. Belknap set the timer for fifty minutes, and they all left the cavern in a hurry. Two of them, Potts and Sanderson, needed to be supported. They'd lost all sense of direction and seemed to be hallucinating. They were mumbling unintelligibly. Their condition only improved as they reached the first cavern again.

Belknap found Badin wasn't waiting for them.

'That son-of-a-bitch guide is gone! Can't trust any of these yellow devils! If the blaggard thinks I'll pay him the second half of his fee, he can go whistle for it!'

'Doesn't matter, Everett. We're not that deep into the forest,' Bellamy said to calm his friend. 'We'll easily find our way back; don't worry, old chap. Let's get away from here before it all blows up.'

They'd retraced their steps to the mangrove when they heard the explosion — a deep underground rumble, followed by the sound of falling rock fragments behind them in the jungle. Their raucous cheers frightened away the birds in the trees. The men felt buoyant wading back through the mangrove and made loud, raunchy jokes about what they'd do with the money this job had earned them. A few of them needlessly threw sticks at a couple of crocodiles that were strictly minding their own business.

When they reached the spot where they'd left the boats behind, a nasty surprise was waiting for them. Their guide had made off with one of the vessels. Belknap was apoplectic with rage. It hardly mattered. The only reason they'd used three boats was because of the explosives they'd needed to bring in. Six men fitted in a single vessel without a problem. The engines started smoothly, and they backed both crafts out of the mangrove into the open water. The weather was still beautiful, not a cloud in the air. The sea was like a mirror.

As they reached the open sea, the men were chatting cheerily and opening bottles of beer to celebrate their success. Potts was sitting on the bench in the first boat's stern. He looked a little pale, but he was relieved it was all behind them. The things he'd seen in the cave continued to make him shudder. There were no words to describe the horrors that unfolded before his mind's eye. He was sure the images would haunt him for the rest of his life. Potts sipped his warm beer, dangling his left hand in the water, while his mates were making jokes at his expense. He couldn't care less. He was grinning distractedly, thinking about what his money would buy him in Sandakan. A lot of pussy, that was for sure. And he wanted to ride the dragon again. He missed that. His finances had been strained lately, ever since his bar had burnt down, and Chinks didn't care much about credit. He suspected those local Muslim buggers. The Sikh police officers had told him there was no evidence for their involvement. What else would they say? A white Christian cannot expect justice from those bloody savages, can he?

A shout from Bellamy interrupted Potts' musings.

'Whoa! What the hell is that?'

Bellamy was pointing to port. His mates came over to look, precariously tilting the small boat with their shifting weight.

'What did you see, matey?' they asked after fruitlessly peering at the water. 'There's nothing to see. You bollocksed already after two beers?'

'I saw a beastly hag sticking her mug out of the waves, I tell ya! The ugly cronk was looking right at me!' Bellamy insisted.

His friends jeered and shouted. One of hem clapped him on the shoulder.

'You saw a dolphin, is all. Get back to yer beer.'

Turning around, they saw Potts had disappeared.

'Where the fuck did he go?'

They moved to starboard to see whether Potts had fallen overboard, tilting the boat to the other side. Eight pairs of scaly, greenish, webbed hands shot out of the water, grabbed the starboard railing, and capsized the vessel. The men tumbled into the sea, screaming. They didn't thrash about in the waves for long as something was pulling them under and tearing them apart. The seething water foamed and bubbled, turning red in an instant like during a shark feeding frenzy.

The men in the other boat were gobsmacked. They saw Bellamy clawing his way back out of the water, trying to climb on top of the capsized fishing boat's hull. His clothes were torn, and he was bleeding from deep gashes all over his body. Again, several arms reached out from the sea and pulled him back in, kicking and screaming. Belknap got his rifle and shot at the pink waves.

After a while, they saw several heads sticking out of the water, all looking menacingly in their direction. The creatures couldn't be mistaken for humans. They had large bulging eyes the size of tea saucers, no noses, and gashes for mouths, filled with a jumble of long, needle-thin teeth.

111

The men were so mesmerised by the feral spectacle on starboard they failed to notice several creatures were stealthily approaching them from the other side. They grabbed one of the men by the ankle and dragged him into the sea. Sanderson drew his service revolver and emptied it at the sea creature. Several slugs hit the merman in the gilled throat and the head, but Sanderson couldn't save his mate. Two other monsters pulled him underwater, and he was gone forever.

Belknap jumped at the wheel and sped the boat away from the danger zone full throttle. The mermen pursued them, their speed an easy match for the accelerating fishing boat. They gave up after three hundred yards after Sanderson proved himself to be an excellent marksman and hit another two of them with rifle shots.

9

Team B, Hawkins Island, Bermuda

Sunday, 11 February 1917

Among the initiated, the precise location where the Outer Gods' 'pickaxe' had struck Earth was a subject of dispute. According to the Standard Model, there was no such thing as a single point of impact: The Outer Gods' initiative had fragmented reality as a high-pitched sound would crack a crystal sphere. The result was a dense network of fractures covering Earth, without an evident 'first-strike' location. The minority faction, called the Impactists, stuck closer to the pickaxe metaphor. In their opinion, there *had* been a first impact, and all fractures in the fabric of reality must radiate from that spot. They argued the fractures' pattern was proof of the single impact theory. If the Standard Model were right, the distribution of the cracks would be more or less even across Earth. If the Impactists were right, the network would show a high crack density around the 'first-strike' spot, gradually diminishing as the distance from the impact zone increased. And sure enough, the Impactists found precisely such a pattern of decreasing density, which allowed them to pinpoint the spot where the 'pickaxe' had hit. The proponents of the Standard Model ridiculed the idea. They pointed out that not all fissures had been charted yet and accused the Impactists of drawing conclusions based on incomplete data. Stalemate.

Professor Eliassen had wavered for a long time. In the end, he became more seduced by the single-point-of-impact theory. According to this theory, the striking point was the middle of a triangle formed by Florida, Puerto Rico, and Bermuda. Nobody could deny it was an area with lots of disturbances in the fabric of reality, as it had acquired quite a reputation for ships vanishing into thin air. In the previous century, the US Navy alone had lost no less than four vessels without a trace in that zone. Another one, the Rosalie, had been found abandoned with only a canary remaining on board. The cognoscenti agreed that the most probable explanation was that these ships had sailed, along a crack, from one plane of existence into another.

The Spanish discovered Bermuda in 1503. They used it for taking fresh meat and water on board, without settling the island. The sailors were frightened away by eerie sounds at night — the screeches of cahow birds, we now know — which they attributed to ghosts and demons. That's how the largest island of the archipelago first became known as the 'Isla de los Demonios', the 'Isle of Devils'.

Professor Eliassen had a copy of the journals of an early, Spanish Jesuit priest, Father Alonso Xabier Altamirano y Panduro, who performed an exorcism on Bermuda in 1550. He claimed to have found a pagan temple on a small island in the archipelago, which was now known as Hawkins Island. Two days after he'd carried out his arcane ritual, the God of Israel's wrath struck the island. There was a terrible earthquake. The island was torn asunder, and a monstrous wave swallowed the half with the temple. The priest considered this a favourable omen. God unmistakably endorsed his servant in his battle against heathendom. Thus fortified, Father Altamirano sailed on to Mexico to christen the remaining Aztec population. Later, he'd travel further north and spread his harsh gospel among the native tribes in what was now Arizona and California.

Eliassen would have lent little credence to the Spanish zealot's self-aggrandising journal without corroborating evidence. In the Mission San Xavier del Bac, a Jesuit church ten miles south of Tucson, an ancient piece of masonry sat in a shrine in the vestry. It was said to be a fragment of the pagan temple on Bermuda. Father Altamirano carried it with him, wherever his urge to convert took him, as a reminder that he was doing God's work. On his deathbed, he'd bequeathed it to his successor, who in turn gave it to Father Eusebio Francisco Kino, the founder of the mission in Arizona. Father Kino wasn't comfortable with the gift — the stone had traces of a disturbing, tentacled being on it — and never wished to exhibit it in his church. Therefore, he opted for a compromise. He ordered an opulent, gilded shrine to be made for the stone and then hid it away in the vestry, a place that was never visited by his parishioners. A century later, an Apache raid destroyed the old mission buildings. A beautiful new church replaced it, and the then-priest followed Father Kino's lead. He decided to conceal the shrine in the vestry and even put it in a niche behind a wooden panel. The writer and journalist Ambrose Bierce could inspect it in the 1890s and wrote a witty newspaper article about it. Bierce's description of the piece of masonry left Eliassen in no doubt about its authenticity.

'Why would you want us to spend resources looking for a Sleeper site destroyed nearly four centuries ago?' a sceptical Fleming asked.

'You've heard what Doctor Mumm said about the creature's resilience,' Eliassen answered, wagging his finger at his boss. 'I can't believe a tumble into the sea would kill the Sleeper. It's probably alive and well beneath the waves, dreaming about heaven knows what atrocities.'

The professor counted on his fingers.

'We have a remarkably exact location, the sea around Hawkins Island is shallow, and Bermuda is a British Overseas Territory. Let's have a look, ask a couple of locals to investigate, and if they find anything, we blow the damned thing up. All it takes is a friendly cable, a bit of money, and a shipment of underwater explosives. You'd wish the other targets were as easy as this one.'

Morton Withers had been a professional diver for the last eight years. He was a treasure hunter, specialised in tracking down wrecks of sixteenth-century Spanish galleons. Withers lived alternately in the Bahamas and the nearby Turks and Caicos Islands. Lately, he'd been doing a bit of work on the Dominican Republic's south coast, near Santo Domingo. The American occupation last year put an end to the political turmoil that plagued the country since its independence fifty years ago. Withers now felt safe to expand his activities to that area.

He'd welcomed Fleming's cable. Withers was happy to hear from one of the few friends he'd made during his short stint at Oxford's All Souls College. Fleming had dropped out after six months, and Withers had lasted only two months longer. He remembered Fleming fuming about the impractical attitude of some of the College's Fellows and the snobbishness of their fellow students. After Fleming's departure, Withers also decided academic life didn't suit him. He wanted adventure and open spaces to explore. First, Withers went to work for a company specialised in marine salvage. Two years later, he owned a small outfit. Life wasn't always easy. His current search for the Santa Maria del Antigua wasn't going well at all. In the first few weeks, stormy weather delayed his exploration, and then his maps proved to be unreliable. Costs were running up. He wasn't getting a return on his investment any time soon. After conferring with his two associates, Gerald Masters and Jarvis Anderson, they'd sailed off to Bermuda, where a crate of underwater explosives was waiting for them.

Bermuda is shaped like a fish hook. Hawkins Island is one of the larger islands in the archipelago in the Great Sound — the body of water nestled in the protective embrace of Bermuda's hook. The boat trip from Hamilton Harbour's docks to Hawkins Island was only three miles. The island was the property of the Royal Navy and functioned as a prisoner of war camp during the Second Boer War. It was now deserted.

Withers' crew had spent two days exploring the waters around the island before striking pay dirt on the south-eastern end, half a mile from the coastline. The azure water was crystal clear, and their trained eyes could see traces of the temple ruins at a depth of thirty-five feet. The building was overgrown with corals and sea anemones, but some angular shapes betrayed the site's artificial origin.

Withers donned the brand-new armoured diving suit he'd acquired a fortnight ago. An American, Benjamin Franklin Leavitt, designed the bronze and rubber contraption, and Withers was delighted with it. It didn't require a separate air-tube anymore. Instead, a tank mounted at the armour's back supplied the air. A caustic soda cartridge, which lasted for about an hour, cleansed the carbonic gas from the exhaled air and sent it back to the tank. A second innovation was the telephone in the helmet. The telephone line was embedded in the steel cable used to lower and pull up the diver. The suit also featured heavy rubber gloves and could function at depths up to one hundred and fifty feet.

When Anderson winched Withers down, the diver marvelled at the underwater spectacle. He was just shy of his thousandth dive. Still, he couldn't imagine he'd ever feel jaded experiencing the ocean's splendour. Dozens of multi-coloured tropical fish darted about him. He even noticed a green sea turtle nearby. These waters were known for the presence of large tiger sharks. Withers knew those colossi rarely represented a danger to humans, and his bronze armour offered him plenty of protection. He saw even less reason to worry because, in the winter season, tiger sharks migrated to warmer waters down south anyway.

It didn't take long to establish this was indeed the Sleeper site. Withers detected a broken-off cornice with a frieze featuring weird, convoluted shapes. Further on, he found the rest of the building surprisingly intact.

Withers called his associates, 'I see the building now. It looks stable. I'll have a look inside.'

The temple had settled on the seabed at a severe tilt, which played havoc with Withers' sense of equilibrium. He rested his right palm against one of the pillars at the entrance and took in the sight. The lack of sunlight hadn't prevented marine life from colonising the building's interior. A hairy type of sea moss, barnacles, and other filter feeders covered the walls. Spidery starfish, small crabs, and shrimp scuttled about on the floor. Among many types of smaller fish, Withers noted the presence of several lionfish. In the middle of the room, stood an equally overgrown pedestal. Ten feet to the right of it, an ovoid shape was lying on the floor.

'I found what we're looking for, chaps,' Withers informed his mates over the inbuilt telephone. 'It's like a huge egg, a life form to all appearances. Not something we've ever seen before. What's peculiar is that it's spotless. I mean, you've seen plenty interiors of wrecks, right? They're always covered in moss and stuff. Same here with the walls. But this thing, this egg, you know, it's immaculate. There's not a single marine organism attached to it, as if it's, well, poison, you know. Just looking at it gives me the creeps. My heart is pounding. I touched the thing, and it feels hard — like stone or metal, maybe. All right, I'm coming out again. I'll tell you when to winch me up. Anderson, better suit up too; we've got work to do.'

Back on board, they changed Withers' caustic soda canister. Anderson put on his diving suit, which was of a classic design. It wasn't armoured — which wasn't an issue, as they'd be working in shallow water — and it needed an air tube and an air pump on the ship's deck.

Anderson and Masters had also lined up the 300-lb depth charges Fleming sent them. There were four of them. The metal, barrel-like casings contained TNT. Typically, a depth charge was set to detonate at a pre-set depth, its detonator triggered by water pressure. On this occasion, Fleming's men had replaced the original mechanism by a detonator linked to a timing device.

Masters winched the four depth charges in place, as close as possible to the underwater edifice's entrance. Then he started up the air pump and lowered Anderson into the sea. Once on the seabed, Anderson detached the cable from his brass helmet and gave a tug. Next, Withers went back in.

'We're in position, Masters,' Withers informed his mate. 'Everything is fine. I'll keep you posted on our progress. We'll manoeuvre the barrels into the building.'

Masters lit up a smoke. There wasn't much he could do now, except keep an eye on the air pump. He didn't even need Withers to report to him about their progress. The water was so translucent he could easily observe the two divers struggling with the heavy explosives. It looked as if the assignment would be easy money. Everything ran smoothly. After a quarter of an hour, Withers and Anderson had already moved two of the bombs inside the building. Masters was looking out over the water. It was a cloudless, calm day — a welcome change after the weeks of storms they'd experienced in San Domingo.

He dropped his cigarette. A huge dorsal fin cleaved through the water less than a mile north of Hawkins Island. Masters grabbed the telephone.

119

'Withers, we've got company. A great white is nearing your position. It looks like a big one.'

'How far?'

'Less than a mile and closing in quickly, mate.'

'All right,' Withers replied, thinking through his options. 'We've got three of the four charges in place. I'll hook up Anderson now — he's less well protected than I am — and then you get him out fast. Maybe three explosives might suffice to blow up that thing inside, but I'll make sure and push the fourth depth charge as close to the target as I can. I've still got air left for about half an hour, probably a bit more.'

The dorsal fin kept nearing. Telephone contact was broken off, which meant Withers had detached the cable. A minute later, Masters felt a tug and winched up Anderson. Anderson's feet had barely hit the deck when Masters saw a large, dark shape passing under the ship's bow.

'Good Lord, what the blue blazes was that!' Masters gasped.

Anderson stood on the deck pointing at his brass helmet. Masters opened the visor and shouted at Anderson, 'Did you see that?'

Anderson nodded, white as a sheet, 'Biggest damn shark I've ever seen!'

They both looked over the railing. Withers had taken refuge inside the building after wrestling the last explosive barrel inside. An enormous shark was circling right above the sunken structure.

'Mother of Jesus, that monster must be sixty feet!'

Masters couldn't believe what he was seeing.

Only now, Anderson truly realised what fate he'd narrowly escaped. He fell to his knees and vomited into his helmet. Masters hurriedly unscrewed the helmet's bolts and lifted it off its base. His mate looked miserable.

Withers hid behind the wall next to the doorway. Whenever he risked a peek, he saw a fast-moving, large shadow dart over the seafloor. The shark swam up to the entrance and pushed its nose between the pillars. Fortunately for the diver, these were too closely spaced for the fish to enter the edifice. Its head was wider than a lorry. Withers hoped, if he kept quiet, the animal would lose interest and leave. After another fifteen minutes, that hope had dwindled. The shark stubbornly kept swimming back and forth, right in front of the temple entrance. Withers marvelled at the animal: A great white had nothing on this shark. Its teeth were bigger than his hand! He estimated the monster's weight in excess of sixty metric tons. There was no escape possible from this terror of the deep. Its powerful jaws would crack his armour suit like a nut. He saw his mates had lowered the cable again and were steadily inching the boat nearer to the entrance. What were they thinking? That he'd hook himself up again, and that they could winch him back on board without the shark noticing? Wishful thinking, that was. Then the monster bumped its nose against the cable. The shark furiously snapped at it and tugged from left to right until it broke. All the while, Withers feared the boat would capsize.

His air supply was running dangerously low, and he had a splitting headache. Something was trying to push him out. Withers had experienced it all the while lugging in the explosives. It wasn't a physical force, more like a deeprooted subconscious urge that was attempting to take over his mind and body to steer him out of the building right into the killer shark's maw. He tried to calm down and clear his mind.

Masters radioed the harbour authorities in vain. It was Sunday, and there was nobody to answer. The skipper wasn't sure whether it would have made a difference anyway. There were no large ships in the harbour, no Royal Navy vessels, nothing that could fire a harpoon at the monster shark or harm it in any other way. They were reduced to sitting and watching how the patient animal cornered their friend until his air supply ran out. As the fish grabbed the cable, Masters and Anderson believed it would drag them to the sea bottom.

The caustic soda canister was exhausted. Withers knew, with every breath he took, carbon levels in his air supply would increase until the air became unbreathable. He had maybe fifteen minutes left. Decision time. He walked towards the egg-like thing, which was surrounded by four depth-charges. If he had to die anyway, he could just as well take the bloody thing with him. And perhaps the shark as well, who knew? He didn't want to endanger his mates. Their boat was right above him. All it took was one piece of stone breaching the hull, and the vessel would sink. Withers set the timers to one hour. Masters and Anderson would assume he hadn't survived, and they'd sail away to safety in, give or take, half an hour. He sat down, unscrewed his visor, and let the water flow in.

'It's finished,' Anderson said. 'He must have run out of air fifteen minutes ago.'

'Let's wait a bit longer,' Masters insisted. 'The thing with those canisters is you can't time them exactly to the minute. They last longer than you'd expect.'

Anderson didn't object. He knew Withers was dead by now. If Masters wanted to wait a bit longer, that was all right by him. The shark hadn't budged. When Anderson looked over the railing once more, it was pushing its snout through the pillars again, as if it wanted to make sure Withers was dead. Masters had been chain-smoking the entire time. Finally, he threw his butt overboard and went to the wheelhouse. The engine started, distancing them slowly from the island.

They were halfway back to the harbour at the moment of the explosion. Anderson watched from the stern how a pillar of water and foam shot in the air. The water coloured red.

'Turn the boat around!' Anderson yelled.

Masters obliged. When they reached Hawkins Island again, sand and debris, lifted from the seabed by the explosion, clouded the seawater. They kept staring at it until the water cleared again. There was a gaping hole where the temple had been. No trace of Withers. The shark had gone too. After they'd turned the vessel and sailed to the most northern tip of the island, they detected a faint blood trail that led to the open sea. Masters and Anderson looked at each other and sailed back to the harbour.

10

SSB Special Branch HQ, Glasgow

Monday, 17 February 1917

Fleming had mixed feelings about the reports from the first two teams he'd sent into the field. Two Sleepers were destroyed. In that respect, he had to consider the missions a success. However, the operations' high death-toll — eight casualties, no less —didn't sit well with Fleming. He was particularly dismayed by Masters' and Anderson's report. Fleming had fond memories of Withers and the Christmas they'd spent together at Withers' home in Yorkshire. On that occasion, Withers introduced him to some old family friends, the Edleys. Fleming instantly fell in love with their eldest daughter, Catherine, which undoubtedly precipitated his decision to drop out of All Souls. Both men kept in touch over the years, off and on, mostly by mail. That was how Fleming had known his friend was active in the Caribbean.

Fleming blamed himself for underestimating the missions' risks, despite Ove's warnings that the Sleeper sites might have some form of protection. Fleming felt personally responsible for all fallen team members, but Withers' case was exceptional. He took it upon himself to write a heartfelt letter to his friend's parents in which he expressed his deepest sympathy and personal grief.

He showed both mission reports to Rebecca and asked for her opinion.

First, she too expressed her concern about the high casualty rates, but then she quickly returned to practical matters.

'I'm especially eager to have a look at the pictures taken by the first team,' she said. 'We now know the sites contain either an egg, a pod, or a chrysalid. The pictures will hopefully give us a better insight. The information confirms our earlier suspicion that, upon release, the Sleeper is a relatively vulnerable juvenile, which validates the early-strike strategy. Additionally, we learnt that the Sleeper, while physically inert, does have a defence mechanism. It can imprint suggestive images and strong emotions upon the psyche of potential assailants, rendering them less effective or even incapacitated. I know of no equivalent in the natural world, and I don't have any suggestions that could benefit the other teams.'

'Hexes or spells could be useful as a defence against these psychological attacks,' Ove suggested. 'We have little to guide us. I haven't found any reliable incantations yet in any of my grimoires that could counteract the influence of an Outer God. Moreover, casting spells requires both talent and experience, neither of which is readily available in the military.'

'As for the creatures that attacked the teams,' Rebecca continued, 'I'm baffled by the so-called mermen. I've seen pictures of one belonging to the Horniman Collection in Forest Hill in London. The owner, Frederick John Horniman, was a tea trader. He brought this specimen back from his travels in the East. I haven't been able to examine it myself, but I'd bet good money it's a hoax. Anyway, even if it were real, it's much smaller than what attacked Belknap's team. I've also been looking at the pictures you've taken of the dead Inuit in Greenland, Fleming. As strange as it may sound, these people weren't fully human. In one of the pictures, I could distinguish the presence of gills below the jawbone. In others, the skin looked distinctly scaly. Also, they didn't have noses to speak of.'

'Maybe they're the next step in human evolution?' Ove supposed.

'I don't know. *Devolution* sounds more likely. It's well known that early-stage embryos of all vertebrates, including humans, possess gills. Darwin built his theory of embryogenesis on that discovery. According to him, the stages of the embryo's development mirror our evolutionary history. Which means it passes through a fish stage, an amphibian stage, a reptile stage, and so on. The human embryo thus possesses the blueprint of each of these life forms. It isn't unthinkable that, in some cases, ancestral features that are normally recessive are expressed in the fully-grown foetus.'

'Like babies born with a tail?' Ove suggested.

'Exactly. It's perfectly possible that, in isolated communities, dormant features of previous evolutionary stages, such as gills or scaly skin, resurface and become a common attribute of the group.'

'Do you think that's what happened to the mermen in Borneo as well?' Fleming asked.

'Honestly, I don't have a clue.' Rebecca admitted. 'Though I'd say that's unlikely. Scientists tend to dismiss sightings of mermaids by sailors and believe they've mistaken seals, belugas, or other cetaceans for these creatures of fantasy. However, I've no reason to doubt Belknap's report. Perhaps they're an alien species stranded here because of the Outer Gods. Professor Eliassen is more competent to give an opinion on that.'

Ove confirmed, 'That's likely indeed. There are several types of water creatures we know of that are half-humanoid and half-fish. They're easily lumped together under the common denomination of siren, mermaid, or merman. There are many different species with widely different origins. The Borneo variety was, until now, unknown to us.'

Rebecca then turned to the transcript of the second mission's report.

'I'm not so much puzzled by the sighting of the large shark. A lot is going on in the oceans about which we know little to nothing. The shark was most probably a Megalodon. We know that species mainly from fossil teeth and vertebrae found in strata dating back from the Oligocene to the Pliocene. That means we believed it had gone extinct some two and a half million years ago. Clearly, it hasn't, which *is* a surprise but not a big one. The real shocker is the animal's behaviour. I've never heard of sharks acting as guard dogs. So either what happened was a coincidence — after Borneo, I'd say it was probably *not* — or the Outer Gods are using different types of dangerous creatures to act as guardians for their Sleeper sites. I think the teams we sent out to discover other sites need to be made aware of that possibility so they can take protective measures to the extent possible.'

After Ove had left Rebecca's office, she casually remarked to Fleming, 'Lately, I've seen some interesting people walking in and out of your office. Would you care to fill me in on what's happening?'

Fleming was startled by the directness of her question. Then he conceded she had every right to ask. She was France's liaison officer, and no doubt her superiors required her to regularly report on the team's progress to the French prime minister. Playing hide-and-seek with her would only alienate both her and the French government.

'Who did you see?'

'Well, there was the seven-foot giant — broad-shouldered, long white hair, full beard. Then a wide-hipped, full-bosomed lady. Not too tall; she wore her black hair in a bun. I'd swear she was French. Ah yes, also a frail-looking elder gent with a fine grey moustache, wearing a Royal Army Medical Corps uniform. And then, the last one, a beautiful lady with silvery hair, who made you cry. Did I miss anybody?'

She stared at him, defiantly.

'Yes, you did. Not that it matters much,' Fleming replied. 'The outcomes of all of those meetings were similar.'

Rebecca didn't react; she waited him out.

'I was looking for allies. The giant you saw was Rod. He's the head of the Slavic pantheon.'

Rebecca couldn't suppress a giggle.

'What's so funny?'

'Nothing. Well, pffff — ', she snickered. 'You know, "*Rod the God*", it sounds funny — you wouldn't be making that up now, would you?'

'No, I would not,' Fleming replied, a bit miffed. 'Rod is a potent being. You could compare him to Zeus, Jupiter, or even Yahweh. If his name sounds too ridiculous, you could also call him Prabog — *"the god who came before all other gods"*.'

'All right, all right, keep your hair on. Why did you call him in, specifically?'

'We had some business together, a couple of years before the war.'

'The Tunguska incident you mentioned to M?' Rebecca asked, hoping to coax some extra information about that event out of Fleming.

'Never mind that,' he rebuffed her. 'Rod had to deal with a bit of a rebellion. A couple of hothead gods wanted to bring the hammer down on humanity, show them who's the boss. I lent him a hand dealing with it.'

'Well, why wouldn't they? I mean, bring the hammer down?' Rebecca argued. 'If they're so powerful, why would they content themselves with living in the shadows instead of taking over Earth?'

'Because there's too many of us and not enough of them,' Fleming pointed out. 'They may be long-lived and mighty, but they're *definitely* not unkillable. Every god-like being in human history who has abused his power suffered for it in the end. Rod was well aware of that. As humanity evolved, became smarter, got better weapons, and increased in numbers, even the most powerful beings saw the wisdom of blending in. They could live long, comfortable lives on Earth if they refrained from standing out.'

'So you did him a favour some time ago, and now you asked him to reciprocate?'

'Yes. But he refused.'

'Why?'

'Our relationship with most of the species brought to Earth by the Outer Gods is fraught,' Fleming admitted. 'Although they were first — the Outer Gods arrived on Earth and left it again before the advent of man — we outbred them and made Earth our own. Coming to an arrangement with them wasn't always easy. As our numbers grew, many of the other beings became increasingly annoyed with us and saw their territories wither. They see us as a cancer taking over Earth. We obliterate everything they hold dear.'

'So they won't help us because they think the Outer Gods will get rid of us,' Rebecca concluded.

'Precisely. They've all survived their previous forced co-existence with the Outer Gods, and they're gambling they can do it again. They didn't like it the first time around — far from it — but, at least, they saw the back of them. When the Outer Gods leave once more, they reckon Earth will be cleansed of all humans and then they can get on with their lives. The Outer Gods are *our* problem, not theirs.'

'And that's the opinion of everybody you've talked to?'

'Not quite. However, in the end, it comes down to the same: They won't help us.'

'Who were the others?' Rebecca wanted to know.

'The hmm... *large* lady is called Belisama,' Fleming said. 'We've established a good relationship with her. In Gaul, before the Romans came, she helped the Celts understand how they could improve their skills in agriculture, pottery, weaving, metallurgy, medicine, you name it. She was one of the few who liked it that humans are a curious bunch, always looking for knowledge. Nowadays, she runs a private school for gifted girls in Toulouse.'

'I knew she was French!' Rebecca cried out, clapping her hands. 'If she likes us so much, why won't she help?'

'She doesn't have the necessary clout,' Fleming answered. 'And because she largely stopped caring when her husband, Belenos, was killed by a stray cannonball in the Napoleonic wars. Belisama resented that a lot. She retired to the province, set up a school, and, on and off, supported pacifist initiatives. After the outbreak of the war, she was bitterly disappointed in humanity. It was the straw that broke the camel's back. It's the same story with the next one, the medic you saw. He goes by the name of Alan Hargrave, but he used to be a Celtic deity called Alaunus. He's a warm-hearted being who always promoted harmony between his kind and man. Alaunus has been a healer since the dawn of time. Last week, he made a disheartened impression. He's working as a field doctor in Flanders, you know, and I don't think he can take much more of it. During most of our conversation, he was telling me about the gruesome mutilations he sees in his field hospital every day. I wouldn't be surprised if he were on his way out. The horror is killing him.'

'And the woman who made you cry?' Rebecca asked, probing further.

'That was Lady Eiluned. She's a long-standing member of the Faerie Council. The Faerie is a collective name for different species that have, throughout the millennia, been able to live, more or less, in harmony with humans. Elves, nymphs, fauns, *lares*, *kami*, brownies, *lutins*, *nisser*, and other "little people". Though they all have different origins, they found one another in their desire to keep a low profile and have a productive relationship with humans. Well, not all of the time — some of them can be quite cruel. Usually, we see eye to eye.'

'That sounds good. Still, that conversation didn't go well either?'

'They aren't keen on the Outer Gods' return, but they feel powerless to do anything about it,' Fleming explained. 'None of them have powers even close to those of some of the god-like species we know. The Faerie also feel we've betrayed their trust. We've breached the covenant that existed for centuries between our species. They blame us for the way we mismanage our planet, encroach upon their natural terrains, and then there's the war. The general feeling is that, with this war, humanity has crossed a line that can never be uncrossed again. In short, regardless of a possible return of the Outer Gods, they've lost faith in us. They see no future for their kind on this planet and have decided to leave Earth.'

'How will they do *that*?' Rebecca wondered.

'I don't know if they've thought this through,' Fleming said. 'They intend to use the breaches in the fabric of reality that brought them here in the first place. I don't think they truly believe they can find their way back to their original universes. They're convinced they can find a better world, though.'

'I didn't mean to eavesdrop, but I couldn't help overhearing you calling her "grandmother",' Rebecca said, coming to the part about which she was dying to know everything. 'When Eliassen said you were partly elf, I thought he was joking. Apparently, he wasn't.'

Fleming stood up and raised his hands in an apologetic gesture.

'Doctor Mumm, I don't want to dodge the question, but I'm running out of time. There's a ship waiting to take me to Ireland. I have an appointment with another "deity". Although it probably won't work out either, the least I can do is try. My story will have to wait. I'm sorry. I promise you that, on my return, we'll take up the thread of this conversation again.'

11

Team C, Madidi Jungle, Bolivia

Monday, 19 February 1917

One of the highest-probability targets identified by Friedrich von Junzt lay in the Bolivian Amazonian jungle. Its location was near the north bank of the meandering Rio Tuichi, between Lake Chalalan and San José de Uchupia-monas. According to the author, a small, degenerate Indian tribe, weakened by centuries of incest, lived in the dense jungle. The writer believed he could trace back their origins to the Tiwanaku Empire, a pre-Columbian culture on the south-eastern shores of Lake Titicaca. The empire had collapsed in the eleventh century for uncertain reasons, and the Inca conquered the region a few centuries later. It was Von Junzt's thesis that a group of Tiwanaku priests and warriors had crossed the Andes, together with their concubines, to escape the new Inca overlords. They spoke an almost unintelligible Quechua dialect, mixed with guttural sounds that didn't belong to any of the known Peruvian or Bolivian languages. The tribe still practised the age-old tradition of cranial deformation and worshipped a dark deity they called the "Destroyer of Worlds". They also believed it was this god who had led their ancestors over the forbidding Andean mountains to where they were living now. Their religious rituals — which involved self-mutilation, cannibalism, and child sacrifice — were so ghastly that the German explorer couldn't bring himself to give a detailed description. They did their worshipping in a building that, according to Von Junzt, pre-dated their arrival in the Madidi jungle by many millennia. In his book, he'd included several sketches of the temple. The octopus theme was omnipresent in the bas-reliefs adorning the great hall. The author also mentioned a lower, holier level in the temple, to which his hosts had denied him access.

The testimony in *Unaussprechliche Kulte* was singularly convincing. Fleming and Eliassen marked the Bolivian jungle temple as a top priority, although they had to acknowledge that reaching this target would be a huge logistic challenge. The British Empire's closest colony was British Guiana, nearly at the northern tip of the continent, almost two thousand miles away from the objective. The French couldn't help out either. Their only colony in South America was French Guiana, practically as far to the north as its British counterpart. The only efficient means to reach the Madidi jungle was an aeroplane that could also land on water. That was, however, a new and scarce means of transport. Not a single flying boat was available in British Guiana. The British deployed all aircraft of this type over the North Sea for tracking U-Boats and other enemy vessels. Fleming got on the phone to pull some strings and call in some favours.

It didn't take a lot of diplomatic effort to convince the governments of Brazil and Bolivia to allow a foreign aeroplane to travel through their airspace and land for refuelling. British diplomats told them Britain wanted to attempt a record-breaking crossing of the South American continent from north to south by flying boat. The event got a lot of publicity in the local newspapers, and the pilots received a celebratory send-off in Georgetown, British Guiana's capital. Nobody wondered why the British would want to spend resources on such a frivolous feat right now when they were involved in a calamitously expensive war of attrition with the Germans. Spectacular sporting events have always had a mind-numbing effect on people, and this one was no different.

Fleming's crew dismantled a Felixstowe F.2A military flying boat and shipped it in from Portsmouth. They repainted the aircraft in garish red and blue colours to emphasise its civilian purpose. Usually, it took a crew of four to fly this aircraft — two pilots and two gunners. The Felixstowe could carry a payload of almost 3,500 lb, and its standard armament was four Lewis guns. For obvious reasons, in *this* plane, the Lewis guns had to go. They removed the gunners' positions and modified the hull to secretly — and uncomfortably — accommodate eight soldiers and all of their gear. That included several 20-lb Cooper aerial bombs, which the pilots could drop by hand. They reassembled the plane in the Georgetown harbour on the Demerara River estuary. The night before departure, they smuggled its cargo aboard without attracting notice by either the press or the local authorities.

The plane's range was only five to six hundred miles, which meant the flight schedule had to include several refuelling stops. The first stop was in the Brazilian town of Boa Vista. Then they flew to Manaus in the northern Amazonas region, where they also stayed for the night. From there, onwards to Porto Velho — a close call: The last twenty miles, they were flying on petrol fumes. Next was Guajara-Mirim on the Bolivian border, and then on to tiny San Ramon, where they also stayed for the night. The following day, they first flew to the city of Trinidad and then to San Borja, another isolated hovel. By then, the soldiers were fed up with their living conditions. They insisted that the pilots immediately find an unobtrusive refuge in the jungle after refuelling. The Felixstowe landed four miles south of Rurrenabaque on the Rio Beni, near the confluence with the Rio Tuichi. In a downpour, the crew set up camp on the riverbank. Their target was within easy reach the next day.

They got up at dawn. At 6 a.m., the temperature was still 70°F. In less than two hours, it would rise to a stifling 88°F. The ominous clouds over the rainforest predicted another day of continuous rain. The men all wore civilian khakis and heavy boots. They checked their guns — each soldier had a Lee-Enfield SMLE MKIII* rifle and a .455 Colt automatic pistol — and donned ammunition belts. On each belt, they hooked six Mills bombs. The pilots transferred all twelve aerial bombs from the hull to their cockpit. The mission leader, Lieutenant George Rushton, made a final inspection before they all climbed into the flying boat.

Captain Francis Porte started the powerful Rolls-Royce Eagle VIII twin engines and taxied to the middle of the river. Visibility was reduced due to heavy rain, making the take-off dangerous. Once in the air, the pilot kept flying the plane at low altitude, no higher than four hundred feet. His co-pilot and navigator, Second Lieutenant Alec Wilcox, held a map with the target's presumed location and carefully observed every twist and turn of the river.

After less than an hour, Wilcox shouted, 'Behind the next turn!'

Porte nodded and stuck up his thumb. They gained a bit more altitude. On both sides of the river, the tropical rainforest canopy was unbroken. There was no sign of habitation. Porte slowly circled over the north riverbank. Wilcox peered down, hoping to find a gap in the green hell beneath them. The pilot flew in ever-larger circles over the area until Wilcox signalled he'd seen a small clearing about a mile from the river. Porte flew back to the Rio Tuichi and landed on the brownish water.

The landing party clambered up the muddy bank, each soldier carrying a heavy backpack filled with explosives and detonators. As the rain stopped, swarms of mosquitoes, eager to have a taste of their exotic blood, assaulted them. Rushton agreed with the pilots that they'd take off and keep circling. Remaining on the river wasn't an option. They'd be eaten alive by the mosquitoes in their open cockpit. Moreover, if the tribe Von Junzt had described did act as a guard for the building they intended to destroy, having some air support might come in handy. Rushton carried a flare gun to call for help.

The calls of hundreds of bird species were deafening. Screaming red-and-blue-coloured macaws flew along the river. Forty yards downstream from where they were standing, a large group of wild boars crossed the shallow river. Three tapirs were watching them from the south bank. An eight-foot water snake swam past the flying boat. A couple of yards further, several pairs of knobbly eyes stuck out of the water. As the eight soldiers marched into the forest, clearing a path with machetes, they were acutely aware of being followed by hundreds of eyes. Progress was slow; it took them almost an hour to reach the clearing observed earlier by Wilcox. Rushton signalled his men to stop at the clearing's edge.

On the other side of the clearing stood a brown-red, stone edifice, overgrown by tropical plants. Two finely sculpted columns topped with a dreadful bas-relief framed the entrance. What struck the soldiers most were the two conical piles of human skulls left and right of the portal. If they needed confirmation of Von Junzt's allegations about horrid rituals involving human sacrifices, this sight left no room for doubt. Moss and other plants covered the piles' bases; the skulls at the very top appeared to be recent. None of the craniums showed the typical deformations described by the German explorer, which indicated the nameless tribe preyed on other locals — such as the Tsimanes and the Mosetenes — for their sacrifices.

Rushton directed his men along the clearing's edge, making sure they kept under cover of the forest's vegetation. The temple seemed unguarded, but needlessly exposing themselves would have been foolish. As the men approached the building's left side, the bird noises ceased. Only buzzing insects and the Felixstowe's reassuring drone broke the eerie silence. The lieutenant signalled two of his men to run to the entrance and provide cover for the others. Before the first one reached his goal, an arrow struck him right through the throat.

'Ferguson!' one of his mates cried out.

The second soldier safely arrived at the entrance. He took cover behind the left column and began firing into the forest. The others broke cover wildly shooting at invisible enemies. When an arrow hit a soldier in the right eye, the lieutenant decided to use grenades. He threw one across the clearing into the forest, and the others followed his example. After a mad dash, they tumbled into the building unharmed — except for the slowest among them. An arrow pierced Private Lowry's right leg moments before the soldier reached the threshold. Rushton grabbed the man by his backpack's straps and yanked him inside.

'We're trapped, Lieutenant,' Sergeant Hix whispered. 'They can simply wait for us outside and pick us off one by one.'

'Not likely,' the lieutenant answered. 'If they want to prevent us from destroying the temple, they'll have to attack now.'

As if to confirm Rushton's intuition, their assailants shot a volley of burning arrows into the temple's hall. They didn't injure anybody. Soon, it became clear that was not the intention. The acrid smoke from the burning substance tied to the arrow tips brought tears to the soldiers' eyes and scorched their lungs. A couple more volleys and they'd be forced to abandon their position. Rushton pulled out his flare gun and shot a flare in the sky, hoping the pilots would notice it.

The aeroplane circled over the clearing right when the second volley of burning arrows flew at the building, revealing the shooters' location to the pilots. The Felix-stowe was an agile plane, and soon, Wilcox was throwing aerial bombs at the hidden attackers. After three passages, the aggressors seemed to be annihilated or, at least, put to flight. Several of them ran out of the forest in a panic and into the clearing. They were easy targets for Rushton's men. Waves of bird and monkey shrieks greeted the bombs' explosions. The jungle sounded like a howling ogre ready to tear the soldiers limb from limb.

The six survivors cautiously left the building for fresh air. Several of them were retching and vomiting. The second volley of burning arrows had filled the hall with nauseating smoke, making it impossible to stay inside. After half an hour, they were able to go back. For the first time, they could calmly take in the sights.

The room was a large rectangular box of sixty by forty-five feet and a height of twenty-four feet. The bas-reliefs on the walls featured the most fantastical creatures — seething masses of limbs, claws, fangs, and eyes, which failed to make sense to human perception. It wasn't clear where one life form began, and another ended. Maybe it was all one entity for all the soldiers knew. Whirling tentacles decorated the ceiling. The same was true for the six pillars supporting the vault. The floor consisted of two types of local granite: blue sodalite and deep black *granito negro chiquitano*. The black granite was laid out in the shape of a labyrinth. Its central chamber held a bas-relief of what looked like a mass of rampant cancer growths and long, writhing tubes of flesh. Some of these ended in toothy muzzles, others in curved spikes or claws. For all the terror these sculptures contained, the talent of their makers was evident. The reliefs were similar to Inca art but appeared far more refined and richer in horrifying detail.

Against the north wall stood a blood-caked stone altar and a six-foot-high statue of a bat-faced deity. Its decaying body was enveloped in a mantle, richly embroidered with gold thread and pearls. Sculpted snakes, lizards, and toads crept over its pustule-covered snout. The idol had bloodshot, leering eyes and a wide mouth with silver fangs. Two stump horns sprouted from its brow. However terrifying the effigy was, it wasn't half as disturbing to the soldiers as the incomprehensible, wriggling masses of weird body parts in the bas-reliefs. Somehow, they could more easily relate to the malevolent bat-deity than to the alien scenes on the walls.

Rushton and two others lit torches. One of the soldiers had a Simplex camera and took pictures of the building's interior. There had to be more than this. Their briefing mentioned a second, underground chamber. There was no trace of a doorway or a staircase leading to another part of the temple. The lieutenant left the building and walked around it. Reaching the external back wall, he saw it wasn't straight. Halfway, there was a five-yard-wide windowless annexe with a slanted roof that touched the ground at the far end, about eighteen feet from the back wall. Rushton went back inside.

'There's a hidden staircase behind that wall,' he said, pointing. 'There's got to be a secret mechanism on this side to reach it. Start looking.'

With some reluctance, the soldiers scrutinised the middle bas-relief on the back wall for suspicious bumps or crags. From up close, the sculptures felt even more lifelike and revolting. It required a conscious effort to touch the images. Two men got on their knees and explored its lower surface while two others tried their luck higher up. After what felt like an eternity, they gave up. The bas-relief consisted of one single alabandite slab. There was no trace of anything that could be used as a lever or button to move it out of their way.

'All right, enough of that,' Rushton concluded. 'Let's blow a hole in this thing.'

Sergeant Hix and two soldiers fetched the backpacks with dynamite, safety fuses, and detonators. As they put them on the ground in front of the bas-relief, one of the soldiers started.

'Lieutenant, Sir!' he called out, pointing at the flagstone next to which he'd put his backpack. 'There is something carved in this stone.'

Rushton came over to look. It was true. Except for the labyrinth's central chamber, there were no carvings in the floor's flagstones. This one was an exception. Was this the lever they'd been seeking? The officer first pushed at the stone and then stood on it. Nothing happened. The same soldier who had found the first carved flagstone called out again.

'There are three more of them over here, Sir!'

'Good job, Private Halversham,' Rushton said. 'You four, each go stand next to one of those stones.'

Then the lieutenant drew his pistol and gave the order, 'Step on your stone! Step!'

Tensely, the soldiers waited with drawn pistols. They kept their guns pointed at the bas-relief, uncertain of what might come out at them. The floor trembled, and they heard a rumbling sound. After a brief shudder, the bas-relief slid downwards and uncovered an impressive staircase leading down.

'Grab your backpacks and rifles,' Rushton commanded and then called to the soldier with the wounded leg, 'Private Lowry, you stay here and guard the entrance. Sergeant Hix, give the man a rifle.'

The stairs led them deep underground to a circular chamber with a diameter of eighty feet. Carved black marble covered the walls. In the middle, surrounded by six pillars, stood an altar with a large, egg-like object on top of it. The ovoid glowed faintly with a steadily fluctuating, hypnotic pulse, which irresistibly captivated the men's gaze. The room appeared to act as an echo-chamber for the creature's dreams. They felt atrocious images seeping into their subconscious. Reality's warp and weft slowly dissolved around them until only the pulsating glow remained. An unspeakable terror built up in their hearts. The marble carvings seemed to come alive, moving in languid undulations.

Under the onslaught of a gut-wrenching panic, Private Pickering stumbled backwards and tripped over his backpack. His rifle came crashing down, and his torch clattered on the floor. Trying to restore his equilibrium, he took hold of the man next to him, unbalancing him as well. This brief disturbance broke the spell. Lieutenant Rushton came to his senses. He shouted orders, shaking and slapping his men until they'd all regained awareness.

It took the soldiers a while to shake off the trance. Then their training kicked in. One of them snapped pictures. The others roped the dynamite and the detonators to the altar and the pillars. They attached the safety fuses to the detonators and then ran the fuse up the stairs. The entire operation took less than half an hour.

Halfway up, Sergeant Hix lit the fuse. They didn't have enough fuse for the entire length of the stairs. They sprinted, trying to reach the ground floor before the blast. When they still had some thirty feet to go, the explosion went off. The blast wave blew the last two of them to the top of the stairs into the first chamber, causing only minor injuries.

Swirling dust clouds poured into the temple, choking the men. The coughing soldiers staggered out while the building's rear wall was collapsing. Walking around the edifice, they saw the blast had created a large hole in the ground and destroyed the foundations of the temple's back wall. The building tumbled backwards in slow motion, filling the opening with rubble and larger stones. The soldier with the Simplex camera documented the destruction. Then he went to the clearing and took some more pictures of the Sleeper site's fallen guardians.

12

Team D, Island of Solitude, Kara Sea

Wednesday, 21 February 1917

In addition to an extensive collection of esoteric volumes, Professor Eliassen's archives also contained a wide array of journals, logbooks, and travel accounts by explorers and adventurers of all eras. The file on Ship Captain Edvard Holm Johannesen belonged to the latter category. Holm had been a famous Norwegian skipper and explorer in the Arctic Ocean. In 1869, he sailed through the Straits of Kara, across the Kara Sea to Belyjøya, and along the east coast of Nova Zembla. He explored the area extensively over the next two summers and was the first to map these waters and chart the coastlines. The Royal Swedish Academy of Sciences accepted research papers with his observations for publication. They rewarded him in 1869 and 1870 respectively with the silver and gold medals of the Academy. In 1878, he was caught in pack ice in the Kara Sea when he discovered an island at 86° eastern longitude. It was twenty square miles in size. Holm baptised it 'Ensomhetens Ø' or the 'Island of Solitude' because of its isolated position. It's situated about one hundred and seventy miles north of mainland Siberia and more than two hundred miles east of Nova Zembla. In December 1901, Holm inexplicably disappeared in the Balsfjord on a short boating trip from Sandøyra to Tromsø in calm weather.

The file's juicy bit consisted of the pictures Holm had taken on the island in 1878. Even in August, the landscape was bleak and barren. The land was flat, mostly covered in snow. In high summer, the temperature hovered around freezing, and the island continued to be surrounded by ice floes. Where the snow in summer had receded, a bit of tundra was showing through on the black earth. It was uninhabited, except for the nesting places of different arctic bird species. At the island's centre, Holm had found a building. It looked like the megalithic burial hills that can be found all over Europe, except for the sophisticated ashlar masonry used to build its entrance. The joints between the stones were so fine as to be nearly invisible to the naked eye. Moreover, the trapezoidal stones had finely sculpted images on them that were far too refined — and too weird — to belong to any Neolithic civilisation. Above the entrance, Holm had found a representation of an octopus carved into the stone. It was an almost perfect match for the carvings found in the flagstones of the church in Zoetevoorde.

These pictures never made it into the Academy of Sciences' official files. An Academy member alerted the Swedish secret service, and they purged the file. They also called in Holm and swore him to secrecy.

Eliassen had been involved in the case and remembered it well. At the time, he tried to gain more information on that part of the world, which was largely unexplored by western scientists. He found an early medieval text written by an Irish monk called Aedh — a disciple of Saint Columba, who converted Scotland to Christianity and founded an abbey there in the sixth century. Aedh had first tried to spread the gospel in Scandinavia and then travelled further east. He ended up in Siberia on the Taymyr Peninsula among a Samoyed tribe, the Nganasan. He learnt their language and wrote in a journal about their animistic beliefs and shamanistic rituals. Eliassen recently looked the book up again. He found that one of the stories Aedh had recorded told of a 'dark shaman' who made the stars disappear from the heavens and called in monsters from the beyond that precipitated the end of times. For Eliassen, the legend about the dark shaman was a further confirmation there was indeed a link between that part of the world and the Outer Gods' return. The mysterious shaman may have been another avatar of the Dream Whisperer. In light of that supposition, the presence of a Sleeper site made perfect sense.

The first moment Eliassen brought up the pictures, Fleming had been reticent — not because he considered Eliassen's analysis unsound but because of the climatic conditions.

'Ove,' he said, '*nobody* will be able to reach that island in wintertime. The Kara Sea is completely frozen. We can't do it until summer. Forget about it.'

Eliassen kept arguing, 'The Barents Sea is far less cold than the Kara Sea; it's navigable even in winter. We could send a ship to Nova Zembla's northern tip and launch an aeroplane from there to our target.'

Fleming called in Admiral Sir Henry Jackson, former First Sea Lord and now president of the Royal Naval College in Greenwich, to discuss the matter. Jackson rejected the idea out of hand.

'Nova Zembla is a place as inhospitable as it gets,' he said. 'There are no airfields, and I wouldn't bet on taking off from an ice sheet. Too dangerous. The Yankees have been experimenting with catapults to launch aeroplanes from ships. We haven't done that yet. So I wouldn't recommend trying it on this mission — certainly not if you intend to send in a large team requiring a big aeroplane. Anyway, even if you can get an aircraft near your Island of Solitude, there are still plenty of problems. We don't have reliable topographic maps of the island. Landing a plane there might be an issue. But the main inconvenience I see is the temperature. The centre of the Kara Sea is much colder than Nova Zembla. This time of year, temperatures can be anywhere between -12°F and -20°F. Even if you manage to land a plane there, you'll never get it back in the air again. Leaving the engine running during the operation won't help you. In poor weather conditions, there will *immediately* be a build-up of ice on the aircraft's wings. The additional weight will prevent the plane from taking off.'

'How about sending in a submarine?' Eliassen challenged the expert.

Both military men laughed.

'To reach the target and make it back safely to a British port without refuelling, we'd have to rely on a K-class submarine. Do you know what the men call our current K-class submarines?' Fleming asked.

Eliassen shrugged. Not his terrain.

'They nickname them "Kalamity-class". We don't even need the Jerries to sink them. They do that all by themselves. And you want to send them into an almost uncharted, frozen arctic sea?'

'The K-Class is indeed a dodgy piece of kit,' the admiral admitted, 'but that's not why I would advise against using them for this mission. The Kara Sea is frozen solid this time of year. Even in summer, ice floes remain. That means the ice thickness may now reach more than fourteen feet in places where the ice hasn't melted during previous summers. A submarine may break through ice three to five feet thick without sustaining too much structural damage — and even that I wouldn't recommend wholeheartedly. Trying to get through anything thicker would be pure suicide.'

'Couldn't you first break the ice with torpedoes or sea mines?' the professor objected.

Fleming and Jackson looked at each other.

'The K-class isn't built to launch sea mines,' Jackson reflected. 'Torpedoes might do the trick.'

The HMS K4 left Scapa Flow in the Orkneys and reached the Kara Sea after a ten-day voyage. The submarine achieved an average speed of about ten knots. It rounded the North Cape and then stopped at the Norwegian port of Kirkenes near the Russian border for re-stocking its coal supply. The K-Class submarine could have made the trip both ways without re-stocking if it made the entire voyage without submerging. That was a risk the captain wasn't willing to take. The Kara Sea would be largely frozen this time of year, which would require the K4 to travel submerged at least part of the way.

Officially, Norway was a neutral country in the war. In practice, it sided with Britain. Germany's unrestricted submarine warfare had sunk more than four hundred Norwegian merchant vessels. That was a crippling blow to a young nation's economy desperately dependent on its fishing industry and merchant shipping. In the Norwegian shipping community, the anti-German sentiment was rife. It didn't take much to convince the Kirkeness' port authorities to allow servicing the K4.

It was the submarine's maiden voyage. The K4 was only commissioned last January, and its first test dive in the Irish Sea hadn't been promising. Its captain ran the vessel aground on Walney Island. It sat there for several days like a beached whale before the Navy towed it away. It could have been worse. The K3 was the first of its class to be commissioned. During a test dive in the British Channel, the submarine nosedived into the muddy sea bed. Its stern stuck out above the water — as its length greatly exceeded the depth of the sea at that particular location — and its propellers whirled uselessly in the air. To make matters even more awkward, Prince Albert, second in line to the

British throne, was on board of the hapless vessel. The K13 was the second to be launched. On its first test dive, the boiler room ventilators failed to close. The flooded ship sank like a stone to the bottom of the sea at a depth of sixty feet. A rescue operation, which lasted for fifty hours, saved the lives of forty-nine sailors. The remaining thirty-one perished.

The K-class quickly gained a sinister reputation for sluggish manoeuvrability, frequent leaks, and boiler explosions. Although British submarine crews all consisted of volunteers, morale was often at a low ebb. The K4 captain, Lieutenant-Commander George Hales, was an old hand. He was a veteran of the war's first naval battle, at Heligoland Bight, and had a low tolerance for demoralising cynicism on board. When Lieutenant Harold MacPherson, the team leader, briefed Hales about the mission's purpose, the captain didn't bat an eye.

The voyage itself was unremarkable, if uncomfortable. The K-Class was unique among British submarines because it was steam-propelled. Fleet Command required its development as they needed a sub that could accompany the Grand Fleet at speeds of up to twenty-four knots — which was entirely beyond the reach of diesel-powered submarines. The K-Class boiler room got so hot that the stokers had to leave it when the vessel submerged. Temperatures throughout the ship were stifling, and the humidity was oppressive. The sailors' quarters were cramped. Lieutenant MacPherson's search-and-destroy team was packed together with the officers in their somewhat more generously proportioned quarters.

As expected, the Kara Sea's surface was mainly frozen. A mile off the Island of Solitude's shore, Hales ordered to empty the K4's fore ballast tanks until the vessel reached a tilt of forty-five degrees at a depth of one hundred and fifty feet. Then they fired a torpedo from one of the four bow tubes. British torpedoes were as wonky as their submarines. The projectile glanced the thick ice layer without exploding and sank to the bottom. After a string of deeply-felt nautical swear words, the captain increased the tilt to fifty degrees and fired another one. This effort met with success. The projectile blew a significant hole in the sea ice. Hales repeated the operation twice until the gap was large enough to fit the 339-foot leviathan's frame safely. After some awkward manoeuvring, the crew positioned the ship right beneath the opening and then allowed it to surface.

When Lieutenant MacPherson emerged from the conning tower, a gusty, ice-cold wind almost cut off his breath. There was hardly any light. The sky was cloudy, and the wind temperature must have been below -25°F. The shore was reachable on foot over the frozen sea, even though the cracks in the ice produced by the torpedo blasts made the surface unstable in the area directly surrounding the HMS K4. MacPherson had planned to ski over the ice, but the forbidding landscape that stretched out in front of him made him reconsider. It wasn't the flat ice plain he'd hoped for. Hundreds of jagged sheets of ice lay scattered about, one on top of another, like shattered beer glasses after a Saturday night pub brawl. Onshore, things looked much better. He returned inside the submarine.

'All right, men. There's no skiing the first mile; the terrain won't allow it,' MacPherson announced. 'We'll use the snowshoes. Once we've reached the island, we can ski. The place looks uninhabited, but we're taking along our guns anyway. The target may be guarded somehow, so let's be careful. Suit up. We're leaving in thirty minutes.'

Even with the snowshoes, the going was tough for the first mile. The soldiers all carried heavy backpacks with explosives, detonators, and fuse cords, which made pro-gress even more difficult. They were, however, lucky en-ough to find a safe path over the ice. When they'd reached the shore, they shed the snowshoes and donned their skis. The trek towards their destination was another four miles.

From the east, rapidly approaching storm clouds were gathering.

Upon reaching their goal, the entrance looked much bigger than on the picture. There was no door, only a dark, square opening.

'Private Partridge, take some pictures. See to it you get the details sharp,' MacPherson motioned towards the convoluted carvings in the masonry. 'And hurry up. A storm is coming.'

The other men quickly shed their skis and readied themselves to go in. They took out torches. Some prepared their rifles; others unholstered their pistols. As they went into the hill, the broad hallway first curved to the right, following the hill's contours, and then spiralled inwards. Wherever they shone their torches, they could distinguish disturbing scenes with unnerving creatures carved in the rock walls. After a five-minute walk, they heard a shuffling sound.

'Careful, men,' the lieutenant warned. 'I think we're not alone.'

They stood still, quietly listening out for any further sound.

'It stinks in here,' Sergeant Plender remarked, sniffing the foul air.

The others had also noticed the rank, fishy stench that became more pronounced as they progressed inside the hill. Their torches showed that, ten feet further down, the hallway curved sharply to the left.

MacPherson pointed two fingers at the curve, 'Bailey and Burns, go ahead and shine a light. We'll cover you.'

The men advanced in a low crouch, shining their torches from the hip and pointing their pistols with stretched arms. Upon reaching the bend, everything went incredibly fast. A colossal shadow leapt from behind the curve with a bloodcurdling roar. Burns' ripped-off arm with the gun still firmly clasped in his hand flew in the lieu-

tenant's face and knocked him over. Bailey uttered a muffled scream before their attacker gutted him. The others
wildly fired at the monstrous shadow coming at them. A
gigantic paw with razor-sharp claws tore off Partridge's
face. Plender slipped in the blood of two other soldiers as
the stinking, hairy shape lunged at him. Five more shots
rang, and then there was an eerie silence.

Blood dripping from the walls made the only sound.
After a minute, MacPherson dared to light his torch again.
The beam uncovered a horrific carnage. Private Merryweather was the only one to have sustained merely superficial wounds. A grey-white bear lay dead among the fallen
soldiers. The animal made a full-grown grizzly look like a
pup. Approaching the beast's body, the lieutenant saw
Pender laying beneath it. The man's right arm stuck elbow-
deep in the animal's maw. The sergeant had emptied his
clip inside the beast's mouth and had blown away the back
of its skull. As MacPherson shone his light on this improb-
able scene, Plender blinked.

'Could use some help here. That damned beast
weighs a ton,' he groaned faintly.

MacPherson and the wounded private rolled the
bear's corpse off the sergeant. Plender had a broken arm
and a few cracked ribs. Miraculously, he'd sustained no
other wounds.

The three men cautiously looked around the hallway's corner and found a dome-shaped chamber. Its floor
was littered with seal carcasses. In the middle stood an
altar with an egg-like object on it. They looked at one another and nodded. They had to go back to their fallen bro-
thers-in-arms to prise the backpacks off their mangled
corpses. MacPherson also took the Simplex camera from
the all-but-headless Partridge. He snapped a couple of pictures of the butchery and the bear. Then he returned to the
chamber with two backpacks. They worked mechanically,
as if in a daze, rigging the explosives. The atmosphere in

155

the room was loathsome. Merryweather puked uncontrollably. He was white as a sheet, likely to go into shock.

As MacPherson shook him by the shoulders, he shouted gibberish. His eyes were rolled back in his head.

'*Ach k'tchuihl ish te'yla in'ngefth! Ach k'tchuihl ish te'yla in'ngefth!*'

He repeated the phrase over and over again until the officer slapped him hard in the face.

Merryweather fell on his knees, snivelling, 'The horror! The horror! They're coming!'

'Help him get out of here,' MacPherson told the sergeant. 'I'll finish up. I'll join you soon.'

It took the lieutenant another quarter of an hour to attach the detonators to the fuses. By the time he'd finished the job, he had a splitting headache. He heard voices whispering in a strange tongue inside his head. The urge to draw his pistol and shoot himself through the head became almost irresistible. MacPherson ran for the exit, unrolling the fuse cord as he went. Plender and Merryweather, recovered but still weak, sat waiting for him inside, next to the entrance.

The storm reached the plain they'd crossed earlier that day. The short arctic day turned into near darkness, and they still had hours to go. None of them considered it an option to spend the night in the building. MacPherson had told the captain to expect them to stay away for six, maybe seven hours, and he wasn't sure the skipper would wait much longer. The water surrounding the submarine must have frozen solid again by now, and Hales was unlikely to risk his entire crew waiting for them.

Plender and Merryweather had already made a head start before MacPherson lit the fuse. The sergeant could hardly use his broken arm while skiing, which slowed them down considerably. The detonation rolled over the plain when the lieutenant was two hundred yards away from the hill. He turned around to watch and saw with satisfaction the hill cave in on itself. Twenty minutes later, he'd caught up with the two other survivors. The howling wind tugged at their clothes and made breathing difficult. Luckily, it didn't snow, and they could make out where they were going reasonably well as the darkness deepened.

It was night when they reached the shoreline. MacPherson shot a flare in the air, to which the submarine crew responded with one of theirs. The lieutenant was glad to see they hadn't veered too far off course. They threw away their skis and donned the snowshoes. The submarine crew shot off flares every ten minutes, spookily lighting up the frozen sea. The moment they were within calling distance, four sailors came out to meet them and helped them to cover the last stretch.

'Is that all that's left of your team?' the captain asked after they were safely on board.

'It was a massacre,' MacPherson replied. 'I'll tell you about it later. Let's get the hell out of here.'

13

SSB Special Branch HQ, Glasgow

Wednesday, 21 February 1917

His session in Dundalk with Badb, the only survivor of the trio of Irish war goddesses called the *Morrigna*, had been worse than awful. During the entire meeting, Badb refused to assume human form. Fleming felt like an idiot, talking to a crow. He'd always known this wouldn't be an easy conversation. Badb was notoriously ill-tempered and fickle. Fleming had hoped the prospect of a battle against the Outer Gods might appeal to her. It did not. She had her mind set on another fight: helping the Irish nationalists repel the British occupiers. Fleming tried to argue reason and only received insults in return. Badb ended the audience with a vengeful prophecy:

> *When Albion withholds Éire's due*
> *And calls upon her youth anew*
> *To sacrifice their noble blood*
> *In a foreigners' country's mud*
> *Behold, its ruling days will end*
> *As Éire's knee shall refuse to bend*

Upon his arrival back from Ireland at his Glasgow office, late on Tuesday evening, a cable sent from La Paz was waiting for Fleming — another success dearly paid in blood. The next day, right before noon, the K4 radioed its account of what had occurred on the Island of Solitude. The list of casualties kept growing. He called M and informed him of the successes of the missions, their death toll, and his failure to secure allies in the coming confrontation with the Outer Gods. Then he went through a new list of priority targets, drafted by Professor Eliassen. Not only was it depressingly long, but the majority of its objectives were also in remote, difficult-to-reach locations. Fleming began to have severe doubts about their strategy's sustainability.

He was about to call it a day when Rebecca swung into his office, carrying two shot glasses and a full bottle of fifteen-year-old Bruichladdich.

'Story time!' she cheerily reminded him of his promise as she smacked the bottle and the glasses on his desk.

Fleming had to chuckle at the flair with which she'd cornered him. Storytelling, indeed. Why not? Maybe it would take his mind off his current worries.

'What do you want to know?' he asked with a twinkle in his eye.

'How about everything?'

Fleming sat back while Rebecca filled their glasses.

'In Britain, you'll find lots of soldiers whose fathers were military men as well, as were their fathers before them,' he began after downing his first dram. 'My ancestors have been with the SSB Special Branch — and whatever it was called before — for generations. The first Fleming who went monster hunting was Adalbert Fleming in 1622. He was a French Huguenot of Flemish descent. His French surname was Flamant, and before that, the family was called De Vlaeminck. France wasn't a healthy place for Protestants. In 1618, Adalbert decided to pack up his family and move to England, where he anglicised his name. There were plenty of Huguenots in London already, and their connections helped my ancestor to become an officer in the King's Guard. These were the latter years of the reign of King James I, the successor to Queen Bess. James I was a smart man, and so was Adalbert. They got talking. Adalbert became the king's trusted advisor on French affairs and finally, the monarch asked him to join the secret service. After him, every first-born son in the family served in the secret service and ended up leading its Special Branch.'

'So you're what? The ninth or tenth of your line?' Rebecca asked.

'The eleventh.'

'Impressive,' she said with a whistle.

'The British monarchs and at least some of the parties the secret service dealt with saw it as an advantage that members of the same bloodline acted as intermediaries between them for centuries,' Fleming explained, 'All Flemings made it a point of honour to leave copious documentation of their dealings to their sons and groomed them from an early age.'

'One would expect a peerage for such loyal and enduring services to the Crown,' Rebecca said.

'In fact, we all carry the title of earl,' Fleming acknowledged, 'but the peerage was never made public. From the outset, my family chose discretion and stayed far removed from the public eye. We don't own lands, don't have a seat in the House of Lords, never use our title, and are never addressed as Lord.'

'Contrary to M,' Rebecca remarked. '*He* has no reservations calling himself *Lord* Holmes.'

'We all make our own choices,' was Fleming's neutral reply.

'Was your grandfather the first of his line to marry a — a member of the Faerie?' Rebecca asked, changing the subject.

'Yes,' Fleming said. 'It was a bold step, much frowned upon by both sides. My grandfather had been married twice before. He lost both wives in childbirth. Lady

Eiluned had been his contact person for the Faerie for years on end, and their long-standing relationship of trust and mutual respect turned into something more affectionate.'

'They must have loved each other deeply to commit to a marriage that was sure to upset both of their communities,' Rebecca mused, and then she asked, 'Did Lady Eiluned have to give up much for this marriage?'

'You mean like her immortality?' Fleming suggested, grinning.

'Well, hem, yes, you know, that's what —' Rebecca stuttered, feeling foolish.

'That's what's told in fairy tales, and that's exactly what it is: a fairy tale,' Fleming said. 'Lady Eiluned is an elf, and elves have life spans of several centuries, but they aren't immortal. And marriage doesn't change any of that. I thought you'd have guessed, being a biologist and all that.'

Fleming had fun teasing Rebecca and watch her cheeks turn a deep pink.

'Anyway, the marriage caused a tremendous shock,' he continued. 'The British prime minister, Lord Melbourne, believed the marriage compromised my grandfather's integrity — which was rich, coming from that philandering, sadistic child abuser. Queen Victoria was very young at the time, only twenty-one years of age, but, in this rare instance, she decided to go against her prime minister. Thanks to the queen, my grandfather retained his position in the secret service. The following year, in 1841, Lady Eiluned gave birth to my father.'

'Being a biologist and all that, I find it remarkable Lady Eiluned and your grandfather were able to have any offspring at all,' Rebecca commented tartly.

'You'd be astounded to know how many of the "imported" species can breed with humans,' Fleming corrected her. 'I suggest you brush up on your Greek mythology: A lot of the most outrageous stuff in those stories *did* happen.'

162

Rebecca blinked in disbelief, and Fleming decided not to pursue the issue.

'My father first wanted to serve in the army before joining the secret service — a choice fully endorsed by my grandfather. He entered the secret service in 1870. He'd spent most of his military career in India and knew the country exceptionally well. He found it teeming with gods, demi-gods, demons, monsters, spirits, and the like. When Queen Victoria appointed him as head of the secret service in 1878, he decided to put more effort into straightening the relationships between the Raj and the *Devas* and *Asuras* — which is what they call gods and demons in India. The *Devas* and *Asuras* belong to many different off-world species, but they were all united in their hatred of the British, as they equated British rule with Christian domination.'

'They saw the British as a threat to the comfortable position they'd enjoyed until then,' Rebecca concluded.

'True. That hadn't always been the case. Initially, the British East India Company fiercely resisted being drafted into any missionary effort whatsoever. For them, the Company was all about trade and making profits. They lobbied the government to keep the missionaries out, arguing the Indians were a civilised people that didn't need to be "enlightened".'

'Amen to that.'

'The Charter Act of 1833 opened the door for the zealots anyway and forced a change in the Company's policy,' Fleming went on. 'Missionaries flooded into the country. Many of them were fanatical Evangelicals, who thought of the Hindu as degenerates needing to be converted to Christianity by all means possible. From then on, all bets were off with the *Devas* and *Asuras*. They used their considerable influence to sow rebellious sentiment among the local population. One of the results was the Sepoy Mutiny in 1857.'

'So your father wanted to calm things down again,' Rebecca supposed.

'Yes. That was a tall order. The missionaries had become immensely powerful by then, and the *Devas* and *Asuras* held little or no trust in my father's good faith.'

'What happened then?'

'My father persevered,' Fleming said. 'He lived the larger part of the year in India. He met my mother in Lucknow, and they married in 1880.'

'And your mother was a "normal" human?'

'Yes, that's why Eliassen told you I'm only a quarter-elf.'

'That's right. Please, go on.'

'As I said, my father worked hard to improve relationships with the Indian gods and demons, but the missionaries' aggressive conversion tactics continuously sabotaged his efforts,' Fleming continued. 'To be honest, a lot of the so-called gods he had to deal with were blowhards as well, which meant he had to use a carrot-and-stick approach to get anything done at all. I was born in Hyderabad in 1882. In that same year, my father got suspicious about what was happening in Thiruvananthapuram, Kerala's capital. The city is home to the richest temple in India, the Padmanabhaswamy Temple, funded by the Travancore royal family. The temple is dedicated to Vaishnavism's Supreme Lord Vishnu and contains an important statue of the deity in eternal yogic sleep while lying on a coiled serpent.'

'Interesting choice of mattress.'

'My father had no quarrel with Vishnu,' Fleming said, ignoring Rebecca's remark. 'He's a tremendously powerful being and, on the whole, played a constructive role in the dialogue my father was trying to establish. The Padmanabhaswamy Temple stands on top of six closed vaults. Most of these vaults contain the temple treasures — gold hoards of mythical proportions — while others have a more sinister reputation.'

'Sinister how?'

'Behind one vault's closed door, legend has it that gods, holy men, and a *yakshi* hold strange rituals in the Supreme Lord's honour,' Fleming said.

'What's a *yakshi*?'

'It's what they call a female vampire in Kerala.'

'Yech,' Rebecca made a face.

'My father found out that, in the region of Thiruvananthapuram, abnormal numbers of young men, women, and also children had disappeared without a trace,' Fleming resumed. 'Now, Vishnu isn't a god who requires human sacrifices. Something darker than the Vishnu cult must have been going on. My father went to investigate, suspecting he had a vampire infestation on his hands. You can't reason with vampires. If unchecked, their numbers spiral wildly out of control. They're a terrible pest. To address the issue, my father took a Company with him from the 94th Russell's Infantry Regiment. He insisted my mother and I stayed behind in Hyderabad, but she categorically refused to be left alone.'

'So your father took his wife and newborn along on a vampire hunt. Seems like the sensible thing to do,' Rebecca agreed in a deadpan voice.

'They arrived in Kerala in August. A member of the local royal family received my father with all honours. The man was horrified at the suggestion something untoward might be happening in the temple his family cared for since many centuries. Three days later, the entire Company of eighty soldiers was found murdered in the city's streets. My parents' bodies were discovered inside the temple. They were lying on Vishnu's golden statue, their breasts torn open and hearts cut out. It had all the appearances of a ritual sacrifice — not something vampires would do at all. I survived because my Indian wet nurse had the good sense to go into hiding while the massacre was taking place.'

'What a horrible story!' Rebecca cried out. 'You never got to know your parents; that's terrible! Did they find out who was responsible?'

'The Travancore royal family was deeply upset by what had happened and offered loyal and active assistance to the British in the murder investigation, but nothing ever came of it.'

'You know, I'm thinking, the combination of a sleeping god, a secret vault, and a murderous sect: It all reeks of a Sleeper site if you ask me.'

'That's what I've been thinking since the event in Zoetevoorde,' Fleming agreed. 'I saw Eliassen also put Thiruvananthapuram on his new list of potential Sleeper sites. Breaking open that vault will be such a scandal, I can tell you now. We'll have an uprising on our hands if we ever try that.'

The bottle was over half-empty, and it was dark outside. Everybody had gone home. Rain clattered against the window panes — another wet night in Glasgow. Rebecca refilled the glasses again.

'What happened to you after that tragedy?' she asked.

'They took me to Irish nuns, who shipped me back to Britain. My grandmother says Prime Minister Gladstone himself informed her about my parents' deaths. And then she told me about an awkward ceremony in Downing Street 10 in October later that year. The prime minister invited her, and she went to see him with two of her sisters. Gladstone was waiting for them, together with a young and inexperienced Mycroft Holmes, my father's successor in the secret service. A catholic nun and the archbishop of Canterbury, Archibald Campbell Tait, were also present. My grandmother thought the archbishop looked gaunt and pale. Later, she learnt he had only two more months to live. The nun held a baby — that was me, as you already guessed. Then Gladstone made a rambling speech, praising my father and the excellent relationships between humans and the Faerie. The nun handed me to my grandmother, but not before M had asked whether the archbishop had performed the iron test.'

'The "iron test"? What's that? I don't understand,' Rebecca asked.

'Elves have a strong allergic reaction to iron,' Fleming explained. 'Putting an iron object on an elf's skin has the same effect as branding him with a hot poker. What M wanted to know was whether the archbishop had verified if I'd inherited my father's elf traits.'

'And have you?' Rebecca asked, tensing up.

Fleming pushed back the sleeve on his right arm and turned the inside of his wrist for her to see. The cross-shaped red scar still looked painful to the touch after all these years.

'That callous son-of-a-bitch branded a baby!' she exclaimed, aghast.

'That's the British clergy for you,' Fleming said. 'May his soul rot in hell. Now you know why I can't stand priests.'

'What's it like to be an elf?' Rebecca asked, changing the subject. 'Is it very different from being a human?'

'The differences aren't extreme,' Fleming said, lowering her expectations. 'Elves' senses are far more acute, though. They have better hearing and sense of smell, sharper eyesight, excellent night vision. An elf is also stronger than the average human and tends to have better motor skills, like superior hand-eye coordination. They have a total absence of fear of heights and exceptional equilibrium. Also, they're immune to a whole range of diseases plaguing humans. I've never had a cold or the flu.'

He raised his glass, smiling.

'Oh, and not to forget, a high tolerance for alcohol.'

'And on top of that, you live longer, you lucky sod,' Rebecca added, grinning. 'Any downsides, except for the iron allergy?'

'The iron allergy wears off a bit with age. Still, I usually wear gloves. The acute senses may seem like a boon, but I can assure you, in an urban environment, they're not. The noise and smells are torture.'

'Poor you,' Rebecca commiserated. 'You were raised by your grandmother then?'

'Yes. Gladstone gave her a speech on how he expected her to raise me like a true warrior "to continue the fight against the forces of darkness on behalf of both humanity and Faerie". She gave him an earful.'

'Bully for her,' Rebecca said, punching the air. 'What did she say to him?'

'That whether I would continue in my ancestors' footsteps was entirely up to me,' Fleming answered. 'She told him then what she told me a few days ago. It isn't the elves' fight anymore but humanity's.'

'Was that the first time she met with M? What did she think of him?'

'She never liked M,' Fleming said. 'She finds him cold and calculating — a cruel man, who isn't to be trusted. Always wheels within wheels, never sure what his endgame is, except that he'll always put human interests first. During his tenure at the Special Branch, relationships with the Faerie cooled considerably.'

Rebecca could see Fleming's grandmother's point. You didn't want Mycroft Holmes as an opponent.

'How was it, growing up among the Faerie?' she asked.

'I think it gave me a perspective on life humans don't usually have,' Fleming said thoughtfully. 'Elves attach great importance to living in tune with nature. You're not supposed to take more than what you need and never more than what nature can provide. That's one of their fundamental rules. Sustainability is a big thing with elves, whereas I feel humans haven't even made a start thinking about the issue. For humans, personal gain and economic growth always take precedence over anything else — damn the long-term consequences. They tend to think there are no limits to what nature can support or, at least, expect we will not reach that cut-off point during *their* lifetime. Humans don't seem to dwell long on the consequences of their behaviour for the next generations. If they give the matter any thought at all, they always seem to nourish the blindly optimistic belief that improvements in technology will solve all problems. I guess there is *some* truth in that, but often technology itself is the root cause of the problem. Anybody who's ever lost his way in our big cities because of the impenetrable smog should understand that. M calls me a Luddite and is always pointing out that life in the past was much shorter and far more brutal. He's an unconditional believer in what he calls "progress". I fear that humanity's future will catch up with them before they've made enough "progress". Well, that is if we can stop the Dream Whisperer. If we don't, it will be over even sooner.'

Rebecca had some sympathy for Fleming's arguments, although she found it hard to share his pessimistic views entirely. As a scientist, she saw both sides of the argument and held great stock in human ingenuity to tackle the hardest problems. However, she felt this was neither the place nor the time to engage in that discussion and decided to change the subject.

'Why didn't you stay with your elf family?' she wanted to know.

'As Eliassen said, I'm but a quarter-elf,' Fleming reminded her. 'The other elves accepted me, albeit only to a certain extent. My entire family history is human.'

'So you became the warrior Gladstone asked for.'

'Not at first, no.'

Fleming let that answer hang in the air for a while before he continued, 'I told you I'm the eleventh of my line. Only four of my ancestors have died of natural causes. That's something to think about.'

This time, Rebecca could see his point all too clearly.

'My grandmother always insisted I had no obligations towards humanity because my family had already spilt enough of its blood for the greater good,' Fleming pointed out. 'I went to Oxford to complete my education. It was the first time in my life I lived in the company of humans. I made a few friends, but I was mostly disgusted by the blustering arrogance and snobbery I encountered in many of my peers. That made me hesitate whether I wanted to be part of a society where entitled boors rule the roost. After a couple of months, I dropped out of university and opted for the life of a gentleman farmer, forsaking my family tradition.'

Rebecca gasped; this was going in a direction she hadn't expected. Since Fleming had ended up in the Special Branch anyway, she dreaded what was coming.

'I fell in love with a marvellous young woman,' Fleming went on. 'We married and had a beautiful daughter. We dreamt we could peacefully live out our blissful lives in splendid isolation on our estate in the Yorkshire Dales.'

'What went wrong?' Rebecca almost didn't dare to ask.

'Eight weeks after my daughter's birth, I went to a nearby market to sell our produce. Upon my return in the afternoon, I found the farmhouse burnt to the ground. My wife and daughter had both perished in the flames. They told me it was a tragic accident, a chimney fire. None of the farmhands had been able to rescue my family. The fire had been sudden and immediately turned into a roaring blaze. My paradise had lasted for less than two years. I sold the estate and joined the secret service.'

Rebecca sat there, speechless for a while.

'How awful —,' she managed to say. 'I had no idea. I don't know what to say. Such grief. And, well, did you suspect foul play?'

'I never heard of a chimney fire turning into a blaze that quickly, but who can tell? Something killed my parents, and then my family was taken away from me again. I don't believe in coincidences is all I can say on the matter.'

Then he poured the last drops of whisky in their glasses.

14

Team E, Khövsgöl Nuur, Outer Mongolia

Thursday, 22 February 1917

Fleming groaned in despair when Professor Eliassen presented him with another of Von Junzt's 'almost certain' locations for a Sleeper cradle.

'Lake Khövsgöl in Outer Mongolia!' he cried. 'Why not the middle of Antarctica or maybe the moon?'

'I told you earlier Antarctica is a likely location as well,' Eliassen said smugly. 'There are several texts in my library that refer to a "nameless city beyond the Mountains of Madness" on Antarctica. Unfortunately, promising though it sounds, its coordinates are a bit too sketchy to send in one of your teams. At least for now.'

Fleming kept scowling at him in silence.

'Von Junzt is supremely convincing,' the professor insisted.

'I agree, and I'm not arguing about that. I simply don't know how we can get a team to that godforsaken place. The closest station we have is in northern bloody Afghanistan. That's *eighteen hundred miles* away from the target.'

Fleming decided to consult with M. During the meeting, M was critical but helpful.

'This Lake Khövsgöl, it makes me wonder,' he remarked while looking at a map of Mongolia. 'It's landlocked. In fact, there are few places on Earth further removed from any sea or ocean. How will this Sleeper meet with its four other siblings if it can't get to the sea?'

'The scale of the map you're looking at, M, isn't large enough to show it. There does exist a small tributary that leads from the Mongolian lake to Lake Baikal in Russia,' Fleming explained. 'From there, the Cthulhu can reach the Kara Sea; it only has to follow the Angara River and then the Yenisei River. It's a two-thousand-mile swim. No doubt the creature is up to it.'

'The Kara Sea again. What a curious coincidence,' M mused.

'It's out of the question to set up an expedition overland,' Fleming went on. 'We'll need a large aeroplane that can carry eight men, weapons, and 500 lb of explosives. The obvious choice would be a Handley Page O/400 bomber: It can carry a crew of four and a 1,600-lb payload of bombs. That'd suit our needs perfectly if we modified the bomb hold for carrying passengers. Alternatively, we could also fly several smaller planes. That'd be even more conspicuous. Also, their range is far more restricted, which means more frequent refuelling stops.'

'We've deployed almost all of our bomber planes in Europe,' M said. 'There's one in Palestine, though. We could fly it to Afghanistan — to Kabul or Kunduz. That won't fail to arouse suspicion with our Russian friends. The entire area is infested with spies. Well, there's nothing to be done about that. What's the range of the O/400? Some eight hundred miles, I'd think?'

'Yes, that's about right,' Fleming agreed.

'Not cutting it too fine, that'd mean three stops each way,' M made the calculations in his head. 'Preferably two of them in the Xinjiang province in China and one in Mongolia. Xinjiang is quiet nowadays. Governor Yang Zengxin

174

runs a tight ship — a ruthless and efficient man, although not well-liked by the authorities in Peking. He relies on the Hui — Chinese Muslims — to run his province. The Han Chinese aren't too happy about that and would like to see the back of him, but it looks as if he's firmly in power. I could talk to a couple of people in London and our ambassador in Peking to smooth the way. It won't be easy. The Chinese invented bureaucracy, and palms will have to be greased.'

Fleming was looking at the maps again.

'I suppose the best choices for refuelling stops in Xinjiang will be Aksu and Ürümqi, where the governor has his seat,' he said. 'I read a description of Aksu by a British officer who visited the city in the 1880s. It's a lively place with a lot of merchants.'

'Ah yes, Sir Francis Younghusband. Quite a character,' M chuckled.

Fleming never ceased to marvel at the depth of M's ready knowledge. It seemed as if there wasn't a single memo or official document written in the service of the Crown in the past century, which he hadn't read and memorised.

'Isn't he a reliable source of information?' Fleming asked, a bit worried by M's remark.

'Certainly, certainly, as long as you don't take him as your moral compass, you can trust his judgement.'

Fleming stared at his boss, waiting him out.

'Some of our chaps go native,' M explained. 'They're so charmed by the local way of life they throw their western upbringing overboard and get assimilated. Start to think and act like the locals. Sir Francis is one of those. Harmless, you know, but he'd find it hard to fit back in, here in Old Blighty.'

M turned back to the matter at hand, 'And then there's Mongolia, an entirely different kettle of fish.'

'Because of the Russians?' Fleming supposed.

'Yes, needless to say, because of the Russians,' M said impatiently. 'In Europe, the Russians are our allies, fighting a common enemy. In Asia, we're bitter rivals. After the overthrow of the Qing dynasty six years ago, the Chinese kept the Xinjiang province under their control. The Mongolians saw it as a unique opportunity to break away from the Middle Kingdom. With some support by the Cossacks, they formed an independent state. The Russians share a large part of their border with the Chinese. So they welcomed an autonomous Mongolia — where they can exert considerable political influence — as a buffer against Chinese expansionism. The most northern part of Mongolia, where Lake Khövsgöl is situated, is entirely under Russian administration. We'll never get permission to refuel a bomber aircraft in those parts. And if we do, I can guarantee the Cossacks will strip-search it.'

'Couldn't we inform the Russians what our mission's purpose is?' Fleming proposed. 'They also have a secret service dealing with un-Earthly species. They might be more amenable than expected.'

'You know better than anyone the current Tsar is a feeble-minded bigot, who cut the funding of your Russian counterpart to such an extent it crippled its operations,' M rebuked him. 'I hear the *skrzaks* — the local imps — are running amok in Kursk and Saint-Petersburg because there is nobody left to keep them in check. Anyway, I predict the Tsar will soon have other fish to fry. The food rationing has sown deep discontent in Moscow, and I expect some serious rioting in the near future. Until now, the army has defeated all insurgencies against the Tsar. However, this time, my sources tell me the army's loyalty is far from guaranteed.'

'Then the operation is a no-go?' Fleming concluded.

'Not so quickly,' M answered. 'The *Bogd Khaan*, Mongolia's current religious ruler, is anxious to see his country internationally recognised as an independent state by foreign governments. He knows the Chinese will never waive their claim that Mongolia is an integral part of the Chinese Republic, and the Russians have been less than straightforward in their support of him. The Russians favour the country's autonomy but diplomatically accept the principle that Mongolia is part of China. Some time ago, the Mongolian government attempted to speak with western foreign ambassadors in Saint-Petersburg to initiate procedures for the official recognition of their country's independence. The Russians have firmly blocked that initiative. If we let the *Bogd Khaan* know Britain might consider opening discussions on this subject, I'm quite sure we could get a landing permit as a sign of goodwill from the Mongolian government.'

When the Handley Page O/400 left Urga, the Mongolian capital, for Lake Khövsgöl, the team was relieved all the official diplomatic functions were behind them. Fleming had asked a high-ranking officer lead the mission, so as not to insult the governor of Xinjiang or the Mongolian *Bogd Khaan*. M made sure of that. Lieutenant-Colonel Lord Bodham was not only a high-ranking officer and decorated war hero, who'd fought at Gallipoli, Egypt, and Palestine. He was also the 6th Viscount Bodham, a title that in the local authorities' perception might carry even more weight than his military rank.

The ceremonies in Ürümqi and Urga took a lot of their time. During banquets, toasts, speeches, exchanges of gifts, military inspections, and discrete diplomatic meetings, Lord Bodham showed himself a suave diplomat. Now he was happy to get out of his gala uniform and back into khakis.

The Handley Page had undergone a thorough redesign. The larger fuel tank extended the aircraft's range from eight hundred to a thousand miles, which allowed them to make the trip from Ürümqi to Urga without a fuelling stop. The former bomb hold now held eight passenger seats. The gun positions had all been removed. In a hidden storage space, where they also concealed the explosives and guns, they kept a Lewis gun with its ammunition and mounting. Bodham intended to fit that gun in the aircraft's nose before reaching the lake. For that purpose, the team made a landing in a deserted area two hundred and fifty miles to the north-west of Urga.

Winters are brutal in this part of the world, and temperatures of -50°F aren't uncommon. Fortunately, the temperature today was a balmy 10°F. The sky was clear; they expected no snow. The lake's surface was frozen solid, and the wild Sayan Mountains on its west bank were all covered in snow. On the eastern shore, vast plains and forests stretched out. From the air, they could observe, among the trees, reindeer herds and several tents that looked like native Americans' tepees. In the middle of the eighty-five-mile-long lake, was a small island.

The plane circled a few times over the island and then landed safely on the ice. While the plane taxied to the island, a group of men gathered on its shoreline. They stood in front of a temple-like structure in dark stone. The pilot stopped a quarter mile from the island, the plane's nose facing the men, so the gunner would be in a perfect position to open fire.

Immediately, the team started unpacking and loaded the explosives on a sledge. The pilot, Captain Hollingsworth, kept the engines running while his navigator, Lieutenant Barber, climbed in the gunner's seat. Bodham took his binoculars and counted thirty men, most of them seated on reindeer. His briefing mentioned nomadic tribes of Dukha or Tsaatan lived in the area. They were reindeer herders and had a reputation as a peaceful people. Bodham could see no weapons and decided they didn't yet represent an immediate danger.

'Sergeant Waterson, are we ready to move to the island?' he asked.

'Yes, Sir, the sledge is packed,' the sergeant replied with a suspicious glance at the island. 'What about the locals, Sir? They don't look all too friendly.'

'The Lewis gun will cover us,' Bodham assured him. 'Tell the men to have their guns at the ready, and then we'll move on.'

'Yes, Sir.'

They set out pulling the sledge over the ice. After the soldiers had covered half the distance, they heard a drum. Bodham had another look through his binoculars and saw two men standing in front of the row of reindeer riders. One was pounding a large drum in a slow rhythm. The other, who raised both hands above his head, was dressed in colourful, ceremonial garb and wore a weird headdress.

They've got a bloody shaman, Bodham thought.

Then the shaman began to dance and chant. He moved slowly and elegantly, making broad, wavy gestures with arms and legs. The fringes on his garb and boots turned the movements into a hazy blur as if the shaman consisted of little else than smoke. His high voice easily carried over the remaining distance, and the men could distinctly hear the words.

'Nt'arthsn och'tse ghui'bsott ylaha fhtàwsz wguhl'nt aich
M'gyenkh ehmend'ni mkeshtr tserph'orn t'yo t'yo ehl'ksch
Azthuzz kiz'get chagguah hoggsu chil'zhokh fh'yettrn'

One of the soldiers doubled over, eyes bleeding and slimy pus dripping from his ears. He was screeching at the top of his voice as if he was being burnt alive. Then the screaming stopped. His skin changed colour and fell in rotten lumps from his face and hands. He dropped to the ice with a soggy thud, his body not so much decomposing as liquefying. A sickening stench of putrefaction oozed from

179

the mushy corpse. A second soldier fell, and then a third. Bodham turned around and gave the sign to the gunner to shoot. The men on the reindeer shouted fierce battle cries and stormed at the panicking soldiers.

The Lewis gun was barking lead. The first attackers fell off their mounts; the others spread to the left and right in a pincer movement. The gunner chose to pick off their left flank first. The soldiers on the ice were shooting as well and took cover behind the sledge as best they could. The riders had small bows and aimed arrows at the team. They were remarkably effective. Two more soldiers lay bleeding on the ice, pierced by several arrows. The Lewis gun was, however, unforgiving. Soon, it had cut down most of the attackers. After a bullet struck the singing and dancing shaman between the eyes — proving he wasn't made of smoke after all — the remainder of the Tsaatan fled.

Bodham assessed the damage. Four of his men were dead, and one had two arrow wounds but would survive. They quickly pulled the sledge towards the island. The officer motioned Hollingsworth to move his aeroplane closer and then disappeared with his team inside the building. The pilot kept glancing nervously at the lakeshore, four miles away. More people appeared from the forest. They were pointing at the aircraft in animated discussion. When they also brought reindeer from among the trees and mounted them, the captain turned the bomber's nose in the direction of the shore and shouted at the gunner.

'Barber! Shoot as soon as they're within firing range!'

Lieutenant Barber stuck up his thumb.

It took another twenty minutes before a wave of sixty reindeer riders hit the ice. The gunner let them close in until they were two thousand yards away and then let loose. The first blast mowed down at least eight of them. The others spread out to avoid being a concentrated target. In five minutes, they would have reached the plane. The

Lewis gun continued to take its toll. More than half of the riders lay dead or wounded on the ice. The remainder of the group had swung to the right and were now out of sight, behind the island. Their plan was to go around the island and then attack the plane from behind. Even if the pilot faced the aircraft the other way, the attackers would be dangerously close after breaking cover. It would be impossible to gun them all down before they reached the plane. Moving the aircraft further away from the island would be safer for the pilots, but it would also increase the distance the returning team had to cover. They'd be cut off and slaughtered. Hollingsworth hesitated briefly before deciding that turning the plane was the best of two unsatisfactory tactical options.

Hollingsworth had just started his manoeuvre when Bodham and his crew emerged from the building. They hastily put the wounded soldier on the sledge and raced towards the bomber. The short distance allowed them to get on board before the attackers emerged from behind the island. The pilot gunned the engines, and the aircraft rapidly picked up speed on the ice. Looking over his shoulder, Hollingsworth saw the first riders chasing the plane from behind the bend. He could relax now because he knew their pursuers were too late to overtake the aircraft.

Right after take-off, the earth shuddered. The island erupted like a volcano. Temple debris and rocks were hurtled high into the sky before raining down on the Tsataan and the icy plain. The largest chunks went right through the ice. They didn't merely punch holes in the plain's surface but destroyed its integrity as well. The ice cracked and fragmented, tipping several riders and their mounts into the water.

The Handley Page circled once more over the area, allowing Bodham to take a few snapshots to document the success of the mission, and then flew off back to Urga.

181

15

SSB Special Branch HQ, Glasgow

Tuesday, 27 February 1917

M sipped his Oolong tea from a delicate bone-china cup as Fleming, Eliassen, and Mumm filed into the meeting room. They'd carefully examined the reports of all five teams. The missions also delivered a wealth of photographic material. The pictures taken in Mongolia were still on the way, but those already in their possession sufficed to establish a few patterns.

'I am all ears,' M announced.

'We've destroyed six Sleepers in total,' Fleming began. 'All Sleepers occupied temple-like buildings. The most complex ones featured hidden chambers and secret panels; the simplest ones comprised only a single, directly accessible chamber containing the Sleeper. All teams found intricate bas-reliefs on the sites' walls. We have many detailed pictures of this artwork. Hopefully, they will help Professor Eliassen in gaining further insights into the Outer Gods' culture and history, and in the circumstances of their expected return.'

The professor agreed.

'Of more direct interest: The sites were all near bodies of water — a sea, lake, or river,' Fleming continued. 'Given the nature of the Sleepers observed in Flanders and

Greenland, the proximity to water may be a necessary condition for a successful awakening.'

'As the Sleeper sites' construction dates from millions of years ago, changes in the Earth's features may have affected some sites' viability,' Rebecca added. 'Marine fossils found in deserts and on mountains prove that, at some point in time, these areas used to be seabeds. We know the Earth's crust moves and reshapes itself according to principles we don't yet fully understand. These geostructural changes may have destroyed a good number of Sleeper sites or moved them too far away from bodies of water. Some Sleepers may have become useless because they'd be unable to reach their preferred watery habitat in time.'

'Dormant Sleepers are inert,' Fleming pointed out. 'None of the Sleepers could *physically* attack our teams. However, they did so *telepathically*, which proves they're somehow aware of their environment. Ferocious animals or local tribes dedicated to the Sleeper cult protected all five sites. In Greenland, we witnessed how such a group of people welcomed the Dream Whisperer.'

'We believe the Dream Whisperer is responsible for setting up these defences,' confirmed Eliassen. 'He's probably instilled — in carefully selected populations — shamanistic traditions or cultist beliefs to increase the Sleeper sites' chances of preservation. Greenland has demonstrated these cultists know and revere him.'

'The tribes selected by the Dream Whisperer aren't fully human anymore — if they'd ever been,' Mumm clarified. 'Both the Greenland Inuit and the Bolivian Indians had gills and scaly skins. Inbreeding or interbreeding with marine species imported by the Outer Gods may have caused those features. The episodes with the shark and the bear demonstrated the Dream Whisperer has the power to make animals obey him.'

'I used the existence of known local cults and the proximity of water as selection parameters to draft a new list of likely Sleeper sites,' Eliassen declared.

'The professor has established a list with another forty sites,' Fleming confirmed. 'We've prioritised fifteen of them, mainly based on their accessibility. As we speak, teams are leaving on search-and-destroy missions. We've learnt from the first encounters. The new crews are larger and better armed than their predecessors, and we warned them about the potential dangers awaiting them at the Sleeper sites. Thanks to Doctor Mumm's briefing of the French prime minister, three of the teams are French military. They'll acquire targets in Africa and Asia.'

'What of the Dream Whisperer?' M wanted to know. 'Any sightings yet?'

'We distributed descriptions of Mathilde von Corvey to all friendly ports, shipping companies, and our intelligence networks,' Fleming answered. 'Up to now, no reports have come in. We don't know for sure whether the countess has survived the shelling in Greenland. If not, the Dream Whisperer may have acquired a different body unknown to us.'

M was eyeing a picture of an egg-shaped Sleeper in one of the sites.

'Doctor Mumm, have these pictures resulted in any new insights?' he asked.

'I've studied them extensively, as you can imagine, M,' Rebecca replied. 'My conclusion is the objects are neither eggs nor chrysalides. I think they're fully-formed juveniles, curled up in a foetal position and wrapped in what I initially and mistakenly considered to be its vestigial wings. These appendages aren't wings. They're protective shields to safeguard its body against the outside world, as would an eggshell or a chrysalid.'

185

'That's hardly consistent with the pictures of this creature taken in Greenland,' M observed. 'The wings on that Sleeper were too small ever to enfold it.'

'Indeed, you're right, M,' Rebecca agreed. 'Neither the wings nor the "eggs" we photographed could contain the creature. May I remind you that, both in Flanders and in Greenland, a blinding flash of light accompanied the Sleeper's awakening? That indicates a major release of energy. As it awakens, the Sleeper must experience a significant growth spurt. The "wings" don't increase in size because they no longer serve a purpose. The sudden volume spike at birth confirms the Cthulhus' enormous growth potential. The "wings" aren't vestigial body parts as I assumed earlier on. *Somebody* engineered them for their specific goal, just like they did the rest of the monster.'

'Hmm, at least we don't have to worry about it flying about,' M grunted. 'Good thinking, Doctor Mumm.'

'Any ideas on how the Dream Whisperer awakens the Sleepers?' he continued his questioning.

'The attacks by the entities on our teams indicate their capacity to establish a psychic link with their immediate environment,' Ove attempted to answer. 'Probably, the awakening involves some sort of mind-link with the Dream Whisperer. This is, however, pure conjecture.'

'Have you made any progress on the composition and function of the green goo in its head?' M inquired.

'Its chemical structure remains a mystery,' Rebecca admitted. 'I did, however, notice a cycle of weight increases and decreases in step with the light pulses we observed earlier. This indicates that matter continuously disappears and then reappears again. A possible — but admittedly outlandish — explanation could be that the green goo exists *simultaneously* in two realities, with matter flowing back and forth between our reality and another one. It's my conviction this is the creature's true essence. If the Cthulhus' raison d'être is to open portals between two parallel universes, they must have access to both universes at the same time. The green goo might be doing exactly that.'

M poured himself another cup of tea.

'Heady stuff indeed, Doctor Mumm,' he said dead-pan. 'Your theory demotes Cthulhus to ambulatory, half-sentient bins for trans-universal green goo.'

16

Agadir, Morocco

Friday, 2 March 1917

Agadir made the European headlines in 1911 when the German *Kaiser* sent a gunboat to its port. It was the emperor's ham-fisted attempt to defend Germany's claim on Morocco and weaken the *Entente Cordiale* between France and Britain. The terms of the *Entente Cordiale* required France to give Britain free rein in Egypt. As a quid pro quo, Britain promised not to interfere with France's designs on Morocco — then the last African country not yet firmly in the hands of any European coloniser. The affair blew up in the *Kaiser*'s face. It strengthened Britain's conviction that the sabre-rattling despot wasn't to be trusted and thus further strengthened the ties between Britain and France. Moreover, crippled by a sudden financial crisis, Germany had to renounce its territorial aspirations. It was fobbed off with a useless piece of the French Congo in exchange for allowing France to take full control of Morocco.

Agadir was a backward spot. Its port remained closed for international trade for a century and a half and only re-opened in the 1880s as a supply point for the sultan's troops. A few fishermen's huts lined its coast. The *Kasbah* on top of the hill was a desolate place where a few local people tried to eke out a meagre living.

The French had, however, well understood its strategic importance. Agadir's bay was the best natural harbour on Morocco's west coast. France established army barracks before the war and built a jetty in Founti as recently as last year. The construction protected the port from the strong south-westerly winds and would allow swift disembarkation of supplies and troops if need be. The French guarded the pier to prevent clandestine arms traffickers from using it. The region remained restless as several local Berber tribes resisted French occupation. At night, two powerful spotlights, installed on top of the citadel's walls, illuminated the jetty.

The sun had already set when a small fishing boat beached itself in the sandy harbour of Anza, a tiny fishermen community a few miles to the northwest of Agadir. It lay at the foot of the Anti Atlas Mountains, safely beyond the perimeter guarded by the French. A tall woman alighted; two men who carried her bags followed her.

On the beach, a small man was waiting for her and deeply bowed in her presence.

'Dream Whisperer, welcome! You make us rejoice! The time to awaken the Sleeper is upon us,' he greeted her.

'Dear, loyal Ouachich,' she answered him in fluent Shilha, taking his hands in hers, 'I knew I could rely on you. When can we leave for the Wadi Al Janat?'

'Everything will be ready by tomorrow morning. We've prepared food and sleeping accommodation for you. Please, follow me.'

He brought her to one of the huts, where they'd readied everything for a comfortable night. An old Berber woman had prepared a fish *tajine*. She kissed Countess von Corvey's hands and left the hut bowing.

The countess smelt the tajine. It amused her people kept assuming she needed sustenance. Many of the god-impersonating species had led humans to believe food offerings were pleasing to them. It should immediately have given them away as frauds. Humans were too stupid to make the correct deductions. She lit a smoke. Now that was an oblation she could appreciate. She grinned and blew blue smoke rings out of the window. The constellation of Orion was visible in the night sky. With her finger, she drew an imaginary straight line from Sirius over Orion's belt and Aldebaran to Algol. Algol — the Demon Star — that was the one to watch. The Dream Whisperer remembered teaching Egyptian astrologers that fact more than three thousand years ago.

The next morning before dawn, five men were waiting for her with donkeys. The caravan left the sleeping village and took the road to Mogador. They followed it for three miles and then turned east into the mountains. The rocky paths were narrow and winding, which made progress slow. The inhospitable, barren landscape gradually gave way to lush greenery as they neared the Tamraght River's bedding. Their journey lasted for about twenty miles, and then they reached the edge of a deep gorge in the mountains.

As they went down the mountain slope, they came upon a body of water more than four hundred feet long, bordered by sheer, red-brown cliffs. The sun was high in the sky — it was noon — and temperatures had climbed to 90°F. The *wadi*'s azure water reflected the bright sky. The men filled their flasks and offered the countess a drink.

Ouachich pointed to the basin's western rim. Beneath the sloping rock layers, right above the water surface, they could see a cavernous opening, visible only to those in the know. The countess patted him on the back and stripped down.

17

SSB Special Branch HQ, Glasgow

Friday, 23 March 1917

Fleming was in an upbeat mood. Over the past few weeks, he received a stream of reports from the teams sent out on search-and-destroy missions. Twelve of the fifteen operations he'd prioritised together with Professor Eliassen were concluded by now. In eleven cases the Sleeper was reported destroyed. One team found remnants of a temple obliterated by a landslide. As that temple's inner chambers were beneath hundreds of tons of rock and rubble, Fleming chalked that one up as a success as well. Casualties remained a worry. Sixteen soldiers lost their lives fighting local cultists, and one French team's aircraft crashed in the jungle of Madagascar before it reached its destination, leaving its ten passengers presumed dead. Another ten missions were decided upon, four on French terrain, two in British colonies, and another four outside either's territory. Planning and organising these assignments became an efficient routine. Some of the soldiers were leaving on their third mission already.

Fleming's major worry was that the Dream Whisperer hadn't resurfaced yet. Greenland was two months ago. It became ever more likely Mathilde von Corvey hadn't survived the bombardment by the HMS Bellerophon, which meant the Dream Whisperer had probably acquired a new host body by now. If that were true, his trace was lost.

He was going through the documents the teams had sent in once more when an excited data analyst knocked on his door. Benjamin Reeve had been with the Special Branch for several years and always struck Fleming as a level-headed chap. Seeing him in such a state, meant bad news.

'You need to see this, Commander,' Reeve began, putting a photograph on Fleming's desk.

It was an aerial view of a bulk cargo ship in clear water. Beneath the vessel, Fleming could distinguish a bizarre, dark shape. Its enormous tentacles were unmistakable.

'This is the Bilswood, Sir, a British collier,' Reeve commented. 'The picture was taken eleven days ago in the Mediterranean as the ship was leaving the port of Alexandria in Egypt. It sank on the same day, nine miles northwest of that location. The crew survived and reported back to the authorities in Alexandria. Their account of what happened was so unbelievable the local intelligence officers brought it to our attention. In the meantime, the entire crew has been sworn to secrecy. The official records show a sea mine sank the Bilswood. The crew is, however, unanimous: A huge sea monster with tentacles and long claws attacked them.'

Then Reeve laid out another four photographs before Fleming.

'I apologise for the quality of these pictures, Sir. The Coast Guard has taken them at Aldeburgh in Suffolk.'

The blurry pictures all showed a sinking ship under attack by a large, looming shape. In three of the four images, Fleming could distinguish giant tentacles.

'This is another British cargo ship, the Pontypridd,' Reeve continued. 'Its crew wasn't so lucky as the Bilswood's. Three men died. We have suppressed he survivors'

194

testimonies and officially attributed the incident to a U-Boat attack. The reports by the remaining crew confirm the pictures taken by the coastguard. A Cthulhu undeniably attacked them.'

'I sense you've got something worse to tell me, haven't you, Reeve?' Fleming asked, knowing what the answer would be.

'Yes, Sir. The Bilswood and the Pontypridd were both sunk on the same day, with less than two hours between them.'

'Well, it was to be expected,' Ove said after Fleming had briefed him and Rebecca. 'Sooner or later, this had to happen. I'm surprised it didn't happen sooner.'

'We haven't got a clue when the second Sleeper was awoken,' Rebecca pointed out. 'All I can deduce from the photograph of the Bilswood is that the creature has reached a length of well over one hundred and eighty feet, including the tentacles. The specimen in Greenland measured twenty-eight feet, so we're looking at an increase in size with a factor six. The pictures of the Pontypridd were taken from a much larger distance and aren't much to go on. I'd wager the tentacles shown in those photographs are much bigger than the ones in the Mediterranean. Our best guess is that it's the monster the countess set free in Zoetevoorde. That'd mean the Cthulhu that sank the Bilswood wasn't older than a month or a month and a half as its awakening must have taken place *after* the Greenland event. This creature isn't a full-grown specimen by any means. Moreover, these pictures only prove there are at least two Cthulhus on the loose. There could be more.'

Fleming had to agree, 'What bothers me most, is that this latest creature was probably released in a Mediterranean country or on Africa's west coast at the furthest and that we haven't noticed a thing. The Allied own all the ports in Spain, France, Italy, the African coast, and the Middle

East except Anatolia; we have spies in all enemy ports, and the Dream Whisperer and his monster slipped us by nevertheless. It's frustrating.'

'Well, our people probably missed the Dream Whisperer because he isn't using the countess anymore to get around,' Rebecca supposed. 'And I think that would make sense. It's something that's been bothering me all along.'

'What is?' Ove asked.

'Well, imagine this. You're an omnipotent being. Your only handicap is that you need to possess a physical being's body to interact with our world. Then you've got a job to do that requires you to criss-cross the globe to release these Sleepers. It's beyond me why you'd want to cling to the same host all of the time! The logical thing to do would be to flit from one host to another and cover the large distances in your ethereal form, wouldn't it?'

'I don't have the answer,' Ove admitted. 'It's certainly something to reflect on. I'll have another look at my books to find out whether the Dream Whisperer is somehow beholden to some rules that prevent him from doing what you said.'

'Do that,' Fleming agreed. 'We're missing too many pieces of the puzzle to understand our enemy. M was right. His behaviour is confusing. There's so much that doesn't make sense. Why did he start a war? Why did he pick a Sleeper site in Flanders with so many witnesses? Why does it take him so long to accomplish his mission? Why did he stick with Countess von Corvey for so long? Why did he allow Von Junzt to reveal any Sleeper locations at all? Why didn't he dodge the HMS Bellerophon, and why did he allow us to follow him straight to the Sleeper site in Greenland? It feels like playing chess against an opponent who has invisible pieces and obeys a different set of rules.'

Fleming's upbeat mood had changed into irritation and frustration. There were too many unknowns.

He stood up, signalling the meeting was over, and added, 'I'll draft a list of all ships that sank without survivors over the past year. I want to know if ships have disappeared without German involvement. It might give us an indication whether more than two Cthulhus are on the prowl and where they've been active. I cannot rule out yet that the Zoetevoorde Cthulhu wasn't the first one to awaken. We might be further behind in the score than we now think.'

18

Catania, Sicily

Sunday, 15 April 1917

A message in Morse code from their agent in Tripoli brought an end to the uncertainty at Special Branch HQ about Mathilde von Corvey's fate. Virgil Drummond was stationed in the city ever since the Treaty of Lausanne concluded the Italo-Turkish War in 1912. The treaty signified the end of Ottoman Tripolitania and brought the region into Africa Settentrionale Italiana, which covered Tunisia and the coastal area from Tripoli to the border with Egypt. As the Ottomans had before them, the Italians soon discovered the Libyans were an unruly lot. Although the Tripolitan area was firmly under their control, the Italians' grip on the Saharan hinterland was non-existing, and resistance in the east by Sunni Muslims was fierce.

The British took advantage of the Ottomans' departure by strengthening their intelligence network. Drummond was working under cover of an import-export firm and spent most of his time in Tripoli's port. He'd sighted the countess last Thursday. She chartered a small private vessel — the Italians had commandeered all other boats for war purposes. Drummond was able to find out her destination was Catania, the second-largest city of Sicily, situated on its east coast.

Drummond's message sent a jolt of energy through HQ. Fleming immediately took steps to mobilise a team to shadow the countess. He knew trying to apprehend her would be useless — and probably extremely dangerous. The best they could do was to follow her every move and hope they could prevent her from waking another Sleeper.

'Who are our field operatives in Sicily, Miss Shylling?' Fleming asked his secretary.

'We have nobody in Catania, Sir. Fielding is in Syracuse. He can get to Catania in under two hours, which would allow him to reach the port well before Von Corvey does. And then there's Postlethwaite in Palermo — not the sharpest pencil in the box, I'm afraid.'

'He'll have to do. Tell them both to get to Catania post haste. Also, contact Fleet Command in Malta to send a speedboat with a support team.'

Fleming called in Professor Eliassen and asked him, 'Professor, I can't remember you pinned down any targets in Sicily.'

'Well, I have,' Ove said in his defence, 'based on ninth-century documents written by a scribe at the Aghlabide court in Tunisia. But it didn't make my highest priorities' list.'

'Why not?'

'Two reasons. I identified a potential Sleeper site on Malta, which one of our teams is investigating as we speak. Its existence lowered, in my opinion, the probability of another Sleeper site on Sicily because of proximity reasons. Malta and Sicily are only sixty miles apart.'

'What was the second?' Fleming asked.

'The Arab text described the Greek and Roman temples on the island, and expressed puzzlement at an edifice south of the Etna,' the professor explained. 'According to the scribe, it was built in an entirely different, much older style than the classical temples. He didn't give any further details. His description could equally well have referred to a Sikanian Neolithic construction, but it stuck in my mind as a potential Sleeper site. I didn't have much to go on; the geographical indications in the text were poor. In the end, it seemed unlikely to me that a building this close to a hyper-active volcano had much chance to survive, and I discarded Sicily from my list.'

'Well, if the Dream Whisperer chose to travel to Catania without stopping in Malta, I think Sicily is the better candidate for a Sleeper site nevertheless,' Fleming concluded.

Fielding was watching as the countess disembarked in the harbour of Catania. Dusk had already set in, and she made no effort whatsoever to hide her arrival. She was wearing a conspicuous green dress and a feathery, broad-brimmed hat. A posh, black 1912 Züst 28HP automobile was waiting for her on the quay in full view. At the wheel sat a meaty colossus. He looked Afghan to Fielding, an impression reinforced by the man's *karakul* hat. He had heavy eyebrows and sported a well-groomed goatee. When he left the car to open the door for the countess, Fielding estimated his height at slightly over seven feet. The man had a wrestler's build. His tightly-fitted, black suit emphasised his broad shoulders and barrel chest. The driver watched smirking how two sailors struggled to put a large travel trunk on the quay and then effortlessly lifted the hefty piece of luggage on the rack at the back of the automobile.

After the Züst drove off, Fielding followed it at a safe distance in his car — a sporty, blue Alfa 24HP — and found out the countess was staying at the luxurious Hotel Royal, near the Piazza del Duomo. He booked a room for himself at the hotel and bribed a bellboy to let him know if their important guest received visitors or left the hotel. That was three days ago, and Von Corvey hadn't moved since. In the meantime, Fielding met his two colleagues — Postlethwaite, who drove down from Palermo on Friday, and Captain Hewitt, who arrived on Thursday night with a team of four in a fast torpedo boat from Malta. Hewitt's team stayed at two different inns in the harbour. Postlethwaite took up residence in a small family-run hotel on Via Manzoni.

Fielding was lying on his sumptuous four-poster bed, preparing for another eventless Sunday evening, when a breathless bellboy came knocking at his door. A man had come into the lobby asking for the countess. Fielding slipped the bellboy a generous tip and gave him some more money to get street urchins to bring the message to Postlethwaite and Hewitt.

The countess wasn't in a hurry. She let her visitor stew for over an hour. By the time she deigned to appear, both Fielding and Postlethwaite sat reading newspapers in the lobby. Hewitt and his men had taken up position in the two local operatives' cars parked on the street in the hotel's neighbourhood, in case their target made a swift exit. Fielding positioned himself in an armchair with its back to the countess's increasingly nervous visitor. Postlethwaite availed himself of a direct view from the other side of the room and sat on a sofa facing the one he expected his mark to take.

As Mathilde von Corvey entered the lobby, the agitated visitor sprang up as if stung by a bee. He kissed her hand and grovelled at her feet. The countess's demeanour was icy.

She took a seat and addressed him sharply in Italian, 'What took you so long, worm? I've been waiting here for you since Thursday. Did you expect I had nothing else to do?'

The small man shrank even further. His face was pallid, although he felt hot under the collar.

'My sincerest apologies, Dream Whisperer. We didn't expect you to come!'

Her poor subject sounded strangled, and he was stuttering.

'The time of awakening has come. Take me to the temple.'

The lackey was now weeping.

'But — but that's impossible, Master!'

'What are you saying?'

Even Fielding felt a cold shiver going up and down his spine. That short sentence held such an unspeakable threat it would have made sturdier men crumble. The countess's visitor was now a mere puddle.

'The Sleeper is lost, Master!' he cried out. 'Seven years ago, we had a terrible eruption. Lava flows went almost as far as Belpasso. It was impossible to evacuate the Sleeper!' he pleaded. 'The lava reached the temple before we could react! The Sleeper has perished without awakening! A thick layer of lava stone covers the site; it's entirely out of reach! There was nothing we could do! Please, Master, please, have mercy on us!'

The countess looked at the quaking minion with all the contempt she could muster.

'You have neglected your duties. You will face the consequences.'

Even though she spoke the words in a soft voice, they couldn't be mistaken for anything else but a death sentence.

Von Corvey looked up and gave a slight nod to her driver, who had appeared soundlessly at the lobby's entrance. He stepped forward, took the snivelling visitor by the arm, and marched him out of the room. The countess touched up her make-up and followed suit minutes later. They went to the hotel's courtyard, where the Züst was parked. Without letting go of their guest, the driver opened the door for his mistress. After she'd taken her place in the backseat, the giant forced the scrawny Sicilian to sit next to him and peeled off.

Fielding and Postlethwaite ran to their cars and followed the countess, trying not to attract attention. They noticed her trunk latched to the luggage rack, which meant she didn't plan to return to the hotel. It was crucial not to lose her trail. The cars took the road to Paterno. When they left the city limits, the pursuers switched off their headlights. After seven miles, the Züst took a sharp turn to the north in the direction of Belpasso. Despite the deepening twilight, the threatening contours of Mount Etna starkly contrasted with the night sky. A faint plume of smoke rose up from one of its many mouths. The Etna was a restless volcano. Its central crater had been continuously active since the end of the previous century before the major eruption seven years ago. In the past three years and a half, both the central crater and a few others on the north-eastern side had shown signs of activity. Specialists predicted an important event any day now. They passed through Belpasso without slowing down. After another two miles, they veered to the right again, on the road to Nicolosi. The traces of the previous disaster were still fresh. Solidified lava streams had turned the landscape into a barren, alien planet. The molten rock had swallowed a few houses further afield; only a couple of crooked roofs were sticking out above the rough surface.

On the northernmost outskirts of Nicolosi, the Züst stopped near the ruin of a burnt-out farm. Some thirty people of all ages were waiting for her. They were of small stature, narrow-shouldered; their broad faces with deep-set, furtive animal eyes had something indefinably primeval. They held torches in claw-like hands, deformed by hard labour in unyielding soil. The scene looked like one of Goya's darkest depictions of witches' Sabbaths. As she stepped out of the car, they all kneeled; not one dared to look her in the face. She waited a long time before addressing her subjects. Fielding and Postlethwaite had cautiously parked their cars a few hundred yards further down the road, and they were observing the scene from a safe distance, together with Hewitt's team.

'Since time immemorial, your forebears have tended to the Sleeper's needs,' the countess began her address in a mournful, solemn tone.

The British didn't understand a word she was saying. She didn't speak Italian or even a Sicilian dialect. Von Corvey used a Palaeolithic language — an archaic tongue with misshapen vowels, guttural consonants, and strange clicking sounds. It was a speech long since lost in the mists of time, which somehow survived in this primitive community.

'During aeons, your ancestors have kept the Sleeper safe from Mount Etna's temper. They moved his resting place whenever circumstances called for it,' the countess went on. 'They have rebuilt his temple over and over again to elude the hungry magma's grasping fingers flowing from the Earth's bowels. Each time Mount Etna made the land shudder with unreasonable fury, your forefathers have repaired the Sleeper's sanctuary and observed the holy rites — secret knowledge, faithfully transmitted from generation to generation, countless times. I entrusted you with the highest responsibility; you were priests serving the dreaming God destined to awaken at the end of times. Unlike your progenitors, you have failed your sacred duty.'

A plaintive howl erupted from the crowd.

'There can be no mercy,' she stated. 'You have let perish the God in your care; there is no crime more heinous. I shall punish you for your shameful neglect and you'll never witness the return of the True Gods.'

The countess raised her arms. A sudden stench of burning meat reached the British team. The Dream Whisperer's followers were convulsing on the ground, screaming and kicking, consumed by an inner fire — as the Sleeper had been because of their carelessness. After half an hour, nothing remained of them but grey husks made of brittle ash.

Postlethwaite and several other team members had difficulties keeping their lunch down. They'd been warned not to interfere with their target because of its terrible powers, but this demonstration of supernatural cruelty was a horror for which they were unprepared.

The countess stepped into the Züst and drove back the way she'd come. The team scrambled to their cars again and followed at a distance with the lights off. At the first crossroads, the Züst's lights went out as well. They had lost her. She must have known she was being followed, which wasn't surprising as there were no other automobiles on the road at all. Fielding swore a blue streak. What to do? Go left, right, or straight on? He got out of his Alfa and told Postlethwaite to go straight on. Fielding chose the road to the left because the right one would have taken them to Mount Etna. It was more likely that Von Corvey would go back to the coast and hop on a waiting boat. They drove as fast as they dared on the unlit, narrow roads. Nobody saw the Züst parked behind an abandoned barn.

The countess tapped her driver on the shoulder, 'Let's go back to the coast, Moloch. Avoid Catania and drive to Pozzillo. I have a guest waiting for me.'

Moloch didn't restart the engine until their pursuers were well out of sight. Pozzillo was an insignificant fishermen village, almost halfway between Catania and Taormina. It took them half an hour over abominable dust roads to get there. Moloch dropped off the countess near the coastline, on the north side of the village.

'You know what to do,' she told him. 'Come back and pick me up here when you're ready.'

The giant nodded and drove off.

Mathilde von Corvey waited for a while at the roadside and lit a cigarette. Then she sauntered to the beach.

The nearest fisherman hut was more than three hundred yards away. Reaching the beach, she saw the light in the house go out. It was thirty minutes to midnight, she noted. Everything was dead quiet. The narrow beach consisted of basalt rocks. The countess walked prudently over the sharp stones to the water, squatted, and patted the water's surface with the palm of her right hand. Then she got up again and waited. Two hundred yards from the shore, an enormous dark shape rose from the sea. Slowly and silently, it walked towards the countess until it stood fifty feet away from her, in shallow water.

What a magnificent monster, she thought.

After millennia of dreams, the creature was destined for only a brief burst of existence. It would burn itself out for masters it had never seen. But not now. Not yet. It was still young and fragile. It needed time to grow and strengthen, to become indestructible.

The Cthulhu had grown to a height of over one hundred and eighty feet, and it wasn't yet adult-sized. There was no wind. Yet it seemed as if its tentacles were gently swaying in the breeze. It got down on its knees — not in a gesture of servility but to look the countess into the face. Its seven eyes burnt in the dark. One of its longest tentacles extended towards her, and she took it without hesitation in both hands.

Neither Fielding nor Postlethwaite had any luck finding Von Corvey. Fielding checked the Hotel Royal, against all hope, to make sure she hadn't returned. To no avail. He sent a telegram to HQ from the hotel, reading:

S + 1910 BY ETNA —STOP—
DW + CULT —STOP—
LOST TRAIL DW —STOP—

The team gathered on the Piazza del Duomo and ended up sitting on the steps of its Elephant Fountain — a graceless, white marble pedestal with fat *putti*, supporting an awkwardly sculpted elephant in dark lava stone with an obelisk on its back, which was topped with a globe, palm leaves, a plaque, and a cross for good measure.

You couldn't make up this stuff if you tried, Fielding thought — Italian baroque wasn't his cup of tea.

'I suppose the countess is finished with Sicily,' Fielding concluded. 'There's a good chance her next destination is Italy. I'll drive to Messina, which is the most likely port she'd use to cross over, and see if I can pick up her trail. I'll leave immediately. I can make it there in under two hours.'

Hewitt agreed, 'We'll have a look in Naples. If we leave now, we may beat her to it. Even if no Sleeper site hides in the vicinity of Naples, she'll probably pass through the city on her way to the north anyway.'

'I'll drive back to Palermo,' Postlethwaite added. 'Maybe she intends to go to Sardinia or Corsica and take a boat from there. Or she could sail to Naples; who knows? I'll check all the expensive hotels and have a look in the harbour.'

Fielding walked back to the Hotel Royal feeling like a complete failure. It was obvious their target knew they were following her. When had she made them? Probably in the lobby with her blubbering servant. She'd spoken Italian to that poor sod, making sure they could understand her. Why would she want that? He shrugged and increased his pace. He didn't believe he'd find her in Messina. She could secure a boat in any village along the coast and had probably sailed already. Maybe Hewitt's team stood the best chance to catch up with her again — if she went to Italy, which was by no means certain. Fielding opened the door to his spacious suite, threw his clothes in his suitcase on the bed, and then went to the bathroom to fetch his toiletries. When he opened the bathroom door, the countess's giant manservant stood before him. Moloch grabbed him by the throat, yanked him inside the bathroom, and crushed his skull against the porcelain washbasin. Once was enough. Moloch stepped over the expanding puddle of blood oozing from Fielding's shattered skull and grabbed a towel to wipe off a few red droplets from his black patent leather shoes. He walked out of the hotel through the lobby, winked at the bellboy, and slipped him a regal tip.

Moloch ambled from the Hotel Royal to the hotel Postlethwaite was staying at, on the Via Manzoni. It was only a three-minute walk. He gave a satisfied grunt seeing Postlethwaite's cream-coloured Lancia Eta parked in the street and installed himself in the car's backseat. The wait wasn't long. Ten minutes later, Postlethwaite left the hotel. Without looking, he got into the driver's seat and put his suitcase on the place next to him. He was still fumbling getting the engine started when two powerful mitts held his neck in a vice and then snapped it.

Hewitt and his four sailors were leaving the harbour in their fifty-five-foot coastal motorboat. The boat was fitted with an 18-inch torpedo and had an anti-aircraft twin Lewis gun mounted on its cockpit. Upon reaching the open sea, Hewitt floored the gas, and the petrol engine gave a mighty roar. It didn't take them long to reach the forty knots maximum speed. These little boats were the Royal Navy's newest toy. Their high speed and manoeuvrability not only made them ideal U-Boat hunters: They could also sink much larger warships. It took them less than half an hour to cover the distance to Taormina on their way to the Strait of Messina, which separates Sicily and the tip of Italy's boot. They never made it. A few miles beyond Taormina, a huge claw ripped their boat in half. A seething mass of tentacles took hold of both halves and pulled them beneath the waves. The sailors were no match for the agile tentacles, which hunted them down in the water and mercilessly drowned them. The tragedy lasted less than half a minute.

19

SSB Special Branch HQ, Glasgow

Monday, 16 April 1917

Fleming had on his desk Fielding's telegram and a transcript of the situation report Captain Hewitt radioed to Fleet Command the previous night.

'The entire team went dark last night,' he said to Ove and Rebecca. 'These are the last messages they sent out. I've tried to contact Fielding and Postlethwaite, to no avail. Fleet Command lost all contact with the torpedo boat after the report. The boat never arrived in Naples. The most likely explanation is they've been compromised and killed.'

Ove agreed, 'I cannot imagine there are a great many motor vehicles on the roads in Sicily. The countess must have spotted them tailing her.'

'Do you think Captain Hewitt may have been right in assuming she's travelling to Italy, Professor?' Fleming asked.

'As you know, I haven't included any Italian Sleeper sites on my list,' Ove pointed out. 'That doesn't mean there aren't any. Still, I prefer to think it decreases the likelihood. If she travels north through Italy, she'll find it hard to reach Austria. There's a lot of fighting going on in the Alps, and it's not getting better any time soon, I expect. Maybe she'll find it easier to travel east over the Mediterranean. There are potential Sleeper sites we haven't targeted yet in Romania, Anatolia, and north of the Black Sea. My money would be on any of those destinations. The Central Powers occupy large parts of Romania, and as the *Sublime Porte* is also siding with the enemy, travelling in Anatolia would be no problem for the Dream Whisperer. He could easily complete his Cthulhu quintet using the Black Sea to reach all three destinations.'

Rebecca was reading the transcript of Hewitt's report.

'Isn't it strange the Dream Whisperer chose Sicily, though?' she wondered. 'He *must* have known that site was destroyed. It's been seven years, no less.'

'Maybe he knew, maybe he didn't,' Ove replied. 'Who's to say? Perhaps he saw it as an opportunity to set an example to the other cultists he's recruited in the past — to remind them not to sleep on the job.'

'I can't get it out of my head that the Dream Whisperer put on a show mainly for our benefit,' Fleming intervened. 'Sending us a message, you know. Reminding us how powerful he is. "Come too close to me, and I'll torch you." That kind of thing.'

'And Von Corvey has a new acolyte, apparently,' Rebecca said.

'She probably has lots of them,' Ove supposed.

'Still. Over seven feet?' Rebecca doubted. 'I've *never* seen anybody over seven feet. Until I saw "Rod the God" walking out of Fleming's office, that is.'

'His description doesn't fit Rod,' Fleming objected.

'No, but it could be a cousin twice removed or some other family member,' Rebecca pointed out. 'You told me, Fleming, the aliens posing as gods don't want to help us because they count on the Outer Gods to get rid of us. Maybe some of them have taken that attitude a little bit further to be on the Outer Gods' good side and are actively assisting them. Perhaps the countess's manservant isn't just a big, dumb lummox she's using for her heavy lifting. He could be an Old God.'

'There aren't that many of them left anymore. I'll ask around,' Fleming promised and then went on to ask Ove, 'Did you make any progress on your research concerning the Dream Whisperer, Professor? Are there any limits to what he can do? The demonstration he gave us on Sicily was a grisly one.'

'Well, we were struggling with the question why he doesn't change hosts more frequently to facilitate his getting around,' Eliassen said. 'You're familiar with the legend that says a vampire can't enter your house unless you've given him permission first? The same thing seems to be true of the Dream Whisperer.'

'Yes, I remember you explained to me on my first day he comes to his victims in their dreams and entices them with all kinds of promises to accept him in their bodies,' Rebecca confirmed.

'That's correct,' the professor continued. 'I went back to my books and found several texts that maintain that the host must actively welcome him to take possession of his body. The implication is that the process of persuading a candidate host can be time-consuming,' the professor explained.

'Which would mean that leaving one victim for another isn't such an effective strategy after all. The time saved in travel could well be lost again in acquiring a new host,' Rebecca concluded.

'Exactly,' Eliassen agreed. 'The strongest-willed targets may not be easily convinced to strike a Faustian bargain. Saint Jerome — the hermit who was tempted by the Devil in different guises in the desert of Chalcis — is a case in point. Only if the host does give in, the Dream Whisperer can invade his body and then becomes a symbiont.'

'A symbiont's life depends on the continued existence of its host,' Rebecca corrected him. 'That's not the case with the Dream Whisperer.'

'The analogy isn't perfect,' Ove admitted. 'What I meant is that the choice is irrevocable, not only for the host but also for the Dream Whisperer. Our foe can't back out of the deal either: He's stuck with his host until the latter dies.'

'That could be easily arranged, couldn't it?' Rebecca argued. 'The Dream Whisperer simply tells his host to jump off a cliff, and he's free to find another one.'

'I don't think it's as easy as that,' Ove objected. 'The possession doesn't mean that the Dream Whisperer takes over his host's mind and body entirely. It's a co-existence where both parties continue to have their say. The Dream Whisperer can't force his hosts to do anything against their will.'

'Then dear Mathilde must be a twisted sister!' Rebecca spat.

'The hosts who give in to the Dream Whisperer's promises have already proven they're corruptible,' Ove advanced. 'In time, that corruption undoubtedly expands as the host will find himself progressively more willing to yield to the Dream Whisperer's desires to continue benefitting from the partnership's advantages. In the end, there'll be almost nothing the host isn't willing to do to make the co-existence last. After a few atrocities, adding another one to the list is only a relatively small step. Compromising one's morality is a slippery slope. Returning to my earlier point: If the host has a desire to go on living, there isn't much the Dream Whisperer can do. That means he's stuck with Mathilde von Corvey until she dies.'

'He could order his driver to kill her,' Rebecca tried again.

'No. That would require her co-operation,' the professor said, finger raised in the air. 'The Dream Whisperer

214

can't make the countess say anything she doesn't want to. The way I understand it, our enemy can only terminate the association by tricking his host — for instance, by feeding her false information — into exposing herself to a fatal event. Unless, of course, Von Corvey grew so disgusted with herself she'd consider suicide.'

'It seems a pretty complex arrangement with a lot of checks and balances,' Fleming mused, sounding doubtful. 'Are you sure about all this, Professor?'

'It's what many independent sources tell me,' Ove declared. 'To me, it sounds convincing. Am I entirely sure? By no means.'

'It would explain why the Dream Whisperer remains in the countess's body,' Rebecca conceded reticently. 'I can't imagine what it's like, having such a monster in my head all the time, pushing me to further its agenda to bring about the end of the world. I'd go insane.'

'Well, it's food for thought. Otherwise, we're back to square one,' Fleming concluded. 'We've lost his trail. I'll send a message to our people in the eastern Mediterranean ports to keep an extra watchful eye out for Countess von Corvey. And I'll inform M. He'll be thrilled to bits, I'm sure.'

'You promised to look into shipwrecks without survivors to determine whether there are more Cthulhus around than the two we're aware of,' Rebbecca reminded Fleming. 'Did you find out anything we should know?'

Fleming shook his head, saying, 'As you can imagine, a lot of ships went to the bottom of the sea since the start of the war. I couldn't find any indication of a Cthulhu's involvement in the cases I researched. I'm inclined to think the Dream Whisperer has only released two specimens. At least we have that to be grateful for.'

20

SMS Loreley, Dardanelles

Sunday, 3 June 1917

Mathilde von Corvey didn't travel east from Sicily as Professor Eliassen expected. After finishing his gruesome business in Catania, Moloch returned to Pozzillo. He found the countess sitting on a rock by the road where he'd left her, smoking a cigarette. Travelling north along the Sicilian east coast, they reached the charming old port of Riposto. They had no trouble finding a fisher who agreed to sail them to Corfu for a hefty fee. There they chartered another boat, which brought them to Durrës, Albania's capital and — although dilapidated and silting up — still a major seaport in the region.

The Principality of Albania gained its independence from the Ottomans two years before the Great War. Soon, it proved itself to be ungovernable. Its German prince fled the country, barely half a year after ascending the throne in the spring of 1914. Albanian warlords immediately moved in to occupy the north of the country, toppling the region in anarchy. Greece reoccupied the south, where the population was predominantly Greek. Soon after that, Serbian and Montenegrin troops invaded the north until the Austro-Hungarian Empire and Bulgaria kicked them out in the winter of 1916. Earlier, in the autumn of the same year, the

Italians established control over the south by removing the Greeks, and they were eyeing even further territorial expansion into Macedonia and Greece. At the same time, the French carved out a protectorate in the southeast. They cynically called it the 'Autonomous Albanian Republic of Korçë'. The front lines had more or less stabilised by now. The *Doppelmonarchie* was firmly in control of two-thirds of the former Principality, a territory that included Durrës.

Even though the Adriatic Sea was only of secondary importance in the naval warfare between the Allies and the Central Powers, fighting was fierce. Both sides bombarded each other's coastal cities from the start of the war. They peppered the Adriatic with sea mines, making it a hazardous environment for ships. While the Allies tried to bottle up the Austrian fleet in the Adriatic, U-Boats wreaked havoc on the Allied fleet, invalidating the Allies' efforts in no small degree.

Immediately after her arrival in Durrës, Countess von Corvey contacted the highest-ranking officer in the Austro-Hungarian army, Infantry General Ignaz Trollmann. Trollmann was a commoner, the son of a police sergeant in Upper Austria. He stood in stupefied awe of the elegant *Reichsgräfin* and her endless family tree. Over dinner, she dazzled the general with her witty conversation and flattered him on account of his military successes. After she explained her need to travel to Constantinople, the general offered to secure her and her manservant a passage on the SMS Loreley. The large yacht belonged to the German Marine. It was for a long time deployed in the Mediterranean for representation purposes. The SMS Loreley transported ambassadors on their diplomatic missions, and the *Kaiser* and his family used it for holidays and official visits. At the outbreak of the war, the *Kriegsmarine* had decommissioned the yacht. The Germans now employed it mainly as a supply ship for other vessels in the Sea of Marmara. However, they also used it for evacuating German civilians from dangerous war zones around the Mediterranean. General Trollmann expected the ship to arrive in Durrës in four weeks. The countess was disappointed it would take that long. As alternatives were few and far between, she took what she could get and thanked the general effusively.

It took her even longer to leave Durrës. The ship needed repairs, and Von Corvey lost another week. She was bored out of her skull. Durrës wasn't exactly Vienna, Berlin, or Paris. Afterwards, to her dismay, the SMS Loreley didn't sail directly to Constantinople. There were severe concerns Greece would soon abandon its position as a neutral nation and join the Allied camp. The ship docked at the ports of Patras and Kalamata, taking several families of German merchants on board.

On 3 June, the ship entered the Dardanelles, the strait connecting the Aegean Sea and the Sea of Marmara. In honour of the military successes achieved by the Ottoman Empire against the British and the French on the Gallipoli peninsula, the north bank of the Dardanelles, *Kapitänleutnant* Meis broke out the bottles of Sekt.

'Let's all raise our glasses at the scathing defeat our Ottoman allies inflicted here on the British and the French,' the captain addressed the small crowd on deck. 'Today, we can sail peacefully through these straits, thanks to the brave Ottoman soldiers who have shed their blood defending the Dardanelles from the brutal attacks by our enemies. They fought valiantly for eight long months against overwhelming odds and gloriously prevailed. Gallipoli will forever be a batch of shame for our enemies, who are now licking their wounds in Egypt. As Ottoman valour has triumphed here, so will our German and Austrian-Hungarian heroes soon defeat the enemies on the western and northern front lines!'

The passengers received the speech with approving shouts, and soon everybody was singing '*Heil dir in Siegerkranz*', followed by '*Das Lied der Deutschen*'. The modest ceremony was welcome entertainment for the families on board. They'd lost almost everything leaving Greece and were now forced to rebuild their lives in unknown Anatolia. The men felt encouraged by the captain's upbeat message, and several women were in tears, struggling with conflicting emotions. The small children ran around, cheering and waving little German flags.

'Nice speech,' the countess complimented the captain.

'Thank you, *gnädige Frau Gräfin*,' said the captain, bowing graciously. 'These people could do with a little cheering up. Most of them are ruined, and they'll almost certainly face hardship in Constantinople rebuilding their businesses.'

'That sounds pessimistic,' Von Corvey remarked.

'Before the war, there was a lively trade in spices and textiles from the East to the West,' Meis explained. 'Now, all these trade routes have been cut off, and commerce has suffered for it. Building new import-export businesses under these conditions will be difficult, to put it mildly.'

'The war won't last forever, Captain. You said it yourself,' the countess admonished him.

'True enough, *Gräfin*,' the captain admitted.

He bowed and clicked his heels before mingling with the other guests. What Meis refrained from saying was that, after a promising start of the Ottomans' involvement in the war, Gallipoli had been their last victory. The Ottoman Empire was weak and crumbling — not the kind of ally that could tip the scales. And neither was the *Kaiserliche und Königliche Doppelmonarchie*. The Habsburgs were at the end of their tether. Their successes in battle in this war were due to German support, not to their own troops'

220

strengths. There were even disturbing stories about Austrian cavalry regiments always galloping away from where the fighting was, keeping themselves at a safe distance from the front line. The captain was doubtful the *Doppelmonarchie* would last beyond the war.

These were things only fools would say out loud, and Meis felt the countess's eyes burning in his neck as if she were trying to read his mind. He'd be glad to see her leave his ship; the woman made him intensely uneasy for reasons he couldn't fathom. Maybe it was her eyes. They continuously shifted colours, from blue over violet to red. He thought it unnerving. Ever since she'd come aboard, he had the strangest nightmares.

'You look tired, Captain,' she greeted him on another night at the captain's table.

She probingly looked him into the eye, and he felt flustered like a schoolboy caught smoking by the headmaster.

'These are *not* safe waters, *Frau Gräfin*,' Meis replied. 'We always must be on the outlook for enemy ships. The SMS Loreley is a slow yacht, and she's poorly armed, no match for British or French Destroyers.'

'We're grateful for your good care, Captain. I'm sure you'll bring us safely to our destination,' she said with a pleasant smile. 'How is Constantinople these days? It's been a while since I've been there.'

'I've always thought it's a strange city,' Meis confided to her. 'I keep myself to the Pera district on the west side of the Bosphorus. It's thoroughly Western; you'd think yourself in Paris or Berlin. Beyond Pera, it's a different world with which I never felt comfortable. No place for a decent white man — or woman — I think. Pera is bustling, despite the war. It's a remarkably wealthy area, and money helps to avoid feeling the pinch caused by war rationing. Pera is full of Europeans, you know. Lots of Greeks; they're doing well in trade. Jews too, unfortunately, but then what would you expect? Those rats are everywhere.'

'It's good to hear Pera is still going strong,' the countess said. 'I'll be staying at the Pera Palace.'

'I'm certain they'll be able to provide you with every comfort you may require,' the captain assured her, raising his glass.

That night, Meis dreamt rats and hideous black creatures overran Constantinople's beautiful westernised quarters. They flowed like boiling tar through the streets, windows, and door openings, and swallowed all the wealthy, white-clad people on their way. The countess, who was no longer Mathilde von Corvey, was watching it happen with a madman's smile. Her eyes shone a bright red.

21

Malta

Saturday, 9 June 1917

The past month and a half, the investigation of ten potential Sleeper sites had yielded mixed results. Seismic events dating back centuries had obliterated one of them. Two proved to be duds — Neolithic graves, which bore no relationship to the Outer Gods whatsoever, one of them in Malta. In seven cases, Fleming's teams destroyed actual Sleeper sites.

'All in all, not too bad,' Eliassen concluded. 'We're descending into lower-probability territory, and our success ratio suffers accordingly — nothing surprising about that.'

They'd worked through more than half of Eliassen's list of forty target sites. Eight more investigations were in progress, which left eleven targets unaddressed. Three of these were centred around the Black Sea.

One was in the mountains near Sinop, an Anatolian port city halfway down the Black Sea's southern shore. Sinop had once been a Bronze Age Hittite port. More recently, it witnessed a violent naval battle during the Crimean War. In 1853, the Russian fleet, under Admiral Nakhimov's command, destroyed an entire Ottoman frigate squadron near Sinop. The town was part of the *Vilayet* of

Kastamonu — one of the most backward provinces in Anatolia, which consisted mainly of farmland and mountains.

Eliassen believed the second site was near the ancient city of Tanais on the most eastern tip of the Sea of Azov in the Don River delta. The Goths destroyed Tanais in the fourth century AD. Its nearby Bronze Age necropolis of over three hundred *kurgans* or burial mounds had attracted the professor's attention. It was his conviction one of the *kurgans* was far more ancient still and contained a Sleeper. He had, however, no idea which one of the three hundred mounds was home to a Sleeper. That — and because it was in Russian territory — had put it low on the list.

The third site was in Romania, in the Danube Delta, an area of unspoilt nature exceeding two thousand square miles. The delta was a warren of rivers, lakes, marshes, and forests. It was uninhabited except by hundreds of bird species. They'd made it their breeding grounds since time immemorial. It was an ornithologist's heaven. However, discovering a Sleeper site, without any other clues narrowing the search perimeter down, looked like the equivalent of finding the proverbial needle in a haystack. It had made the list — barely — at number forty.

Fleming was looking at maps to figure out a practical approach to the problem at hand. Once more, M strongly advised against involving the Russians. Tsar Nicholas II had abdicated last March, and his designated successor, Grand Duke William, wasn't keen to take the mantle. The provisional government led by Minister-President Lvov was notoriously weak and in disarray. The Russian secret service tasked with the supervision of alien populations on Russian soil was all but dismantled. None of the acting ministers were familiar with the challenges the secret service used to handle. There was no one either M or Fleming could talk to with a reasonable chance of success.

Moreover, opening hundreds of burial mounds in search of a Sleeper was out of the question.

Despite indications being sketchy at best, Sinop offered the highest chance to knock out a Sleeper site in the region. They could reach the area by air from the Romanian Black Sea coast — a Handley Page bomber could make the journey both ways without refuelling. As they hadn't yet identified the Sleeper site's location, the aeroplane would have to make several scouting flights over the mountains. Only then, they could dispatch a ground team to take out the site. They needed to drop off the landing party in the lowland area nearest to the Sleeper site. Then the aeroplane had to take off again immediately after dropping off its cargo and fly back to Romania. Leaving the aircraft on the ground in enemy territory for hours on end wasn't an option. Whatever happened, the team would be on its own for at least twelve hours. Fleming didn't like the odds. Then again, he didn't expect the Ottoman army to have too many troops in the region. The actual fighting was happening three hundred miles further to the east. In February of last year, the Russians captured Erzurum and Trabzon. After the victory at Gallipoli, the Ottoman V Corps was hastily redeployed to Erzincan to strengthen the Third Army and prevent the Russians from advancing further west. It didn't help. In June, the Russian General Yudenich took Erzincan after a two-day battle. Everybody expected the Russians to go on the offensive again and chase the weakened Ottoman army to the west. That didn't happen. The Russians suffered set-backs up north, and their General staff decided to reduce General Yudenich's army to reinforce the vulnerable northern position. The front line hadn't budged since.

Upon hearing the plan, Rebecca wasn't overly impressed.

'Why are you overcomplicating things?' she asked Fleming. 'Once you get a fix on the Sleeper location in the mountains, simply send in a bomber plane to level the site.'

Fleming disagreed.

'Remember Zoetevoorde?' he asked. 'The Germans had bombed the church to bits, and the Dream Whisperer still got a live Cthulhu out of it. Some of the Sleeper sites have several levels deep underground. They're as good as bomb-proof. That's why we need to have a team on the ground. We need to do things properly or not at all.'

Fleming set the wheels in motion for an operation on Ottoman soil.

On 6 June, Fleming received a radio message from Hafiz Hifzi, a local British agent in Constantinople. It confirmed the arrival of Mathilde von Corvey and her manservant. She'd booked rooms at the Pera Palace Hotel for the next four weeks, which came as a surprise, as Fleming expected her to move more swiftly towards one of her targets. This further delay in the countess's search for Sleeper sites increased the window of opportunity for the team that was scheduled to destroy the site in the area of Sinop. The day before, a converted Handley Page bomber had taken off in Thessaloniki with destination Constanta, the largest Black Sea port in Romania. M had cleared everything with the Romanian authorities.

In the previous weeks, Fleming had several conversations with Eliassen and Mumm. Fleming had been thinking hard about the implications of Eliassen's theory on how the Dream Whisperer was dependent on a willing host, and he came up with a daring scheme.

'Sooner or later, the Dream Whisperer will succeed in releasing three additional Cthulhus. It's bound to happen — even if we eliminate one of the Sleepers in the Black Sea area,' Fleming said to Ove and Rebecca. 'It's only a question of time. We've almost reached the bottom of the professor's list, and honestly, the last five or six locations are sketchy at best. Our current strategy has almost run its course. The

Dream Whisperer doesn't have this kind of problem; he knows *exactly* where all the Sleepers rest. He can elude us again and make a bee-line for the next Sleeper sites. The only way to win this game is to eliminate the Dream Whisperer himself.'

'Killing his host won't solve your problem,' Eliassen objected.

'That's not what I'm proposing. The Dream Whisperer needs an interface with our reality, and that's what his host's body provides him with. You told us the Dream Whisperer can neither access nor leave this body without the host's consent. If we disable the interface, the Dream Whisperer is trapped.'

'You mean to inflict a non-mortal, crippling wound on the countess, which would prevent her from travelling?' Rebecca tried to clarify.

'That was my first idea,' Fleming replied, 'but that would leave the interface, his means of interacting with our reality, intact. We've heard what he's capable of without making physical contact. He set fire to his minions in Sicily without even touching them. What I propose is to make his entire interface *inert*. More simply put: I want to drug Mathilde von Corvey and slip her into a chemically induced coma.'

'You'd still have to keep her alive,' Rebecca remarked. 'Even if you injected her with a paralysing toxin or a somnifacient, you'll need to feed her. Otherwise, she'll die of starvation, and the Dream Whisperer would be free once more. Moreover, the drug won't be active forever. You'll have to drug her again and again.'

'Exactly. We need to perform an extraction. We drug the countess and smuggle her back to our facilities, where we can continue to drug and feed her,' Fleming agreed.

'The Dream Whisperer would be a captive in a body that doesn't allow him to interact with our reality anymore. His mere presence in the body prevents it from ageing. He could be imprisoned in there forever. That's smart thinking,' Eliassen concluded admiringly.

'It sounds brilliant enough, Fleming. I wouldn't bet money on it, though. Too many unknowns for my taste,' Rebecca said, remaining doubtful.

'Desperate times,' Fleming said. 'What have we got to lose? It's either that or the end of the world.'

Later that day, Fleming called in Desmond Quayle, Master Gunsmith.

'Master Quayle,' he said, 'I need your skills to build me a .50 calibre muzzle-loading airgun that allows a clean shot at a range of at least fifty yards. I don't want it to fire bullets but tranquilliser darts. The projectile's velocity needs to be exactly sufficient to plant a hypodermic needle in the target's body. It must release the tranquilising fluid without inflicting any other damage.'

Master Quayle raised one eyebrow.

'And I need it the day after tomorrow,' Fleming added.

Master Quayle rolled his eyes and left Fleming's office.

Fleming spent the rest of the day on the telephone — first with M, and then with Fleet Command and the Royal Air Force.

On 9 June, around noon, two Handley Page bombers landed at the British military airbase in Malta. A team of twelve, including Fleming, descended from the aircraft and began unloading. Royal Navy Commander Cunningham was present to meet them.

'Welcome, Commander Fleming,' Cunningham greeted him. 'As requested, we have two E-Class subs ready for your team. The captains received instructions to take you through the Dardanelles into the Sea of Marmara. They haven't been briefed about the nature of your mission and will await your further instructions after you've left port. We have two lorries waiting here to get your team and your gear to the port.'

Fleming thanked the commander, and Cunningham waved at the Thornycroft lorries to drive up to the aircraft.

By dusk, the HMS E26 and the HMS E33 left port. They were both third-generation versions of the E-Class design, which initially dated to before the outbreak of the war. One hundred and eighty-one feet long, they were far smaller vessels than the enormous K-Class. The diesel-propelled E-Class also had a shorter operational range and a maximum surface speed barely exceeding fifteen knots. They were, however, well-suited to the purpose of the mission, which required them to pass unseen through the Dardanelles. Comfort on board was rudimentary. Living space was even more cramped than on the K-Class. The three officers had to share one bunk, and the rest of the thirty crew members slept where they could. The additional six men of Fleming's team and their gear stretched living conditions in each vessel beyond what would generally be considered bearable. Fortunately, the trip wouldn't last longer than three days — four, if they had to travel submerged longer than foreseen. As Ian Thomas, captain of the HMS E33, was confident they'd encounter no German warships or U-Boats, he decided to travel mostly on the surface. It allowed them to save fuel and proceed at a higher speed.

Fleming explained the mission to the captain soon after they left port. He described the countess as a spy for the Central Powers in possession of crucial information.

'You're risking the lives of more than seventy men, including your own, to catch this spy alive in enemy territory,' the captain replied in disbelief. 'That must be some secret she's carrying with her.'

'Believe me, it is,' Fleming assured him, without revealing anything further.

The captain didn't believe a word of it. Fleming doubted whether he would have swallowed the truth any better. What was coming next would be bad enough.

'Are you aware of any recent unusual events in the Mediterranean?' Fleming asked the captain.

'Could you be even less specific?' Thomas retorted, not even trying to conceal his annoyance with Fleming.

'You know, like ships disappearing without a trace.'

'In case you hadn't noticed, Commander, there's a war going on. Ships get sunk every week.'

Fleming sighed. He was getting nowhere with Captain Thomas. Still, he needed the skipper at the top of his game. Fleming suspected the Dream Whisperer was in contact with the Cthulhus he'd released. Their enemy had probably instructed one of his monsters to sink Captain Hewitt's torpedo boat in Sicily. Then why wouldn't he use his creatures again to keep any pursuers off his trail? Especially, if he had the possibility in the Black Sea to finish the game once and for all, the Dream Whisperer wouldn't want to have any killjoys around. Posting a Cthulhu, or maybe even both of them, as gatekeepers guarding the entrance to the Dardanelles straits looked like an obvious move to Fleming. It was what he would have done.

'All right, you didn't believe me the first time around, I get that,' Fleming tried again. 'I could have told you the truth, and you wouldn't have believed me either.'

'Try me,' Thomas challenged him.

'Are you a religious man, Captain?'

'What's that got to do with anything?'

'Humour me, please. Do you believe in the existence of God and His Angels?'

'Yes, I'm an Evangelical Christian,' Thomas said, jutting out his chin.

'Then you also believe in the existence of the Devil — not as a metaphysical concept but as an actual physical being walking among us, plotting man's ruination,' Fleming

230

concluded. 'What we're chasing is a woman *literally* possessed by the Devil. He's using her as his vessel to walk the Earth and to initiate the Great Tribulation. If we let him have his way, there'll be no Rapture or Second Coming of Christ, no Millennial Age. Maybe you think Pestilence, War, Famine, and Death are already roaming the land as harbingers of the Last Judgment? Make no mistake. The Devil's intervention won't bring about a divine apocalypse that conducts the Just to their rightful places at the Lord's side for all eternity. No, the Prince of Darkness will unleash the full powers of hell on Earth. He aims to turn the Lord's Creation into a blasphemous mockery. Humankind will suffer the Lords of hell's everlasting rule.'

The captain stared at Fleming in shocked silence.

'The Fiend will do anything in his power to foil our attempt to capture and neutralise his vessel,' Fleming continued. 'He's called his infernal vassals from the bottom of the oceans to second him — unspeakable monsters from the deep that'll try to prevent us from reaching Constantinople. One of them has already been roaming the Mediterranean for weeks, sinking vessels while biding its time. It's a tentacled Leviathan that lies in wait to tear us asunder without pity.'

'What do you expect simple mortals to do against the forces of hell?' Thomas replied in despair.

Fleming's flowery biblical speech had struck the right tone with the profoundly religious captain, but he suspected he might have overshot his mark. The captain losing his nerve was just as bad as facing danger unprepared.

'Keep the faith, Captain. God is always on the side of the righteous,' Fleming comforted the shaken skipper, 'We aren't going down without a fight. Chance favours the prepared mind. Keep a watchful eye at all times, and have all torpedo tubes loaded and ready.'

Thomas nodded and got on the radio to confer with the captain of the E26.

22

Aegean Sea

Monday, 11 June 1917

Captain Thomas was right to assume that the chances of encountering enemy vessels were limited. They travelled on the surface unhindered for most of their voyage. The diminished Ottoman fleet was mainly active against the Russians in the Black Sea and only sporadically present in the Aegean Sea. It was 6 p.m. They'd been travelling for about forty-six hours, and the voyage had been unexceptional. Both submarines maintained an average speed of fourteen knots. They rounded the Greek peninsula and weaved through the Aegean archipelago. Five hours previously, they left the Cyclades behind, sailing between Mikonos and Naxos, and set course for the north. Now, the Island of Lesbos was disappearing slowly on starboard. It would take them another three hours before they reached the Dardanelles. The captain was verifying his calculations. In two hours, they'd submerge to keep out of sight of Ottoman coast guards. The strait itself was lined with fortifications and heavily mined. The passage would be hazardous as there was little room for evasive manoeuvring if they were detected. At their narrowest, the Dardanelles were less than a mile wide. The maximum depth was only three hundred feet. Except maybe for the Bosphorus, it made the thirty-eight-mile stretch of water the easiest to defend strategic maritime area in Ottoman territory. The battle for Gallipoli had taught the British and French this lesson to their great detriment.

Two hours later, the captains gave the order to submerge to periscope depth, and they cut the speed to a sluggish three knots. Fleming found the confinement in the cramped submarine hard to endure. One look at his men sufficed to assure him he wasn't the only one. In his febrile imagination, Fleming felt the hull warping and the bolts groaning. He hated the sea. Rebecca's rhapsodies to the oceans' beauty didn't convince him. As far as Fleming was concerned, the most dreadful creatures on Earth lived in the seas. He didn't even like regular fish; their glassy eyes and slimy, scaly skins were enough to turn his stomach. It was no surprise to him that sea creatures had colonised the land four hundred million years ago. Given a choice, in their stead, he would have scampered out of the water as well. When Fleming learnt in Greenland that the Dream Whisperer's minions had gills and scales, it confirmed his worst prejudices. Nothing good could come from the sea. Ever.

The crew member at the periscope interrupted Fleming's dark thoughts.

'Captain, the 26 is in trouble!' he shouted.

Thomas moved quickly to the periscope and, after one glance, motioned to Fleming.

'It's on, as you predicted,' the captain confirmed.

Fleming looked through the periscope and saw how a tangle of tentacles enveloped the E26. The attacker pulled the submarine's bow downwards, and the E26's stern stuck out of the water. The sub tilted heavily to port as the Cthulhu was locking one arm and its tentacles around the hull and repeatedly smashed one of its claws into the conning tower. Fleming saw each blow leaving a dent. It wouldn't take the monster long to breach the hull.

Suddenly they were shaken by an explosion. The captain of the E26 had given the order to fire a starboard broadside torpedo at the assailant. It hit the Cthulhu in the abdomen. The explosion cracked open the submarine's hull, and the ship was going down fast.

Fleming pulled Thomas by the sleeve and told him urgently, 'Captain, the 26 is lost. We'll be next if we don't act quickly. Give the order to fire both bow torpedoes at the 26 and the monster. If we explode the 26 and deliver a direct hit to the creature, we might stand a chance.'

Thomas positioned himself at the periscope and shouted a short burst of orders in his speaking tube. The E33 corrected its course by twenty-three degrees port and fired two 18-inch torpedoes at the sister ship and its attacker. One struck the Cthulhu in the back; the other narrowly passed by the creature and slammed into the E26's bow. The explosion detonated all torpedoes stored in the submarine's bow in a terrible conflagration. The captain hadn't waited for the hit to turn his ship back to starboard. He still had spare torpedoes left to fire another blast from the bow, but loading the tubes would have taken more than fifteen minutes. That was why he turned his ship ninety degrees instead and fired a port-side broadside torpedo at the Cthulhu. Without stopping, he continued the turning manoeuvre until the stern was aligned with the target and fired again from the single stern tube. Fleming was hanging on against the control room's wall, feeling completely useless. Each explosion shook the submarine in a nauseating, rolling movement. The last one was the worst. The stern torpedo missed the monstrosity but smashed into the E26 amidships, and the explosion ripped the ship further apart. Large pieces of its hull tore into the Cthulhu.

The E33 surfaced, and the captain and Fleming hurried up the conning tower's ladder. Another crew member followed them to take position at the twelve-pounder Hotchkiss gun on the foredeck. There was nothing left to shoot. The E26 had already sunk, leaving a black oil slick on the waves. A large amount of green goo was mingling with the oil on the water surface.

'What's with the green stuff?' the captain asked.

'The monster's innards,' Fleming explained. 'You got it good, all right.'

'You've seen one before, haven't you?' Thomas suspected.

'Yes, straight from the egg,' Fleming admitted. 'A tiny tod compared to this one. I was worried the torpedoes wouldn't harm it anymore.'

'I saw it getting hit,' the captain said. 'It took the 26's torpedo full-on, and it *still* survived the blast. One of our first two torpedoes hit it in the back. The exploding bow took its right arm and part of its head clean off. The third one got it again in the back — I saw the explosion leaving a gaping hole. The stern torpedo missed the creature, but the hull's shrapnel gutted it. I think it's safe to say it hasn't survived.'

'The green goo was in its head. If the explosion in the bow blew part of the head off, that would have sufficed to kill the creature,' Fleming confirmed.

'Well, better safe than sorry, my grandmother used to say.'

'That was some nifty manoeuvring you did,' Fleming complimented the captain.

'I had to fire at my own,' Thomas said in a toneless voice. 'I'll never get that out of my head. I killed thirty fellow submariners.'

'They were dead already,' Fleming pointed out. 'The captain of the 26 made that decision for you firing his first torpedo. He knew the blast would tear his ship apart.'

'I failed them. We should have noticed the monster before it attacked.'

'Your man at the periscope was constantly on the lookout, and the hydrophone couldn't have detected the beast either,' Fleming said. 'It was swimming noiselessly. There was no sound to pick up. It came out of nowhere. There's no need to blame yourself. You did what was necessary.'

The captain didn't reply anymore. He was praying in silence.

Fleming wiped his brow. It was good to be out of that tin can for a while and breathe some fresh air, even if he knew they couldn't stay on the surface long. Maybe the explosions had been seen or heard from the coast. They needed to get away from this spot as quickly as possible.

'Are you still on?' the captain asked.

'What?' Fleming replied, not understanding the question.

'You lost half your crew. Is the mission still go, or do you abort?'

'We're still go. I'm not letting the bitch run.'

'You better pray then there's only one of those sea monsters around. We won't survive another encounter,' the captain said, descending the conning tower's ladder.

Fleming knew Thomas was right. Hopefully, its sibling had remained in the North Sea. He wondered how strong the bond between these creatures was. Would one know when the other was in trouble or had died? And what about the Dream Whisperer? Would he have sensed, all the way in Constantinople, his attack dog was dead? Maybe killing the Cthulhu had given them away, and now the Dream Whisperer knew for sure they were coming for him? No use crying over spilt milk: There'd been no other option. Just be glad they were around to fight another day. Well, half of them were. The captain had a point: He was operating with a skeleton crew now. Luckily, the tranquilliser gun and the team's sharpshooter were on board of the E33. Otherwise,, he'd have had to abort the mission anyway. Killing the Cthulhu bought them some time, Fleming comforted himself. Even if the Dream Whisperer were successful in awakening all of the three Black Sea Sleepers, that'd still fail to complete the quintet. Their enemy was back where he'd been when he released the Sleeper in Zoetevoorde. By now, the bastard must be slightly miffed at his lack of progress, Fleming supposed with some grim satisfaction.

23

Sea of Marmara

Tuesday, 12 June 1917

Captain Thomas decided to wait until dark before entering the Dardanelles. The strait was too heavily guarded to risk a passage during the day. They neared the coast at periscope depth and submerged to eighty feet some five miles out. The E33 entered the strait at 9.15 p.m. The captain and his navigator were continuously checking and marking their progress on a detailed nautical chart. Thomas gave frequent instructions to the petty officer steering the ship — slight adjustments of the course and depth, depending on the particulars of their position. Their speed didn't exceed four knots. At this rate, it would take them about nine hours to reach the Sea of Marmara, which meant they'd emerge from the Dardanelles around 5 a.m. when it was still reasonably dark.

The passage was a claustrophobic nightmare for Fleming. His heart was pounding in his throat. He felt the control room's walls coming at him and had all the trouble in the world not to hyperventilate. The damp, metallic air was scorching his lungs. Sweat soaked his clothes and stung his eyes. A foul reek — a heady mix of diesel, un-washed males, shit, testosterone, and fear — pervaded the entire ship. Fleming felt his head throbbing. How had he ever believed he could live through this ordeal? Being help-lessly enclosed in a metal coffin dunked in a hostile sea was as close to a personal hell as he could imagine. Part of his education as an elf warrior had consisted of hand-to-hand combat in underground tunnels. It was considered the most challenging training module. The environment nulli-fied any physical advantage an elf might have against a po-tential enemy. The passages were low and narrow. Their taskmasters forced the trainees to fight in half-crouched stances and made lithe bounds, zigzagging darts, and sweeping movements impossible. The crushing claustro-phobia saw to it that the subterranean combats were more about facing one's darkest inner fears than confronting an external foe. Compared to travelling in a submarine, those training sessions had been a walk in the park.

The diesel engines' muffled drone and the captain's short, sharp instructions were the only sounds during the passage. More than the weight of the water pressing on the submarine's hull, the dead silence and the presumed inky darkness of the sea surrounding them made the experience neigh unbearable. They didn't belong here, Fleming kept thinking. Humans had spurned their cradle of life aeons ago. They'd forfeited their right to dwell below the waves and stripped themselves of the means for survival in a world without sun or breathable air. The sea kept calling them ever since, stirring the blood of sailors yearning to return to its salty womb. It was a treacherous appeal, shorn of maternal tenderness, that lured them to an early, watery grave.

Fleming forced his breathing to slow down. An an-xiety attack wasn't an option. Not here, not in front of his men. He tried to empty his mind and failed. The elusive countess's features kept resurfacing with a vengeance. She — or rather, her hostage-taker — was waiting for him. He felt it in his every bone. The Dream Whisperer was a being he had no means to comprehend. A God — not the pretend kind he used to deal with on an almost daily basis. No, a *real* God with boundless power, who had inexplicably linked himself to a frail human frame, deceiving his opponents into believing he was frail and human too when he was neither. Rebecca was right. The chances this expedition would succeed were infinitesimally slim. And even if they achieved success, would it be more than a reprieve, an insignificant postponement of the inevitable — the return of omnipotent beings even more alien, more inscrutable than the Dream Whisperer, and whose sole presence on Earth would end human existence?

He couldn't allow these thoughts. Fleming concentrated on elfish meditation techniques, clearing his mind, reducing his pulse, normalising his breathing.

'There is nothing but Self, and Self is nothing.'

The mantra his teachers had drilled into his mind repeated itself over and over again. It finally soothed his nerves.

Entering the Sea of Marmara, the captain brought the submarine to periscope depth and increased the speed to eight knots. It took them another eight hours and a half to reach their rendezvous coordinates, less than twenty miles from the port of Constantinople. A small cargo ship was waiting for them. The E33 surfaced right next to it, startling the skipper.

Hafez Hifzi leaned over the railing and lowered a rope ladder. As Fleming and his team boarded the ship, their host looked concerned.

'There's only six of you? I expected a larger team,' he asked.

'Change of plans. This is all there is,' Fleming confirmed. 'A small group will attract less attention.'

He didn't want to alarm Hafez. The less the agent knew, the better.

'Could we have some water and soap to wash off the stink?' Fleming asked, changing the subject.

'Certainly. I also have hair dye and clothes,' Hafez said.

'Hair dye?'

'Sure. There's only one among you who has black hair. How many Turks, do you think, have blond, brown, or red hair? You need to blend in, or you won't even make it off this boat. There are police officers and soldiers all over the port.'

After they'd finished washing up and dyeing their hair, Hafez inspected them critically. He pointed at Phineas Shaw, the sharpshooter.

'You won't do at all like that. You're too fair-skinned. You have freckles. Turkish men don't have freckles.'

'Well, I sure as hell won't get a bloody tan before we reach Constantinople,' the pasty-faced Shaw said. 'I never get a tan. All the sun does to me is turn me into a boiled lobster.'

'Come here,' Hafez told him.

He took a container from a duffel bag.

'Rub this on your skin.'

'What's that?' Shaw asked, suspiciously eyeing the pot Hafez had pushed in his hands.

'Face paint. Used in theatres all over the world. It'll darken your skin. Rub it on your face. Better yet: Rub it all over your body.'

The other men laughed.

'You two,' Hafez pointed at Eugene Bradley and Hiram Dunn, both deeply tanned veterans of the Sinai and Palestine campaigns. 'You forgot to dye your eyebrows.'

Hafez turned to Fleming.

'You don't have a moustache.'

'No, I don't,' Fleming had to admit with a grin.

'Every Turkish man has a moustache.'

242

The duffel bag again. Hafez came up with three moustaches.

'Pick one.'

Fleming chose a handlebar moustache, and Hafez carefully glued it on.

'Good. Much better. Don't roll up your sleeves and don't unbutton your shirts, or the hair on your arms and chests will show and betray you. That's all I can do. Pity I can't do anything about the eyes.'

'Let me guess: Turkish men don't have blue eyes?' Fleming said.

'No, they don't. But it'll have to do. You should have chosen your team more carefully,' Hafez admonished him.

'Well, you know, one has to make do with whatever one has got,' Fleming said grinning, to loud protests from his crew.

After a frugal meal, Fleming took Hafez to the ship's bow, so the rest of the crew couldn't overhear their conversation.

'Tell me, Hafez, what's going to happen next?'

'It'll take us about four hours to reach the port of Constantinople. We'll dock at the Galata Quay, close to the centre,' Hafez explained. 'We've picked up cargo in the port of Bandirma, which we'll unload. That'll take the rest of the afternoon. I don't expect strict inspections. The bill of lading is perfectly in order, and the captain knows the police officers in the port well. If they're intent on boarding, he can easily bribe them. You and your team will be safe. You'll keep out of sight until nightfall, and then we'll leave the ship.'

'The captain and his crew are trustworthy?' Fleming wanted to know.

'I can vouch for them,' Hafez said without hesitation. 'The captain is an old smuggler. There's no love lost between him and the regime.'

'Did you secure transport?'

'We'll leave the port on foot. I don't want to attract any attention. From the quay to the Pera district is a twenty-minute walk, no more.'

Hafez took a city map from his pocket and pointed out where the Galata Quay and the countess's hotel were situated.

'We have medical supplies, guns and ammo, and a rifle that's key to the mission. I'd feel distinctly uncomfortable carrying all that stuff with us on the street,' Fleming objected.

'I understand. We'll put a couple of men and the luggage in a horse-drawn cart, no problem,' Hafez reassured him.

'I thought we'd agreed to have cars?' Fleming insisted.

'You'll see cars are exceedingly uncommon in the city. We do most of our transport by horse and carriage. For leaving the port, cars would be too — What's the word? Conspicuous?'

'I get that. We need them for the extraction operation, though,' Fleming repeated impatiently.

'Sure, sure, no problem,' Hafez waved away Fleming's concerns. 'I got us two cars, a large one and a smaller one. Perfectly good vehicles. Don't worry.'

'All right, I'll want to see them before the operation. How about the flat?'

'The Pera Palace Hotel is situated on a large street, *Mesrutiyet Caddesi*,' Hafez said, pointing at the map again. 'When the target leaves the hotel during the day, she'll be travelling in an open carriage along that street. I've rented a flat on the second floor in a building on the corner of *Mesrutiyet* and *Asmali Mescit Caddesi*, across the street, not far from the hotel's entrance. Your man will have a perfect shot, and the intersection provides the extraction team with several exit opportunities.'

'Sounds great, Hafez, well done indeed,' Fleming complimented him.

Hafez accepted the accolade impassively. If Fleming's insistent questioning had ruffled him in any way, he didn't show it.

'I've also rented a safe house west of the city,' Hafez continued, 'where you can keep the person you plan to abduct until your rendezvous with the submarine. It's close to a fishing boat harbour. I'll have a boat at your disposal to make your escape.'

'Well, that covers our needs perfectly. We'll take one of the cars and go have a look. I'm a bit worried that, in the heat of the moment, we might get lost in the city. It's better to familiarise ourselves with the surroundings as quickly as possible.'

'You don't need to worry. A friend and I will drive you. We know the city like the back of our hand.'

The thoroughness of the preparations satisfied Fleming. Hafez seemed like a reliable chap, he thought. That bloody moustache itched, though. Why other men believed they needed to prove their manliness by sporting a dead furry animal on their upper lip was beyond him.

24

Constantinople, Ottoman Sultanate

Thursday, 21 June 1917

Everything happened according to plan. After the ship had docked, Hafez disappeared to secure a horse and cart. The police officers didn't bother to search the cargo hold after the skipper generously plied them with arak and dirty jokes. After nightfall, they strolled into the city. Shaw and Hafez's assistant, Ilhami, piled all of their gear in the cart and then put sacks with onions on top of it. They took a different route to Pera, with their horse trotting at an unhurried pace.

Mesrutiyet Caddesi was unfortunately not as wide as Fleming had hoped. It was a busy street, cluttered with pedestrians, hand and horse carts, carriages, and mules. *Asmali Mescit Caddesi* was hopelessly narrow. They couldn't risk using that street — wagons and mules would most certainly prevent a fast exit. Getting away quickly after sedating Von Corvey would be a challenge, Fleming saw. On the positive side, the flat's location was perfect. It was on the second floor of a modern building in the ornamental French Beaux-Arts style. Best of all, its corner was a round tower with large windows on every level. The view of the intersection was excellent: Shaw would have no problem taking out his mark from this vantage point. The Pera Palace Hotel was a six-storey building that took up an entire block. Near its main entrance on *Mesrutiyet Caddesi*, two or three carriages were permanently waiting for guests needing transportation. Fleming's men could comfortably survey the hotel entrance from the flat's corner window.

They observed the countess being driven back and forth in open carriages several times a day. No doubt about it: She led a hectic social life. They saw their target often in the company of the German ambassador to the Ottoman Empire, *Graf* von Bernstorff. Mathilde von Corvey graced an endless stream of receptions, functions, parties, and concerts with her presence. Surprisingly, she always travelled unaccompanied. Her gigantic manservant was notably absent. Hafez found out he was holed up in room 411 while Von Corvey occupied an extravagant suite on the third floor. Fleming was cautious enough not to shadow her all too frequently or from too close a distance. He knew how alert the countess was and wanted at all cost to avoid that she noticed their presence. They took turns jotting down her comings and goings. Countess von Corvey followed the same schedule every day. She left the hotel at lunchtime, came back around 3 p.m., sailed off an hour later to return at 5.30 p.m., and then reappeared again shortly after 8 p.m., returning only late at night. Early on, Fleming decided not to risk an abduction in broad daylight. They'd get her the instant she left for her dinner appointment. Fleming considered grabbing their target upon her return at night. Then he decided against it, as the poor light conditions might hinder Shaw taking his shot.

Shaw had been practising with his new airgun in an open field outside the city and was now confident he could hit his target as she trundled down the street in a carriage. The tranquilliser darts contained a drug powerful enough to drop an elephant. Shaw would be alone in the flat taking his shot. He would then immediately leave the premises, hurry down *Asmali Mescit Caddesi* to the west until he reached the street parallel to *Mesrutiyet Caddesi*. A small car with Ilhami at the wheel would be waiting there to take him to the safe house. Fleming would have preferred a more nearby position for the shooter's getaway car. After reviewing the alternatives, he decided none of the other options were satisfactory. The neighbouring side streets were too busy and narrow. Having two vehicles waiting at the same time in *Mesrutiyet Caddesi* might easily arouse suspicion. It couldn't be helped. Shaw would have to cover the seventy-yard-long distance to the next wide street on foot, as inconspicuously as possible.

Fleming was satisfied with the cars Hafez had provided. The smaller of the two was a sporty La Buire two-seater roadster, the large one a nine-year-old Delauney-Belleville, a six-cylinder, top-of-the-line, French touring car. It had seen better days, but the 5,900cc engine was running smoothly and would effortlessly manage sixty mph on an open road. It was a great getaway car, offering enough room for a driver and five passengers. Fleming particularly liked that a canvas top covered the entire seating area and that the doors reached to the top. He had curtains installed to cover the side glass panes to obscure the interior from curious glances.

The idea was that, after Shaw had shot the countess, a team of four would drag the unconscious target from her carriage into the car and then drive off to the safe house. Fleming hadn't yet made up his mind whether it would be better to approach the carriage from behind and escape speeding down *Mesrutiyet Caddesi* in a southerly direction or take the opposite route. He was leaning towards the latter, as he'd observed that northbound traffic was somewhat lighter. It also would avoid overtaking the carriage and potentially getting blocked by vehicles coming from the other direction.

Captain Herbert Lawton was the team's medical doctor. It was his mission to keep the countess sedated during the whole trip. He was a Barts alumnus and spent his entire career before the war at Saint Bartholomew's Hospital in Smithfield, London — except for three years in South Africa, where he served as a doctor during the Second Boer War. He'd been the hospital's leading anaesthesiologist until the war and maintained an intensive correspondence with his peers in France, Germany, and the United States to keep abreast of the latest developments in his field.

He was already at the safe house and had outfitted a room with a hospital bed and a sophisticated anaesthesia system — invented three years earlier by Dennis Jackson, an American doctor with whom Lawton corresponded. It fed the patient nitrous oxide anaesthesia through an inhaler fixed over the mouth and reused the exhaled gas in a closed system. Oxygen and small amounts of nitrous oxide were continuously added to the circuit via two separate canisters. An absorber removed the exhaled carbon dioxide. An identical set-up remained on board of the submarine. Lawton considered it unlikely the countess would wake up in the first four hours after being shot. They'd installed the system in the safe house anyway, since they couldn't take any risks while waiting to board one of the fishing boats. In case of necessity, Lawton also had a container with chloroform, to be used while shipping their captive to the waiting submarine.

The safe house had a radio transmitter they'd use to fix a rendezvous with the submarine that was to carry them to Thessaloniki. The submarine refuelled in the port of Kamariotissa, on the Greek Island of Samothraki, and lay waiting in the Sea of Marmara. It was positioned twenty miles off the coast and was to move to the rendezvous point upon reception of a coded radio message.

250

Fleming decided to strike on Thursday evening. Captain Thomas was duly informed with the code message 'Cupid', which referred to the dart they'd aim at the countess's heart. Hafez volunteered to drive the Delauney-Belleville. Ilhami took the La Buire's wheel. They'd emptied the flat on *Mesrutiyet Caddesi*, leaving nothing that'd be traceable to them.

Right before 6 p.m., Hafez parked the touring car in the street, facing in the hotel's direction, one hundred yards from the corner where they expected to intercept their mark. Shaw took up his position. He cracked open the window, just far enough for the airgun's muzzle but kept the curtains drawn. Fleming and three team members — Bradley, Dunn, and Schofield — loitered in the street below, keeping an eye on the Pera Palace's entrance.

At 8 p.m. sharp, Mathilde von Corvey appeared. She was wearing a scarlet silk dress and a feathery hat. The doorman bowed to her and then snapped his fingers at one of the waiting cabbies, who immediately drew his carriage in front of the entrance. Fleming and his team took their positions near the corners of the intersection. Hafez started his car's engine and moved slowly forwards. With the doorman's assistance, the countess climbed aboard and settled on the leather couch in the carriage's rear quarter. It was a two-horse open landau, which kept both its heads folded. As the coachman sat upfront, this put him in Shaw's line of fire at first. Shaw knew the angle from his position on the second floor would allow him a clear shot when the carriage reached the intersection. The carriage moved away from the hotel's entrance while the pedestrians ignored its presence.

A mule loaded with copperware stood stubbornly rooted in the middle of the street, encouraged by laughing bystanders. The animal wilfully ignored its owner, who was by now beyond apoplexy. From his box seat, the coachman joined the crowd haranguing the mule driver. Soon, several hotel valet attendants rushed out to push the strong-willed animal out of the way.

Moloch observed the amusing pantomime from the fourth-floor windows on the landing of the Pera Palace's opulent staircase. Behind him, the large, wooden lift cage was descending — filled to the brim with a portly matron, her frazzled manservant, and eight hysterically yapping *borzois*, all eager to be taken on their outing. Temporarily diverted, Moloch thought *borzois* were indubitably the most idiotic dogs on the planet. He felt it must take a special kind of temperament to keep eight of those mutts. If he'd been a more compassionate man, he probably would have pitied the valet, who was inextricably tangled up in the dogs' leashes.

He returned his attention to the entertainment on the street. The mule had been shoved aside — not without having kicked one of the valets in the hip, narrowly missing the groin, and bitten another. The carriage now had free passage. The coachman clicked his tongue to urge his horses to speed up. Moloch detested his mistress's frequent outings, even though he knew she was perfectly capable of taking care of herself. This stay was a waste of time, he fretted. He could easily have arranged transport to the Black Sea more than a week ago, but his mistress appeared to have all the time in the world and had carelessly rebuffed him. Moloch wondered how long it would take the British to pick up their scent again. They weren't stupid; they had spies everywhere, and it wasn't as if his employer was inclined to live discreetly. Then some new turmoil at the intersection caught his eye.

Shaw patiently waited for the carriage to make its way around the headstrong mule. As the landau neared the intersection, the coachman's head steadily shifted away from his line of fire, and the countess became an easy target. Shaw pulled the trigger when the horses reached the crossing.

The airgun hardly made a sound. Von Corvey's upper body contorted in a spasmodic move; the tranquilliser dart firmly stuck in her left shoulder. Her mouth and eyes .popped wide open. She stared directly at Shaw. Her face first acquired a startled expression, before her features relaxed as she slumped backwards.

Fleming and his three acolytes jumped at the landau. Schofield knocked the unsuspecting coachman down with the butt of his pistol, and the three others dragged the countess from her seat. Hafez had driven the car next to the coach. Fleming yanked open the door behind the driver; Dunn and Bradley pushed her inside. Fleming and Schofield ran to the Delauney-Belleville's other side. Schofield sat down next to the driver while Fleming positioned himself on the backseat and helped to pull their victim further inside. All this took them scarcely twenty seconds. Before Dunn had even closed the door on his side, Hafez floored the gas pedal. They roared away, passing the hotel's entrance, where the valet attendants were still catching their breath after the struggle with the mule. The pedestrians darted away from the speeding car as Hafez aggressively honked his horn.

Moloch immediately turned from the window to rush down the staircase, taking three or four steps at a time. As he reached the ground floor, the lift door opened, and the eight Russian wolfhounds frantically spilt out, pulling the hapless manservant along with them. They also tripped Moloch, who maintained his equilibrium only with difficulty. Cursing, the giant grabbed three dogs by the collar and threw them out of his way while the matron was shrieking abuse at him. By the time he reached the street, the abductors had shot by the entrance and disappeared behind the corner.

After taking the shot, Shaw closed the window and waited behind the curtains until Fleming's team had pulled their target into the car. Then he returned his gun to its casing and ran downstairs. By the time he reached the street, the intersection was teeming with agitated people. Some of them had climbed on the landau to proffer help. The coachman was pitiably groaning, holding his head in both hands. Shaw strolled by without attracting attention to himself, carrying his gun case wrapped in a piece of cloth under his left arm, and descended *Asmali Mescit Caddesi*. Near the next intersection, Ilhami was waiting for him in the roadster.

Moloch ran to the landau, pushing through crowds of shouting people who were also making their way to the spot where the abduction had taken place. Upon reaching the carriage, he saw Shaw disappearing down the side street. As Shaw was the only person walking away from the incident and was carrying a bundle under his arm that could contain a firearm, he immediately aroused Moloch's suspicion. The countess's manservant hurtled after him.

Shaw reached the La Bruine idling near the street corner and was about to turn its door handle to take his place next to the driver when he was thrown against the wall with great force. It was no contest; Moloch was easily two heads taller than the Irishman. He put a huge hand over Shaw's mouth and took his lower jaw in a vice, jerked his victim's head forwards, and crashed it back into the wall, shattering the skull. Before Ilhami knew what happened, Moloch slid next to him. His bulky frame filled two-thirds of the car. His head pushed against the canvas top. While stepping into the car, he pulled a gun, which he drove into Ilhami's crotch.

'Take me to where they're keeping the countess,' he snarled, 'or lose your balls and bleed to death.'

At first, Hafez drove like a maniac through the narrow streets of Pera and then Galata, sowing panic among the pedestrians until, from the back seat, Fleming put a hand on his shoulder and urged him to slow down.

'Take it easy, Hafez, we're attracting far too much attention. Ease off the gas; make it look as if we're taking granny out for an evening stroll. There's nobody following us, and I'm sure that, even if the hotel has alarmed the police, they don't have a clue where to look for us.'

Hafez took a deep breath and shifted down to five miles per hour as they arrived at the densely populated Galata Bridge and crossed the Golden Horn. At a higher speed, they followed the road bordering the Golden Horn to the west until they came upon the Cibali tobacco factory in the Fatih district and then turned left. They passed the Fatih Mosque, drove further south through Altimermer and on to Samatya. The population of both these neighbourhoods was almost exclusively Greek Orthodox and Armenian. They followed the Marmara Sea shoreline further west for another ten miles until they reached Avcilar, a sleepy village, home to some fifty, mainly Greek families, who made a living as farmers and fishers. The Ottoman capital was well behind them. The place consisted of weathered single or two-storey houses in stone and wood, plus some sheds and barracks used to store fishing nets, buoys and crates, and to repair fishing boats.

The house Hafez had rented was a bit isolated from the rest, next to a barrack. After he parked the car in front of the house, Captain Lawton hurried out to have a look at the countess. He felt her pulse, opened one eye, and shone a light into it.

'Everything went as planned, I gather?' he asked after his brief inspection of the abductee.

'Couldn't have gone better,' Fleming confirmed. 'Do you think she needs another dose?'

'She's out cold. Slow but steady heartbeat, no reaction to visual stimuli, and low muscle tone. It'll depend on how long we need to get her to the sub.'

'Schofield, get on the radio and hear where the 33 is at,' Fleming ordered.

He looked at the small fishing boats on the beach.

'Which one is ours, Hafez?'

'I'll get the fisher,' Hafez replied.

'All right. Let's get the countess inside and put her on the bed while we wait.'

Dunn and Bradley lifted the woman out of the car and carried her in the house.

'If you're taking me on a wild goose chase, you'll regret it,' Moloch warned his driver as they were approaching the western outskirts of Constantinople.

Ilhami took a more circuitous route than Hafez, hoping they'd reach Avcilar after the rest of the team had already sailed off. He was scared out of his wits because of the ogre sitting next to him. The crunch of Shaw's skull against the wall was still ringing in his ears. He cursed the day he'd agreed to assist Hafez. Times were hard. Hafez paid him well, and he had a wife and three children to feed. Truth be told, he'd enjoyed the last week. He'd driven Fleming around to visit the safe house, helped Lawton to set up the hospital bed and the anaesthesia equipment, brought Shaw to a spot where he could exercise with his new gun. Sure enough, there were risks. He was aware of that; he wasn't stupid or naive. These chaps were so well organised, he thought, and that had lulled him into a false sense of security. Now, he was sitting next to a monster that wouldn't think twice about squashing him like a bug.

He'd never see his wife or children again. They'd never know what had happened to him.

'No, I told you. I wouldn't lie. The British agents are in a small village west of the city,' Ilhami tried to calm down his captor.

'They'd better be. I'll take my sweet time shredding you to pieces if they aren't,' Moloch hissed in his ear as they passed in front of the Armenian Church of Saint George of Samatya.

'I swear, they'll be there. Only fifteen miles to go; please don't hurt me. I have a family, a wife, children.'

'Floor it. Mess with me, and I'll be going after them too.'

Back in the house, Schofield was on the radio. He took off his headset when Fleming entered the room.

'The 33 is in position, five miles out,' he reported.

'Good. Shaw will be arriving any minute now, and then we'll leave. What's taking Hafez so long? I want to go.'

Fleming went to check on the captive and found Lawton positioning the inhaler over her mouth as he entered.

'Is she waking up already? I thought you said she was safely under?' he asked with some concern.

'Well, I'm not taking any risks. She's still unconscious, don't worry, but she's sturdy enough to take a whiff of nitrous oxide while we're waiting,' Lawton calmly answered as he opened the gas canister's valve.

'Hafez is back,' Dunn called out.

Hafez had an elderly fisherman with him.

'This is Dima. He'll take you on his boat,' Hafez introduced his companion.

They shook hands and grinned at each other. Dima didn't speak a word of English.

'Great. Tell your man we're still waiting for one person. Maybe you two could already push the boat into the water?' Fleming suggested.

Hafez nodded and took Dima out again.

The La Bruise hurtled over the bumpy, narrow, unlit road. Ilhami was clenching the roadster's steering wheel so tightly his knuckles turned white. His passenger sat silently next to him, the gun still aimed at the driver's crotch. They reached the banks of Lake Küçükçekmece, a brackish lagoon that bordered Avcilar to the east.

'There! There's Avcilar,' Ilhami cried out, pointing, when they were a mile from the village. 'See, just as I told you. I'm co-operating, right?'

'Kill the lights,' Moloch said.

A couple of hundred yards away from the village's edge, Moloch told Ilhami to turn off the engine and point out the safe house to him. Avcilar lay at the bottom of an inclination. Moloch gave the car a push. They silently rolled down the hill into the hamlet and parked the vehicle behind the barrack next to the one where the safe house stood.

'I did everything you told me. Please, don't kill me,' Ilhami begged in a whisper as they were both sitting in the parked car.

'Right,' Moloch answered and snapped Ilhami's neck before getting out.

Fleming was getting ever more restless, pacing back and forth inside the safe house. The wait for Hafez and Shaw was taking its toll on his nerves. Everything had gone according to plan. There was no reason to get all worked up, he told himself to little avail. A nagging voice in the back of his head kept reminding him that, as long as they were on Ottoman soil, they were in grave danger. What if the local police came calling? What if something had happened to Shaw and Ilhami? How long could they afford to remain cooped up in the safe house?

'Schofield, go outside and watch the road. The moment you see the headlights, we'll get the countess on a stretcher and carry her to the beach,' Fleming ordered, before checking back on their captive.

'No worries, she's deeply sedated,' Lawton commented without looking up.

He was still feeding her nitrous oxide. Fleming observed the doctor and had difficulties believing his plan had worked. The demon they'd been chasing for so many months lay helplessly bound in the inert body on the hospital bed. Mathilde von Corvey looked radiant in her festive red dress. Her peaceful and beautifully sculpted features gave no indication whatsoever of the evil she harboured inside her. Fleming wondered whether the Dream Whisperer was sedated as well or fully aware of what was happening to him, incapable of doing anything about it. Maybe he now felt what Fleming had experienced in the submarine: being captured inside an unresponsive envelope, which cut him off from any awareness of the outside world — buried alive.

Dunn and Bradley were sitting at the kitchen table, imperturbably smoking cigarettes in silence. They and Schofield were consummate professionals. Fleming had been fully transparent with them about what they were up against because he wanted to avoid at all cost that they underestimated the challenge facing them. They hadn't batted an eye and only asked technical questions about the mission. Shaw was cut from the same cloth. He'd seen action both in Flanders, France, and the Middle East, and was one of the most highly decorated soldiers in the war. Three months before this mission, the British monarch had presented him with the Victoria Cross, the highest award offered by the United Kingdom for gallantry in the face of the enemy. He'd never even mentioned this to his teammates.

After a couple of minutes, Schofield walked back in.

'Finally,' Fleming said.

Schofield shook his head and said, 'Bad news, Commander.'

He'd been standing next to the house from where he had a good view of the road. After a while, he began pacing back and forth, around the house, and to the back of the barrack. There, he noticed a front fender sticking out from behind the nearest construction.

'Ilhami's roadster?' Fleming asked, already knowing this was the case.

Schofield nodded.

'Did you investigate?'

'No, I came right back in.'

'Good, better not take any unnecessary risks. It's almost completely dark by now; he could be anywhere.'

Fleming didn't have to specify to whom he was referring. They were all thinking about the countess's oversized bodyguard. The realisation this bogeyman was skulking around the house, intent on liberating his employer, was a chilling one.

Fleming did some digging after Rebecca had suggested Von Corvey's driver might belong to the same species as 'Rod the God'. Even Fleming's usually most forthcoming informers were reluctant to share any intelligence about the individual. After persistent prodding, one of them dropped Moloch's name. Professor Eliassen confirmed this was one of the vilest Old Gods, shunned even by his peers. He'd belonged to the Canaanite pantheon before Yahweh routed all his competitors. Moloch was worshipped throughout the Phoenician empire, along almost the entire coastline of the Mediterranean, except for Egypt. He was one of those rare and cruel gods who exclusively required child sacrifices. He demanded that, without shedding a tear, his victims' parents watched them being burnt alive in large, bronze braziers or on his own blazing-hot, brass effigies. Little was known about him after he fell from grace and child sacrifices were prohibited throughout the region. Eliassen suspected Moloch went on to be a series of near-mythical, vicious potentates who ruled small Middle Eastern kingdoms from the fifth to the fourteenth century. Later, their foe was involved in rumours about serial murders and child abuse networks in larger European and American cities. The Dream Whisperer knew how to pick his acolytes.

As Dunn posted himself near the back door, and Schofield and Bradley guarded the front entrance, Fleming and Lawton lifted the countess on a stretcher. Hafez and Dima were still on the beach, readying the boat and unaware of the impending danger. Moloch was still keeping out of sight. Fleming cracked the front open door and listened. Even with his heightened senses of perception, he was unable to detect their nemesis.

'We can't stay here,' he decided back inside. 'Hafez and the fisherman are too vulnerable out there, and we need to leave while it's dark. To wait until the morning isn't an option. Maybe we can surprise him. The car is parked at the front door. We can shove the stretcher with the countess on the back seat. Lawton drives the car to the beach. The rest of us grab a hold on the outside, ready to shoot if he comes running at us.'

The men agreed, not entirely convinced, but they all knew they couldn't come up with a better plan. Dunn kept guarding the back door while Fleming and Bradley carried the stretcher to the door. Lawton preceded them. He opened the car's front door and then the rear one on the right. After they'd pushed the stretcher in the back seat, Lawton took the wheel. Fleming, Schofield, and Bradley stepped on the running boards, pistols ready. As Lawton fired up the engine, they heard a crash inside the house.

'Step on it, Lawton! Drive!' Fleming yelled.

Dunn was taken by surprise when Moloch crashed through the door. He splintered the wood as if it was balsa and immediately caught hold of Dunn's throat, steamrolling him backwards into the room. Dunn grabbed Moloch by the wrist. It was impossible to shake him off. In a couple of seconds, he'd smash into the wall behind him, and then he was done for. Dunn pulled the pistol trigger and pumped five rounds into his attacker's stomach before being slammed through the room's wooden inner wall. Moloch was unstoppable. With one backhand blow, he broke and dislocated Dunn's jaw. The second punch crushed his skull. Moloch scarcely glanced at the empty hospital bed, the gas canisters, and tubes, and rushed to the front door. The touring car was speeding away. Bullets whistled past his head. He charged in pursuit, pulled his gun out of his coat pocket, and returned fire while running. His first bullet pierced the rear window, grazed Lawton's shoulder, and shattered the windscreen. The second caught Scofield in the chest. The three others went wide. Bradley and Fleming emptied their clips at the thundering giant, hitting him several times without slowing him down. The car reached the tideline near the boat and stopped. Hafez and Dima looked on in horror at the unfolding drama. Bradley had reloaded and was firing again at Moloch, the impacts showing clearly on his upper body. The Old God stopped thirty feet from the car, calmly took aim, and shot Bradley between the eyes. He threw his empty gun away and turned to Fleming.

'Little elf,' he grinned, 'I'm going to enjoy this just as much as killing your wife and daughter. They squealed so nicely. I hope you'll sing as beautifully as they did.'

Fleming stepped off the running board, staring hard at the smirking would-be god, and ran straight at him. Moloch's murderous right swing only met with air. The 'little elf' somersaulted over his head, drew a 12-inch serrated knife behind his back from the sheath on his belt, and thrust it straight through the giant's skull. Moloch was still standing when Fleming landed on both feet behind him and then tumbled over like a felled tree. Fleming put his boot on the head and retrieved his knife.

'I always gathered you were weak in the head,' he spat.

To Hafez' dismay, he then proceeded to cut off the head. Even with his razor-sharp blade, it took Fleming a while to saw through the cervical vertebrae.

'What are you doing?' Hafez asked, appalled.

Fleming threw the head as far as he could into the sea, before cutting Moloch's shirt and jacket open to expose his torso.

'Look,' he said, pointing at the unscarred skin. 'He was hit by at least twenty bullets. They didn't even leave a mark on him. Not because he has unbreakable skin — I'm sure, if I cut him open, I'd find all the slugs inside — but he heals extremely quickly. If I left him lying there, he'd recover from the knife in his brain as well.'

He walked to the car, retrieved a can of gasoline from the boot, and doused the headless corpse.

'That's for all the children who died in fires because of you,' Fleming mumbled, setting the fuel-soaked body alight.

His thoughts were with his wife and daughter. The notion that they'd ended up as burnt offerings on this maniac's altar was more than he could endure. All the unhealed old wounds their parting had left him were torn wide open again by Moloch's words. He sank to his knees, tears streaming down his cheeks.

Lawton gently touched his shoulder, 'We need to leave, Fleming. We woke up the entire village.'

Fleming followed him wordlessly.

25

Thessaloniki, Greece

Saturday, 23 June 1917

The submarine captain's first words were, 'Two survivors? You've outdone yourself, Fleming.'

Captain Thomas did, however, temper his cynicism by offering his passenger a broad grin and punching him on the shoulder.

'Glad you made it and that you got the bitch, mate.'

Fleming turned to Hafez.

'Thanks, Hafez, we couldn't have done it without you,' he said. 'Are you sure you want to go back? We left an awful mess. You're welcome to come with us, you know.'

Hafez declined with some regret.

'I have a wife and two daughters, Fleming. I can't leave them behind. I'll clean up. We'll give your three companions a decent burial in the village's cemetery, and I'll make that brute's body disappear as well.'

'Make sure to crush to dust whatever is left of his bones and scatter his ashes to the four winds,' Fleming warned.

'I'm sorry I can't do anything for Shaw,' Hafez said.

'Take care of Ilhami's widow and children. Money can't bring him back, but at least they shouldn't have financial worries,' Fleming replied.

They briefly hugged. Fleming hoped Hafez was right and that he could indeed efface all traces. Deep in his heart, he knew, if the police made enquiries into who rented the flat and the safe house, and who bought the cars, evidence would soon point to his collaborator. They'd caused quite a spectacle in Avcilar. All it took was one snitch to inform the authorities. Even if Hafez survived, Fleming realised the British would never call on his services again for fear the Ottomans would have turned him and made him a double agent.

They installed Von Corvey in the officers' bunk. Lawton immediately hooked her up to the nitrous oxide. Keeping her sedated wasn't a problem at all. However, it didn't take them long to experience that, while the Dream Whisperer was effectively a helpless captive within the countess's body, his presence was tangible throughout the submarine. The crew found it hard to concentrate on the tasks at hand. Sleep kept eluding them, and if they did get some shut-eye, their dreams were troubled by unsettling visions impossible to describe after they woke up. A pervading sense of doom clung to the men's subconscious. They grew irritable, and the captain had to intervene several times to break up harsh altercations and even, on one occasion, fisticuffs.

It made Fleming's voyage — and especially the passage through the Dardanelles — even more of an ordeal than the first one. Bouts of paranoia and panic attacks compounded his natural proclivity to suffer from claustrophobia. He felt an almost uncontrollable urge to open one of the hatches. Inexplicably, the insane thought of letting seawater flood the submarine held a powerful attraction to him — a deliverance from unbearable suffering. His wife and child were always on his mind. He heard them crying for help, saw them writhing in the flames, imagined the

266

cruelties Moloch had inflicted upon his loved ones before setting them alight.

When he could no longer endure it, he grabbed Lawton by the arm and whispered to him, 'I can't take this anymore. Please, restrain me before I do something stupid.'

Lawton had been observing Fleming, and even though he was far from immune to the Dream Whisperer's pernicious influence, he understood his team leader's agony was much more profound than his. After some discreet consulting with the captain, he used his belt to tie Fleming to the pipes in the control room.

'Well, dear Ulysses, you'll remain tied to the mast until we surface again in a couple of hours. For the rest of us, I'd put wax in our ears if I expected that'd work,' Lawton grinned at Fleming with a levity he hardly felt and patted him on the shoulder.

The voyage was surprisingly tedious. Fleming's gravest concern failed to materialise. He had half-expected the remaining Cthulhu to make its way to the Aegean and cut them off on their emergence from the Dardanelles. Instead, they found the sea devoid of monsters and ships, both military and commercial. This absence allowed them to cover most of the one hundred and thirty miles on the surface or at periscope depth, averaging a speed of thirteen knots. The submarine reached the port of Thessaloniki on Saturday, 23 June, at 3 a.m., with a crew on the brink of insanity but otherwise unharmed.

Greece was a country in deep political turmoil. After his blood relative Tsar Nicolas II abdicated in the Spring of 1917, the Allies forced the Greek King Constantine I also to relinquish his crown on 11 June. Next, they reinstated his former Prime Minister Eleftherios Venizelos to power. While the Greek king always advocated the neutrality of Greece in the war and hindered Allied troop movements in his country, the Allies knew Venizelos favoured joining the war effort on their side. In previous years, the disagreements between Constantine I and Venizelos almost toppled the country into a civil war. That risk was now averted, and the Allies soon expected the new government to declare war on the Central Powers and to remobilise the Greek army.

The front line on the peninsula stabilised after the push of the Bulgarian army in 1915, which cost Greece all of the territories it had acquired during the Second Balkan War. The front was almost four hundred miles long. It started in the south of Albania, ran first along the Serbian border to the border between Central and Eastern Macedonia, and then along the Thracian coastline, ending at the border with the Ottoman Empire. The Allied Army of the Orient, commanded by a French general, was stationed along the front line and comprised twenty-four divisions consisting of British, French, Serbian, Italian and Russian brigades. They'd hoped to initiate a counter-offensive in the spring. The volatile political situation in Greece delayed the operation.

Thessaloniki was barely thirty miles behind the front line. During the daytime, an eerie calm reigned over the city as everybody was waiting for the inevitable resumption of hostilities. At night, the place was buzzing with energy. The harbour was the most critical hub for getting supplies and Allied troops into Macedonia. The centre was teeming with British and French soldiers in search for entertainment, tripling the population of what had been a sleepy port before the war.

When the E33 docked, a British officer accompanied by four soldiers was waiting for them on the quay. It took Fleming a moment to recognise Lieutenant-Colonel Lord Bodham, who'd returned from his second Cthulhu hunt, on the Black Sea coast.

'I'm sorry, Sir, I'm afraid I'm not quite myself after this trip,' Fleming apologised.

'You do look a bit frazzled, old chap,' Bodham said, clapping him on the back. 'Everything went well, I gather?'

'We've got the Dream Whisperer,' Fleming said

'Jolly good show!' Bodham exclaimed.

'How about you?'

'We dealt with the Sleeper in the mountains near Sinop. Best of all, we did it without any of the good guys getting killed, which must be a first,' the lieutenant-colonel announced proudly.

'That's great! Wasn't there any resistance at all?' Fleming asked, pleasantly surprised.

'I wouldn't say that exactly. It was mostly old goats and kids.'

'Come again?'

'All vigorous youngsters in the area have been drafted into the army, which mucked up the Sleeper site's defences,' Bodham explained. 'We only met with a few old codgers and a bunch of striplings, poorly armed at that. I'd learnt my lesson in Mongolia and brought a larger team along, armed to the teeth. I took no risks. We killed them all. God will know His own.'

'I wish I could say the same about my team,' Fleming sighed.

'Lost a few chaps, did you?' Bodham said as he looked in vain for Fleming's teammates to emerge from the submarine's conning tower.

'Eleven killed out of fourteen and a sub lost with all hands,' Fleming confessed. 'A nightmare. Speaking of nightmares, I think it's best to get the countess back to Britain as quickly as possible. I couldn't keep a plane waiting for us all this time in Malta. The aircraft that brought you back would do just fine. Is it still available?'

'Well, yes, but there's a hitch,' Bodham warned. 'The Handley Page is our mission's only casualty. When we'd almost reached Thessaloniki, the starboard engine decided to blow up for no reason. The pilot only just managed to keep his crate aloft until we reached the landing strip here. It's beyond repair I've heard, and we've been told not to expect a replacement engine before a week or three. So Old Blighty will have to wait.'

'Damn, that's a long wait,' Fleming cursed. 'We'll have to get the countess to a safe place for the duration of our stay. I was thinking about a hospital.'

'There are plenty of military hospitals in Salonika,' Bodham assured. 'I know of a good one, right in the city centre. It's called the Hirsch. Frightfully modern. It has all the works; sits right in the Jewish quarter. Well, I suppose that isn't saying much. Most of Thessaloniki is of the Hebrew persuasion.'

In the meantime, Captain Lawton had joined them and heard Bodham mentioning the Hirsch.

'Is it one of ours?' he asked.

'We share it with the Frogs,' Bodham said. 'They'll make no bones about it, I gather.'

'Can you take us there?' Fleming asked.

'Thought you'd never ask. We've got a lorry waiting for you, right over there.'

The Hirsch's building was indeed a modern one. It was erected in 1907, as the Roman numerals on the facade proudly announced. Before the military commandeered it, the hospital had been exclusively serving the Jewish community. The Star of David over the entrance didn't leave any doubts about that. It was a gift to the city by the wife of philanthropist Baron Maurice von Hirsch, a wealthy German-Jewish banker who lived in Austria and had made a bundle developing railways in the Balkans. Clara von Hirsch had lavished two hundred thousand gold francs on the construction, and it showed. They drove through the

270

gate, under a sign that said '*HOPITAL TEMPORAIRE N° 14*', up to the stairs of the main entrance.

Bodham walked up the stairs and knocked imperiously at the front door as if he owned the place. A nurse appeared. Fleming saw Bodham briefly arguing with her. Then the officer motioned to bring their charge inside. They installed Mathilde von Corvey in a comfortable single room on the first floor, usually reserved for wounded high-ranking officers. As hostilities had been on the back burner in the previous months, the hospital's occupancy rate was low. There was no problem to accommodate the sedated patient.

'This room needs to be guarded at all times,' Fleming told Bodham. 'I'll make sure to pull some strings. It would be of great help to me if your men took guard duty for the next few hours.'

'That goes without saying. I'll see to it,' Bodham promised.

'Listen, what we experienced in the sub was awfully similar to what you may have felt in the Sleeper's proximity,' Fleming warned Bodham.

'I know. Beastly images somehow popping up in the noggin, anxiety attacks, and other such unpleasantness,' Bodham recalled.

'Exactly. We spent less than two days with the Dream Whisperer on board, and he ran us ragged,' Fleming said. 'By the end of the voyage, we were ready to rip each other's throats out. I had myself tied down for a while because I felt an irresistible urge to open a hatch and flood the sub. This is an enemy who preys on our deepest fears and traumas. Each time he tears away the veil from himself and the other Outer Gods in the visions he projects into our minds, it's more than we can take. Even as the countess is out cold, the Dream Whisperer remains a threat.'

'I'm with you,' Bodham agreed.

271

'The same thing is liable to happen to the guards,' Fleming predicted. 'There always needs to be more than one of them on duty, and we need to rotate the teams frequently to avoid them falling under his spell.'

'There's fourteen of us,' Bodham said. 'That should be enough until you can find other soldiers to relieve us. I recommend you talk to Major-General Croker of the 28th Division, very decent chap. He'll help us out for sure. Give him my regards. We went to Eton together.'

'Thanks for the tip,' Fleming replied. 'I'll get on it first thing at dawn.'

26

Thessaloniki, Greece

Thursday, 19 July 1917

Fleming was growing restless. The wait for the replacement engine lasted forever. He contacted M to report on the success of the two missions in Anatolia and to ask him whether he could speed up matters. M had to disappoint him. The battles in Flanders and France had reached new levels of intensity and received full priority. The General Staff insisted they couldn't miss a single bomber at present, and M concurred since their captive seemed relatively safe in Thessaloniki. The new Greek government under Prime Minister Venizelos was as good as its word and immediately declared war on the Central Powers. It reconstituted the Greek army, and two hundred and fifty thousand Greek soldiers landed in Macedonia to join the Allied forces in early July.

Major-General Croker was remarkably forthcoming in his response to Fleming's appeal for support. He dispatched twenty soldiers from the First Battalion of the Suffolk Regiment for guard duty. They formed five teams of four and relieved one another every three hours to limit their exposure to the Dream Whisperer's pernicious influence as advised by Fleming. Two guards stayed in the countess's hospital room while the other two stood outside at her door. They were weathered fighters; each carried a Lee-Enfield rifle, a Webley revolver, a bayonet, and even a trench club.

Captain Lawton remained personally in charge of their captive. He quickly struck up friendly relationships with both the British and French medical officers in the Hirsch Hospital. His ability to speak French fluently — his mother happened to be from Le Havre — made him popular with the French nurses as well. The day after their arrival, he called on Fleming.

'We need to talk about our options for feeding the patient,' he told Fleming. 'If we don't do anything, she'll get dehydrated and undernourished, and ultimately, she'll die.'

'I'm not the specialist here. What are the options to get fluids and food into her?' Fleming asked.

'We keep her in a comatose condition, which means she's lost her swallowing response,' the doctor began. 'Trying to force food or water down her throat would send it straight into her lungs because the oesophagus is a closed tube whereas the trachea is wide open. There have been experiments to introduce diluted nutritional elements directly into the bloodstream via the arteries. None of them have succeeded in keeping patients alive over a longer period.'

'Then I'll ask you again: What are the options?' Fleming repeated.

'I'm not a surgeon myself,' Lawton said. 'So I talked this through with my colleagues at Barts before we left on this mission. They proposed a surgical procedure that'd consist of making an incision in the patient's abdomen and stomach wall. Then they'd feed a tube into the stomach, which would allow injecting nutrients and liquids via the tube directly into the stomach.'

'Have they done this before?' Fleming asked.

274

'I'm afraid not. The procedure is highly experimental,' the captain had to admit. 'There's a significant risk of gastric fluids leakage, internal haemorrhages, and infection. We could somewhat reduce that risk by performing the procedure on the small intestine instead of the stomach. Anyway, transporting the patient any time soon after the operation isn't advisable. I'd hoped to have this procedure performed at Barts after getting back to Britain. The delays caused by the defective aircraft engine are forcing my hand here. Honestly, I don't like the odds too much.'

Fleming sighed and pinched the bridge of his nose.

'We can't risk staying here too long.,' he reflected. 'We've got plenty of troops along the front line, and no doubt the Greek reinforcements are strengthening the Allies' position, but we're far too close to where the fighting will be happening during the impending counter-offensive.'

'We're caught between Scylla and Charybdis; I realise it all too well,' Lawton said.

'Well, we took care of those two a long time ago. I suppose there might be another alternative,' Fleming suggested.

'And that would be?'

'Do nothing.'

As Lawton wanted to protest, Fleming held up his hands.

'Wait, hear me out, please,' he pleaded. 'The possession of Mathilde von Corvey's body by the Dream Whisperer has obvious physiological consequences. She stopped ageing, for one. She also survived what must have been a gruelling hike through Greenland in wintery conditions after we shelled the first Cthulhu and destroyed her local acolytes. No normal human being could have gone through all that and live to tell the tale. Sure, she engaged in a lot of wining and dining in Germany and Constantinople — we know she does eat. The real question is: Does she *need* the food to subsist?'

'We don't know,' the doctor admitted.

'No, we don't,' Fleming repeated. 'Why don't we adopt a wait-and-see attitude? If she does need sustenance, it'll show after a couple of days, won't it?'

'Dehydration would have more immediate consequences than malnutrition,' Lawton said. 'It would result in a measurable drop in her blood pressure. I could do some regular blood tests as well. Sodium and potassium levels in the blood are reliable indicators.'

'Good. It sounds like we have a plan,' Fleming concluded.

'We need to have a contingency plan as well,' the captain insisted. 'I'll talk to Major Leroux about placing a feeding tube into the stomach or the small intestine. He's an experienced surgeon. He taught surgery at the Sorbonne before the war. I'll walk him through the procedure; see if we can cover all eventualities so he'll stand at the ready if the situation requires it.'

In the next few days, Lawton carefully monitored his patient's vital signs, and as days turned into weeks, it became undeniably clear. Mathilde von Corvey didn't need sustenance. Lawton performed several blood tests, and their outcomes baffled him. He couldn't come up with a scientifically valid explanation of the phenomenon, but he had to admit Fleming's gut feeling had been right all along. Their captive's survival wouldn't have to depend on experimental surgery.

In the spell between battles, the primary source of patients at the Hirsch Hospital was pub fights. Soldiers were bored stiff and looked for pleasure. Since the troops' arrival, pubs and bordellos had mushroomed in Thessaloniki, and they were doing a brisk business. Every night, the military police and regular police officers rounded up drunk brawlers. Those needing stitches or worse ended up in the hospital closest to the harbour, which happened to be the Hirsch.

Fleming got to know the chief of police, Kostas Pagiatis, picking up Private Morecambe, one of Bodham's men, after a night in the local jail. Pagiatis was a lank forty-something with an Egyptian cigarette permanently screwed in the right corner of his mouth. He had intelligent brown eyes and an unruly mop of black hair, which covered an old scar on his forehead. He was glad to share his eleven-o'clock Ouzo with Fleming, and the men had a pleasant conversation. Pagiatis had been around and had some tall tales to tell. He'd been the first mate on a cargo ship that visited most of the ports on the African coast and in the Orient. The men parted on the best of terms, and Fleming wasn't too surprised by the chief of police's phone call a week later. He told Fleming he had again somebody in his jail who'd mentioned his name. This time around, it wasn't a drunk British soldier but an unknown Bulgarian man. Fleming's interest was piqued since he couldn't fathom how the man might have gotten hold of his name.

Pagiatis pointed him out in a cell, sitting among twenty other occupants, who all looked the worse for wear. Last night had been a busy one.

'He says his name is Amid Agush,' the chief of police informed Fleming. 'He's a Bulgarian — more specifically: a Pomak.'

'I've never heard about Pomaks, and I've never seen that man before. I can't imagine where he got my name from,' Fleming wondered.

'Pomaks are Slavic Muslims,' Pagiatis explained. 'Most of them live in the Rhodope Mountains on the border between Bulgaria and Macedonia, some hundred miles from here. The Bulgarians don't like them much. I heard they were rounding them up before the war to convert them. In Greece, we don't usually see them as far west as Thessaloniki. They live in small numbers in eastern Mace-

277

donia and Thrace. Pomaks speak a Bulgarian dialect. This one is fluent in Greek. I can translate what he says for you if you want to.'

'How did you catch him?' Fleming asked.

'We didn't,' Pagiatis said. 'Last night, he walked into the police station, asking where he could find you. The officer on guard duty threw him in the bin because he's a Bulgarian, and we're at war with Bulgaria. He's suspected to be a spy.'

'He certainly didn't behave like one last night. I'd like to talk to him if you allow me,' Fleming proposed.

'Sure, that's why I called you,' Pagiatis agreed.

Pagiatis had the Pomak brought to a separate interrogation room. He was a greying man of middling height, with rosy cheeks. Fleming estimated he was in his late sixties, not a threatening figure at all.

'Amid, this is Mister Fleming,' Pagiatis introduced his guest to the prisoner.

The man's eyes widened. He remained silent, unmistakably intimidated.

'Mister Agush, I'm Fleming,' Fleming repeated in a comforting tone of voice. 'What did you want to tell me? Why did you make the long journey to Thessaloniki — in times of war, no less?'

The answer came in gulps. Agush was excited, and Pagiatis frequently had to ask him to slow down and to repeat some of the things he said. As the tale unfolded, the chief of police grew more and more disconcerted.

'What is he saying?' Fleming asked, waiting in vain for his host to translate the Pomak's narrative.

Pagiatis held up his hand to stop the torrent of words from the old man.

'I'll try to summarise. He says you're under threat. You're holding an extremely dangerous person captive. He called him Shai'tan, the Devil. There are people from his

278

tribe, young men, who are on their way to Thessaloniki to free your prisoner. They're fanatics who cling to age-old beliefs, held from times before the tribe was converted to Islam, centuries ago. It's a sect within his tribe, shunned by the other Pomaks. Its initiates don't pray like Muslims, and they don't read the Koran. They have another book — written by some Arab — and it contains dark, horrifying knowledge. Some time ago, the sect's members went into a frenzy because their elder, the one who acts as the cult's priest, received visions in his dreams. Their god talked to him in his sleep. He told the priest about his captivity and where the man could find him. He also mentioned your name.'

Pagiatis stopped talking, at a loss for words. It took Fleming a moment to let this sink in. The Dream Whisperer wasn't only able to influence the dreams and thought patterns of those in his immediate surroundings. Apparently, he was also a radio beacon that could broadcast messages far and wide to his disciples. Additionally, Fleming made a mental note there was probably a Sleeper site somewhere in the Rhodope Mountains, which had escaped Eliassen's attention.

'Does this make any sense to you at all? Please, tell me this old fool is talking nonsense!' the chief of police pleaded with Fleming.

'Could you ask him how many of his tribesmen are coming?' Fleming asked as calmly as possible.

Pagiatis stared at him aghast.

'That means you believe what he's been telling us?'

'As I told you, I've never heard of any Pomaks nor of this cult,' Fleming repeated. 'I do know of similar Satanist covens elsewhere. So what he's saying, yes, it does make sense to me. I wish it didn't, but it does.'

The chief of police didn't know what to think of this. It gradually dawned on him that Fleming wasn't your run-of-the-mill British army officer — his business obviously had nothing to do with the war. What had Fleming brought to his doorstep? A demon? Satanists? Homicidal religious fanatics? Something weird was going on, and it made Pagiatis feel out of his depth.

'These cultists are coming for us, and we need to prepare for their attack. How many of them are there? We need to know,' Fleming insisted.

There was a knock on the door. When Pagiatis answered it, a police officer urgently whispered something in his ear.

The chief of police turned around and announced, 'There's a shooting reported at the Hirsch Hospital!'

The Thessaloniki police didn't have cars yet, so Pagiatis and Fleming caught a taxi and rode to the Hirsch together. It was a short, quick ride. Thessaloniki had ceased to be a crumbling bazaar-city with crooked, narrow streets after the fire of 1890. It had been rebuilt as a modern European city with wide roads and avenues, such as the splendid Hamidye Boulevard.

Upon their arrival, several police officers were already present. Nurses and doctors stood outside, discussing in great agitation. Fleming ran up the stairs to the entrance with Pagiatis in his wake. On the first-floor landing, a police officer wanted to stop him. The chief of police curtly waved his subordinate aside. Two men were lying in the hallway in dark pools of blood. They were the guards posted outside the countess's door. They had their throats cut before they'd detected the intruders. Their revolvers were still in their holsters; the bayonets had remained in their sheaths, and the trench clubs attached to the belts. The door to the countess's room stood wide open. Six men were on the ground, only one of them alive — and severely wounded at that. It was one of the guards. The private clenched his Webley firmly in his right hand, even though he was about to go into shock. He was bleeding from wounds to his chest, abdomen, and arm. His breathing was laboured.

Fleming called out, 'We have a man down here! Send in the medics! What are you waiting for? Hurry!'

After medics had rushed away the man for medical care, Fleming took in the scene inside the hospital room. His captive was lying in bed with the breathing apparatus firmly in place. Her eyes were closed. She seemed a picture of serenity. On the floor lay the fourth guard, a corporal. He was dead — he had a gaping wound in the throat, where an expert knife thrust had severed the carotid artery. His uniform was blood-soaked. Given his rifle's position, the soldier had probably fired it. The autopsy reports would have to clarify that issue. The four other bodies were all young men, none of them older than thirty. They wore dark clothes, which made their wounds hard to distinguish — except for the attacker whose brains had been splattered all over one of the walls. The floor was slippery with blood. Fleming left when the forensic photographer arrived.

'If you don't mind, I'd like one of the hospital's surgeons to perform the autopsies on these bodies as soon as possible,' Fleming proposed to Pagiatis, who agreed silently, spellbound by the bloody mess.

Then Fleming went to phone Major-General Croker, who immediately agreed to send more men to guard the building, and Bodham, who also promised to round up his men and come over to the hospital.

In the late afternoon, the hospital informed Fleming that Private Hurlock, the injured guard, was no longer in a critical condition. He'd lost a lot of blood. The doctors at the Hirsch had fortunately set up blood banks in the previous year and were proficient in transfusion techniques. Hurlock suffered from a punctured lung and four broken ribs. The two knife stabs to his abdomen had miraculously missed all internal organs. The doctors had sutured the deep cut in his arm without further complications. Although he was in a coma, the doctors expected him to regain consciousness later in the evening.

In the meantime, Captains Lawton and Scrivener, one of the British surgeons at the Hirsch, had finished the autopsies. They called on Fleming to discuss their reports.

'The causes of death of the three British guards are straightforward; you've seen it for yourself,' Lawton began. 'Privates Lamond and Sutton had their throats cut. Corporal Radford sustained several knife wounds. The fatal one was the knife thrust that severed the carotid artery.'

'Private Hurlock fired five shots and killed three attackers,' Scrivener continued.

'That means Corporal Radford took care of the fourth one,' Fleming commented.

The doctors exchanged a significant glance.

'The fourth attacker didn't sustain any bullet wounds,' Lawton stated.

'How did he die, then?' Fleming asked, surprised.

'It took us a while to find out. Doctor Lawton and I concur he died of massive thrombotic ischemic stroke. We detected a large thrombus or blood clot lodged in the cerebral artery,' Scrivener explained.

'How peculiar,' Fleming said.

Scrivener misconstrued Fleming's quizzical remark as a criticism of his professionalism, and he replied slightly piqued, 'Granted that it's an affliction one usually associates with elderly patients, who suffer from high blood pressure and obesity issues. I can, however, assure you it's not unheard of in young and seemingly healthy individuals.'

'I'm not questioning your judgement, Doctor,' Fleming replied. 'I find it a bizarre coincidence that this man suffered a massive stroke at the same moment he would have overpowered the last remaining guard. It sounds almost too good to be true.'

The next morning, Private Hurlock was sufficiently recovered to be interviewed by Fleming and Pagiatis. His account didn't add much new information. Hurlock hadn't been aware of any struggle in the hallway, which meant both guards at the door must have been swiftly dispatched. The attackers kicked in the hospital room's door and rushed inside. Hurlock immediately killed one with a head-shot and wounded another one. The rest of his tale was understandably confused. He'd been wrestling with two aggressors, getting off a few shots. One of the men took his right wrist in an unbreakable grip and stabbed Hurlock several times. As he raised his knife for a last, fatal thrust, the assailant collapsed, falling over his victim. Hurlock pushed the body aside and fired his revolver one more time at another attacker, who was already wounded.

'You did well, Private,' Fleming praised him. 'You killed three of them; you're a crack shot.'

'It all went so quickly,' Hurlock mumbled faintly.

A nurse appeared at the bed, indicating the interview was over.

'One more thing, Private,' Fleming insisted. 'The attack occurred approximately one hour into your watch.'

Hurlock nodded in confirmation.

'Did you experience any exceptional sensations during your watch? I mean, like anxiety attacks, frightening visions?'

'No, Sir. I was there on guard duty several times before, and it was always — well, I don't know how to describe it. Stressful? The feeling somebody wants to get into your head; you understand what I'm saying?'

'Yes, I know what you mean,' Fleming encouraged him.

'Yesterday, I felt nothing of the sort. It was — calm.'

Tears were running down Hurlock's cheeks, and his body was shaking. The nurse decisively pushed Fleming and Pagiatis out of the room.

The army transformed the hospital into a heavily secured fortress. Twenty soldiers permanently walked the grounds. The front, back, and side entrances were guarded by two infantrymen each, and there were eight guards both on the ground floor and the first floor.

While Fleming was walking Pagiatis to the gate, the chief of police told him, 'I talked to the Pomak again. He confirmed there were only four men dispatched by the cult's priest, but there's no saying what that man will do if he gets wind of what's happened here. We cannot exclude a second rescue attempt.'

'What are you going to do with the old geezer?' Fleming asked.

'Keep him in jail for as long as you lads remain here,' Pagiatis said. 'I think it's safer for him if we don't let him return to his mountain tribe. By the way, how much longer will you be staying in my beautiful city?'

'Still waiting for the damn engine to arrive. Could be weeks,' Fleming grumbled.

'Plenty of time for an Ouzo and a story, then,' Pagiatis concluded and clapped him on the shoulder.

It was to be the start of what would become a daily routine during the remainder of Fleming's stay in Thessaloniki.

27

Thessaloniki, Greece

Thursday, 16 August 1917

It took even longer for the engine to arrive than Fleming had assumed in his most pessimistic moods — until the second week of August, to be precise. There had been no new attack on the Hirsch Hospital. The countess remained nicely sedated and caused no problems whatsoever — except for the bad dreams. Fleming slept fitfully, often waking from nightmares screaming and hyperventilating. The image of his wife and daughter burning in the house continued to haunt him. Their terrified voices were always in the back of his mind. Killing their murderer brought Fleming no relief. On the contrary: The confrontation with Moloch reopened doors he'd prefer to remain closed forever. The life he could have led with Catherine and Emily — those thoughts were too painful to dwell on. What had happened couldn't be altered. Still, it was impossible not to brood. Every day anew. The idleness was killing him — that and the Thing inside Mathilde von Corvey.

Pagiatis's daily yarn over a glass of Ouzo became the highlight of Fleming's waking hours. The chief of police was a consummate storyteller with an extensive collection of road-tested corkers. The one-eyed chimp in Mombasa, the veiled lady in Lourenço Marques, the juggling twins in Port-Bouët, and the all-female gambling den in Macau were among Fleming's favourites. When, after four weeks, Fleming announced he'd be leaving the next day, Pagiatis had a request.

'Listen, I get it, you're not to talk about your present business, but we both know what you've got upstairs in the Hirsch is no lady. It's some kind of monster. And I was thinking: If you're a monster hunter by trade, there must be some great stories *you* can tell. I've been spinning all these tales in the last few weeks; how about you telling me one for a change, as a parting gift?'

Fleming chuckled as he watched Pagiatis making goo-goo eyes at him.

'All right, all right,' Fleming said, giving in. 'But I can't tell you about anything recent, you must understand. What my department does is very hush-hush. So this story happened way before my time. Tell me, who's your favourite Greek goddess?'

'Well, Aphrodite, the goddess of love, of course. Who else? We were both born on the same island, did you know? I'm originally from Cythera,' Pagiatis answered with a broad grin.

'Yes, you told me before. That's why I knew you'd choose Aphrodite. Unfortunately, I have to disappoint you, old boy,' Fleming replied. 'That "goddess" is far more ancient than you think, and like you, she's been around a bit. Her name changed as she went from one place to another. Aphrodite always loved stirring up trouble; she's probably one of the wiliest creatures I know. People think she's all about love. Nothing could be further from the truth. Her business is *lust*. Now, especially men are bound to confound love with lust — that's in our nature. Yet they are two different things. One is a short-lived flame, which dims the moment we've conquered the object of our desire. The other is a smouldering fire that lasts for a lifetime and beyond. It even keeps on burning even if our loved one isn't around anymore to share our passion. Love is a constant agony when we cannot be with the person who occupies that special place in our heart. Lust will take its pleasure from whoever is nearest and loses interest as distance increases. Aphrodite has always left a trail of mayhem in her wake — driving men into madness, wrecking households, ruining reputations, careers, and lives. She feeds on our grief: That's her true nature. Lust is merely her instrument for enslaving and tormenting us. She's a wicked predator. As vampires need our blood to sustain their undead existence, Aphrodite thrives on our tears and heartbreaks. She's the ultimate trickster: The mortals whose lives she destroys blindly adulate her. Aphrodite was never my bureau's priority. We deal with threats that could jeopardise human society or affect the balance of power in the world. Aphrodite's doings were always too petty to be of our concern. That is: until she got her talons deep into a future king of Britain. We have a history of members of the royal family not exactly being paragons of virtue, but this case defied all imagination. Under Aphrodite's spell, the crown prince became a serial womaniser and sex-addict. He found his mistresses in all levels of society. He both slept with wives of members of the House of Lords — wrecking quite a few marriages in the process — and with singers, dancers, actresses, and prostitutes. He even felt compelled to frequently travel to Paris to slake his lusts in the Hindu Room of *Le Chabanais*, the swankiest bawdy house on the *Avenue de l'Opéra*. Over the years, his behaviour became so outrageous that the queen feared she couldn't cower the press into silence for much longer. As she felt her days coming to an end, her worst nightmare was that her oldest son's dissolute lifestyle would not only prevent *him* from succeeding her to the throne. She dreaded it would damage the royal family's reputation beyond repair and provoke the establishment of a republic in Britain. So my predecessors at the secret service had to intervene.'

'Tell me, what did they do?' Pagiatis asked, riveted by Fleming's tale.

'Besting a god isn't easy, as you can imagine,' Fleming continued. 'Luckily for them, Aphrodite had made some powerful enemies, and Hephaestus happened to be one of them.'

'Sorry, mate, my mythology is a bit rusty. Those two were a couple, right?' Pagiatis interjected.

'Hephaestus used to be Aphrodite's husband for a while,' Fleming confirmed, 'and he has a grudge against her the size of Mount Olympus. Hephaestus has hands of gold. He was the smith of the Greek gods and turned out marvellous objects from his forge — swords, helmets, shields, breastplates, even jewellery. He was also the butt of jokes from the Olympians, who never considered him their equal. Hephaestus is an ugly son-of-a-bitch — he's club-footed and hunchbacked, and he's got a face like pig's snout. His marriage to a beauty like Aphrodite and his expectation that she'd love him back had his peers in stitches. Needless to say, Aphrodite had many suitors. One day, Hephaestus caught her making love to Ares, the god of war. The cuckold threw a net over them, so finely forged it was invisible. Then Hephaestus exposed them, both still trapped naked in his net, to the other gods to shame his wife. It only earned him further ridicule, and the incident pains him to this day.'

'Where did they find him?' Pagiatis asked.

'There aren't that many Olympians left,' Fleming said, 'and those who survive usually live discreetly among us. Hephaestus is no exception. They found him in Saint Petersburg. He's the right-hand man of Fabergé, the Russian jeweller.'

'And he was willing to help them?' the chief of police asked.

'Delighted. Hephaestus still had his invisible net. With his help, they caught Aphrodite in it and dragged her out of her 12th arrondissement flat in Paris, kicking and screaming. She used the vilest language imaginable. Anybody who'd seen and heard her then would have never fallen for her charms again.'

'Where is she now?'

'That's classified information,' Fleming replied, and seeing the comically disappointed look on Pagiatis's face, he added, 'They stuck her on a small island off the west coast of Ireland, in an abandoned farm, with a dog and a couple of sheep. Only a few old couples and some pixies are living there, and they're immune to Aphrodite's charms.'

'You British are cruel men,' the chief of police joked. 'Anyway, walking the streets of Thessaloniki at night, I don't have the impression she's stayed on her Irish islet for long.'

'We don't need Aphrodite to feel horny,' Fleming said. 'It's simply a trait in humans she exploits to her advantage. It's the way of the gods; remember that. They prey on our weaknesses, desires, and fears. It's a one-way street. They hardly ever give something in return.'

'What are your plans with the devil countess in the Hirsch?' Pagiatis wanted to know.

'Put her as far away from humanity as possible,' Fleming answered. 'An Irish rock in the sea won't do. She must never again be set loose upon the world.'

'Good luck with that. Never is a long time,' the chief of police warned.

28

SSB Special Branch HQ, Glasgow

Wednesday, 22 August 1917

Fleming and M exited the lift at -3. In the five-hundred-square-foot concrete hall, eight armed guards stood to attention. There were three doors. The one to the left led to a room with listening equipment, the one to the right to an office with medical supplies and an emergency operating theatre. The door straight ahead was an imposing, twenty-inch-thick steel affair with a tiny, square, bullet-proof window in it. The door had no hinges; it slid open to the right on a steel rail. A vertical steel girder, aligned with the door's right side, prevented it from opening. An electrified mechanism, operated by two separate keys, allowed the girder to slide down into an opening in the floor and back up again. On the door's left side, four heavy latches bolted into the concrete wall provided additional security. Behind the door was a sixty-foot-long, vaulted concrete corridor.

In that passage, after the sliding steel door had closed behind them, Fleming pointed at fifteen round, evenly spaced openings in the walls, five inches above the floor.

'In case of an emergency, we can flood this hallway in under five seconds with either nitrous oxide or a mix of chlorine and phosgene,' he explained. 'The guards release the gas by flipping a switch in a control box in the guard room. Note, M, that there are no handles on this side of the door: It only opens from the other side, and the guards have immediately locked it behind us.'

At the end of the hallway stood what looked like a massive, round, steel bank vault door.

'The door swings open to the left,' Fleming continued. 'We use the handwheel to retract its fourteen sliding bolts. The handwheel is locked as well, and we need two separate keys to unlock it. Both for this vault door and the sliding door behind us, the commanding officer of the guard keeps one set of keys. The other set remains upstairs. The system doesn't allow to unlock both doors at the same time. The moment we enter the room with the Dream Whisperer, the guard here will close the vault door behind us.'

Fleming slid his key in the lock and waited for the accompanying guard to introduce the second key. Then he turned the handwheel and opened the vault. The guard remained outside with both keys and shut the door after M and Fleming had entered the room.

Inside, M noticed the walls were all covered with thick sheets of steel. The room was bare except for a hospital bed with the countess and the Jackson anaesthesia contraption. M observed their captive from a distance. Mathilde von Corvey's serene appearance was entirely irreconcilable with the evil residing inside her, M thought. He hadn't anticipated Fleming would succeed. M had always considered the extraction plan a desperate last-ditch effort against an invincible enemy. And here she lay, against all his expectations. For the first time, M personally experienced the oppressive, ethereal force that radiated from their prisoner's inert body. He'd read about it in several reports, without being able to imagine what it would feel like to be in the immediate vicinity of an Outer God. He felt nauseous. Even though his mouth went dry, M felt a compulsion to swallow frequently. His throat appeared constricted, and he thought there was a distinct lack of air in the room. M sensed an ominous, subsonic thrumming throughout his body. For the first time in his life, he had trouble concentrating on information provided to him.

Fleming continued his tour inside the room at a quicker pace. He didn't want to be here — any place but here. As always, he couldn't shake the feeling that the Dream Whisperer was acutely aware of his presence and relished in telepathically igniting his darkest phobias.

'The floor around the bed consists of separate steel plates, mounted on springs. We installed a pressure-sensitive device underneath each plate. If the countess leaves the bed, her weight will set off an alarm in the guard room. The guards can then release a sleeping gas through the vents normally used to provide the room with breathable air,' Fleming said, pointing at the small openings lining the bottom of the walls. 'They do so by flipping a switch in the control box in the guard room.'

He then pointed at several minute holes in the ceiling, 'We installed microphones to monitor sounds inside this room. They connect with listening equipment in the room next to the basement guard hall and in the central guard room on the ground floor. We operate both listening stations around the clock.'

After a furtive glance at M — whose eyes were bulging, and his breathing was laboured — Fleming called out to the microphones, 'That's quite enough; let us out of here.'

The man at the basement listening station pushed a button on his control panel. The green light next to the vault door lit up, and the waiting guard opened the door again. When they were back in the corridor, the guard closed the massive door behind them. Its bolts slid into their slots with a reassuring click.

M was catching his breath and wiped the perspiration off his brow.

'How often are the guards changed?' he wanted to know.

His voice sounded shrill.

'Every two hours, and there are three days between guard duties — all this to restrict their exposure to the monster to an absolute minimum,' Fleming replied.

'Good. How often do people need to come in here? How frequently do we need to replace the canisters in the anaesthesia system?' was M's second question.

'It's a daily routine, M. The timing of this procedure is, however, different every day. The canisters could easily last for three days, but we want to minimise any risk of a technical malfunction.'

The answer was visibly unsatisfactory to M, and he made a conscious effort not to sound too harsh in what he said next.

'Why bother with those canisters at all? We should flood the entire room with sleeping gas. This cumbersome daily procedure needlessly puts people at risk. It's the Achilles' heel of the entire set-up. Better do away with it entirely. The less frequently people need to enter that chamber of horrors, the better.'

Fleming knew M was right — he'd thought precisely the same thing accompanying Von Corvey for the first time into her containment chamber. Nevertheless, Fleming considered the question a bit unfair, and he struggled to keep the irritation from his voice.

'Please remember, M, we designed this underground layout still assuming the captive needed water and nutrients. That would have required daily access to her chamber,' he pointed out. 'In those circumstances, keeping the room permanently flooded with sleeping gas wouldn't have been practical. We can only use the vents to pump gas *into* the room. It's by no means a closed circular system. We need to set up a circuit that allows for a continuous supply of the correct mix of nitrous oxide and oxygen, while, at the same time, it also eliminates the carbon dioxide from the process. I'm sure our engineers will soon figure out a way to upscale the Jackson anaesthesia system. Only then, we'll be able to keep the doors forever closed. Unfortunately, we're not there yet.'

'I'd also feel more at ease if our patient could be visually monitored at all times,' M remarked, pretending he hadn't picked up Fleming's vexed tone.

'I agree with you, M. It's an oversight in the original plans,' Fleming admitted. 'I requested drilling a viewing hole in the ceiling. That would allow constant monitoring from the floor above. Our engineers are looking into the matter as we speak.'

'What happens, heaven forbid, if the Dream Whisperer somehow makes it into the basement guard hall?' M asked.

'If the Dream Whisperer steps on a floor tile or opens one of the doors leading to his chamber, alarms go off and block the lift at ground floor level. The lift *never* waits in the basement. After delivering its load, the lift carriage always automatically returns to the ground floor. In the basement, next to the lift, there is a telephone that directly connects with the central guard post on the ground floor. It requires a daily changing password to have the carriage sent down. So the Dream Whisperer would still be stuck in the basement. We can also flood the guard hall with gas. You'll notice the vents in the ceiling when we'll get back there.'

Fleming was all too aware the real question on M's mind was a different one. Would the remaining safety measures even matter if the Dream Whisperer circumvented all of the controls in his chamber and the corridor? It was a rhetorical question. The two doors and the gas *had* to be sufficient. They'd have to work around the clock to avoid having to open the doors in the basement ever again. As far as Fleming was concerned, after they managed that trick, they could pour concrete down the lift shaft until it filled up the entire basement guard room.

Upon leaving the basement, M remained concerned.

'Are you aware, Fleming, of what happened in Thessaloniki the day after you left?' he asked.

'Yes, M,' Fleming replied, 'I heard a fire burnt down a third of the city. The seafront and the centre have both gone up in flames. Seventy thousand people lost their homes. I don't know if the Hirsch Hospital escaped the fire. It must be pandemonium.'

'A coincidence, you think?' M suggested.

'Hardly,' Fleming disagreed. 'The fire's origin is as yet unknown. It was most certainly not caused by any act of war by the Central Powers. We learnt in Thessaloniki that the Dream Whisperer can establish long-range telepathic contact with his followers, even in his current diminished capacity. I suspect the fire was part of a belated effort by his Pomak acolytes to rescue him from the hospital or, failing that, release him from his mortal envelope.'

'Which means we must not only prepare against a jail-break attempt from the inside,' M pointed out, 'but also against outside endeavours to liberate our captive. Imagine the Dream Whisperer's minions burning down Glasgow to set this monster free.'

Fleming tried to reassure his boss.

'We took several measures to secure this facility against attacks from the outside,' he said. 'Forty soldiers guard the building and the grounds at all times. We raised the garden walls to eighteen feet and topped them with barbed wire and glass shards. Twelve trained dogs permanently roam the grounds. The entrance is guarded by another eight infantrymen, and three teams of six soldiers each continuously patrol the streets in a half-mile perimeter. You're right to raise the broader issue concerning the city's safety, M. I'll take it upon myself to talk with the city authorities. I'll make sure the police department is on permanent alert, and fire fighting capacity is up to the highest standards.'

M wearily looked at the soldiers bustling about the building.

He sighed, 'I never thought I'd say this. I wish my brother were around to review all the safety measures. He'd immediately see any flaws and weaknesses.'

Fleming immediately picked up on the uncharacteristically melancholy tone of M's remark, 'I'd welcome him with open arms, M. I've never met your brother.'

'And you never will. Sherlock is dead,' M replied curtly.

Fleming didn't know what to say.

'I'm sure that would have made headlines in the press. I can't believe I missed it,' Fleming wondered, surprised where this was going.

'He died twenty-four years ago at the Reichenbach Falls in Switzerland,' M declared.

'But he survived that incident,' Fleming argued. 'His presumed death was a hoax to fool his opponents, wasn't it? Didn't I read about his further feats in *The Strand* until recently?'

M smiled wryly before saying, 'The moment the press announced Sherlock's death, British crime rates shot up to unseen levels. Scotland Yard was unable to stem the surging criminal tide, and Lord Asquith, who was home secretary at the time, decided to "revive" my brother. The return of his adventures in *The Strand* had a remarkably calming effect on the country's underworld elements, and the newspaper continues to publish new stories to this day for that same purpose.'

'Reading these stories, knowing your brother has long since departed, must be extraordinarily painful for you,' Fleming commiserated.

Another sad smile.

'We live to serve our country's best interests.'

'And how about his friend, Doctor Watson?' Fleming asked.

'Watson never existed,' M said. 'He was merely a literary device used by the author to offset my brother's brilliance and to explain the outlandish methods by which he reached his far-fetched conclusions. My brother could never have worked together with anyone, let alone with such an inferior intellect as Watson.'

'I always assumed Watson was a pseudonym for Sir Arthur Conan Doyle.'

'Mister Doyle is a bloated oaf, whose endless stream of facetious letters to The Times shows he has little or no understanding of how the world really works. I'll never forgive him for the way he painted the relationship between my brother and me, nor for divulging Sherlock's cocaine habit to the general public.'

M took a deep breath. He didn't like to talk about these things. It brought emotions to the surface he preferred to keep under lock and key. Conan Doyle's stories didn't do justice to Mycroft's relationship with his brother, although M had to admit it was a complex one. Sherlock and he didn't always see eye to eye, and there had been bruising arguments. Sherlock's untimely death and his ensuing literary resurrection prevented Mycroft from achieving closure. His brother's absence left a festering emptiness in M's soul, but he considered it was *his* burden to bear and nobody else's business.

He congratulated Fleming on the success of his mission, and admonished him again, 'Get on the engineers' case. They need to fix the gas system. Then we seal the damned place off for good. We can't have a moment's rest before we get it done.'

29

He didn't have a clue about how he got there. He was deep under the sea. Even if the water were clear, sunlight was but a faint memory. His surroundings bathed in deep shades of blue. Extravagant fish were swimming all around him. An undulating sea snake proudly displayed its complexly textured skin design. Fleming suspected that, in the even dimmer distance, more dreadful marine life was lurking between the rocks.

Why was he swimming? He couldn't remember the last time he'd swum. The sea disgusted him. All the fish disappeared. As Fleming slowly turned around, he saw a dark shape closing in on him. He felt unable to move an inch from where he was floating. Fleming noticed he still had his shoes on — actually, he was fully clothed, wearing a dinner jacket, a heavy woollen overcoat, and even a homburg hat. The approaching shape turned out to be a huge basking shark. Its outsized mouth was wide open and came right at him, sucking him in with the rest of the plankton. While he was gliding unresistingly into the animal's gaping maw, Fleming touched its conical snout and noticed it was metal. Lucky he was wearing his leather gloves, he thought.

The inside of the fish looked like a gothic cathedral's nave. While Fleming couldn't see where it was coming from, there was a light inside the fish that mimicked the effect of sun rays on a late-summer afternoon transformed into playful spots by a stained glass window. He stood up, brushed the krill from his sleeves, and walked down the nave. Where the altar ought to be, a man was sitting at a desk. The Tiffany desk lamp only illuminated his hands and a large folder. The hands opened the folder.

'Think carefully, Mister Fleming,' a stern voice instructed. 'Are any of these faces familiar to you?'

Pictures flew up from the folder and circled Fleming like moths around a flame. They all contained faces of men who'd fallen in the Sleeper missions. Fleming couldn't count them; there were more than a hundred of them. They stared directly at him with reproachful gazes. As he looked back at them, he saw their skin growing transparent and peeling off their skulls. Caught in the vortex of these flittering images, Fleming felt his feet lifting from the ground. Again, he floated helplessly. The image overload was compounded by an atonal sound burst that combined the deepest tones of a church organ with the shrieks of humans in mortal fear. The pictures turned into actual faces and then entire bodies, writhing in flames. The din abruptly ended; all human forms melted together into that of his wife holding their baby in her arms.

'Why did you do this to us?' she whispered.

He couldn't answer. Tears streamed down his cheeks. After the lights went out, he remained behind in total darkness for what seemed like an eternity.

By the time an eerie glow illuminated the place again, it had turned into the central chamber of a Sleeper site. The walls and pillars all glistened with contorting, hellish forms. Fleming sensed the obsidian reliefs were alive with malignant creatures, whose shapes he found impossible to distinguish as they merged and disjoined again in a never-ending cycle. On the altar where the Sleepers usually await their awakening, a masked woman sat. The mask showed two fiery red eyes above a mass of frantically writhing tentacles. Fleming felt irresistibly pushed towards the woman. When they were nearly face to face, the woman slid the mask aside and showed her true countenance. It was the Countess von Corvey. Her beautifully sculpted features decayed immediately. Tentacles grew out of her cheeks and chin until her face was a replica of the mask she'd removed. The rest of her body also transformed into squirming coils of slimy tentacles. Her slithering tongue licked Fleming's face.

'Sweetheart,' she hissed, 'why do you keep me waiting for so long while I yearn for you with all my heart? Don't you know we are a match made in hell?'

Fleming awoke in a pool of sweat, his heart pounding in his throat. It was 4.15 a.m. He'd slept for three hours, although he felt as if he'd spent an eternity in agony. These troubled nights were a repeating pattern ever since he captured the countess. It didn't matter whether he was sleeping in a room next to hers or in his town house, miles away. The dreams kept coming, relentlessly — each one never an exact copy of the previous one, all of them equally horrifying. Fleming went to the bathroom and looked in the mirror. His face was gaunt with dark circles around the eyes; he'd lost several pounds. Some mornings, he had to wait until his hands stopped shaking before he could shave. He splashed cold water on his face.

He comforted himself with his engineers' assurances. They were in the final testing stages before they could install a ventilation system that kept their captive in a coma without anybody ever needing to enter her room again. His men drilled the spy hole in the ceiling a week ago. Von Corvey hadn't moved an inch. Keeping an eye on her was a strenuous task. The guard had to be relieved every half hour. In less than a week, Fleming hoped to permanently seal the countess in her concrete tomb and forget about her. If only she let him.

Rebecca was particularly gentle with him. She patiently listened to his stories. Moloch's taunt that *he* was the one who'd killed Fleming's wife and child chilled her to the bone.

'It's as if the Dream Whisperer is hunting *you*, instead of the other way round,' she commented.

Her remark had been on Fleming's mind ever since. For him, the hunt started with the investigation in Zoetevoorde, almost a year ago. At which moment did the Dream Whisperer begin *his* persecution? Twelve years ago, when Fleming lost Catherine and Emily? Or thirty-five years ago, when his parents were murdered?

Ove had presented him with yet another list of remaining potential Sleeper sites. It was a much shorter one than the previous one. This time, the focus shifted towards the USA. The professor recently acquired a few sinister tomes, which originated from New England. By the looks of it, something more troubling had been going on in that area than the hysterical Salem witch trials in the late seventeenth century. Eliassen suspected these trials were merely an attempt at obfuscation, with the intent to turn attention away from far more ancient and deep-rooted cults related to the Outer Gods. He appeared convinced certain east-coast villages hid terrible secrets among their populations. Fleming promised to look into the matter. However, he made it immediately clear that sending over British agents to the former colony to investigate these matters would be decidedly ill-advised. He'd insist with M that he speak about this with his American counterpart — if there was one. Since the Americans joined the war effort last April, contacts between the US government and M had greatly intensified.

Fleming knew it was useless to return to bed. He got dressed and left for HQ. It was his daily routine to visit the guard room first thing in the morning and to have an informal chat with the soldiers on guard. Their job was hard. It motivated them to know their boss was well aware of that fact and appreciated them for their perseverance. He saluted the guards at the entrance and walked over to the guard room on the ground floor. After the usual chat and banter, Fleming took the lift down to the basement.

Upon opening the lift door in the basement, he was immediately snatched out of the cage and thrown to the floor with great force. Dazed, it took Fleming a moment to realise he was on his hands and knees in a large puddle of warm blood and entrails, in the middle of the guard hall. The lift door automatically clanged shut, and the cage returned to the ground floor. The walls were smeared with streaks of gore. Behind him, the sliding door leading to the corridor stood wide open. What was left of the eight guards lay scattered all over the place. Their bodies were torn and tattered. Instinctively, Fleming unholstered his gun. The sight and smell were nauseating — severed limbs, gutted torsos, shattered skulls. It was a vision from the seventh circle of hell, rivers of blood, a crimson orgy. He could hardly keep his balance on the slippery floor. Right beside the lift stood the countess, soaked in blood, a menacing grin on her face.

When she saw him pointing his gun at her, she taunted him, 'What are you going to do, Fleming? Shoot me? What do you think that'll achieve?'

She licked the blood off her fingers and coquettishly rearranged her hair. Fleming didn't move and kept his gun pointed at the ghoul.

'You know what'll happen if you shoot me. You can't win, little elf.'

Fleming shuddered. *Little elf.* Moloch had used precisely the same words. He expected to go up in flames or to be disembowelled. The Dream Whisperer was relishing the moment. Von Corvey made a slow pirouette.

'Did you really believe your silly scheme ever had any chance of success?' she chuckled. 'Did you even think you came up with that plan yourself?'

'Why did you let me abduct you?' Fleming wheezed. 'Why did you let us destroy all those Sleepers?'

'You don't know the first thing about me,' the countess mocked him. 'You think you do because you believed everything that Swedish dunce told you about me, but you're wrong. So damned wrong. I've been around for aeons. I was there when your forefathers climbed down from their tree. I whispered in their ears something bigger than them was watching out for their kind. I taught them how to worship, how to fear the wrath of the gods. I wrote all their holy books. I dictated everything there is to read about me. It's all bogus. The learnt professor only told you fairy tales, and you gobbled them all up. You wanted to believe there are limits to my power, that I need to obey rules, that you could beat me. You *never* stood a chance. Your grandmother is smarter than you. She left Earth through the cracks. She won't be here anymore to see the place crackle and burn.'

'Then didn't the other Outer Gods leave you behind to make their return to Earth possible?'

'I'm nobody's servant, boy,' the Dream Whisperer snarled. 'They'll return if and when *I*'ll let them and not a moment sooner. *I* am the Key. The choice is with *me*.'

'You never intended to wake up five Cthulhus to open the gate.'

It was a sober statement. It finally dawned on Fleming that the Dream Whisperer had no intention whatsoever to let his peers — or maybe his masters — return to Earth. Earth was *his* playground, only for him to enjoy. He was happy to be rid of his kin. Now, *he* ruled the roost. Nobody could challenge him. All this was a game to him. He made up the rules, and he decided whether to break them. The Outer Gods' decision to leave the most human-like among them behind to facilitate their return had been a terrible error of judgement.

'High and mighty humankind has grown. Though I fought well, I have been vanquished!' the Dream Whisperer moaned theatrically, one hand to the countess's forehead, tearful eyes staring aloft. 'Unsparing in my efforts have I been. Alas, my dreaded foes are legion. They swarm in untold numbers over this benighted globe. Our unborn Saviours' cradles suffered desecration and smothered in their deathless sleep they were! No more will Cthulhu howl at the starry expanse. No more will this noble race tear the cosmic veil that hinders our brethren's return! The Demon Star winks in vain in the inkiest of nights. The passageway remains shut for eternity and a day. Alas, how the mighty have fallen! My grief lies all within, and these external manners of lament are merely shadows to the unseen grief that swells with silence in the tortured soul!'

Von Corvey knelt silently and spread her arms, like a leading actress bowing for her audience at the end of the play.

'What do you think?' she asked, grinning slyly. 'I know it still needs some work. The gist of it is there, right? There's nothing like a bit of old Will to lift the senses. I almost believe it myself.'

Fleming was feverishly thinking about his options. It was clear as day to him what the Dream Whisperer's next step would be. All events in the last thirty-five years had one purpose, and *he* was at the centre of it all. He put the barrel of his gun under his chin.

'Ahahah, we won't have any of that, dear boy!' the Dream Whisperer warned him.

Fleming lost all control over the muscles in his right arm and hand. The gun moved away from his chin.

'That was a selfless and foolish move. You have my respect, but I can't allow you to take my prize,' the countess berated him, wagging her finger. 'Now, let's finish this.'

Fleming saw a blurry shape detach from the woman, and it flung itself at him. A bolt of black energy, full of cold rage and spite, pushed Fleming aside in his own body. Before drowning in a tarry pool of oblivion, he felt for an instant the full extent of the Dream Whisperer's immeasurable power.

Mathilde von Corvey blinked, startled. She turned her head left and right, taking in the carnage around her, wild panic in her eyes. The woman seemed lost, clueless, and fragile. She stared at her bloodied hands with a look of utter disbelief.

'You've served me well, darling,' Fleming said to her, his eyes featuring a reddish sparkle, 'but this one here will be so much more fun. All the toys I'll have to play with! I almost can't wait. Farewell, my dear, sweet dreams.'

He raised his gun and shot her between the eyes. Then he walked to the telephone and shouted in the mouthpiece in an almost hysterical voice, 'The Dream Whisperer has escaped! I had to shoot the countess! Everybody is dead!'

30

M's Office, London

Friday, 13 September 1917

'How did this happen?'

M's voice was trembling with ill-contained exasperation. It was true he'd felt an unshakable sense of dread in the Dream Whisperer's presence. Nevertheless, this setback was difficult to stomach. More than forty people died in the effort to capture this monster. Now, it was on the loose again, and they didn't have a clue where it was or in what guise it would resurface. Fleming looked both rueful and frustrated.

'The investigation showed that the nurse responsible for changing the canister with nitrous oxide must have made a mistake,' he explained. 'She took an empty canister from the stockroom and hooked it up to the system. The countess regained consciousness, and the Dream Whisperer was once more in full control of his interface with our reality. He was able to override all of our safety measures. He slid back the vault door's bolts without triggering the alarm, walked down the corridor, and opened the next door. No traces of brute force. He did it purely by psychic means.'

'How could that dumb cow make such an unforgivable mistake? I'll see to it her negligence doesn't go unpunished,' M raged. 'And why didn't the guard who was supposed to keep an eye on the captive sound the alarm when he saw Von Corvey leaving her bed? Was he asleep on the job as well?'

'We found the poor man slumped over his viewer. His eyes were burnt out, and his brain was cooked.'

M considered this fresh horror in silence.

'I don't understand it,' he sighed.

'After the Dream Whisperer regained his grasp on reality, he was impossible to retain,' Fleming said. 'We know what he can do from the Sicily report. He doesn't need to touch something to bend it to his will.'

'Not that!' M cried out, exasperated. 'I don't understand why the Dream Whisperer went through this entire charade of getting captured and locked up, only to escape again and kill a few guards in the process. What's the point? He lost months! He could have done so much more damage by immediately leaving Constantinople and waking up all of the Sleepers around the Black Sea. If this is all the result of some cunning plan on his part, I don't get it.'

'I'm not convinced it was a charade, M. I remain of the opinion we took him by surprise,' Fleming replied defensively. 'Maybe — I'd even say: probably — he telepathically influenced the nurse to choose the empty canister to allow him to escape. On the other hand, I can't imagine any good reason why he purposefully would have allowed us to capture him. That doesn't make sense at all.'

'Don't be so obtuse, Fleming. He was able to manipulate the nurses like a master puppeteer, and still he chose to stay shackled to that bed for weeks,' M countered. 'He could have escaped from day one. I'd wager he was never even sedated in the first place. He's been playing with us. But why? It doesn't add up, and it drives me mad. I already told you before that the Dream Whisperer's behaviour isn't logical. We don't understand his real purpose. By now, I'd be inordinately surprised if it were setting free those Sleepers and opening the gates of hell. He's so powerful that he could have done that a year ago — without us even noticing it before it was too late. There must be more to his actions than that.'

'Maybe you're giving him far too much credit,' Fleming suggested. 'Being immensely powerful doesn't necessarily mean having a superior intelligence or being good at organising things. On the contrary, his superhuman abilities may have lulled him into carelessness, underestimating his opponents.'

'I think it's *you* who underestimate our opponent, Fleming. We're talking about a being that's been toying with humans as a pastime for millennia. He knows us far better than we know him.'

M was disappointed in Fleming's stubborn failure to recognise the obvious. He realised this setback must have hit his subordinate harder than anybody else, given his investment in the countess's abduction. Nevertheless, he wasn't used to Fleming showing such patent lack of acumen. Rebecca told him Fleming suffered from sleep deprivation and horrid nightmares ever since he returned from his Constantinople mission. The man sitting in front of him looked haggard, exhausted, emaciated even. Perhaps a couple of days off would do him good.

'What do you suggest we do now?' M asked.

'We're back to square one, although not quite,' Fleming answered. 'The Dream Whisperer's identity is again unknown to us, but we've annihilated an important number of Sleepers. Professor Eliassen came up with another list of potential sites we need to investigate, and that's what we'll do. Hopefully, it'll take our enemy some more time before he can seduce another host. Once he possesses a new body, he'll be physically limited in his travels again. Time may be on our side. Eliassen told me the time window available to open the portal for the Outer Gods isn't unlimited. The Dream Whisperer has now been at it for about a year. Maybe his opportunity is passed or will be soon.'

M didn't even try to hide his sarcasm anymore.

'Hunting Sleepers once again!' he snorted. 'Don't you think the fiend would have made more haste if he *actually* planned to release the Sleepers within a restricted time-frame?'

'We know he's made truly significant efforts to awaken Sleepers on several continents. That's *all* we know. All the rest is pure speculation. I've not heard any theory yet that offers a better insight into our enemy's actions,' Fleming retorted as if stung by M's biting remarks.

That shut his boss up, and Fleming took advantage of this to put Eliassen's latest list on the desk, 'As you'll see, M, the list is short. The majority of the eight target sites are on American soil. We'll concern ourselves with the two remaining identifiable sites in Europe and the one in Africa. We should approach our American allies to have them take care of the Sleepers on their territory.'

M studied the list. Eliassen had added a site in the Bulgarian Rhodope Mountains, in the home territory of the Pomak tribe that executed the attack in Thessaloniki. The second one was in Kraków, under Wawel Hill. A Greek philosopher and wonderworker, Apollonius of Tyana, who was a contemporary of Jesus Christ, had already noticed the site. Apollonius was a preacher as well, and his followers believed in his divine origin. He identified 'positive radiation' coming from the Wawel Hill and left a talisman to mark the place. The hill was right next to the Vistula River, which made sense as well. As in Zoetevoorde, an old church marked the spot. In this case, it was even a cathedral. In Africa, Eliassen identified a site near the Congo River in Belgian Congo. Quite appropriate, M thought, as one of his favourite authors had called the area the *Heart of Darkness*. Joseph Conrad's intuition couldn't have been more on the mark. The other five locations lay scattered along the coasts of the United States.

'We cannot risk a diplomatic incident by sending teams over to the States,' Fleming repeated. 'The Americans need to investigate these sites themselves.'

'I'm meeting with their president in a few months,' M said. 'I'll broach the subject, although I'm afraid it'll be a difficult proposition: He has different priorities on his mind now, as you can well imagine.'

'The Dream Whisperer only needs to convince an American victim, and then he's free to roam the country. There are five Sleepers according to Eliassen. Our enemy can awaken them while the president is otherwise occupied, and it'll be the end of our world,' Fleming insisted.

'If it were so easy to compose his desired quintet exclusively in the USA, he would have done so. He wouldn't be mooching about in war-torn Europe, don't you think so?' M replied icily. 'I'll talk to the president, but I remain unconvinced of the urgency.'

'As we concluded ourselves at the beginning of this affair, our enemy plays on a global scale. Large and powerful though the British Empire is, we need allies,' Fleming pleaded. 'We've solicited the French's co-operation, and it's been exceedingly useful. They've destroyed several sites we'd be hard put to reach without creating a diplomatic outcry. We need to have a similar alliance with the Americans, M. As a matter of fact, I strongly advise establishing a well-funded international organisation to deal with the global threat posed by the Outer Gods' return.'

'I see your point; it's a valid one,' M conceded. 'Nevertheless, it'll have to wait until a more imminent global threat is squashed. First, we deal with the Central Powers, and then we'll discuss setting up an international agency. In the meantime, I'll talk with President Wilson and give him some pointers on where to find Sleeper sites on American soil. If he decides to do something about them, and the raids are successful, he'll be all the more amenable to seeing the value of international co-operation on this issue.'

M stood up, signalling the meeting was over, 'Dispatch teams to destroy these three remaining sites in Europe and Africa. Do not, I repeat, do *not* participate in any of them yourself. You've gone through a taxing experience, and you need rest. Take some time off; restore yourself; sleep and eat well. That's an order.'

He amicably clapped Fleming on the shoulder and ushered him out.

Epilogue

Jardin du Luxembourg, Paris

Sunday, 27 April 1919

The war ended with the German capitulation on 11 November 1918. A four-year war of attrition and bloodshed on an unprecedented scale left many European nations' economies and state finances in tatters. In its main protagonists — Germany, France, and Britain — the war practically wiped out an entire generation of bright young men. The end of the war laid the foundation for a new world order, as it caused the collapse of the Central and Eastern European Empires, and of the Ottoman Empire. In Russia, one brand of authoritarianism replaced another as the Bolsheviks firmly established themselves in the seat of power. The ugly beast of nationalism, which raised its head before the war, gathered momentum in Eastern Europe and the Balkans. It created increasing tensions in areas where many different ethnicities co-existed. There, the rise to power of national majorities created disaffected minorities. These minorities began to look for support in neighbouring countries dominated by *their* ethnic group and thus planted the seeds of future conflicts.

The USA emerged as a new world power. Its economy benefited hugely from the war, and the country now was the Allied nations' most important creditor. As the

Americans entered the war only in a late phase, they paid a lesser toll in human lives. Thomas Woodrow Wilson, who served as president since 1913, was eager to weigh in on the negotiations at the Paris Peace Conference. The Conference opened in January 1919 in the Palace of Versailles, a few miles outside the French capital. Twenty-seven nations participated in these talks, which addressed numerous issues — the most important being the allocation of responsibility for the war. With many nations' state finances in terrible disarray because of the war effort, this wasn't merely a moral issue. It also had significant practical consequences, since especially France and Britain had every intention of presenting the culprits with stiff demands for both financial and territorial compensations.

A year before, President Wilson had made a lofty speech to Congress. He outlined fourteen points as the basis for a just and secure peace that'd be more than a new balance of power. Although Wilson did succeed in introducing these fourteen points as a basis for the Versailles peace negotiations, he found the going tough. The American president had disembarked in Brest in December 1918 and stayed in Europe for two months, then went back to the USA, only to return to Paris three weeks later. He struggled to come to grips with the complexities of European politics and was often exasperated by them. Georges Clemenceau, the French prime minister, openly derided the naivety of Wilson's fourteen points. Lloyd George, Britain's prime minister, was keen to secure his nation's dominance over the seas. That's why he fought tooth and claw against the American president's proposal to accept absolute freedom of navigation in international waters. Moreover, both Clemenceau and Britain's representatives in the talks on reparations, Lord Sumner and Lord Cunliffe, were determined to coerce Germany into paying astronomically high war reparations. This inflexibility was something Wilson consistently advised against as he rightly foresaw this would become a future element of tension between European nations.

Early April, President Wilson fell victim to the influenza pandemic raging through the world. The pandemic caused far more casualties than the war. When Wilson met with M for an informal Sunday walk in the *Jardin du Luxembourg*, he'd recovered from the illness, although he still felt weak.

Wilson lamented the lack of progress in the peace negotiations, and more particularly, Britain's unhelpful stance. Naturally, M was aware of this as he closely followed the procedures from behind the scenes. It was on *his* instruction that Sumner and Cunliffe adopted an intractable attitude in the compensation debates. M's hidden agenda was to cripple the vanquished enemy's economy. He wanted to prevent Germany from ever building a high sea fleet rivalling Britain's. M realised, however, it would be unwise to let the president of the emerging new world power lose face in the peace negotiations.

Wilson's fourteenth point was the creation of a League of Nations — an intergovernmental organisation that would maintain world peace through negotiated disarmament and conflict arbitration. Although it was a controversial idea at the time, rejected even by several influential American politicians, M saw its merits. He intended to put Britain's weight behind it if Britain got its way in the compensation dispute. He said as much during their walk, which improved President Wilson's mood considerably.

Wilson's idea of international co-operation to maintain world peace also provided M with an opportunity to segue into his next subject smoothly.

'Mister President,' he said, 'do you remember, last year, I provided you with some coastal locations your secret service might usefully look into?'

317

'Why, yeah, sure,' Wilson replied. 'They found some profoundly weird stuff, as I recall. In a couple of those towns, people were turning into fish! Can you imagine? We can't have that, of course. It's decidedly un-American — as if we haven't got enough problems with our darkies.'

'What did you do about it?' M asked.

'I had them rounded up and put them into camps,' the president said. 'Scientists are studying them. It ain't easy. There were riots in some camps and outside attempts to set the fish heads free. The army had to intervene and use proportionate force.'

'Meaning?'

'Shot most of them,' Wilson said.

'Did your scientists learn anything from the captives?' M further inquired.

'A lot of mumbo-jumbo, basically,' Wilson grunted, airily dismissing the findings of his services. 'About waking up sleeping gods and returning to the sea while all life on land will be wiped out. I don't have time for these lunacies.'

'What if I told you these findings are consistent with ours, and that, during the war, we had to spend considerable resources to contain an alien threat endangering the survival of humankind?' M suggested.

'I'd say, "Pull the other one",' Wilson gruffly answered.

'There's more to it than that, Mister President,' M insisted. 'I bet you regularly receive reports about inexplicable events from local police and federal agents. I'm talking about strange cults, unnatural events at old burial sites, mythological monsters lurking in your mighty nation's sparsely populated areas. I could go on, but I'm sure you get my drift.'

'Are you *spying* on me, Holmes?' Wilson asked, irritated by the turn this conversation was taking. 'You're referring to top-secret files nobody knows about, except a few of my most trusted collaborators.'

Wilson eyed his companion suspiciously, but M kept his poker face.

'I don't need to spy on you to know that, Mister President,' he said. 'Don't forget that, before you kicked us out in 1776, we had plenty of time to get acquainted with your country's peculiarities. We had this kind of reports in our files long before Washington even considered the creation of a specialised secret service. Let me tell you that *every* civilised country has an intelligence agency that deals with the abnormal and the inexplicable. There are plenty of things we don't want the general public to know about but that governments ignore at their peril.'

'Where are you going with this, Holmes? Come to the point,' Wilson said.

'The events we confronted in the previous years have led us to understand that humanity faces a global and imminent threat to its survival,' M explained. 'There's no single nation equipped to independently and successfully deal with this menace. As you pointed out in your visionary Fourteen Points document, we need a League of Nations to contain conflicts between humans. But what of the dangers to our existence coming from elsewhere, from obscure powers existing at the fringes of our awareness, powers whose origins go beyond our comprehension? These menaces don't care about borders traced by men. They are global, and they need a global response. In the past two years, Britain has allied itself with France to fight a fiend who, if left unchecked, would have opened the gates of hell and doomed humanity. Only a secret collaboration between two great nations has succeeded in averting worldwide disaster. I'm inviting you to consider co-founding a well-funded international body with far-reaching executive authority, manned by operatives of the three major nations that emerged victorious from this war.'

President Wilson considered this proposal in silence for a long while.

'Then the USA shall want to take the lead of this endeavour,' he finally replied.

'Mister President, your nation has emerged from this war as a future world power,' M flattered his partner, 'but Britain has been running an Empire for over *five* centuries. We have networks of field operatives both in Europe, the Middle East, Africa, and the Far East. No doubt, in the years to come, your nation will build a network that will be a match to ours. But not yet, my dear friend, not yet.'

'So you claim the lead for yourself,' Wilson said.

'Not for *me*, good grief, no,' M replied, waving the suggestion away. 'Processing information is what I do best, not running field operatives. Trust me; I acquired that nugget of wisdom the hard way. However, I do have an excellent man, who's been running Britain's Special Branch of the secret service in a remarkably competent manner. His name is Fleming, and he's an impressive chap. I'll introduce him to you shortly if you want to.'

'I look forward to meeting this prodigy,' Wilson muttered.

'You won't regret it, Mister President.'

'How about the French?'

'Clemenceau already agreed yesterday.'

'And what do you propose to call this agency?' Wilson asked.

'Janus,' M answered.

'Jane's?' the American said disapprovingly. 'That sounds more like a seedy saloon than a bona fide league to fight the unholy powers of darkness.'

'No, Mister President, "J-a-n-u-s",' M spelt out. 'It's the name of the Roman god of doorways and passages, beginnings and endings, past and future, change and transition. I think that's appropriate, don't you? And as it's Latin, it'll please the French. Always make sure you please the French.'

'The French? I can't stand them,' Wilson growled.

'Neither can I, Mister President, neither can I,' M
agreed.

.

PART 2

31

Oskarshamn Cemetery, Sweden

Saturday, 12 February 1921

It was freezing. A razor-sharp east wind was blowing the first snowflakes of what was to become a heavy shower over the tombstones in the cemetery of the coastal town of Oskarshamn in the Swedish Kalmar region. It had been snowing for weeks. The weather all but paralysed train traffic and blocked most of the roads. The funeral service in the unheated, yellow, neo-gothic church in the town centre had lasted for an interminable two hours. The pastor, undeterred by the weather, was delivering a lengthy eulogy at the open grave for a small crowd of shivering mourners. Next to the pastor stood a pint-sized, older woman, all dressed in black. Her face didn't so much express grief as grim determination and triumph.

'Glad to see you, M. I didn't understand a single word of the service,' Rebecca complained, 'and the people next to me in the church only spoke Swedish, so that wasn't much of a help either. I can't understand why they give a life-long atheist a funeral service in the church.'

'A dead man's voice doesn't carry much weight in these matters,' M whispered back. 'His sister is Eliassen's only remaining family. She, being a parson's wife, decided to haul his body over to his native town and bury him with all the proper rites.'

'Ove couldn't stand his sister,' Rebecca said. 'They constantly feuded over his lack of religion. One would reckon she'd have respected his convictions in this instance. She did nothing of the sort. Instead, she looks like the cat that got the cream.'

'Well, that's understandable. Eliassen's sister believes she saved her brother from the eternal flames of hell,' M pointed out.

'She's a Lutheran. She believes no such thing,' Rebecca dismissed M's suggestion. 'In their view, only God's grace can grant salvation. It has nothing to do with how the deceased has lived his life, let alone with funeral rites imposed upon the deceased against his will. What you see on her face is the satisfaction of having prevailed over her brother in his final moment.'

The pastor finished his eulogy and invited the family and mourners to pay their final respects to the plain casket in the open grave. Afterwards, Ove's family offered the mourners a frugal post-funeral luncheon. Neither M nor Rebecca knew anybody present, and they felt no particular inclination to make Ove Eliassen's sister's acquaintance. They left and went to M's car, which his driver had parked near the church grounds.

'How did you get here?' M asked.

'I was in France, visiting my mother, when I heard the terrible news,' Rebecca said. 'I went by train from Paris to Sassnitz, where I took the ferry to Trelleborg. Then it took me another two trains to first get to Linköping and then to Västervik. Finally, I travelled the last thirty-five miles by bus over horrible roads. At some point, I was sure I wouldn't make it in time. I'm glad I can travel back to London with you, M. You didn't come here all the way by car, did you?'

'That would have been difficult, wouldn't it?' M chuckled. 'I have a private yacht — it's moored in Kalmar. I didn't want to arrive in Oskarshamn in too conspicuous a fashion, so I thought it wise to dock in a bigger port, forty miles south from here. I must say I've regretted my choice. The roads in Sweden are a bit of a nightmare with these perpetual snowstorms.'

Rebecca looked up at M with a mocking glint in her eye. She could only imagine how gruelling M's journey must have been on his luxury yacht and in his chauffeur-driven Rolls Royce.

'How did poor Ove pass away?' Rebecca asked. 'I was so busy travelling here that I never got the opportunity to inquire. In the last few months, I felt something wasn't all right with him, but he refused to talk about it. I never expected him to die so suddenly, though.'

'He was found dead at his desk. The coroner's report states heart failure as the cause of death, which doesn't tell us much,' M said. 'It's what doctors write when they're clueless. Did you say Eliassen behaved strangely lately?'

'He seemed stressed, a bit short-tempered even, which I thought unusual, as he was the most gentle person I ever knew,' Rebecca reflected. 'I remember trying to hear him out over dinner last Christmas, but I couldn't get anything out of him. He remained oh-so evasive and rebuffed any direct questions.'

'Did he have any problems with other members of the bureau? Maybe Fleming was a bit too demanding?' M insisted.

'I wouldn't know, M,' Rebecca said. 'Fleming is hardly around anymore; he's continuously travelling. The co-operation with the Americans absorbs most of his energy; those Yankees sure appear to need a lot of pampering. Fleming spends more than half of his time across the pond. Is that why he didn't come to the funeral?'

'I'm afraid so. Fleming had to catch the ocean liner in Southampton three days ago,' M confirmed her assumption.

They'd reached M's car. It was a pre-war monstrosity — a Silver Ghost Double Pullman Limousine. The driver immediately jumped out and opened the door for them.

When they'd settled comfortably in the back seat, a distinguished, elderly gentleman knocked on the car window. M remembered seeing him at the funeral and rolled down the window. It was a tall and reedy fellow, with a long, narrow face and large teeth. His hair was white, and he had spectacular, old-fashioned mutton chop whiskers.

'Lord Holmes, I presume?' he inquired.

'The same,' M answered. 'With whom do I have the honour of speaking?'

'I'm Ormger Lagergren, Professor of Comparative Mythology and Nordic History at the University of Gothenburg,' the stranger said. 'I am — or better: was — a good friend of the deceased. A month ago, Professor Eliassen sent me *this*.'

Lagergren showed M the large package, all wrapped up in brown paper, which he'd been carrying under his arm.

'In the letter that went with it,' the man continued, 'my friend asked me to hand it over to you in case something should happen to him. He was confident you'd have the decency to come to his funeral, and you've proved him right.'

He proceeded to shove the package through the car window.

Then he took a step back and made a slight bow, 'As I've acquitted myself of my duty to my late friend, I bid you farewell and good luck, your Lordship.'

'Just a moment, dear Professor,' M withheld him. 'Are you travelling back to Gothenburg?'

'Yes, your Lordship, indeed, I am.'

'We're travelling in the same direction. We're driving to Kalmar, and then we'll sail on to Malmö. Would you grant us the pleasure of your company, Professor Lagergren?' M proposed.

'I'd be gratified, your Lordship!' Lagergren answered, pleasantly surprised.

They drove to the inn to fetch the professor's and Rebecca's luggage and embarked on the journey to Kalmar. The snow intensified. The chauffeur had to drive slowly to keep the humongous automobile on the slippery, narrow roads.

'How did you know Professor Eliassen?' Rebecca wanted to know. 'Your domains of expertise seem to overlap. Did you study together?'

'No, we did not, Doctor Mumm. I'm five years older than Ove,' Professor Lagergren corrected her. 'We read each other's publications. The world of Swedish academia — certainly in our field of study — is a tiny one, so I knew Ove from an early stage in his career. We got in contact because we were always chasing the same antique books and dealt with the same book dealers. One day, we were involved in a bidding war for a precious medieval copy of the *Liber Juratus*, a grimoire authored by Honorius of Thebes. Through a dealer's indiscretion, we got to know the other bidder's identity. We met, compared our purchases over the last few years, and came to the conclusion we'd cost each other a small fortune. So we decided not to engage in such foolish behaviour anymore and share our finds. It was a sad day for Swedish dealers specialised in occult books.'

'Were you aware Professor Eliassen was working for the secret service?' M asked.

'Yes. After a while, when Ove knew me better, he wanted to recruit me as well,' Lagergren replied. 'Ove confided in me about what he called "*the secret world order*" and how governments of different countries were struggling to contain alien races that preceded humankind on this planet. At first, I had difficulties taking these notions seriously, but the evidence he showed me was convincing. I took on temporary assignments from the secret service myself, as a consultant. I have Ove to thank for that; it was riveting work.'

'Was there a division of labour depending on your respective expertise?' Rebecca inquired.

'Our specialised knowledge overlapped to a large extent,' Lagergren acknowledged. 'Ove pushed assignments my way because, at times, he couldn't cope with the work-load. On the whole, one could say I'm more knowledgeable about magic. At least, the theory of magic that is. I've never been much of a practitioner.'

'Would you say magic yields *practical* results then?' Rebecca asked, sounding predictably doubtful.

'Surprisingly, yes,' Lagergren confirmed. 'Magic has a bad press because most grimoires are written in a convo-luted, hermetic style, which is deliberately used to confuse the non-initiated. To casual readers, it all may sound like pompous rubbish, but there's more to it than you'd expect at first sight.'

After a slight pause, he asked, 'All those alien races are so much older than humankind. Did you never wonder, Doctor Mumm, why *they* didn't invent cars, aeroplanes, and all other modern technological marvels ages ago?'

'As a matter of fact, I did. That question has been on my mind a lot, I must say,' Rebecca admitted.

'Well, to begin with, some species are simply too stupid. Our native trolls are a good example, I'm afraid. There are plenty of brutes around that don't have the wits to develop a scientific tradition of their own. Other races, like the elves, deliberately chose to stay clear of mechanisa-tion for reasons of principle. They believe it's a path that leads straight to perdition,' Lagergren explained.

'Fleming told me about that. Elves maintain that mechanisation and industrialisation inevitably disturb our natural environment's subtle balances. They fear that these new developments will lead to our planet's destruction,' Rebecca added, noticing M's sarcastic smirk.

'Exactly,' Lagergren continued. 'And there's a lot of truth in that philosophy. One of the most important reasons why we haven't encountered races with superior technology is that they all annihilated themselves ages before *we* showed up.'

'But you're saying there are *other* reasons why we don't see such species?' Rebecca wondered.

'Most of the surviving intelligent species haven't chosen the path of technology because there was no need,' the professor continued. 'They tend to operate by magic. Magic is, as it were, an alternative, altogether different form of science, which doesn't require or promote the development of machines. For most humans, it's almost impossible to grasp because we're not wired that way. Still, the magic developed by certain species offers surprisingly practical solutions in healthcare, nutrition, communication, transportation, and so many other issues our modern society is struggling with.'

'It isn't a path without dangers of its own,' M remarked, 'There's a dark side to magic as well, which has caused untold misery over the ages.'

'In that, technology and magic resemble each other,' Lagergren agreed. 'They're both tools that can be either beneficial or harmful, depending on the user's purpose. If greed or lust for power is the practitioner's dominating drive, both paths will ultimately lead to ruin.'

They sat in silence for a while, considering what Lagergren had told them. Despite the man's self-avowed interest in magic, he didn't strike M or Rebecca as a sinister individual. They'd both taken a quick liking to this elderly gentleman.

'Well, since we have a long drive ahead of us, I propose to open the package you so kindly delivered to us,' M announced.

He first retrieved a large envelope from the package. Upon opening it, M found a handwritten letter addressed to him. M quickly read the first page and then decided to read the letter out loud to his companions.

Dear M,

When you hold this letter in your hands, it means my worst fears have come to pass and that I am no longer among the living. Your frequent travels have prevented me from confiding in you in person, and Doctor Mumm is staying in France. Because of the recent substantial staff turnover, I do not know whom to trust anymore in our organisation. That is why I have decided to entrust this package to the excellent care of my long-standing friend and confidant, Professor Ormger Lagergren.

Two months ago, I came upon information that has convinced me Janus's operational integrity is severely compromised. Although I am thoroughly discomposed, I shall try not to get ahead of myself in this narrative.

While hatching the plan to abduct the Countess von Corvey, we assumed the Dream Whisperer could only possess willing hosts. We believed that only the victim's consent or death could break that covenant. I, personally, made this assessment based on numerous occult sources and assume full responsibility for it. Now, however, I fear I was misled on both accounts by our cunning adversary.

332

Last November, one of my most trusted sources of ancient manuscripts contacted me. He wanted to sound me out about whether I would be interested in a particular document. He was on the verge of acquiring the journal of an Arab geographer, shipwrecked in 788 AD near the Andaman Islands in the Indian Ocean. These islands have been inhabited for more than twenty millennia. Their civilisation was already decrepit when the Spartans were fighting Xerxes. The geographer encountered the degenerate descendants of this race after washing up on the shores of what is now called Havelock Island, the largest of the Great Andaman chain of islands. He found his hosts worshipped unspeakable gods in cannibalistic rituals. Naturally, I immediately declared my keenest interest and obtained said document in early December.

The Arab's journal describes a ritual performed at the full moon. Fierce warriors hold down a frightened slave on a dais while six bearers carry another man on an ornate palanquin, dressed up as a god, to the same stage. The whole tribe is chanting the name 'Dream Whisperer' during the entire procedure. When the man dressed up as a god has taken his place on the stage, he performs a wild ritual dance. The dancing god, accompanied by a constant beating of drums, drives the worshippers into a frenzy. At the end of the dance, a spirit leaves the dancer's body and enters the cowering slave. The warriors release the slave and give him a sword. The slave beheads the man who was, only a moment before, a god. Then the cultists dress him up as a god himself and will worship him as such until they repeat the ritual the next full moon. The crowd tears the old god to pieces and eats him

333

while the new god launches into his first terrible dance.

M sighed, 'Oh dear, I don't like where this is going.'
Rebecca and Lagergren speechlessly waited for him to continue.

I have included the original manuscript and a full translation in the package for your perusal.

The description of this horrible ceremony made me realise that my original assumptions concerning the Dream Whisperer's limitations were entirely unfounded. <u>Our enemy can enter and leave a body without his host's consent!</u> This new awareness sheds a disturbing fresh light on the occurrences in 1916 and 1917. The Dream Whisperer duped us into believing he intended to wake five Cthulhus to bring the Outer Gods back to Earth. I now understand his actual intention was to seize control of the Special Branch and to convince you, dear M, to broker an international alliance. You have created with our allies, France and the USA, an agency with near-unlimited means at its disposal. We must assume our foe has taken an unwilling Fleming as host and has been leading the Special Branch since September 1917 and Janus since its creation right after the war. He has carefully bided his time, arousing little or no suspicion. The Dream Whisperer has seen to it that Janus could present an impressive string of operational successes over this period, such as the destruction of several more Sleeper sites, the eradication of a few sinister cults, and the containment of mutated populations. However, I fear there is much that has eluded us. You know very well that the Agency's internationalisation greatly complicates its supervision. President Wilson's illness is another negative factor that has substantially weakened oversight of Janus's oper-

ations by our American friends. I have no doubt that the Dream Whisperer has profited from that situation and has been misusing his nearly unchecked authority to fund secret projects that only serve _his_ purpose.

For millennia, the Dream Whisperer has authored or corrupted my source materials. In the light of current circumstances, we must assume that none of the ancient tomes in our libraries have escaped the manipulations of this Fiend. We cannot rely on them any longer. I suspect, as in every clever forgery, they contain a crafty mix of objective information and cunning lies, which makes it onerous to separate fact from misdirection.

The bas-reliefs in the Sleeper sites illustrate the age-old history of the Outer Gods and remain, in my opinion, a trustworthy source of information. In the package, I have included all the pictures taken during the search-and-destroy missions and my analysis thereof. The depictions in the bas-reliefs confirm that an ancient and tremendously powerful race inhabited Earth. It left before the advent of man with the firm intent to return. I suspect it is correct to assume that the Dream Whisperer and the Sleepers were indeed left behind to facilitate their return. Even if it is difficult to establish a strict hierarchy among the Outer Gods, I believe the Dream Whisperer's position is but a lowly one. Frustration motivates him to act against the interests of his kin. If the Outer Gods were to return, the Dream Whisperer would be a bottom-rung member of their pecking order once again. It is only natural that he does not want to relinquish his current position as Earth's single most powerful being.

The Dream Whisperer could have destroyed the Sleepers himself, but he is covering his tracks by 'allowing' us to do the dirty work. If the Outer Gods ever find a way to return to Earth without relying on the Sleepers, there will be a reckoning. Our enemy is setting up humankind as his scapegoat. He will not hesitate to shift the blame for the Sleepers' demise to us.

I have been torturing my brain to find a reason why the Dream Whisperer would be attracted to the leadership position in Janus. As an all-powerful being, he has no need whatsoever for Janus's resources to wreck our world. Then I remembered he is a typical trickster god. He does not relish the use of raw power. He is forever playing games, and playing games is no lark if the same party always wins. That means he intentionally limits his abilities while playing the game; it is why he introduces obstacles that make it harder for him to win. He is balancing the scales, as it were, to make the game more interesting. In the end, I do not even believe he considers winning to be of primary importance. The end-result matters little to him as long as the game itself is entertaining. He is an eternal, immortal being. Nothing is ever entirely lost to him. Once a game is over, he can always start a new one.

A few days ago, I found Fleming going through my papers. I suspect he has found the Arab geographer's manuscript and that he is well-aware of its implications. I fear I have little time left to live and shall bring this package to the Post Office myself today. I implore you to take the necessary steps to remove the Dream Whisperer from his position of power in Janus and to inform our Allies about the threat we are facing.

In the envelope you opened, you will find another, smaller one, addressed to Doctor Mumm. I would be grateful if you could deliver it into her hands.

I wish you strength and fortitude in the trying times that will no doubt follow.

Yours sincerely,

Ove Eliassen
London, 7 January 1921

Visibly affected, M looked up from this last page and reached for the envelope from which he retrieved the smaller one addressed to Rebecca. She hesitated before opening it with trembling fingers. Reading its content, tears sprang into her eyes.

Last Will and Testament of Professor Em. Ove Eliassen

I, undersigned Ove Eliassen, declare I am sound of mind and body. This last will and testament replaces any earlier version thereof.
I hereby declare it is my final wish to leave all my earthly belongings to Doctor Rebecca Mumm, for her to dispose of as she sees fit. It is my sincerest hope that this will allow her to undertake the scientific oceanic expeditions she dreamt of as an aspiring scientist and that she may write the books that will earn her a well-deserved position as a highly-regarded member of Academia in France or any other country fortunate enough to have her.

Ove Eliassen
London, 7 January 1921

After a three-hour drive, they reached the harbour of Kalmar. M's yacht stood out among the other ships. The Brizo was a sleek, white, one-hundred-and-eighty-foot, steel steam vessel, which could accommodate twelve guests and had a crew of ten. Its main deck featured three sitting rooms and a dining room. The head steward led Rebecca and Professor Lagergren to spacious below-deck guest cabins, whereas M had his quarters on the top deck. The exterior woodwork on the ship was teak; all the interior woodwork consisted of rich, red mahogany. Rebecca marvelled at her luxurious cabin, which stretched out over the ship's full twenty-three-foot width. It had two portholes on each side, a double bed, a sitting room with a three-piece leather sofa set, and a private bathroom with water closet, porcelain sink, and bathtub. More comfortable by a stretch than her Glasgow flat, she thought.

Once the Rolls Royce was loaded on the foredeck, secured, and covered in protective tarpaulin, the crew prepared for departure. They left Kalmar around 6 p.m. in complete darkness. It hadn't stopped snowing since they'd left Oskarshamn.

'I always thought Glasgow had a rotten climate,' Rebecca admitted when they convened for pre-dinner drinks in one of the main deck's sitting rooms. 'Yet I must say it's no match for Sweden.'

Lagergren laughed heartily and said, 'Swedes don't even consider this part of the country as the "real Sweden". They think of us southerners as wimps, who moan about the weather when it's barely freezing. You should visit Lapland to experience what a *real* winter feels like.'

Then he turned to M and complimented him on his beautiful ship.

M smiled modestly and said, 'I had the opportunity to acquire her two years ago from the original owner. He felt she was a little cramped and had ordered a larger boat. I'm not much of a sea-enthusiast myself, although I must admit it's a wonderful place for having discreet meetings. At sea, it's impossible to leave the negotiation table in a huff. I've put that quality to good use in the final stages of the Versailles Treaty discussions. Also, the ship doesn't have a telephone. I find that relaxing. I like to pour over written reports and take my time to reflect on them. The telephone is too conducive to spur-of-the-moment-type decisions. It kindles the impulsive side of one's nature, which, in politics, is the worst possible trait a decision-maker can have. If I'd received the horrible news about the Dream Whisperer in my London office, I might have been tempted to pick up the phone and give orders immediately. Now, we have time to think the matter through. I propose we brief Professor Lagergren over dinner on what happened since the unfortunate events at Zoetevoorde in 1916 and take advantage of the tranquillity of the night for further reflection. We can share our thoughts over breakfast tomorrow morning.'

32

R.M.S. Berengaria, Atlantic Ocean

Saturday, 12 February 1921

Fleming peeked at his five cards and gave the other three players at the table a broad grin.

'Gentlemen, the gods smile upon me,' he declared.

He took a crocodile-leather cigar case from his pocket and slid out a seven-inch *Hoyo de Monterrey Double Corona*. He smelt the *puro*, taking in its robust, beefy aroma, and used his cutter to make an opening at the cigar's head. Then he put the *Monterrey* in his mouth and took a draw before lighting it to check whether it wasn't too tightly rolled. Satisfied, he lit a wooden match and toasted the cigar's foot, not letting the tip of the flame touch the oily wrapper while rotating the *Habano* between his fingers. When the end began to glow, he took a series of small puffs. Fleming tilted back his head and let the smoke curl escape from his lips ever so slowly, rolling the subtle taste of roasted wood and hickory around in his mouth. The other men patiently watched the ritual.

'I'd like to open with one hundred pounds, gentlemen,' Fleming said.

'Too rich for my blood,' the thick-set man on his left declared, folding his cards.

The two other men called.

'I'll draw one card, please,' Fleming continued, sliding his discarded four of clubs face-down towards the dealer.

He got a queen of spades. The other two drew two cards each.

'I'll raise by another fifty,' Fleming announced.

The next man called. The third man in the game hesitated. His name was Tobias Dolton, and he'd already lost a significant amount of money that evening. They all had — except for Fleming, who was sitting behind a comfortable stack of chips. Dolton was emigrating to the States. His father's textile business had foundered, taking most of his inheritance with it. He'd hoped to supplement his dwindled capital with some gambling gains during the crossing. Dolton had fared poorly. Except for some family jewels and a satchel with antique gold coins he'd left in his cabin, his entire fortune sat on the table. Of his original fifteen hundred pounds, he had only one hundred and twenty left. A pittance. He should have walked away from the table after his first few losses, but he'd been hell-bent on recuperating them and dug himself deeper in the hole. The story of his life, he thought grimly. Dolton looked at his hand. It was the best he'd held all evening: four nines.

'I'll go all in,' he decided and pushed all his remaining chips to the centre of the table, 'and raise you to two-twenty.'

'I'll see you,' Fleming answered without hesitation. 'How about you, Mister Honeysett?'

Abbott Honeysett owned a meatpacking plant in St. Louis, Missouri. Money was no object to him — but he hated losing it, as he'd been doing all night. He suspected Fleming of cheating, although he had no idea how. He'd been looking at his opponent's hands for the last five games and was none the wiser. Fleming made him shudder. The Brit had an inscrutable face, oozed self-confidence, and his eyes, well, his eyes were just plain strange. One moment, they were a regular grey-blue; the next, they were tinged with a red gleam. It was spooky as hell. He was an arrogant son-of-a-bitch and lucky to boot. A third of Fleming's stack of chips had been Honeysett's two hours ago, and he was lusting for pay-back. Honeysett happened to have the hand for it: three kings and two sixes.

'I'm already in for one-fifty, might as well go the whole nine yards,' the American said with a shrug, pushing his chips towards the middle.

'Care to show us what you've got?' Fleming asked.

Honeysett laid out his Full House on the table and looked Fleming defiantly in the eye.

'I'll do better than that,' Dolton announced, showing off his Four of a Kind.

Fleming kept them in suspense for a while and then put four queens on the table. The others groaned. Dolton was wiped out completely; Honeysett had lost three thousand pounds in the course of the evening, and the elderly, obese man, Doctor Seward Paisley, a retired surgeon from Renfrew, another thousand.

Fleming made a show of looking at his watch.

'Gentlemen, it was a pleasure playing cards with you. Alas, as the midnight hour approaches, I'd like to retire for the evening.'

He cashed in his gains. With a bow, he left the Tudor-styled First Class Smoking Room and saluted a few admiring fellow passengers, who'd been following the high-stakes game from nearby tables.

Fleming climbed the stairs to the Upper Promenade Deck. He was only wearing his evening jacket, and it was freezing. Fleming didn't seem to mind as he walked in the open air on the starboard side towards the stern. Festivities in the Ball Room were still going strong, he noticed, looking through the windows. There were at least thirty couples on the dance floor, showing off their best twists and shakes in time with the intoxicating ragtime rhythms. Most of them had drunk more than their fill of the free-flowing alcohol on board — a lot of the American passengers made the nine-day trip between the States and Europe mainly for the availability of booze. Since the beginning of last year, the Volstead Act prohibited the production, sale, and use of alcoholic beverages in the United States. Party-animals and shipping companies alike had quickly discovered that selling and drinking liquor was perfectly legal outside the three-mile territorial limit.

Fleming took his time smoking his cigar, looking at the stars. It reminded him the time window for the Outer Gods' return was closing. Another eight months and the opportunity would be lost for several millennia. He looked at forever-winking Algol in the constellation of Perseus. The star had puzzled astrologers and astronomers since its discovery until forty years ago. Then they believed to have established that Algol was an eclipsing binary star system, which explained the variations in its light intensity. The Dream Whisperer knew it was, in fact, a giant triple-star system. The orbital plane of two of those stars contains the line of sight to Earth, resulting in the observation of eclipses occurring roughly every two years. The eclipses did, however, not matter at all. They weren't what made Algol so special. There were plenty of triple-star systems in this universe. The reason why Algol was key to the return of the Outer Gods was its unique magnetic cycles generating huge x-ray and radio-wave flares. When these were perfectly in sync with those of their unseen counterparts in the Outer Gods' universe, a gate between the two worlds could be forced to open. That was the real significance of the Pythagorean concept of the *Music of the Spheres*. Typically, humans were unable to grasp it and lost themselves in fanciful theories.

These trips across the Atlantic had been a regular feature for the last year and a half. Fleming's hands-on approach to managing Janus's American branch required him to spend eight months per year across the pond. The Dream Whisperer had been carefully covering his tracks, making sure Janus could chalk up several notable successes.

During his tenure, Janus had destroyed four Cthulhus on American soil and five more elsewhere. The Dream Whisperer knew this left only seven intact Sleeper sites in the entire world — one of them deep under the sea. A couple more successes and it would become impossible to assemble a complete Cthulhu quintet to open the gate for the Outer Gods' return ever again.

He helped organise raids on the outskirts of New Orleans and Tampa, and also in Innsmouth. These places were hotbeds for Cthulhu cultists and hybrids — people who acquired amphibian traits as they got older. They were the offspring of humans interbreeding with Deep Ones. The Deep Ones lived in the oceans and worshipped Dagon, an old ally of the Dream Whisperer. Many hybrids rotted in secret detention camps, where Fleming's goons interrogated them and subjected them to horrific medical experiments. The Dream Whisperer didn't care. It was a small price to pay to divert any suspicion from him while he was furthering his actual agenda.

To that purpose, he'd been siphoning vast amounts of money into a secret project unbeknownst to M. He limited his direct contacts with M to an absolute minimum, using the intensity of the efforts required for establishing Janus in the USA as an excuse for his protracted absences in Britain. Supervision by the American authorities was almost non-existent after President Wilson collapsed in September 1919. Wilson never recovered from a stroke that paralysed his left side and left him nearly blind. He was in no condition to perform his presidential duties. Nevertheless, Wilson clung on to office with the help of his wife, physician, and a few trusted aides. The last year of his presidency had been shambolic. The economic depression, which started in January 1920, made matters even worse. The Wilson administration was so overwrought it left Fleming entirely unsupervised. In a fortnight, Warren G. Harding would succeed Wilson as the new president of the United States. The Dream Whisperer was confident he could make his next move before Harding knew what was going on.

He also avoided being around Rebecca and Ove, since the Dream Whisperer suspected they'd pick up on inevitable, small changes in Fleming's behaviour. Especially Rebecca knew Fleming far too well to be fooled by his impersonation for a long time, even if he had access to all of Fleming's memories. As luck would have it, a tumultuous love affair with a young sculptress thoroughly distracted Rebecca. The sculptress's name was Phyllis Boyd, and she was specialised in animal sculptures. Last year, Rebecca had liked the small statuettes of a puma and a timber wolf Boyd exhibited in a Glasgow gallery, and the two hit it off immediately. Fleming smiled. Rebecca's infatuation amused him immeasurably. Her lover was high-strung and overly jealous. The sculptress saw rivals everywhere, which regularly led to epic rows. The two couldn't live together because Phyllis was working on a Scottish War Memorial in Edinburgh, and Rebecca was occupied in Glasgow. In early December, relations became so strained Rebecca decided to break off the affair. Phyllis wasn't easy to get rid of. She physically stalked Rebecca in the week-ends and pursued her with tearful telephone calls during worktime. The situation drove Rebecca up the wall, which suited the Dream Whisperer perfectly fine.

Surprisingly, the actual threat to his assumed identity hadn't come from Rebecca. During the Christmas season, he first noticed Ove's aloofness towards him, and he became intrigued. Ove's behaviour was suspicious. The professor was a good-natured, jolly chap, always up for a drink and a chat. Although Fleming avoided extended pub crawls with Ove, they used to spend quite some time together whenever he happened to be in Glasgow. Ove suddenly grew sullen and distant. He started locking his office door when he was out. A few days after New Year, Fleming broke into Ove's office and went through his papers, finding the Arab geographer's journal. The Outer God remembered his stint in the Andaman Islands all too well, although the stranded Arab had escaped his attention. Manifestly, Ove had put two and two together and no longer believed the Dream Whisperer had to obey rules for entering hosts. The logical conclusion was that he'd found out their enemy was possessing Fleming. What followed was inevitable, and the Dream Whisperer had enjoyed it immensely. He walked into Ove's office without knocking and reached across the desk to put his hand on the professor's forehead. That was an unnecessary gesture, but it added drama to the situation — the Dream Whisperer was all for drama. He channelled a stream of devastating images into Ove's mind. His father's disappointment in him when he proved himself unable to go into business for himself. His brothers' contempt as he failed his army physical and opted for useless studies at the university. The enduring quarrels with his sister and her parson husband, who forbade him to enter their house ever again. His physical shortcomings and all the mocking glances and poisonous remarks behind his back from disdainful beauties and their handsome suitors. His failure to see through the Dream Whisperer's deceptions and the weight of his responsibility in Fleming's current plight. The emotional bombardment was shattering, and Ove's heart failed as a result. Dying in the conviction one's entire life had been an abject failure must be the worst of all deaths, the Dream Whisperer reflected with petty glee.

When his cigar was all but smoked, it was a couple of minutes past 1 a.m. Fleming descended the stairs between the Ball Room and the Lounge Room — where a few drunken revellers were lying unconscious in armchairs — to his port-side State Suite on the A Deck. Turning the corner on the A Deck, Fleming noticed puddles on the floor, which was strange as the sea was calm and the decks were dry. His cabin door stood ajar while he clearly remembered locking it going for dinner at the captain's table of the Ritz restaurant. He pushed open the door, cautiously remaining in the doorway.

A hideous being with a creepy deep-sea-fish head sat on the bedroom sofa facing the entrance. It had the body of an enormous, fat conger eel and a scaly, square-built torso with long sinewy arms ending in webbed claws. From its thick lips protruded a mass of stringy feelers. Several rows of needle-thin teeth sparkled in its wide maw. The horror didn't have a nose, and its large, deep-set eyes glowed in the dark. The stench of rotten seaweed and decaying fish in the cabin was overwhelming.

'Dagon? What the hell are you doing in my cabin?' Fleming exclaimed in Ugaritic.

'The real question is: What are *you* doing, Dream Whisperer?' Dagon shot back. 'For the first time in aeons, the stars are right for the Outer Gods' return, yet you chose *not* to act on the moment. Instead, humans massacre the Sleeping Gods and persecute my worshippers. Enlighten me, please, Dream Whisperer, what's going on?'

'Get out of my cabin, Dagon. You don't know what you're talking about,' Fleming replied, not budging from the doorway.

In the blink of an eye, Dagon darted off the sofa, grabbed Fleming by the throat, and dragged him inside, slamming the door shut with his tail. Electricity crackled from his skin, throwing Fleming into spasms.

'Don't try your tricks on me, Dream Whisperer,' Dagon warned. 'They were always useless against me. What are you up to? And don't presume that, because the oceans are my domain, I don't know what's happening in the rest of the world. You've been playing your silly games again as you've always done, haven't you?'

'Let go of me!' Fleming croaked.

'You've been cloaked in human flesh for so long you've forgotten what it is to be a God!' Dagon spat. 'You had *one* mission: Azathoth himself entrusted you with the Outer Gods' return, and you failed. Do you have any idea what awaits you? The Blind Idiot God will pick you apart, atom by atom. In a process lasting for all eternity, He'll disperse your particles over the countless dark stars that comprise his unfathomable being. The pain and suffering will be inconceivable as you are re-absorbed by the mindless entity that once fathered you. Is *that* the price you are willing to pay for your trivial fun and games in this world?'

He threw Fleming to the ground and towered menacingly over him.

'You are Azathoth's first-begotten. You could have ruled over all the Gods as His mind began to fade, and He retired into oblivious sleep at the Void's centre. Instead, your volatile character brought you down to the very fringe of your pantheon — a despised and mocked buffoon, a mere foot wipe of the Gods. You had this opportunity to redeem yourself, and you squandered it.'

'You believe humans are still the primitive, little apes they used to be millions of years ago,' Fleming sneered. 'Look around you, Dagon. This ship can easily cleave your biggest ocean behemoth in two. They have weapons that can destroy a Cthulhu, one of my race's proudest achievements. I've awakened three Sleepers, only to see two of them being ripped apart by the hand of man. All over the world, humans have uncovered and annihilated Sleeper sites. Their species now numbers in the billions, and they're aware of us, matching us in every step we take. I've plunged them into a war the likes of which this world has never seen. Millions have died, and it won't take them but a few years to replace the fallen. Humankind is a virus; it spreads like a disease. We cannot stem the tide of man so easily.'

'You are a disgrace to your kind,' Dagon sighed. 'When my race was washed upon these shores by the Outer Gods' colonising initiative, I was in awe of your kin's capabilities. I gladly subjected myself to them, knowing their power had no bounds. They allowed me to thrive in these rich oceans. For that, they've earned my undying loyalty, and I'm counting the days until their return. You, however, are an abject failure. You've already resigned yourself to defeat. The Gods *will* find a way to return, with or without your help; don't fool yourself into thinking they won't.'

Fleming got to his feet. Internally, he was smiling. That idiot Dagon had taken his bait and was convinced his failure to assemble a Cthulhu quintet wasn't by design but caused by his incompetence. He could now make his next move.

'I haven't given up on my mission, Dagon,' he said. 'There are eight months left to achieve my goals. And I suggest you watch your mouth. You'd best remember who's helping you to swell your ranks.'

Dagon had no reply to that.

Fleming straightened his back and dusted off his sleeves before he continued.

'I want you to know that, in the past months, I've been designing a device that'll allow me to wipe out humankind. After its deployment, I'll have free rein to awaken four more Sleepers without having to fear humans will immediately destroy them. Trust me: The stars favour us. Man is living his final days. Your legions of Deep Ones will come out of hiding and take what's rightfully theirs. My brethren will return as planned.'

Dagon eyed him distrustfully. He knew the Dream Whisperer was all lies, but was he indeed such a fool as to wilfully risk his existence trying to trick the Outer Gods? The fish-god decided to give him the benefit of the doubt. The burden wasn't on *his* shoulders. If the Dream Whisperer failed, on his head be the consequences. Dagon would continue to provide him with every assistance required. No Outer God would be able to infer he hadn't done his utmost to keep their stray sheep on the straight and narrow.

33

Brizo, Malmö Harbour, Sweden

Sunday, 13 February 1921

When they met again at 8 a.m., the skipper was manoeuvring the Brizo into Malmö's harbour. It was a grey day; the lead sky promised more snow to come before noon. The purser had set the breakfast table with porcelain decorated with M's coat of arms, and a diligent waiter was pouring their host's preferred Chinese Oolong tea. Before she moved to Glasgow, Rebecca's breakfasts — if she had any at all — had consisted of a large bowl of coffee and a croissant or a piece of baguette with jam. The British tradition of serving kippers in the morning turned her stomach. She limited herself to some omelette with mushrooms and toast. Lagergren possessed a sturdier constitution and happily allowed the waiter to serve him the full range of the ship's ample breakfast buffet, as did their host.

After they'd cleaned their plates, M looked at his two guests in turn and asked, 'Well, what counsel did the night bring?'

Lagergren had been overwhelmed by the information of the previous evening. The professor had passed a restless night and preferred not to pronounce himself first. He glanced pleadingly at Rebecca.

'We should warn the Americans as Ove urged us to do,' she said. 'We can't allow the Dream Whisperer to appropriate Janus's funds for his designs. Who knows what he's been up to in the past three years?'

M remained sceptical.

'The timing is decidedly unfortunate, though,' he replied. 'Poor President Wilson has been ailing for a long time, and he's on his way out. I haven't yet met his successor, Mister Harding, who'll take up the presidency next month. It's hard to see who'll be willing to take any initiative at all before the new president is firmly in the saddle. And then the question is: What options are open to us to remove the Dream Whisperer from his current position of power? I prefer a solution that'd spare Fleming's life. If we tell the Americans about the situation, they'd probably shoot him on sight. If not, the Dream Whisperer will sense he's been discovered and expedite whatever plans he's been hatching.'

'Yesterday evening, I was startled to hear the Crawling Chaos himself was the enemy Ove and yourselves have been struggling with,' Lagergren confessed. 'I can hardly imagine a more deadly or redoubtable foe. I've come upon that name many times in the most terrible books I've had the displeasure of reading. If even a fraction of what these tomes say about him is true, there's no weapon on Earth that can counteract him.'

'Then what would you suggest?' Rebecca replied, fiercely. 'That we roll over and let him have his wish?'

'No, I meant that trying to capture or kill him by the usual means of science or force, is doomed to fail. We need to choose another path,' the professor said.

'And that is?' M inquired.

'Magic,' Lagergren replied. 'I told you yesterday I've spent my career acquainting myself with the subject, and I believe we may find a solution in that field.'

'Then you'll have to explain to me how magic works, Professor,' Rebecca told him. 'I can't see how potions made of wolf's tooth, hemlock root, shark's stomach, goat's bile, and Jew's liver would help us. Even though I'd love to assist with the latter if considered useful in any way.'

Lagergren laughed softly at the reference to the witches' brew in Macbeth.

'You're right, Doctor Mumm. Potions weren't what I had in mind. You have to understand humans have lumped all kinds of notions together under a single label of "*magic*". True magic has nothing to do with witches' potions or even with obscure alchemical concoctions. In real life, witches combine useful herbal knowledge with superstitious nonsense, just as alchemists mix up sound chemical principles with mystical hocus-pocus.'

'Are you then maybe talking about spells? Is that what magic is about?'

Lagergren sighed, struggling to find words that'd have any meaning at all to a scientific mind like Rebecca's.

'If all you did was read page-long spells or incantations from musty grimoires, the results wouldn't fail to disappoint you, Doctor Mumm. Such spells don't work on others; they only work on yourself.'

Rebecca stared blankly at Lagergren. He wasn't making any sense to her.

'The mage has to reach into his subconscious to perform magic,' Lagergren patiently explained. 'How to get there is entirely up to each practitioner. For some, reciting long spells, endlessly repeating the same mantra, burning candles and incense, or ingesting mind-altering substances are ways to reach this level of the mind. Others can do it purely through meditation or by focusing on one specific point in space — be it a crystal scrying ball or a nail in the wall. It doesn't matter all that much. Each individual can create his specific rites. Anything that works for that particular person is fine. There are no hard and fast rules about how to do it. A creative, supple mind is a great asset, obviously. The objective is to reach a state of deep trance — what some call *"the Gnostic state"* — which gives access to the most profound level of reality, where everything is connected to everything else, and the traditional rules that govern our physical universe don't apply. At that level, there's neither time nor space. Everything occurs at the same moment, and there are no distances. The sorcerer can instantly reach out to anybody and anything — provided he knows the true name of the entity he wants to influence or ask for help. His actions at this most occult level will translate in changes in our environmental reality. Some of these changes will be instantaneous. Others will cause a slow ground wave that will gradually affect the world we're living in and all beings in it.'

'Have you ever experienced this state yourself?' Rebecca asked, always the empirical scientist.

'I understand — more or less — the principles,' Lagergren answered. 'As I said before, I'm more of a theoretician than an actual practitioner. Ove and I have tried many times to reach the Delphic level of our subconscious. Ove was terrible at it. He usually ended up laughing hysterically at himself after a while. I reached the Gnostic state a couple of times, but I was unable to hold on to it for long. It's like walking a tightrope. The skilled adepts keep their balance almost effortlessly for as long as they choose to. Others take a few faltering steps, then inevitably thrash about, and tumble off the rope. However, the short while I was able to stay in this state has convinced me that the primordial level of reality — where the entire universe can be affected by our deepest thoughts — does indeed exist.'

'Do you believe a being like the Dream Whisperer, whose immense psychic power can drive normal humans to madness and even physically destroy them, can be affected in that realm?' M remarked critically. 'I'd think he'd be a peerless adversary there as well.'

'I don't know. We'd have to call in an expert,' Lagergren suggested.

'Do you know anybody who'd qualify?' M asked.

'Humans are usually poorly skilled at this exercise,' Lagergren had to admit. 'There are several alien species that excel at it. Unfortunately, as I understood yesterday, they aren't keen to act as champions or even allies of the human race. I do know of one exceptionally gifted human, and he happens to be a compatriot of yours.'

'I hope you're not referring to that charlatan Crowley. He used to work for the secret service for a while, but I had to let him go. The man is totally unmanageable, and I have my sincerest doubts about his magical abilities,' M grumbled. 'I first met him in a pub. His behaviour was downright weird. He was hopping from table to table and grimaced horribly. Nobody minded him. When I asked a waiter who that buffoon was, he answered me not to mind too much: It was Mister Crowley pretending to be invisible. Apparently, he did it so frequently that everybody had gotten used to his antics.'

Lagergren and Rebecca had to laugh heartily at M's anecdote.

'I've heard of him,' Lagergren sniggered. 'It's not him I had in mind, though. I was thinking of a young and talented artist who currently lives in London. His name is Morris Selman Wheeling. He's well known in certain circles. Still, he's what one would call a struggling artist. His drawings and paintings don't appeal to the current general public's taste. I'm sure he'd be interested if you made him an interesting financial offer.'

'Do you know him personally?' M asked.

'Yes, I've met him a couple of times and exchanged letters with him. He's a nice chap.'

'Well, Professor Lagergren, you have now heard what we're up against,' M said, taking a final sip of his tea. 'The demise of our regretted friend and colleague Eliassen

357

has considerably weakened our team and increased our plight. What would you say about taking your friend's place as the permanent scholar of the occult in the British branch of Janus?'

'A — Are you serious, your Lordship? Considering my age...,' Lagergren stuttered.

He was taken aback by M's sudden proposal. Lagergren was used to working as an independent consultant. What M proposed was an entirely different level of commitment.

'It's not as if we'd require you to jump out of aeroplanes or accomplish any other acts of derring-do, Professor,' M assured him. 'We require your knowledge in the fight against our nemesis. What say you?'

'In that case, I'd feel honoured to join you in this endeavour,' Lagergren beamed. 'Allow me a couple of days to make some arrangements in Gothenburg with my landlady and pack my things. Then I'll gladly join you.'

34

American Janus HQ, Warwick, Rhode Island

Tuesday, 15 March 1921

The American Janus HQ was a white, single-storey building in the middle of the woods, right next to the Spring Greene Burial Ground, near the Occupessatuxet Cove on the Providence River. Providence lay six miles to the north; the nearest town was Warwick, with a population of twenty thousand souls.

In Britain, Glasgow had been chosen as the location of the Janus HQ because the secret service could operate there far from the questioning gazes of uninformed politicians and official bodies. Moreover, Glasgow offered all the facilities and anonymity of a large city and port. As far as Glaswegians were concerned, the HQ building housed a large import-export firm, and they asked no further questions. Similarly, Warwick was far away from Washington, D.C., and its isolated location in the green Rhode Island countryside guaranteed the utmost discretion and secrecy required for Janus's operations.

It came as an unpleasant surprise to the Dream Whisperer that, almost immediately after the new president's inauguration, Janus was up for a review by the US secretary of state, Evan E. Hughes. Fleming had proposed to travel to Washington, yet Hughes insisted on visiting the facilities near Warwick in person. Hughes was a formidable man, who'd been a high-profile anti-corruption attorney in New York before being elected state governor. He was appointed to the supreme court by President Taft and resigned from that position to run as the Republican candidate against Woodrow Wilson in the 1916 presidential elections.

Fleming worried about Janus's future, as Wilson's lofty internationalist ideas were by no means shared by his successor and his team. The ailing Wilson hadn't even succeeded in convincing the US Senate to ratify the Versailles Peace Treaty. The Senate's refusal to let the USA join his brainchild, the League of Nations, had profoundly humiliated the president. International co-operation was at the very bottom of the new government's agenda. Janus might bear the consequences of that policy shift.

When Hughes and his three aides sat down in Fleming's office, the secretary of state didn't mince his words.

'I'll come to the point straight away, Mister Fleming, and I'll be blunt,' Hughes said. 'I've gone through your numbers and reports, and I'm far from impressed. Your operation has consumed fifty-eight million dollars in the previous year, and you've precious little to show for it in return.'

As Fleming wanted to protest, the secretary of state silenced him with one stern look.

'Over eighteen months, only four Ch — .'

Hughes had difficulties to wrap his lips around the outlandish name and tried again.

'Only four Cthulhus have been destroyed on American soil. Already more than four years, one of these creatures is roaming the seas, and you haven't tracked or killed it — talk about ineffectuality! In the meantime, the monster is making an unacceptable number of casualties. It has sunk no less than thirty-eight American cargo ships and four Navy vessels. Hundreds of innocent people have died, and you've done *nothing* about it. You've dispatched four twelve-men-strong teams on numerous wild goose chases within and outside the USA without notable successes. Nevertheless, they've sustained significant human losses. I've done a quick count, and the tally stands at seventeen fatalities.'

Hughes was consulting his papers again.

'The raids on eight coastal towns from Louisiana to Maine have cost another twenty-three lives. And for what? We now detain hundreds of in-bred individuals in secret camps and they're costing the nation thousands of dollars, all without proof these prisoners represent an actual threat to national security. You've acted virtually without over-sight, and the results are abysmal. If an American general had presented us with these kinds of results, we would have fired him on the spot for sheer incompetence.'

Hughes paused for effect, and Fleming knew what was coming next.

'Even if all of these activities were useful and justifi-able — and that is, in my opinion, a big "if" indeed — there's no way, Mister Fleming, they could have cost the taxpayer fifty-eight million dollars. Therefore, I'm asking you to justify immediately the attribution of those funds. Make no mistake about the gravity of this issue. We have severe concerns about potential misappropriation of funds. This government won't hesitate to take legal action against you, even though you're a British civil servant. Am I making myself clear, Mister Fleming?'

Fleming leaned back in his chair and smiled pleas-antly.

'Mister Secretary of State, your questions are per-fectly understandable,' he said, 'and it'll be my pleasure to answer them. First, I'd like to familiarise you with my ac-tual and complete service record. I've been fighting this threat to our nations since the end of 1916. I've eliminated no less than fifty-three Cthulhus, most of them in their un-awakened state. Two of them, I killed in live-combat situations. I'm responsible for the capture and temporary detention of our main enemy, the Dream Whisperer — the only being who, to our knowledge, can awaken the Cthulhus. I've also eradicated untold numbers of nefarious cults all over the world, including the USA. These were all minions of the Dream Whisperer, who assisted him in preparing for the Outer Gods' return. These Outer Gods are unimaginably powerful creatures, for whom we're but specks of dust and whose arrival on Earth would signify the end of humanity.'

Fleming took his time to give his words the necessary weight.

'We are now in the final phase of the struggle for the continued existence of humankind,' he continued. 'No doubt my previous actions have significantly reduced the Sleepers' remaining number. It isn't surprising that, currently, successes are few and far between. All the low-hanging fruit — and, dare I say it, much more — has already been picked. I need to point out that no additional Cthulhus have appeared in our seas since 1917. That is a significant success in itself. It proves my actions have effectively thwarted our foe's intentions. The high casualty rate in our search-and-destroy teams is regrettable indeed. At the same time, it illustrates the danger posed by the legions at the Dream Whisperer's beck and call. We need to obliterate them at whatever cost. The captives made during our raids on American coastal towns are no mere inoffensive, in-bred idiots. These towns were the recruiting grounds for the armies of hell, bent on the destruction of man. By now, the seas teem with this infernal aquatic breed. You can expect them to invade our cities at any moment. Therefore, we vigorously need to cut off their supply of recruits. That's why these raids were not only essential: We need to increase them even further.'

Fleming stood up and pushed back his chair.

He continued while looking down on his guests, 'As far as the one remaining active Cthulhu is concerned: You're more than right to be worried. The creature roams our oceans at unimaginable speeds. Even if we were able to track it, it is by now indestructible. Our heaviest ordnance, our largest bombs are all ineffectual against this being. The only reason why I could defeat the creature twice is that it was still in its vulnerable fledgling state. In the meantime, it's grown to full maturity and has become immune to all of our conventional weapons. That's why we need to upgrade our arsenal with unheard-of weapons — and that, gentlemen, costs money. I've started up a research programme aimed at the creation of an innovative weapon that exploits our opponent's weaknesses. I admit: I didn't consult the previous administration in this matter. You know that, in his final year, President Wilson was in no condition to take on the heavy responsibilities of his office. I've taken the initiative to do what had to be done, whatever the consequences.'

He walked towards the door and invited his guests to follow him, 'If you're kind enough to follow me, I'll show you your tax dollars at work.'

They walked down the hall and stopped at a lift door.

'The first floor, where I have my office, is only the tip of the iceberg. There are several floors underground,' Fleming informed his visitors. 'We have a large library, a detention centre, extensive research facilities, a cafeteria, and living space for all of our staff on these premises. We have a workforce of over two hundred here. We kept the above-ground facility fairly limited for reasons of discretion. We didn't want to arouse suspicion or rumours in neighbouring Warwick. The building doesn't reach above the treetops. All there is to see from the highway to Providence is a small dirt road leading into the woods and ending at a rusty gate. Admittedly, it added to the building's price tag. The grounds are close to marshland. The soil is waterlogged, and the building's lower levels are below the groundwater table. That's why we had to install powerful water drainage pumps.'

The lift stopped at -4. A stark, concrete corridor led to a large hall filled with machinery, where several men in white lab coats were waiting for them.

'I'd like to introduce you to our leading biochemist, Professor Israel Steiner. He's the acting Dean at the New York Homeopathic Medical College, and spends a third of his time at this facility.'

Professor Steiner made a slight bow. He was a diminutive man in his late thirties, who was already balding. His round face, with a full-lipped mouth and protruding eyes behind metal-rimmed glasses, shone with keen intelligence.

'Our British colleagues provided me with a series of Cthulhu-tissue samples,' he started his exposé. 'They collected these samples early in 1917 and kept them in salt water in refrigerated containers all this time. They've allowed us to ascertain the Cthulhu species' alien origin since these tissues are not carbon-based. The tissue analysis report written by Doctor Mumm in Glasgow was comprehensive and identified the presence of compounds containing tungsten, titanium, oxygen, phosphorus, and acidic hydrogens. The samples dissolve in alcohol, which led to the primary assumption that we could successfully attack the creature with projectiles dousing it in large volumes of alcohol.'

The secretary of state nodded. Thus far, he could follow what the professor was saying.

'Apart from issues with the practicality of this approach — the creature lives in the sea: The surrounding water would immediately dilute the alcohol — there's another flaw in this reasoning,' Steiner pointed out. 'It was established that, as the creature gained maturity, it became less and less vulnerable. The two creatures destroyed in action were very juvenile specimens. The samples harvested by Mister Fleming belong to a specimen that had "hatched" — if I may use that term — shortly before large-calibre shells killed it. In the meantime, both the British and US Navies have lost several war vessels to the remaining mature specimen. Their guns and torpedoes were unable to harm the creature in any way. The Cthulhu's maturing process involves profound changes in the biochemical compounds of its tissue. In other words: The study of the juvenile tissue samples available to us doesn't provide us with reliable information about the biochemistry in an adult specimen.'

The professor led the guests to a separate lab. When he opened the door, they saw rows upon rows of Petri dishes.

'While studying the samples at our disposition, we became aware of the surprising fact that the cells in the tissue were somehow still alive,' Steiner said. 'Their development was suspended in the seawater medium. They didn't grow or change, but this was not inanimate tissue. We had no way of knowing how the Cthulhu feeds and which nutrients it requires for its spectacular growth. That's why we proceeded to cut up a tissue sample into tiny pieces and put each of them in differently composed nutrient baths inside separate Petri dishes. For the nutrient baths, we used cocktails of elements naturally found in an oceanic environment. As you can see, we experimented with hundreds upon hundreds of different cocktails and isolated the cultures that reacted well.'

'By "reacted well", you imply they started to grow?' Hughes asked, visibly impressed.

'Exactly,' Steiner replied. 'Of the hundreds of cultures in this room, only four showed any growth at all. Among those four, there was one clear winner, which matched the Cthulhu's growth rate as observed in the wild. Once we'd identified the winning nutrient mix, we produced cultures on a larger scale and observed the changes in the growing tissue samples' biochemistry.'

In the next lab room, they could see how Cthulhu tissue samples were cultivated on a quasi-industrial scale. The largest ones had grown into slabs with an eight-inch diameter.

'As the successful samples grew and aged, we established that significant changes indeed occurred in the cell tissue biochemistry,' Steiner continued. 'Ultra-complex chemical bonds — the nature of which is unseen in Earth's natural environment — developed at a staggering speed. While the result defies our analysis, we could observe a systematic tissue strengthening. The process continued until the cells became indestructible, no matter which level of kinetic energy we applied.'

'In simple terms: They tried to blow it up and failed,' Fleming explained.

'Indeed. Our most extreme experiments in the Nevada Desert involved the use of several tons of TNT,' Steiner acknowledged.

'Not a scratch, not a dent,' Fleming concluded.

'We tried to find another way to attack the full-grown tissue and subjected it to hundreds of chemical substances — all to no avail. Even alcohol, capable of dissolving juvenile tissue, did not affect it,' Steiner went on. 'However, six months ago — while analysing a mature tissue sample — we experienced an accidental short circuit in our measuring apparatus. The tissue sample was briefly subjected to an electric charge and appeared to be slightly affected. This observation led us to further experiments with electricity. We found that, at high voltages, we could inflict substantial damage to the sample.'

'This was the breakthrough we'd been hoping for all these months,' Fleming took over the narrative from Professor Steiner, 'and I called in another team of experts. Please follow me.'

The delegation thanked Professor Steiner for his testimonial and followed Fleming into another room. There, a different team of scientists was waiting for them. One of them was a greying, slender man in his late sixties, with a narrow face, prominent cheekbones, chevron moustache, and wild, blue eyes. He was wearing a heavy rubber suit.

'We needed to weaponise electricity,' Fleming continued, 'and I found the right man to do that. Let me introduce you to Mister Nikola Tesla.'

Tesla was well known to the US secretary of state, who had dealings with him in his capacity of governor of New York. The scientist made a fortune with the invention of his alternating current induction motor and polyphase alternating current patents in the late 1880s. In the next decades, he conducted high-voltage, high-frequency power experiments, working on ideas for wireless lighting and wireless electric power distribution. At the beginning of the century, Tesla built a huge metal tower in Shoreham, New York. He designed it as an experimental wireless transmission station to improve on Marconi's radio-based telegraph system. Tesla's alternative would have allowed the wireless transmission of messages and voice communications to Europe and ships at sea, using the Earth as a conductor for the signals. Nothing came of it. Tesla ran out of funds before he could obtain tangible results, and his banker pulled the plug. The tower was scrapped to pay his debts, and Tesla was left floundering. Fleming's proposal to design an electrical weapon came as a godsend for him, and he'd jumped on it without a second thought.

'Welcome gentlemen,' Tesla greeted them — after all his years in the USA, he still retained a Serbian accent. 'Actions speak louder than words. Instead of going through a boring technical exposé with you, I propose immediately to skip to a practical demonstration of the prototype electrical gun I and my team have developed. This demonstration aims to destroy a mature Cthulhu-tissue sample at a distance of seventy feet.'

Tesla pointed at a concrete pedestal at the other side of the room, which had a large slab of tissue on it. He motioned to his aides, who helped him put on a heavy, metal backpack. A tangle of electrical cables joined it to a large generator. Two assistants screwed a cylindrical glass helmet onto his rubber suit, and Tesla donned heavy rubber gloves. Next, they connected a device that looked like a small anti-tank gun to Tesla's backpack with thick, rubber-insulated wires. Fleming guided his guests to take place behind a thick plate of protective glass. Tesla thumped a red button on the gun, and they heard a high-pitched, whining sound, which quickly turned into a wail. When the noise stopped after half a minute, Tesla shouldered the gun, took aim, and flipped a switch. A blinding burst of electricity crackled from the weapon's business end in an erratically zigzagging beam that hit the mark and then smacked into the wall behind it. It was over in a fraction of a second. The backpack was smoking. Tesla's aides came to his rescue with fire extinguishers and pulled the contraption off his back before it burst into flames. After they'd unscrewed the glass helmet, and the frightened spectators emerged from behind their protective wall, an unfazed Tesla walked them to the concrete pedestal.

'As you can see, gentlemen,' Tesla said, scooping up a handful of black dust from the top of the plinth, 'there's almost nothing left of the tissue sample. The electrical beam thoroughly destroyed it. We're now well beyond our proof-of-concept phase. The device exactly works as I predicted.'

He pulled off his rubber gloves, wiped his brow, and pointed at the smouldering backpack, saying, 'I still need to iron out some design weaknesses. That's a minor issue, which I can solve in a matter of days. The next important step is to upscale the design. My goal is to build an electrical gun that's a thousand times stronger than this prototype. My engineers will mount it on a battleship, which will allow us to transport the gun to a spot where the US Navy can use it in a face-off with the monster. The ship will be a huge generator powering the gun. In principle, the gun can be re-used an unlimited number of times, as long as the generator holds up.'

The secretary of state and his aides were speechless. The demonstration exceeded any expectations they might have had.

Back in Fleming's office, Hughes' combative mood had passed completely.

'As you can see, Mister Secretary of State, I've put Janus's important budgets to excellent use,' Fleming concluded. 'Soon, we'll have a weapon at our disposal that can deal with a threat that was up to now intractable, and we can make our seas safe again. Moreover, this weapon will decisively tilt the balance of power in the post-war world in favour of your country. You'll be the only world power with access to this new technology. It's been developed with American money and with American scientists, so it's rightfully yours to make use of as you see fit.'

'I must say that's a remarkable statement coming from a British civil servant,' Hughes wondered.

'We must build the co-operation between our two nations on fairness, or it won't last,' Fleming went on imperturbably. 'You'll be happy to know I've made contact with Admiral Wilson, Commander of the Atlantic Fleet. We need him to provide us with a vessel we can transform to accommodate an upscaled version of our electrical gun. I'll be travelling to Norfolk, Virginia, to discuss this matter with him tomorrow.'

Hughes took his leave an hour later and parted with Fleming on the best of terms, deeply impressed by what he'd seen. Janus's budget issues were a thing of the past as far as Hughes was concerned.

35

M's Office, London

Thursday, 17 March 1921

M cast a sceptical look at the scruffy young man slouching in one of his office's armchairs. He was in his early thirties and strikingly good-looking, with a full head of brown, wavy hair, an oblong face, and a pouty mouth with full lips. He wore a threadbare herringbone tweed jacket and vest; his shirt collars were ragged; the hems of his trouser legs were filthy, and his shoes had never been polished. The sole of his left shoe had a hole in it the size of a shilling.

Lagergren unearthed Morris Selman Wheeling in a small flat in Bloomsbury, where he lived in bohemian squalor since his return from the western front. Previously, Lagergren had provided M with a folder containing the artist's etchings and copies of three self-published books he'd written on magic. M could appreciate the virtuoso draughtsmanship of the prints. They were mostly self-portraits. Wheeling liked to surround himself with strange objects and animals that undoubtedly all had deeper occult meanings that escaped M — as did the intricate monogram-like line drawings that adorned several of the prints. M found the reading of Wheeling's books tough going. The fellow had an impenetrable style and often relied on obscure aphorisms to convey his clouded ideas.

'Mister Wheeling, thank you for taking the time to visit us,' M welcomed him. 'I assume Professor Lagergren has informed you of our predicament?'

Wheeling nodded imperceptibly but kept his silence.

'Could you share any of your insights on the matter?' M asked, without showing his profound annoyance at his guest's poor manners.

'Your man is fucked,' Wheeling answered, purposefully being rude.

Toffs like Holmes, with their carefully turned phrases and expensive accent, pissed him off no end, and it amused him to get on their nerves.

Lagergren intervened before things could get worse.

'I went through our options with Mister Wheeling, and even though the situation is bad, we concluded there might be ways to remove the Dream Whisperer and save Fleming.'

Rebecca joined the conversation.

'How would you go about it?' she asked.

'And who are you?' Wheeling asked in return.

'Doctor Mumm is a prominent French marine biologist, who's been with the British secret service for years,' Lagergren hastened to reply, with an apologising glance at Rebecca.

'A fucking scientist? That's all we need,' Wheeling snorted.

'I beg your pardon?' Rebecca asked.

'Science won't help your man for shit, lady. Better pack it in and go home for all the good you'll do here,' Wheeling sneered at her.

'Mister Wheeling, you made it perfectly clear you are *not* a gentleman. I'd appreciate it if you at least try to behave like a civil person. If that's beyond your reach, you might as well return to your hovel in Bloomsbury and forget about the stipend you've agreed with Professor Lagergren. I'm sure your creditors will be delighted to learn you've forgone a splendid opportunity to pay them back,' M barked at Wheeling, waving a little notebook. 'I hear the gents at Kiely & Sylvester's are short on patience and long on ways to inflict hurt. One of my men will happily inform them how this meeting went, and no doubt they'll be keen to hear *your* version at your earliest convenience.'

Wheeling sat up a bit straighter and glowered at M.

'What I'm saying is you're facing a tall order, and there's no way traditional science will help you achieve your goal,' he muttered.

'That's why we came to you,' Lagergren interjected, trying to mollify his guest. 'Please, tell Lord Holmes and Doctor Mumm what you told me.'

'The subconscious is the doorway to the Dreamlands,' Wheeling began hesitantly. 'That's my name for the fundamental level of reality — or the "*Gnostic state*" if you want to be pretentious about it. What happens in the Dreamlands has consequences for our reality as well.'

'That's what Professor Lagergren already told us,' M confirmed.

'An able adept can dispense little nudges in the Dreamlands to realise changes in our world. For instance, if a mage wants to get rid of somebody, he'll try to find a way to edit that person out of the Dreamlands' reality. As a result, the subject will lose his foothold in our reality as well and disappear, either by an accident, a disease, violence, or — ideally — by dissolving into thin air. There are two conditions. First, the mage needs to obtain his target's real name to gain power over him. Secondly, the mage's desire to impose his will on the target must be stronger than the target's own wish to hold on to the status quo. Facing an opponent as powerful as the Dream Whisperer, there are limits to what one can do. A full-scale reality edit is most certainly undoable in this case.'

'Then what can you do? How does this "editing" of the Dreamlands' reality work?' Rebecca wanted to know.

'It's hard to put into words. The more I try it, the less sense I'll appear to make to you. It all has to do with channelling will, desire, and fantasy via one's subconscious. It starts with establishing an entity's Dreamlands' address, a location where it can be reached. Basically, the address is a combination of the subject's real name and its coordinates in Dreamlands' space.'

'That almost sounds like geometry, where three coordinates can define the position of any point in Euclidian space,' Rebecca remarked, happy she at least recognised some of the principles in the mage's thought process.

'Yes, well, except that the coordinates in the Dreamlands have nothing to do with Cartesian geometry,' Wheeling said, tempering her enthusiasm. 'Don't ask me to explain Dreamlands' coordinates; I can't find the words for it. They've more to do with emotions and desires, rather than with specific, measurable positions in space vis-à-vis three perpendicular axes. Try to imagine space with forty dimensions. You cannot because you don't have the words to describe the nature of each dimension. Because of this lack of words, you also fail to visualise it. That's what the Dreamlands are like: Its dimensions are different from ours.'

'Mmmm, you almost made sense a moment ago,' Rebecca said with a pout.

'As I travel in the Dreamlands, reaching my destination and influencing it — nudging it — is practically the same thing,' Wheeling tried to explain. 'As I reach my target's coordinates, I'm also altering them. The perception of a thing alters its very nature.'

'How do you do that? That — "reaching" and "altering"?' Rebecca insisted.

'However I want. I use sigils because I find them convenient. They work for me. For somebody else, a different approach might work better. There are no rules.'

'It's all awfully confusing,' Rebecca sighed. 'What are *sigils*?'

Wheeling had to think about how he could explain this. To him, magic was intuitive — it all came naturally, without complex cerebral processes. Putting his approach into words in an easily understandable way was hard for him, even though he'd written several books on the subject. Most people in his circle had high praise for his work, yet he suspected only a tiny fraction among them were able to grasp its true meaning.

'Sigils form a written language,' he said. 'Which means they're a convention, not the thing itself — just as words aren't the things they designate. They're mnemonic tools that help us to understand and denominate what surrounds us. As with words, there's no unique sigil that's "right". When I take a walk in the park, I see trees. At least: *I* do. A German would see *Bäume* and a Frenchman would see...'

'*Arbres*,' Rebecca completed his sentence.

'Right,' Wheeling said. 'These three words are totally unrelated — trees, *Bäume, arbres* — they're completely unlike. Still, they designate the *same* object, and — in their respective languages — they work equally well. The only thing that remains unchanged is the object itself. The English, Germans and French, they all see the same thing, which proves the object isn't the word. Words help us to make sense of the world we're living in, but they're not the world itself. Words are conventions, and in writing, they're constructed with other conventions: letters. Letters aren't sounds; they're representations of sounds. Different languages not only use different words for the same object; they also use different modes of representation for the sounds that make up these words. Our Roman alphabet differs from the Greek, the Cyrillic, the Hebrew, or the Arabic one. In the end, it doesn't matter because they're all accepted conventions. Sigils somehow fulfil the same role.

They identify the entity one wants to do one's bidding. A sigil is the entity's detailed description within its Dreamlands' context. It also describes what you want it to do — or what needs to happen to it.'

'That sounds absurdly complicated. To do that in English or French, you'd have to fill an entire library,' Rebecca marvelled.

'Remember that a sigil is merely a mnemonic tool,' Wheeling pointed out. 'It concretises your will, your desires, your vision. It's your subconscious that imbues the different elements of a sigil with meaning. It works both ways. The writing down of a sigil, its very construction, forces your subconscious to define in great detail what its purpose is. However complex one's designs may be, the sigil itself may be relatively simple. You've probably seen illusionists at work in the theatre, who perform incredible memory feats. For instance, they can remember every card's position in a deck after flipping through it only once. For that trick, these parlour magicians construct a memory palace where they allocate every object a room and then define a path to reach that room. A sigil does the same thing. It's the key to the memory palace of a subconscious will or desire.'

'I think I've seen some of those sigils in your works of art. They're made up of intertwined Roman letters,' M remarked.

'Yes, mine usually are,' Wheeling agreed, 'because that works for me. Others might use something completely different. I make them up along the way, as *you*'ve done at least once in your lifetime.'

'I'm not sure what you mean?' M said, sounding confused.

'Your family doesn't belong to ancient nobility, does it?' Wheeling asked M. 'You are the 1st Earl Holmes and you were ennobled for your services to the Crown as the first of your line. On that occasion, you had to design your coat of arms. The purpose of a coat of arms is to let the world know who you are, what you stand for — your ideals and principles, your goals in life — why you were ennobled, what makes you exceptional. All this information is translated into codified designs that make up your coat of arms. In other words: Your coat of arms is a sigil. It gives a complete description of who Lord Holmes is, and what he aims to achieve.'

'Yes, I see. This example helps me to understand better what you've been saying. Thank you,' M said.

'Now, before I can even begin to do anything, I need your enemy's true name,' Wheeling continued. 'Without it, there's no way I can locate him in the Dreamlands, let alone exert some influence over him.'

'The problem is that the Dream Whisperer goes by so many different names,' Lagergren clarified. 'I have to find the most ancient sources that mention this being, and I need to certify our enemy hasn't tampered with them. I'll have to discard all books written by humans. Our kind came to the stage so late that anything *we* have written down is no more than unreliable hearsay. I either need to find manuscripts belonging to species that drifted into our reality at the same time as the Outer Gods or else get access to whatever other types of memory carriers they use to store their information.'

'It's a pity the elves have left Earth,' M said, 'They were a reasonably reliable source of information — and they didn't like the Outer Gods either. I'll ask around; I maintain several contacts with other species. They might not *all* side with the Dream Whisperer.'

'What'll you do once you've obtained the Dream Whisperer's true name?' Rebecca asked.

'I'll visit the Dreamlands and try to gauge his strengths and weaknesses,' Wheeling replied. 'I'll need to tread carefully since I don't want to make him aware I'm looking for him. Depending on what I learn, I'll establish a strategy to separate the Dream Whisperer from your man Fleming. I've got a couple of approaches in mind, but I need more intelligence first.'

Outside, Lagergren asked Wheeling, 'What has gotten into you? Why did you have to be so rude to his Lordship?'

'I couldn't help myself,' Wheeling said. 'It's upper crusters like Holmes who got poor buggers like me killed in their thousands during the Great War. I can't stand them, and I've earned the right to have my say. *I* am the one who was knee-deep in mud, gassed, and shot at — *he* was not.'

36

Oval Office, White House, Washington D.C.

Thursday, 24 March 1921

Warren Harding, the twenty-ninth president of the USA, was still a bit uncomfortable in his new surroundings. His candidacy had been a long shot, and nobody was more surprised than he to find himself the Republican nominee for president. It took the convention no fewer than ten ballots to agree on his nomination. All his life, Harding had been living in rural Ohio. His home stood in Marion, an insignificant town with a population of not even thirty thousand, where he owned the local newspaper. Even after his nomination, he never seemed to believe in his chances of winning the election. His Democratic opponent, James M. Cox, criss-crossed the country by train to gain support for his programme, which consisted of a continuation of the incumbent President Wilson's policies. As governor of Ohio, Cox earned the reputation of being an effective, progressive reformer. During the campaign, Harding didn't budge from his front porch and won the election by a landslide anyway. His one campaign promise was '*a return to normalcy*'. The average American was sick and tired of America's costly and bloody meddling in European affairs. Voters had little interest in American statesmen taking up the role of world leader: They wanted to go back to things as they were before the war. Harding's down-to-earth, conservative attitude skilfully tapped that vein of discontent with current policies and got him the ticket to the highest office.

His presidency was only twenty days old when his secretary of state presented him with a report he found difficult to digest.

'Well, that was a humdinger of a report you wrote last week, Mister Hughes,' Harding began, addressing his secretary of state, who was sitting across the desk from him. 'Truly instructive, I must say. I learnt that — apart from the SIS, the OP-20-G, and MI-8 — we have yet another spook department called *Janus*. And even better: It's so secret even Congress isn't aware of it, and it's spending taxpayers' money as if there's no tomorrow. How did you even know the darned thing existed?'

'My predecessor informed me of the agreement with Great Britain and France to set up such a secret service. I investigated it immediately because, as you said, Mister President, it's been spending a surprising amount of money, and supervision by the previous administration lacked entirely,' Hughes replied.

'And good ole Wilson didn't think it necessary to ask for approval, neither from the Senate nor from the House of Representatives? That's a doozy!' Harding cried out. 'Now, I'm saddled with this sheisty thing that's supposed to hunt monsters and aliens. I couldn't believe my eyes reading it!'

'Well, you can hardly blame Wilson,' Hughes pointed out. 'It isn't something you'd want to advertise in the newspapers. The other nations all have similar organisations, and their Parliaments have been left in the dark as well. Imagine the panic and the outrage if we told our voters the truth.'

'The truth? I don't know what to believe,' the president said, shrugging off Hughes' argument. 'Do we have any proof at all that these so-called monsters Janus is pretending to hunt are anything more than the figment of a diseased mind?'

'I've been told there are stacks of secret files, which accumulated over the last century and a half. They corroborate the existence of alien species on American soil,' Hughes said. 'I've also seen pictures taken by a US Navy aeroplane of a sea monster ripping apart one of our battleships. We've got several detention camps, in Louisiana, Mississippi, Virginia, and New England, filled to the brim with people that look more like fish than humans. So, yes, Mister President, I'm convinced there are plenty of reasons to believe there's some truth to it all.'

'And what about this electrical gun business? That's where the bulk of our taxpayers' money went to, right?' Harding asked.

'I must admit I was impressed by the demonstration Mister Tesla gave me,' the secretary of state said. 'I knew him from my days as governor of New York. He's a brilliant man — difficult to handle but a true genius. I believe his technology will give us the military edge.'

Harding looked as if he were about to have a seizure.

'Are you completely bughouse, man?' he exclaimed. 'Have you forgotten the *one* campaign promise I made, and that got me elected? I promised a return to normalcy to the voters! I committed myself to a disarmament programme, to cutting the defence budget back to the size it was before the war! Not to enter into any new arms race! I'm working my ass off to organise an international conference next fall. I hope to convince the major naval powers to reduce their military fleets. And you'd want me to go on a spending spree, installing new-fangled guns on our battleships that'd scare the bejesus out of every single nation in the world? That's insane; it's gotta stop right now!'

The secretary of state shifted uncomfortably in his chair. He'd expected the president to be upset by the suggestion to push a new armament programme. On the other hand, he wasn't much of a believer in America's ability to convince other nations to reduce their fleets. It was true that the Europeans were crippled by war debts — most of them to the USA. But if Harding expected Great Britain to reduce its fleet, the very thing that ensured its might as a world power, that seemed incredibly naive to Hughes. It painfully showed the president's total lack of experience in international politics.

'We at least need to be able to rid ourselves of the threat this sea monster is posing to our ships, Mister President,' Hughes argued. 'We've already lost several merchant vessels and battleships to it. That cannot continue. We can't hurt it with conventional weapons. I think the electrical gun is the only viable solution available to us. Mister Fleming has already made a deal with Fleet Command. He has obtained a battleship to equip it with an upscaled version of the prototype I've seen in Rhode Island.'

'Sure he has!' the president raged. 'Fleet Command must have thought his proposal was the cat's pajamas! Did you think the top brass were going to applaud me while I reduce their budgets? Did Fleet Command contact the secretary of the Navy or the secretary of War before agreeing to give this Fleming a battleship? The hell they did! They simply want to pre-empt my plans to cut their wings! They'll have to learn that it's us politicians who call the shots! *We* make the rules! *We* are the policy-setters, and they'll have to do as they're told! And if they don't like it, they can go looking for another job! And as far as this Janus-thing is concerned: If that Limey thinks he can go behind my back and do whatever he wants, he's got another thing coming! I'm done with it! I'm pulling America out of Janus! I'm not having any of it! If we need to deal with alien threats on American soil, we'll do so all by ourselves. We don't need snooty foreigners to tell us how to do it and then let us foot the bill!'

Harding finished his rant, red in the face and panting.

'How do you propose we do *that*, Mister President?' Hughes cautiously asked, pulling an official document from his briefcase. 'I've got the original agreement signed by President Wilson right here. The commitment is unusually clear. It won't be easy to work our way out from under the promises your predecessor has made to Britain and France.'

'Haven't you heard a word I've said, Hughes?' Harding shouted. 'As far as I'm concerned, this document doesn't even exist! Wilson didn't have the authority to sign it without the approval of Congress! It's null and void! And what will the others do about it? It isn't as if they can feed it to the press to make an international stink about it. They don't want their constituents to know about Janus either! So we sit around the table with them and tell them where it's at. Janus is dead, and so is the electrical gun. Got it?'

37

Great Queen Street, London

Tuesday, 12 April 1921

M's Rolls Royce drove down Drury Lane and then took a left on Great Queen Street. It passed the Freemason's Hall of the United Grand Lodge of England and stopped in front of an antique shop called *'Deere Antique Furniture'*. It was a stately white building adorned with four Corinthian columns. When the driver opened the car door, M and Lagergren stepped out into the chilly fog.

As he'd promised, M tried to get in touch with his contacts to find out whether they had any information on the Dream Whisperer's true name. Just as Fleming experienced before him, none of his contacts were forthcoming. At best, they made some vague promises; most of them denied having any helpful information whatsoever. It irritated M having to spend so much time on this wild goose chase while other sensitive matters required his attention. The situation in Ireland was quickly spiralling out of control. Only last Tuesday, the Irish Republican Army ambushed a train carrying British troops near Killarney, killing nine British soldiers and three innocent civilians. The press was in an uproar about the 'Headford Ambush'. M hoped the owner of this antique shop would be of some assistance. It was a long time since he'd last seen him.

An elegant woman greeted them in the vast salesroom chock-a-block with furniture ranging from the Queen Anne style to late Regency and early Victorian.

'Mister Deere is expecting us, I assume,' M said.

'He certainly is, your Lordship,' the woman answered with a smile. 'You know your way.'

M nodded curtly and walked without hesitation to the back of the room, where he opened a door on the right.

Lagergren gasped entering the next room. It was filled with artefacts, none of them more recent than the Early Dynastic Period in Ancient Egypt. Some of them he could identify, like a Mesopotamian Proto-Elamite copper sculpture of a horned demon with the wings of a bird of prey, a gold-inlaid stone sculpture of a muscular being with a human face and reptilian skin from Bronze-Age Persia, or a Neolithic Early-Cycladic marble sculpture of a wide-hipped, naked woman. Others were alien to him, including a few that looked precisely like the bas-reliefs found at the Sleeper sites. Lagergren was gaping at a larger-than-life stone sculpture of a four-winged female with lion legs, a fearsome head with terrible eyes, and a grinning mouth full of pointy teeth when a man appeared to greet them.

'Holmes, welcome, it's been a while. Who's your friend?'

M introduced Lagergren, who was fascinated by their host. Deere was a tall man, with broad shoulders and a rough face with a crooked nose. He had a well-groomed, white beard and piercing, blue eyes. At first, Lagergren failed to notice Deere's prosthetic right hand. The prosthesis wasn't the typical clumsy affair one often saw on war amputees. It was a remarkably life-like mechanical marvel, which allowed Deere to move each of his artificial fingers separately. With each motion, Lagergren heard a soft buzzing and whirring, as if minute electric motors coordinated the hand's delicate movements.

'It's considered bad form to stare,' Deere told Lagergren with a mischievous grin.

'I'm sorry, I couldn't help myself,' the professor apologised, a bit flustered. 'How did you lose your hand if I may inquire?'

'A big bad wolf bit it off,' Deere replied while making a clawing motion, and then he turned again to M, 'What brings you here, dear friend? Your secretary wasn't quite clear.'

As they walked to Deere's office in the back of the room, M and his companion explained what they needed.

'I've got plenty of old books and manuscripts that date from before you folks lost your tail,' Deere said, making a broad gesture towards the vast library behind his desk. 'I doubt whether you'll find what you're looking for in there. Although they may be time-worn, they're not written by people who experienced the Big Piercing that brought the Outer Gods here.'

With Deere's permission, Lagergren took a few volumes from their shelves and leafed through them.

'Even if the information were in here,' he sighed, 'I wouldn't be able to read it. I've never seen these types of script. Unless you also have a Rosetta Stone, I'm afraid it's hopeless. Can *you* translate them?'

'Most of them, yes,' Deere answered. 'There are over seven thousand volumes. How much time have you got?'

'You've read them all over the ages, Deere,' M insisted. 'Can you remember anything that might be useful to us?'

'I told you. I don't think there's anything in there. To most of the species that have been swept along the Outer Gods forever remained a mystery.'

'We have hundreds of pictures, taken in Sleeper sites, of texts cast in stone, written by the Outer Gods,' Lagergren told him. 'We've had dozens of linguists looking at them, and we're still none the wiser. Probably, the true names of all the Outer Gods are somewhere in these pictures, if we could only recognise them.'

'I can't read their scribbles either,' Deere confessed. 'I was born long after they left. And anyway, for your purposes, you'd also have to know how to *pronounce* the name. Even if you recognise the characters used by the Outer Gods, it won't bring you much further along.'

They sat for a while in silence.

'I can think of only two peoples that have the information you're looking for. They're both able to get into anybody's mind, including those of the Outer Gods, and they're truly eternal. Time means nothing to them,' Deere said.

He stood up to fetch a modified Marconi radio receiver from a closet and put it on his desk. He plugged in the earphones and fiddled with the wavelength and frequency dials.

'Here, listen,' he said, offering the earphones to his guests. 'What you hear sounds like white noise, only it isn't. It's the endless chatter of a species that lives on wavelengths between fifteen and twenty miles, and frequencies around ten kilohertz. Those radio waves go right through us, and so do these creatures. They know everything about every being that lives or has ever lived on this planet. They form a hive mind; not a scrap of information ever gets lost. They were already around long before the Outer Gods broke through.'

'Interesting,' M said. 'And how do we get information from these beings?'

'That's the problem. You don't,' Deere answered. 'As far as I know, information flows only in one direction. From us to them.'

'So this is useless,' M concluded.

'Yes, it is,' Deere admitted. 'I needed you to hear this, to make you understand how limited your options are. Because you're not going to like what comes next.'

'Let's hear it anyway,' M said resignedly.

'When the Outer Gods arrived on Earth, they brought a slave people with them that performed all kinds of menial services for them. It wasn't so much a people as a single individual. It's a fungus. It establishes itself in the soil in the form of a mycelial mat. The mycelia form a huge network that grows sentient fruiting bodies that can take diverse forms depending on the duties they're required to perform. It's also an unimaginably vast data repository. The being is called the Qohl'Hotl.'

'And this is a species we can communicate with?' M asked.

'Yes, it has strong telepathic abilities,' Deere confirmed.

'This — this Qohl'Hotl knows the Dream Whisperer's true name?' Lagergren wanted to know.

'It knows everything there is to know about all of the Outer Gods,' Deere assured them. 'It lived in a sort of symbiotic relationship with them, and it read their minds like a book. The Outer Gods could keep no secrets from their slave. Did you mention pictures taken in the Sleepers' cradles? I've seen several of those locations. The walls are covered with bas-reliefs representing the Outer Gods' history. The Qohl'Hotl sculpted all of those based on its knowledge of its masters.'

'The Qohl'Hotl is the Sleeper sites' architect?' Lagergren exclaimed.

'Yes, it is,' Deere said.

'If it's so close to the Outer Gods, why would it be willing to share any information about them with us?' M asked.

'Because it was betrayed and almost killed by the Dream Whisperer,' Deere explained. 'When the Outer Gods decided to leave Earth, they wanted to make sure they could return if they so desired. They designed a creature that could open inter-universal gateways and built a large number of them. To keep these beings safe, the Outer Gods commanded the Qohl'Hotl not only to erect sanctuaries all over the world; they also demanded their servant guarded all of them. The Qohl'Hotl grew its mycelial mat to such an extent that it covered most of the globe. It sprouted fruits to construct the buildings, and then, in every Sleeper location, it grew still other fruits that acted as formidable guards.'

'That means that, originally, the Dream Whisperer wasn't in charge of the protection of the Sleeper sites?' Lagergren asked.

'Correct. That task was confided to the Qohl'Hotl because it had the ability to be everywhere at the same time,' Deere said.

'I can imagine that must have bothered the Dream Whisperer immensely if he had no intention to let the Cthulhus open the gates for the other Outer Gods' return,' M remarked.

'Exactly. I wasn't aware of the Dream Whisperer's agenda until you told me what has occurred in the past five years,' Deere agreed. 'His actions always puzzled me. Now, it all makes sense.'

'Our teams have never encountered fungous guards at the Sleeper sites, which means the Dream Whisperer must have found a way to rid himself of the Qohl'Hotl,' M supposed.

'You can say that again,' Deere grinned. 'Sixty-six million years ago, less than a century after the Outer Gods left, he created a cataclysmic event that scorched the entire mycelial mat of the Qohl'Hotl to a cinder. What saved the Qohl'Hotl was its enormous size. It couldn't be destroyed in the blink of an eye. It took several years to burn its root system on Earth, which gave it ample opportunity to expand its mycelia through a number of inter-dimensional cracks before severing its connection with its doomed parts on this planet.'

Deere lit a thin cigar and then continued with a twinkle in his eyes, 'By the way, the Dream Whisperer's initiative caused a mass extinction that wiped out three quarters of all plant, animal, and extra-terrestrial species on the planet. All large dinosaurs disappeared. Small, furry mammals survived and took over the world. You have the Dream Whisperer to thank for creating the ecological niche that, in the end, allowed humankind to evolve.'

'Well, I'm sure the father of humankind hasn't finished yet making us pay for that privilege,' M replied. 'But, once more, you brought us to a dead end. The Qohl'Hotl is nowhere to be found on Earth anymore. We've never made any serious attempts at exploring the cracks, and there are so many of them. How can we even hope to speak to this being?'

Deere got up and led them down a staircase to his basement, past a large boiler to a locked room. He took a key from his belt and swung open the heavy iron door. When he'd switched on the light, they were standing in a bare room with a single piece of furniture. A large, ornate mirror leaned against a wall. Deere put his hand through the mirror's surface, which seemed to liquefy, and softly spoke, eyes closed, a series of unintelligible phrases.

'This mirror has allowed me to travel the cracks for centuries now,' Deere told his guests after finishing his mumbling.

'You expect us to step through the looking glass?' Lagergren asked, amazed.

'I'd offer you a rabbit hole if I had one,' Deere joked. 'But, yes, the looking glass will have to do.'

'The Qohl'Hotl is on the other side?' M asked cautiously.

'I've arranged it so, and it'll certainly answer your questions. You need to be aware there's a price. There's always a price,' Deere warned them.

M became even more suspicious.

'What's the price it'll ask?'

'It won't *ask* anything. It'll simply *take*,' Deere said. 'I told you it's a strong telepath. The moment you step through that mirror, it'll immediately read your mind. It'll know all about you. It'll be aware of all your secrets, all your memories, your deepest desires, your most heartfelt regrets.'

M's face turned pale.

'I'm carrying all of Britain's state secrets of the last few centuries in my head!' he whispered hoarsely. 'If I were to step through the mirror, I'd be committing treason. I can't do this.'

'My secrets are far more trivial than yours,' Lagergren said, without thinking twice about it. 'I'll go.'

'Then that's settled,' Deere concluded. 'Before you embark on your journey, I'd like you to put this on.'

Deere put an overall with a hood in Lagergren's hands.

'Upon your return, you'll be covered in spores,' Deere warned the professor. 'The Qohl'Hotl won't miss a trick to return to this world. We'll burn the overall and give you a thorough rinse.'

M shook Lagergren's hand and said, 'Thank you for doing this, Professor. I appreciate this more than I can say, and I wish you the very best of luck.'

After discarding his clothes and putting on the overall, Lagergren slowly approached the mirror. He tentatively touched the mirror's surface with his left hand's fingers. The surface felt cold and gave way as if made of quicksilver. After one look back and a thumbs up from Deere, he stepped into the looking glass.

Briefly, it felt as if he was drowning. As he opened his eyes again, he stood on a hilltop overlooking an empty plain. Two moons lit up the cloudless night sky. One of them was much larger than ours; the second was smaller and coloured a deep brick red. Lagergren didn't recognise any of the constellations in the sky. Behind him, the opening he'd stepped through remained a silvery shimmer. He looked around and noticed something was growing from the ground in front of him. At first, it was a greyish, shapeless blob. As it increased in size, it took a human shape. After a couple of minutes, Lagergren was staring at his lookalike. It was entirely dressed as he'd been before donning the overall.

'*Välkommen*, Professor Lagergren.'

Although the replica moved his lips, Lagergren heard the Swedish words in his head. It was speaking with his voice.

'How are you?' the voice continued in the same language.

'I think you already know,' Lagergren answered.

'You are the first human I have the pleasure to meet,' the Qohl'Hotl said. 'I've heard about your species from earlier visitors. Nothing surpasses an actual encounter, though. So many fresh data. Delightful. And you are such a beautiful specimen too. You carry the knowledge about so many cultures and so much history in your head.'

Lagergren had the feeling he was an insect under a microscope. He expected an entomologist's pin piercing his spine at any moment

'I must admit I'm fascinated by sexually reproducing species. I've never had the pleasure to multiply myself in that fashion,' the voice went on as if it hadn't picked up on his guest's discomfort.

'It's an overrated experience,' the professor answered.

'Is that why you're attracted to specimens belonging to your own sex?' the voice asked innocently.

'I don't want to be rude, but there's a specific reason I made this journey through the cracks to visit you,' Lagergren said, trying to change the subject.

'We share a common enemy,' the voice confirmed. 'Even though I see he's moderated his manners considerably since he disposed of me.'

'He plays games with us, like a cat with a mouse. All fun ends when the mouse dies,' Lagergren said.

'I can imagine,' the voice agreed. 'The Dream Whisperer, as you call him, was already bored stiff a few years after his kin left Earth. Inhabiting carnivorous dinosaurs gets old awful quickly. He always needed something new to occupy his over-active mind.'

'We cannot defeat him in our reality. That's why we want to go into the Dreamlands to find a chink in his armour. We need his real name to do that. Can you please help us?' the professor pleaded.

'A bold plan. I could do more than that,' the Qohl'Hotl boasted. 'I can give you a full understanding of the Outer Gods, although I'm afraid that wouldn't do much good.'

'Why is that?' Lagergren asked.

'It would drive you to despair, and you'd be stark raving mad after a short while. I honestly wouldn't want that on my conscience,' the fungus declared. 'I'll give you the Dream Whisperer's true name, though. Also, I see you're seeking to complete the list of Sleeper sites. I can help you with that as well. You've missed thirty-eight of them, although I'd be surprised if all of them still existed today. Earth has an active crust — I tried to explain it to my masters. Of course, they wouldn't listen, as one could have expected. I'll also teach you to read my masters' script and speak their language. Mind you: It'll be rather taxing. So I'd advise patience and moderation. The texts in your possession give only a superficial insight into the Outer Gods' nature, though I may have included a few helpful warnings.'

Lagergren felt the information filling his head, and it dizzied him. When he saw clearly again, the replica had shrunk like a deflated balloon, and it diffused a musty smell. The air was thick with spores. The audience was over.

Lagergren staggered back through the mirror. Deere immediately made him put his overall in a tray and then dumped it in his boiler's fire. Next, he made the professor stand in a deep basin, doused him with water and scrubbed him with a foul-smelling substance. Deere burnt the towel he'd used to dry his guest and added a pesticide to the basin's content before boiling it.

'Better safe than sorry,' Deere said. 'The Qohl'Hotl might present itself as a reasonable chap, but it could easily overrun and control this planet. Best to keep it out.'

After Lagergren had related his encounter with the alien fungus, M was satisfied.

'I should have looked you up much sooner,' he admitted to Deere. 'It would have been of tremendous help if we'd possessed the complete list of Sleeper sites right from the beginning. I must be getting old.'

'Lately, I've been occupied travelling the cracks almost full-time. It would have been a lucky strike if you'd found me in my shop. Fleming tried several times, I heard, but Herja,' Deere pointed upstairs, where the lady in the salesroom was, 'she sent him packing each time.'

'Oh, did she now?' M asked, as if that piece of information surprised him.

'You know full well there's no love lost between them after what Fleming did to her sister Sigrun,' Deere reminded M.

'Well, *she* was the one plotting an invasion of the Shetland and Orkney Islands, remember?' M pointed out while taking his leave.

Back on the sidewalk, Lagergren asked, 'That lady in the salesroom... Was she— Is she—?"

'A valkyrie?' M finished his sentence. 'Yes, indeed, she is. Not a lady to be trifled with, I'd say. We caught her on a good day.'

'What happened to her sister?'

'She's at the bottom of the sea, together with her small Norwegian invasion army of five hundred berserkers and twenty-five ice giants. Valkyries are notoriously bad swimmers.'

38

M's Office, London

Thursday, 14 April 1921

Wheeling grunted approvingly when Lagergren told him the Dream Whisperer's true name.

'I can go to work now,' he confirmed. 'I'll hear around, speak to my contacts in the Dreamlands. It shouldn't be too hard to trace a heavy hitter like him.'

Rebecca coughed. She knew Wheeling didn't like scientists, but she had to ask.

The moment he looked in her direction, she said, 'I'd like to go along with you to the Dreamlands if that's at all possible.'

Wheeling sceptically eyed Rebecca.

'I don't need a chaperone, thank you very much,' he answered. 'You still believe what I do is hogwash, don't you? The only reason you want to tag along is to prove I'm a fraud.'

'Well, then prove me wrong,' Rebecca retorted.

'You're the brainy type, doc,' he told her, 'all ratio, voice of reason, and all that. You don't trust your own emotions; you suppress them as much as you can. Don't take it as a criticism. All I'm saying is that it's inordinately difficult for the likes of you to get into the Dreamlands. It would mean you'd have to disobey your strongest instincts and convictions. I don't believe you have it in you.'

'I'm sure you could do something about that,' Lagergren intervened. 'You promised me I could follow you one day on your journeys in the Dreamlands. Maybe that day has come. It would help us understand what we're up against.'

'You're all ganging up on me,' Wheeling whined. 'What do I look like? The Cunard Line?'

It looked as if Wheeling was about to stomp out of the room. Then he changed his mind. With a resigned look, he sat down in the middle of the sofa and invited the two others to sit next to him.

'If you really want this, you need to let go,' he warned them. 'I can help you reach the deepest level of your subconscious only if you allow me to, trust me, give yourselves over to me.'

He'd taken their hands into his and was speaking in a soft, mellow voice, 'The Dreamlands are only accessible if you empty your minds of petty thoughts and worries. You have to stop thinking of yourselves as individuals and go with the flow. It's like being in a canoe on a calm river. The weather is sunny, and you're drifting with the current. Down the river you go, not a care in the world. Everything is fine, nothing to worry about. Time is all you got. You're enjoying the moment, and the moment lasts for an eternity. A light slumber overwhelms you. You're now ready to go on a journey. Look ahead. A steep staircase stretches out in front of you, to the most profound areas of the subconscious. Take the first steps and feel how liberating it is to leave all of your false certainties behind you. The unknown welcomes you. It waits to be shaped by your dreams and desires.'

As he spoke, his voice deepened, and the words came ever more slowly. Rebecca and Lagergren felt drowsy. It didn't last long before the three of them dropped away in a deep sleep, still holding hands.

When Rebecca opened her eyes again, she was standing in a poorly lit, cobbled street. The narrow houses were all in Tudor style or older and stood at awkward angles to one another. The tavern she was facing tilted menacingly forwards as if it intended to gobble her up in an instant. Inside, raucous singing was going on. Through the filthy windows, she could see men and women dancing on the tables. They had bronze skins and long black hair, their clothes a strange mix of western and oriental garments that had long gone out of fashion. Several women wore gauzy veils in glittering colours.

She looked at herself. She was wearing a tight black leather jerkin over a full-sleeved burgundy shirt with a frilled collar, black velvet knee-breeches, with vertical slashes and a lining of the same colour as her shirt, over a black, tight-fitting hose, and loose boots of smooth, black leather. She had a black, tall crown hat adorned with black feathers on her head, and over her shoulders hung a hooded cloak trimmed with genet fur, fastened with an elaborate, silver, phoenix-shaped broach. The phoenix's chest was an exceptional forty-carat ruby. Two quillon daggers were stuck in her broad belt; a rapier with a swirling hilt hung at her left side.

Her two companions were equally dressed as Elizabethan gentlemen. She was surprised to see Lagergren was thirty years younger than in real life. Wheeler had lost his adolescent, gawky bearing. His back was ramrod straight, and he'd acquired a shiny mane of shoulder-length hair. Rebecca realised she'd added at least eight inches to her height.

'You can be anything you want in the Dreamlands,' Wheeling said, grinning at her. 'This is how we see our ideal selves. Enjoy it while it lasts.'

'Why are we dressed like this?' Rebecca wondered.

'Because that's the fashion in Anhur-Lud,' Wheeling answered, 'and I'm the expert. I dreamt up the place myself. It started as a couple of houses on the banks of an estuary. Over the years, it's grown into a vast harbour, visited by vessels from all parts of the Dreamlands. It's my point of entry into the Dreamlands. All my journeys originate from here.'

He opened the tavern's door and motioned them inside.

'Come on in. We have an appointment to keep,' Wheeling said.

He led them to a back room, where the din of the singing and dancing was but a dim echo. At the only table sat an elderly man nursing a tankard of ale. He had a long, narrow face, with jutting cheekbones and a pronounced overbite. When he looked up, Rebecca noticed his eyes were expressionless, except for a long-suffering weariness.

'I want you to meet my good friend Randolph Carter,' Wheeling introduced him. 'I met him in France during the war. We both fought in the Battle of the Somme.'

'I'm pleased to make your acquaintance,' Carter welcomed them with a distinct New England accent.

'You're an American,' Lagergren remarked, slightly surprised. 'Didn't the Battle of the Somme *precede* the American entry into the war?'

Carter made a sour face.

'I had the honour to fight in the French Foreign Legion,' he said, 'after my compatriots made it abundantly clear to me they didn't consider me fit for duty in the United States Armed Forces. Also, I didn't care for my nation's vacillation in the face of Teutonic barbarism. Joining the Legion was the quickest route to enter the fray.'

'Carter here is a dreamer extraordinaire,' Wheeling enthusiastically continued his introduction. 'He's been everywhere in the Dreamlands. He's spent more time here than on Earth.'

'There's little that binds me to Earth, except for my childhood memories of New England,' the old man agreed. 'For a while, after the war's atrocities, I lost my innocent capacity to yearn for the overwhelming vistas of the Dreamlands. After all the bloodshed, it seemed like an immature, selfish thing to do. That sorry state of mind needlessly deprived me for a long time of the means to visit these wondrous places I'd wandered around in my youth. I allowed myself to be fettered to a humdrum existence without perspectives. I count my blessings I found my way back.'

'I'm glad for you it didn't take too long to overcome the barriers that prevented your return,' Rebecca said. 'The war ended not yet three years ago. A lot of fellow soldiers and bereaved families are still struggling with its consequences.'

'It took me longer than those few years, I can assure you,' Carter countered. 'If you'd sought me up at Miskatonic University instead of here, you'd have found a despondent shadow of a man.'

Rebecca looked baffled at Wheeling. Was this old man delusional? And how could he, at his age, have fought in the Great War? It made no sense.

Wheeling pointed out with a smile, 'Remember, time in the Dreamlands isn't as we know it on Earth. There's no past, present, and future. Everything happens simultaneously. The Randolph Carter we're speaking to here, isn't the Randolph Carter who's currently living in Arkham, Massachusetts. For him, our present day is a thing of a distant past. He's been living here for ages. In a couple of our years, he'll definitely have disappeared from the face of Earth to take up permanent residence in the Dreamlands, where he's become a king in his own right.'

Rebecca rolled her eyes and complained, 'Jesus, when did dreaming turn into the theory of general relativity? Did anyone bother to tell Freud?'

Then Wheeling gave Carter a full account of their struggle against the Dream Whisperer and told him their opponent's true identity. Hearing the name, Carter tensed up and furtively looked about him.

'*Never* utter that name again,' he warned. 'The one you seek is an ever-spreading blight on the Dreamlands. He has ears and eyes everywhere, even in your beloved Anhur-Lud. In my youth, I saw him from afar, silk-clad, on a golden throne in primordial Sarkomand on the arid plateau of Leng, amidst his toad-like worshippers, as the High-Priest-Not-To-Be-Described. Once, I even met him face to face in the onyx halls of unknown Kadath. It nearly cost me my life. He misled me — as he's wont to do — and sent me off on a misguided quest to the sunset city of my own making. The fiend pretended he wanted me to return the Dreamlands' original gods, the Elder Ones, to the cold waste of Kadath. He sent me hither on the back of a monstrous shantak-bird, which flew me straight into the dreamless, bubbling Void. There, at infinity's centre, the demon-sultan resides, who — in time immemorial — spawned the abomination that is your enemy.'

'But you did survive,' Rebecca reminded him. 'How did you escape the trap he'd set for you?'

'I woke up screaming, I did,' Carter replied soberly. 'It happened at a time when I still had a body to return to in your world — which isn't the case anymore, and that's why I cannot accompany you on your journey, even if I wanted to.'

Carter paused before adding, 'Which I do not. It's a foolish venture, and I strongly advise against it.'

'Where can we find him?' Wheeler asked unperturbed. 'Is he in Sarkomand, or do we need to travel onwards to Kadath?'

'I told you. Nyarlathotep – because that's the sobriquet he tends to go by in these parts – is an ever-spreading blight. He makes his influence and presence felt in an increasing number of places. Once, with the help of ghouls and night-gaunts, I defeated his cronies, the hideous, tentacled, toad-like moon-beasts that travel in fearsome black galleys. Now, I see those dreaded vessels docking again in the ports of Dylath-Leen, Thran, Hlanith, Oriab, Ilarnek, Baharna, and even in Celephaïs, where my old friend Kuranes is, unfortunately, more and more lost in reveries about his native Cornwall. The only places where his influence hasn't taken any foothold yet, are Ulthar, where cats reign supreme, and my town and kingdom, Ilek-Vad. His stronghold remains the cursed, windowless monastery in Sarkomand, where he officiates as the terrible High-Priest. His cult attracts growing numbers of disciples, who leave their homes on pilgrimages to Leng, uncertain whether they'll ever return.'

'Why would people be attracted to worshipping a being so patently evil?' Rebecca asked, incredulously.

'Lies and promises never meant to be kept,' Carter sighed wearily. 'People feel a desperate need to believe and have lost faith in their rulers and their silent gods. Nyarlathotep's ruthless power beguiles and enchants them, even though, in his eyes, they're only altar-fodder. None of their expectations will be met as they stumble to their inevitable doom.'

'If we need to go to Sarkomand anyhow, it might make sense to join up with the pilgrims who are making their way to the monastery,' Lagergren suggested. 'We wouldn't stand out among the masses.'

Wheeling and Rebecca agreed as Carter shook his head with a disapproving mien.

'What'd be the ideal departure point to associate ourselves with the throngs travelling to Sarkomand?' Wheeling asked.

'They tend to convene on the outskirts of Inganok, the Dreamlands' northernmost city before the plateau of Leng,' Carter answered reluctantly. 'In my youth, that would have been unthinkable. Now, Inganok's great Temple is decaying, and the wise priests, who were once versed in the mysteries and cults of the Elder Ones, have all but left since Nyarlathotep keeps their powerless gods hostage in inaccessible Kadath. Though I never liked the haughty Inganokians, who pride themselves on being descendants of the gods, the city's decline and the degeneracy of its denizens pain my heart more than I can say.'

'How do we get to Inganok?' Wheeling insisted.

'You could perhaps board one of the black galleys in your port,' Carter teased him. 'I doubt you'd ever end up at your destination. The moon-beasts have a particular craving for fine human meat. Or you could travel on board of my ship, and I'd take you there. But I warn you: That's where the journey stops for me. Once I drop you off in Inganok, you're on your own.'

39

Inganok, The Dreamlands

In the alleys on their way to the port, Carter pointed out strange-looking individuals. They wore turbans that covered up bumps on their foreheads. They had rough, leery faces with mouths that were far too wide, and their feet were tiny.

'You'll meet more of these where you're going,' he warned. 'Nasty critters. Don't trust them and *never* drink their wine. It's a mistake to let them enter Anhur-Lud, Wheeling. You'll find out that running a city in the Dreamlands is a full-time business. Turn your back, and the vermin creeps in.'

In the harbour, Carter's three-mast, cream-coloured galleon eclipsed all other moored ships. It was larger, more majestic than any of the clippers, barques, frigates, and cutters docked at its side. The only crafts that could remotely compete in stature with the king's vessel were the two ominous black galleys lurking in a remote spot at the end of the docks. Rebecca noticed large numbers of enormous crates being loaded onto them by sinister longshoremen, despite the late hour. She wondered what might be in those crates.

Before she stepped on the galleon's gangplank, she was startled by its peculiar figurehead, which seemed like an ill fit with the rest of the ship. It was an entirely black creature with horns, wings, and a tail. The most striking feature was the absence of a face. The smooth head lacked eyes, nose, and mouth. It was an altogether uncanny and disturbing sight. When she asked her host about it, he showed some embarrassment.

'It's — it's a form of atonement,' he said.

'How so?' Rebecca asked, her curiosity piqued.

'That's a night-gaunt,' Carter replied. 'Terrible creatures. Yet they were my allies in my foolish confrontation with Nyarlathotep. He made them disappear with as little effort as a mere snap of the fingers. Wiped out the entire species, just like that, demonstrating his might in an off-hand manner as an illustration of how ill-advised I'd been to seek him out in remote Kadath.'

Carter sighed, his mind dwelling on the terrible event.

'Making their effigy the figurehead of the royal galleon is my tribute to them, even if it's an awkward one,' he explained. 'Night-gaunts were notoriously reluctant to fly over water, and now I have one strapped to the prow of my ship, forever a couple of feet above the waves. Still, I always found it a useful reminder to pick my future battles more wisely and with more consideration for those who are willing to ally themselves with me.'

On board, three luxurious cabins had already been prepared for them, which made Rebecca realise Carter knew about their undertaking before he met them. They sailed an hour before dawn. Although there was hardly any wind at all, the square sails ballooned, and the galleon left the dormant port at a brisk pace. Out in the open sea, they encountered a stiff breeze, but the galleon rode the waves windward without the crew making any effort to adjust their sails. Rebecca thought the sailors on board were an unlikely bunch of handsome, young men — as if Carter had used a male-model agency to hire them. She'd half-expected a crew of weather-beaten, gap-toothed, and bow-legged shipmates — she wasn't complaining, though. They travelled to the east — if that notion had any meaning in the Dreamlands — over smooth seas. Late in the afternoon, Lagergren noticed a toothy sea snake, with a cyclopean eye in its forehead, following the ship. Carter ordered his men to throw a large basket of spicy fishcakes in the water, and the snake disappeared. Around sunset they sailed past Dylath-Leen, a foreboding city whose thin towers built in black basalt jutted high in the sky. The galleon steered clear from its shores as the port teemed with black galleys.

'That's what'll happen to *your* city as well if you don't put a stop to it,' Carter warned Wheeling. 'Dylath-Leen has long since fallen for the siren's song of the black galleys' merchants. At first, they sell spectacular rubies at impossible prices, holding out to their trading partners the prospect of wealth beyond imagination. Once greed has the buyers firmly in its grip, those hideous creatures tell them that mere coin can no longer purchase their gems, and soon a darker bargain is struck.'

'They're slave traders,' Wheeling guessed.

'They exchange their goods for humans, yes. They have that in common with slave traders,' Carter answered.

The next days, the galleon was surrounded by shoals of flying fish, which melodiously whistled while jumping out of the water. After a week, the ship headed north, and another week later, they reached the Cerenarian Sea. On starboard, the city of Celephais appeared, with its elegant minarets and turquoise temples. Although they were too far away to see it clearly, Rebecca was convinced she'd discerned colourful, swan-necked sailing ships gliding through the air among the city's spires. Carter told them about his visits to the city and how time has no hold within its walls. Men don't age there, and buildings don't crumble under the weight of the years. Rebecca and Lagergren would have loved to visit the place. Carter insisted on sailing on. He couldn't stand the sight of his friend King Kuranes. Like Carter, Kuranes had willingly traded his life on Earth for the marvels of the Dreamlands, but he had come to regret that choice bitterly. The wretch was now wasting away in his fairy-tale castle, hankering for his native Cornwall.

From then onwards, the weather grew colder and greyer as the days shortened. A stiff breeze turned the waters choppy, and they spent most of their time inside. Only the sight of a vast herd of white-haired, whale-like creatures could entice them to remain on deck for longer than a few minutes. In the evenings, over dinner, Carter still tried to dissuade them from continuing their journey. He told them over and over their mission was pointless and had no chance of succeeding.

'Nyarlathotep is a chaos monster,' he pointed out, one night. 'You know what that is, don't you?'

Rebecca only shrugged and raised her eyebrows; Lagergren knew exactly what Carter was talking about.

'In many religions, the original state of the universe is chaos, and it takes the intervention of a god to create order out of chaos,' he explained. 'Often, chaos is personified as a monster — a snake, a dragon, an evil giant — that has to be vanquished by the god. Legends featuring heroes slaying mythical beasts to bring wealth and prosperity to their country are variations on the same theme.'

'Precisely,' Carter continued. 'All these stories have their facts backwards. Chaos didn't reign at the beginning of time: There was a state of absolute order. Perfection. Ever since, as time progresses, that perfection has been steadily eroded. Chaos incessantly gnaws at its roots — like the serpent Nidhöggr at Yggdrasil's — until the tree, which represents Law and Order in the universe, topples over and dies, and only chaos remains.'

'The Second Law of Thermodynamics!' Rebecca interjected. 'Disorder increases with time. An isolated system always tends towards a situation of thermodynamic equilibrium, which is the state with maximum entropy.'

'Exactly!' Carter exclaimed. 'I thought I could be the hero who slew the monster. You know, like Theseus with the Minotaur, or Perseus with Gorgon and Cetus. Rid the Dreamlands of this cancer that eats it from the inside! I know better now. Nyarlathotep is the Crawling Chaos, entropy incarnated. He cannot be overcome. Not by the likes of us anyway. He'll only grow stronger over time.'

Wheeling remained unconvinced.

'Our aim doesn't necessarily have to be to destroy him,' he pondered. 'Stalling him for a while could be enough to save Fleming. I need to observe him from close up. I can't tell now.'

It took them another three weeks to reach their destination. As Inganok's shoreline rose over the horizon, a sentiment of impending doom pervaded among the travellers. The entire city was built in the blackest onyx, giving it an air of impenetrable gloom. The region was renowned for its onyx quarries. It had always been a magnet for ambitious stonecutters who wanted to earn above-average wages. The many-storied buildings came in all shapes. Inganok bristled with bizarre towers, spires, and minarets. Some of them were arrow-straight and ended in sharp, pointy roofs; others bulged into onion-shaped domes. Terraced pyramids with huge flames flaring at their tops loomed among the tallest constructions, lending the skyline a fascinatingly alien feel. On a hill towering over the city, sat the palace of the Veiled King — a brooding place, awe-inspiring and inaccessible. As their ship entered the basalt harbour, they heard a cheerless bell tolling, which seemed to summon them to a funerary service. Eerie, mournful music and dissonant chants resounded over the water. A forbidding mountain range, whose peaks were obscured by grey clouds, overshadowed Inganok. The dying daylight was entirely insufficient to penetrate the murky veil of smoke and shadows hanging in the city's joyless streets.

Carter pointed at the quays on the east side. An enormous crowd had already gathered. It increased in size as hundreds of people continued to alight from twelve ships of different origins, which had moored in that area of the harbour. Three ships had unloaded their cargo and were leaving the port; several other vessels were waiting to enter. The pilgrims had all donned brown cowls and were waiting meekly on the quays. Rebecca observed the mob through a spyglass. She saw they were being herded into several queues by dozens of beings that weren't wearing any clothes at all, despite the near-freezing temperature. She zoomed in on one of them. The guardian had a lewd face with an overly-large, full-lipped mouth and two small, curved horns protruding from the forehead. His shoulders were broad, combined with a squat torso and long, inordinately muscular arms. Reddish fur covered his hips and thighs; the creature had goat legs and an insignificant tail. He was holding a short, two-pronged spear, used as a cattle prod to push the pilgrims along.

'That's what the black-galley merchants really look like,' Carter whispered in her ear. 'They're the Men of Leng, and — like their masters, the moon-beasts — they're beholden to the Dark Lord Nyarlathotep. They round up the pilgrims in the harbour before sending them on their way to the monastery of Sarkomand. Their grim destination sits proudly on the plateau of Leng, on the other side of the mountain range.'

'Those mountains look forbidding,' Lagergren said. 'How will all those people reach the other side?'

'I don't know for sure,' Carter replied. 'I made the journey on the back of an infernal shantak-bird a long time ago. Much has changed in the meantime. Inganok is now firmly in the claws of Nyarlathotep's minions. The secretive Veiled King is a prisoner in his palace. The priests once worshipped Dreamland's original gods, the Elder Ones, in that sixteen-angled tower over there. They have all gone and been replaced by something unspeakable.'

As if to emphasise Carter's words, the chanting turned into an inhuman howling that sent chills down their spines.

'Are you still resolved to continue on your foolhardy journey?' Carter asked one more time.

The three nodded.

'Then you'll need these.'

Carter turned around and opened a wooden linen chest. He extracted three brown cowls, identical with those worn by the pilgrims on the quays.

40

Plateau of Leng, The Dreamlands

Rebecca, Lagergren, and Wheeling walked cautiously along the quays in the direction of the bustling crowd as Carter's galleon left the harbour. A goat-man shouted angrily at them and pushed them towards a waiting throng of pilgrims. The devotees all wore vacant expressions and were softly chanting a mantra the three didn't understand at first until Lagergren recognised the words.

'They're praying in the Outer Gods' language,' he said.

'Can you understand them? What are they saying?' Wheeling asked.

'They're chanting, *"i'Hrii mnahni' i'Shogg athg i'vultlag'n Gnaiih uaaah y'hah"*,' Lagergren told him. 'It translates roughly as, "Accept your worthless followers into your realm of darkness, we pray to you, oh Lord".'

'Charming, good to hear. Religion always gives a person such a grand feeling of self-esteem,' Rebecca remarked. 'Well, your visit to the Qohl'Hotl is paying off, Ormger. You're the perfect tour guide, knowing the locals' lingo and all.'

After standing around in the cold for the better part of an hour, the Men of Leng prodded the worshippers in their group into motion. They walked in the direction of the mountains nearest to the coastline. Rebecca estimated there were approximately three hundred people in their party. They were shepherded by twenty armed goat-men bearing torches and accompanied by fifteen yaks carrying food supplies. The daylight was gone. Once they'd left the city, they were marching under a starless night sky. The terrible chants coming from the former Elder Ones' temple accompanied them, as the winds blowing in from the sea carried the incantations along. Progress was slow. The journey led them uphill over uneven rocky paths. After what must have been a march of six hours, the first pilgrims showed signs of exhaustion. Two rows in front of theirs, an older man collapsed. Immediately, a goat-man grabbed him by the scruff and dragged him aside. They couldn't see what was happening to the man because they were forced to continue their march. Rebecca distinctly picked up the crunch of a rock smashing a skull. She wasn't sure whether she heard or only imagined a vile, slurping sound and beastly growls. Her worst suspicions were confirmed half an hour later when they passed two bodies alongside the road — a woman's and a small girl's. Their heads had been caved in and their brains sucked out. They also had bite marks on their arms and legs, and their bloodied cowls were torn open, exposing ripped-out remains of entrails. The three travellers shuddered, horrified. They were grateful for Carter's foresight — thanks to which, they were carrying ample supplies of hardtack and water beneath their cowls.

Four hours and many victims of exhaustion later, the cortège stopped. Dawn was breaking, and their guards allowed them to rest. They haphazardly distributed chunks of stale bread from the packs on the yaks' backs. There were no tents or blankets. The pilgrims were left in the open as freezing winds blew over the barren plain. The mountains were still distant, and the three worried about what was yet to come on this journey. The mountainsides were high and sheer, a challenge to even experienced mountaineers. There was no way this group would be able to scale those cliffs. Yet everybody knew Sarkomand lay on the other side. Rebecca and her two companions looked around them. Their ranks had thinned significantly. The Men of Leng had swollen bellies and smears of blood on their hands and faces. They had haughty, satisfied looks on their foul muzzles and watched their herd with a predatory glint in the eyes. The pause was brief. Less than an hour later, the pilgrims were forced back on their feet. Several older people couldn't get up again and were slaughtered for everybody to see.

Welcome to your realm of darkness, Rebecca thought.

It took them just over three days to reach the foot of the mountains. Wheeling estimated hardly two-thirds had survived the debilitating march. Rebecca more or less expected the horrible shantak-birds, which Carter had mentioned, to wait for them. Instead, they saw a large fissure in the mountainside. The goat-men set free the yaks, which carried the last remains of the mouldy bread supply with them. Then the keepers drove the pilgrims towards the gaping hole in the mountain. Inside, they discovered a long and deep cavern, whose height rivalled that of the largest gothic cathedrals. The place was riddled with giant, milky selenite crystals, which stood at all possible angles. Their presence indicated that, at some point in time, there'd been volcanic activity in this area — as these crystals can only originate at high temperatures. The floor felt warm, no doubt heated by an underground magma chamber. The largest crystals measured over fifty feet in length and twenty feet in diameter. The cave was moist and hot. Soon, everybody was gasping for air, and their clothes were soaked with sweat.

The goat-men prodded their human cattle on. The stream of people laboriously weaved its way between the translucent pillars. Deeper into the mountain they went. As they progressed, the cave became narrower and lower, forcing them to stoop. In the end, they could only pass in a single file. The crystals were no longer pillars; the corridor's walls and roof consisted of rows upon rows of jagged glassy rocks that looked like over-sized teeth. It felt as if they were struggling inside the maw of a monstrous lamprey. The air became ever more difficult to breathe. Rebecca had to fight off spells of dizziness and nausea. Lagergren and Wheeling were hardly doing any better. After a long while, the passage widened again, and they arrived in another cave. It was impossible to keep track of time during this journey. They felt as if they'd spent an eternity underground. All the time, a choking feeling of despair had weighed them down. Upon their arrival at the other end of the mountain, they were exhausted. Their clothes were torn and tattered by the crystals' razor-sharp edges. Many suffered from bleeding hands and feet, cut on the rocks.

It was with a sigh of relief they saw the evening sky again. The joy didn't last. A cruel draught howled along the cavern walls, instantly cooling their sweaty bodies. Ice crystals formed on their sodden garments, and several pilgrims succumbed to heart failure from the sharp drop in temperature. The Men of Leng exulted. This place was their home, the merciless plateau of Leng, and they appeared impervious to the climate change. They danced around, taking silly goat-like leaps, grunted, and yowled.

The goat-men drove their herd of believers out of the cavern on to a wind-swept, barren plain. Rebecca heard the sea before she saw it. The Northern Cerenarian Sea's towering waves crashed into the wild shore's sheer basalt cliffs. The roar of the surf was deafening. She understood now why the unfortunate pilgrims all passed through Inganok. Even though the plateau of Leng bordered on the seashore, it was inaccessible via the water. On their journey over the table-land, they passed several hamlets — usually no more than a couple of primitive huts — where Men of Leng lived their meagre existences. They stood in their doorways to watch the caravan of hapless faithful pass by. Sometimes, they were engaged in savage rituals, dancing and howling around bonfires or totems with inscrutable idols. Above them, vulture-like, circled large flying creatures. They knew instinctively these were the shantak-birds Carter had referred to. Except for their ability to fly, these creatures had little in common with ordinary birds. Larger than elephants, they had leathery, bat-like wings and scaly skins. Their heads resembled those of flayed horses, with horrible teeth that could leave no one in doubt whether they were carnivores. Whenever pilgrims fell by the wayside, Lagergren noticed the goat-men no longer butchered them. They left them as a tribute to the shantaks, who swooped down to claim their prize. The rocky desert was strewn with human bones and carcasses. Hideous shrieks of worshippers being ripped apart alive by the nightmarish scavengers punctuated the entire death march.

Eternal twilight enveloped the plateau of Leng. Before the pilgrims reached the crumbling walls of primeval Sarkomand, they had long lost all sense of time. The ragged convoy entered the dilapidated city through a high, arched gate, crowned by weather-beaten effigies of monstrous entities. A broad, straight road led past numerous ruined buildings and shattered pillars. The scale of these edifices had nothing to suggest human proportions. In the distance stood a low, windowless building in the centre of a circle of primitive, tall monoliths. Within the circle, many groups of pilgrims, which had arrived earlier, were waiting in silence. They looked every bit as pitiful as their own company. The worshippers stared listlessly at nothing in particular, forever mumbling their terrible mantra, *'i'Hrii mnahni' i'Shogg athg i'vultlag'n Gnaiih uaaah y'hah.'*

Once they'd delivered their flock within the confines of the stone circle, the guards turned back. They left the pilgrims in the care of other goat-men, who were their equals in casual cruelty. They prodded the weary believers with their sharp spears until they'd reached their designated spot. Although they must have marched for several days, they were offered neither food nor drink. Each time exhausted travellers tried to sit down, several horned men viciously stabbed them while shouting abuse until they were back on their feet.

Not a shred of human dignity was left to them. The pilgrims were cattle. Rebecca didn't doubt they'd be led to the slaughter soon. She could only hope, against her better judgment, that this awful experience was worth the effort — that it would allow Wheeling to devise a winning strategy against the Dream Whisperer. She was feeling despondent. One glance at her companions told her they were in no better shape. Lagergren looked as if he could faint instantly; Wheeling was hollow-eyed and ashen, and he had an ugly gash in his right cheek.

They saw the groups that'd arrived before them leaving for the monastery one after another. Soon, it was their turn. Right after they'd been marched through the building's arched doorway, the Men of Leng divided them into two groups. They directed Lagergren and Wheeling to the left; Rebecca was pulled to the right. Both groups reached the structure's inner court via different entrances. The monastery looked squat and diminutive from the outside. Still, its courtyard was a stupendously vast, round forum, surrounded by towering windowless walls with garishly-coloured, ornate frescoes. On the broad ledges, hundreds of drummers and flute players drenched the scene in insane rhythms and shrieking noises. In the middle of the plaza was a huge, gaping black hole, flanked by gigantic statues of malevolently snarling, winged lions in mottled diorite. Along the circular court's outer edge, six blood-soaked altars stood evenly spaced. Gutters in the altars and the black granite floor drained the sacrifices' blood via elaborate patterns towards the central pit, which was situated slightly lower than the court's edges. On a throne, which hovered above the abyss, sat the larger-than-life, yellow-robed High-Priest. A veil that only left his fiery eyes visible covered his face. Shimmering above the priest, was the diaphanous image of a spread-eagled, naked man, floating unconsciously in the air. He was tethered to the throne or the priest with what looked like an umbilical cord.

One stream of victims was directly driven in thirty-men-wide rows towards the black hole. The other one was diverted towards the courtyard's edge. There, the goat-men evenly divided their victims over the six altars. Teams of priests, in floor-length, red robes with pointed hats and full-faced cloth masks with eyeholes, were waiting for their sacrificial lambs. Lagergren and Wheeling were headed towards the pit, whereas Rebecca gyrated in the direction of one of the altars. The noise was unimaginable. The drummers were beating their instruments in ever-changing patterns, sometimes in wildly diverging rhythms and then suddenly in sync, like a monstrous heartbeat.

Lagergren was fascinated by the colourful frescoes. With the knowledge provided to him by the Qohl'Hotl, he could read them like a book. He found the depicted Outer Gods easily identifiable. There was Yog-Sothoth, the all-seeing, who — appropriately, Lagergren thought — looked like a bunch of glowing orbs that functioned as eyes. Then Shub-Niggurath, a dark, seething mass of tentacles and drooling mouths, forever spawning small monstrosities that immediately slither away into different dimensions.

Azathoth, the blind, idiot god, father of all Outer Gods, enthroned in the deepest recesses of ultimate chaos, an all but formless, bubbling mass, utterly inscrutable. Five Cthulhus joining their writhing tentacles to open a portal in the skies, allowing their masters to travel from one parallel universe to another. Tsathoggua, a many-legged, toad-like abomination, devouring the sacrifices offered to it by fanatical cultists in temples scattered over different universes and dimensions. The frescoes also represented some creatures that had allied themselves to the Outer Gods. Among them, featured the eyeless moon-beasts sailing along on board of their black galleys. Dagon was another prominent accomplice. He was a fish-like entity with a horrific head, who was kneeling in subservience before the Outer Gods. Behind him, was a swarm of aquatic warriors that were half-fish and half-human. Other races had chosen to battle the Outer Gods and were crushed without mercy — among them the Elder Things, the first sentient inhabitants of Earth, with their Shoggoth slaves.

Wheeling focused his attention on the Yellow High-Priest hovering over the abyss. Carter had told him Nyarlathotep had many avatars in the Dreamlands. His seat of power was here, in the benighted monastery of Sarkomand, where endless streams of sacrifices were offered to the ever-hungry Outer Gods. The stench of blood and fear was an invigorating tonic for the awe-inspiring godhead floating over the carnage. He relished the ceremony with all his senses. As he was pushed closer and closer to the brink of the pit, Wheeling tried to scrutinise the translucent naked man tethered to the High-Priest. While he'd never met Fleming in person, he was nevertheless convinced that was the identity of the phantom-like shape drifting over the Yellow High-Priest. The man didn't appear to be conscious; he was plunged into a deep trance. In this state, he was a mere vessel, a passive doorway to human reality for the Dream Whisperer. The umbilical cord linking them glowed with a steady pulse. Wheeling knew he had to find a way to cut the cord to sever the parasitic bond that existed between Fleming and his unwanted guest. He wouldn't be able to do it here as he was five rows away from the edge of the pit. He had to concentrate on waking up if he weren't to be sucked down the ghastly hole.

Only three pilgrims separated Rebecca from certain death. The red-clad priests grabbed their prey by the arms and legs and swung them on the blood-stained altar. Two priests pushed their victims' shoulders down on the sacrificial slab while two others immobilised their legs. The fifth priest would then raise a curved obsidian blade and cry out, '*Ch'Nglui Shogg-Nith uaaah!*', before plunging the knife in the pilgrims' chests. If Lagergren had been near her, he could have told her this meant 'Cross the threshold, servant of darkness'. The general gist was, however, more than clear enough to her. The priest carved open his sacrifice's thorax and cut out the heart. Involuntarily, Rebecca had to think back to Fleming's narrative of his parents' murder in an Indian temple. Only then she recognised the ghostly shape floating over the Yellow High-Priest's head. Once the victim had bled out, two horned men grabbed the corpse off the altar, carried it to the pit, and threw it unceremoniously over the edge. Rebecca had no idea where Lagergren and Wheeling were. All she knew was that her time was running out fast. Wheeling had told her the risks attached to a stay in the Dreamlands were limited because one could always leave by regaining consciousness. The snag was that he'd omitted to teach her how to do it. When a goat-man pushed her towards the priests as the next in line to be gutted, she reached under her cloak and retrieved her two daggers. She plunged one in the brute's throat and scratched the arm of a priest who was reaching out to grab her with the other knife. Six more guards overwhelmed her. Despite Rebecca wounding another two or three, it

421

didn't take them long to disarm her and pin her down on the altar screaming.

'Now would be a good time to wake up!' Lagergren yelled at Wheeling as he was toppling into the black abyss.

41

M's Office, London

Thursday, 14 April 1921

M waited impatiently for his collaborators' return to consciousness. In spite of Wheeling's warning that their stay in the Dreamlands could take a while, he hadn't expected them to be gone for quite so long. They'd been in deep sleep for the better part of three hours. M noticed their eyes moving frantically under closed eyelids. Their faces showed rapidly changing expressions, and their bodies were twitching as if in pain. Wheeling had warned him explicitly not to wake them up since this might undo all of their efforts. The warlock had assured M he was able to wake up on his own if the dangers in the Dreamlands became too dire. Still, M was worried. The journey to the Dreamlands was fraught with peril. Death in a dream state might result in irreversible trauma or even heart failure in the real world.

When the three had been under for about an hour, M's secretary brought him a disturbing telegram from the US secretary of state. The message made it quite clear time was running out quickly for a successful intervention. M hoped Wheeling could bring back the information needed to clip the Dream Whisperer's wings. He didn't dare to think of the alternative.

Wheeling jumped upright with a loud gasp as if he emerged from an extended underwater stay. Rebecca and

Lagergren were still unconscious. Lagergren's head was moving wildly from left to right, and Rebecca's body was convulsing.

'Help me wake them up!' Wheeling shouted at M while shaking Lagergren by the shoulders.

M grabbed a carafe of water from his desk and emptied it over Rebecca's face, who was immediately wide-awake and sputtering. Lagergren woke up screaming, arms thrashing and legs kicking.

It took them a while — and some of M's best whisky — to calm down again and recover from the extreme emotions their stay in the Dreamlands had put them through.

'It was incredible,' Rebecca sighed, shaken by the experience, while Lagergren remained mute.

Wheeling briefed M on what they'd seen in the Dreamlands, focusing mainly on the events in the monastery of Sarkomand.

'You told us events in the Dreamlands have consequences in our world,' M reminded him. 'How do you interpret the mass slaughter in the monastery? What does it mean for our reality?'

Wheeling made a helpless gesture.

'Remember that Dreamtime and our time aren't directly linked,' he began. 'We stayed in the Dreamlands for approximately two months, whereas here, only three hours elapsed. Time in the Dreamlands is an altogether different concept. No doubt the sacrifices in Sarkomand are related to a major massacre in our world. However, I can't tell with any degree of confidence whether it's a thing of the past or a future cataclysm. At first, it reminded me of the senseless slaughter in the Great War because I personally experienced that hecatomb. On the other hand, it might just as well have been the Mongol invasions under Genghis Khan or the Black Death in the fourteenth century. For what it's worth and for no sound reasons whatsoever, it's my conviction that it relates to a future event. Probably the next holocaust you've been planning with your mate Clemenceau.'

'What?!' M exclaimed, outraged at Wheeling's suggestion he was planning for another war.

'You didn't seriously think your Versailles Treaty was to be the end of all wars?' Wheeling sneered. 'Humiliating the Germans in the peace process and imposing ridiculous reparation payments on them that'll cripple their economy for the years to come have only planted the seeds for the next conflict in Europe. A blind man can see that. Another war is coming, which will be fought with even more terrible weapons than the previous one. And it's all on *you*, Holmes. On you and your short-sighted political allies. *You* wanted to eliminate Germany as a world power once and for all. Well, I'm sure the next generation will pay for your mistake in blood. Again.'

Rebecca and Lagergren expected M to punch the defiant Wheeling in the face.

The professor quickly intervened by saying, 'This falling out with one another is exactly what the Dream Whisperer would want us to do. It doesn't matter what you think about the Peace Treaty, Wheeling. The only question of importance is whether you've learnt what you hoped to embarking on this journey through the Dreamlands. Do you now know how to stop the Dream Whisperer and liberate Fleming?'

Wheeling keenly eyed M, who was seething a couple of feet away.

'I'm sure if I can pick your brain some more for information passed on to you by the Qohl'Hotl, Professor, I'll be able to create a powerful sigil that'll limit the Dream Whisperer's presence in our reality. At least for a while,' he answered.

'How much more time do you need?' M asked through gritted teeth.

'Why?' Wheeling wanted to know.

'Because we haven't got much time left,' M replied while turning to his desk. 'This is a telegram I received two hours ago. The US secretary of state informs me that Fleming has illegally commandeered a warship from the US Navy. Also, he installed a doomsday weapon on it — one he developed in secret with Janus funds, unbeknownst to the American authorities. The ship has left the harbour for an unknown destination. The Americans will attempt to sink it if Fleming doesn't surrender the vessel to the American authorities. Earlier this week, Mister Hughes informed me of his president's displeasure concerning the financially reckless way Fleming has been running Janus's American operations. Harding intends to cancel the USA's involvement in the programme. A formal letter is underway to clarify their position. The Americans will propose the dissolution of the Janus co-operation agreement during next May's board meeting. Today's events will make it entirely unfeasible to salvage our international collaboration, I fear.'

'What the hell does the Dream Whisperer intend to do with a single battleship?' Rebecca asked, unbelievingly.

'A single battleship *with a doomsday weapon*,' M specified. 'I have no idea, my dear. Apparently, he's sailing somewhere along the east coast in the direction of New York.'

42

USS Tennessee, North Atlantic Ocean

Thursday, 14 April 1921

The meeting Fleming had with Admiral Wilson three weeks ago went swimmingly. The commander of the Atlantic Fleet was fascinated by the new weapon. Fleming showed him minutely detailed blueprints of how Janus could retrofit a traditional battleship with Tesla's groundbreaking technology. To the secretary of state, he deliberately underplayed the advances Tesla's team had made in upscaling the prototype. They'd finalised most of the design already months ago. Fleming had secretly sent out production orders to many different factories for components of the electrical gun's ship-size version. These were waiting in dozens of crates stored in a civilian warehouse in the Norfolk harbour. Transporting them to the US Navy base, after obtaining the go from the commander, was a matter of hours. Tesla and his engineers travelled to Norfolk with Fleming. They stayed in a nearby hotel, ready to be deployed immediately. Tesla estimated that, if everything went well, they could achieve the ship's retrofitting in two weeks, three weeks tops.

Even for a fleet commander, releasing a ship on active duty for the implementation of an experimental weapon design was a big thing. At first, Wilson was inclined to choose an older vessel — which would have to be scrapped anyway if the president got his way in the matter of fleet reduction. However, under the Dream Whisperer's mesmerising influence, the admiral swiftly agreed to relinquish a modern ship and cut all red tape. Fleming left the fleet commander's office with all the necessary papers signed in under three hours.

The USS Tennessee had been launched in 1919 and commissioned barely a year ago. Its design was brand-new and still suffered from teething troubles that needed to be ironed out. With its six-hundred-foot length and four turbo-electric transmission engines it was the largest and fastest battleship of the American fleet. Moreover, no other ship could match its firing power. The USS Tennessee had no less than twelve 14-inch guns, sixteen 5-inch guns, forty 40-millimetre anti-aircraft guns and another forty-one 20-millimetre cannons. The 14-inch turret guns could be elevated to an angle of thirty degrees, rather than the fifteen degrees of battleships of earlier designs. This feature added ten thousand yards to the guns' range — more than enough to blow any attacking ship out of the water long before the USS Tennessee came within its firing range. The vessel was conveniently docked at Hampton Roads in Norfolk, Virginia, where the US Navy had its most important naval base since 1917. Fleming was planning on replacing only two of the anti-aircraft batteries with electrical guns — one on each side of the ship. The rest of its armament he would leave unchanged.

The conversion under the expert guidance of Tesla, assisted by his team and a dozen extra Navy engineers, had proceeded propitiously. That morning at 6 a.m., the refurbished ship left the harbour for a first short test run, carrying a full crew of over one thousand men. However, it didn't return after five hours as scheduled. The ship spent three hours testing its equipment some thirty miles off the

Delaware shoreline and, around 9 a.m., suddenly changed course. The USS Tennessee crew, which until then reported at regular intervals on the progress made in the test programme, broke off all radio contact.

Seven hours later, the ship reached Atlantic City. Naval Command was in a frenzy. No warship currently docked in Norfolk was able to catch up with the USS Tennessee. Moreover, none of the available vessels had a firing range that could match the rogue ship's, which meant an engagement with the USS Tennessee would amount to suicide anyway. As the battleship continued its course parallel to the New Jersey coastline, fears mounted it would attack New York.

The only US Navy ship in the area was the USS Langley, which happened to be experimenting with launching aeroplanes from its flight deck. It was a former collier that had carried American troops and coal to Europe during the Great War. Two years after the war, it had been decommissioned to be converted into the first US aircraft carrier at the Norfolk Navy Yard. A five-hundred-and-forty-foot flight deck had been mounted on top of its existing structures. When fully operational, it was expected to carry more than thirty planes. The ship wasn't commissioned yet because it still had to undergo several proof-of-concept tests. It had only four Vought VE-7 biplanes on deck. Not only did the USS Tenessee outgun the USS Langley, but it could also muster a top speed that was twice that of the aircraft carrier. Naval Command wisely ordered the USS Langley to stay well out of the enemy's twenty-mile firing range and send in the Voughts to attack the battleship instead. It was a desperate move. The single-seater biplanes with their laughable .30-inch Vickers machine guns couldn't hope to inflict real damage on the heavily armoured ship.

Earlier, Naval Command had also alerted the submarine base in Groton, Connecticut. It was the home of the New London Submarine Flotilla, which counted twenty vessels. Only a few ships were on full standby, however. At 1 p.m., three fully armed and refuelled S-class submarines left the base. In optimal circumstances, it would take them nine hours to reach the New York Bight. The USS Tennessee was expected to reach the area a full hour earlier. One hour was an eternity. It would provide ample time to the rogue ship's powerful 14-inch guns to inflict significant damage on Manhattan. Moreover, there was no telling what the new-fangled electrical weapons were capable of.

'Mister President,' the secretary of state said during a hectic crisis meeting in the Oval Office, 'I strongly advise you to inform the New York mayor of the impending danger to his city.'

'And pray tell what would that achieve in your opinion, Mister Hughes?' President Harding scoffed. 'Do you honestly expect that meathead Hylan to come up with a workable evacuation plan for Manhattan in what? Eight hours? I'll tell you what'll happen: Mayor Hylan will flee the city with his Tammany cronies in tow and leave his constituency to perish in the onslaught.'

'That would then be Mayor Hylan's responsibility entirely,' Hughes replied. 'You'll have performed your duty as president, and the New York Democrats will have failed theirs, improving the Republicans' chances in the next mayoral and gubernatorial elections.'

'You're a sly dog, Hughes; I'll give you that,' Harding admitted, 'but let's not kid ourselves. It's *my* head on the block. How could I explain that, on my watch, some foreign crook absconded with our top-of-the-line battleship? I'll tell you. It's simple: I cannot. Our only hope is that our submarines sink the USS Tennessee before it can do any damage. A sunk battleship is something I can explain, but I'm not feeding myself to the likes of Hylan and his gang of profiteers.'

Fleming — or better: the Dream Whisperer — was enjoying himself tremendously. Even though the ship had a crew of over a thousand, mind-controlling them was easy. He only had to manipulate the fifty-or-so officers. The rigid chain-of-command structure on board did the rest. Soldiers were trained to obey their superiors unquestioningly. That was how the Dream Whisperer liked his subjects best.

His initial plan had been to attack Boston. The Dream Whisperer had a particular soft spot for New England. It was a place where many secret cults in his honour had established themselves over the centuries. Regrettably, in the past few years, he had to sacrifice a few of them to ensure his credibility as Janus's commanding officer with the Americans. The irony of Janus's leader having two faces was not lost on him. No doubt disrupting a city like Boston would set in motion a series of events that, in the end, would wipe out human dominance in the area. Large colonies of Deep Ones were laying in wait to invade the city since ages, and their numbers had been increasing rapidly in recent years. The attack would keep the Boston police, fire-fighters, and state troops occupied for quite a while before they could re-establish some semblance of law and order. In the meantime, the sea creatures could swarm the harbour and take over the entire city unopposed. Massachusetts, New Hampshire, and Maine were his for the taking.

That, however, would have to wait. The Dream Whisperer wasn't about to pass up on an opportunity to destroy the biggest city in the USA. Levelling downtown and midtown Manhattan wouldn't only kill hundreds of thousands; it would probably also mean the end of the country's rule of law. If the political classes were unable to prevent such a catastrophe, they'd lose all legitimacy in the eyes of the American people. Democratic governance structures painstakingly built over centuries would crumble in a matter of weeks. Chaos would rule the land. Man would revert to the animal he truly is. Nature, red in tooth and claw, would impose the law of the jungle once more. Only the strong and unprincipled would survive, and America would turn into a fun place again, the likes of which he hadn't seen since the wholesale slaughter of the Indian tribes by the white colonists, the times of slavery, and the Civil War. That was, indeed, something to look forward to. And if destroying New York didn't do the trick, well, after Boston, there was always Philadelphia and Baltimore and Washington and Charleston and Miami and New Orleans and Houston. So much entertainment ahead. He was on a roll, and nobody was going to stop him.

But first things first. His acute senses detected the distant drone of aeroplanes. The USS Tennessee reached the New York Bight at sunset. In the fading daylight, the Dream Whisperer could make out three, no, four biplanes coming his way. How delightfully droll! He strolled up to the conning tower behind the second forward main gun turret and amicably clapped the captain, who stood rigidly frozen on the spot, on the shoulder.

'Dear Captain Leigh, we have a couple of insects visiting us,' he whispered in the expressionless officer's ear. 'I propose we let them strike the first blow to show them how absurdly inadequate they are — if that's all right with you. Let's already warm up the Tesla guns. It'll be an interesting test to see if we can blast those silly contraptions out of the sky.'

In a toneless voice, the captain gave the order in the speaking tube to spin up the electrical guns. Immediately, they heard a faint hum.

The four biplanes came in from the east at an altitude of ten thousand feet. They didn't carry any bombs, which meant they couldn't inflict any meaningful damage on the heavily armoured ship. After circling once above the battleship at high altitude, one of the Voughts dropped out of formation and came in low, strafing the USS Tennessee from bow to stern. Several bullets hit the conning tower's 16-inch armour. Fleming didn't even flinch. The next two planes attacked from the port side; the fourth one chose the starboard side before regaining its original altitude. All they managed to do was to chew up a few of the wooden upper-deck planks.

'Fine, now that's out of the way, let's see if *we* can do some damage,' Fleming said. 'Please, man both Tesla guns and give the order to fire at will, Captain.'

Again, Leigh woodenly gave the orders. Fleming left the conning tower for the port-side superstructure deck-house, the level where the main anti-aircraft armament was located. On each side of the ship, one of the four anti-aircraft turrets had been replaced with a Tesla gun, mounted on a free-standing rotating platform, which was entirely rubber-coated. The port-side gunner wore dark sunglasses. He was sitting behind a large curved plate of tinted, bullet-proof glass. The command centre at his fingertips allowed him to control the direction and elevation of the gun manually. The Tesla gun itself was a twenty-foot-long, sleek, rectangular tube. It ended in a convex bowl containing a miniaturised Tesla coil. A metal rod protruded from the bowl.

'Show me what you've got, son,' Fleming told the gunner.

The four aeroplanes were circling above the ship at ten thousand feet, uncertain what to do next. The gunner took aim at one of them and hit the red button on his command centre. After a brief, high-pitched whine, a powerful electricity burst shot from the gun's rod into the air with a blinding flash. The lightning dart fell, however, at least two thousand feet short of its aim. The starboard-side gunner wasn't any luckier in his attempt to take down one of the other planes.

'Well, that's a bit disappointing, I must say,' Fleming pouted. 'Let's give our toy some more juice.'

He climbed over the glass plate and straddled the gun's tube, holding on to it firmly with both hands.

Looking back over his shoulder, he shouted to the gunner, 'Let it rip, boy!'

Again, the gunner aimed and hit the red button. The blast was deafening, and the sunglasses only just prevented the gunner from going blind. With a fierce crackle, the lightning bolt pierced the sky and skewered the hapless aircraft, which immediately went up in flames. Fleming was whooping with laughter.

'Let's do that again!' he yelled.

The three remaining aeroplanes scattered in all directions. Two of them tried to put more distance between them and the battleship. The third made a broad downward curve and came in low over the water intending to take out the port-side electrical gun. Its Vickers machine gun started rattling when the aircraft was still more than two thousand feet away from the ship.

Fleming jumped off the gun and took refuge behind the bullet-proof glass plate.

He put his hand on the gunner's shoulder and told him, 'Steady now, let her come… and NOW!'

The bolt hit the biplane right on the nose, the engine exploded, the pilot instantly burnt to a cinder, and the aircraft turned into a fireball before hitting the waves.

Fleming whooped and yelled, and jumped around like a madman. After that, to his disappointment, the two remaining aeroplanes wisely chose to retreat and disappeared over the horizon.

'Spoilsports,' he grumbled and went back to the conning tower.

There, he consulted the nautical maps. Given the USS Tennessee's heaviest guns' range, New York would come within reach in about fifty-five miles. He ordered a course to the northwest that'd lead the battleship past Sandy Hook into the Lower Bay. Then they could steam towards the Upper Bay. Soon, New York would be a smouldering slag heap from Battery Park up to the Bronx.

The Dream Whisperer already looked forward to aiming his Tesla guns from the East River or the Hudson River at the panicking masses in the streets and scorch them into oblivion.

43

M's Office, London

Friday, 15 April 1921

M's secretary delivered another telegram from the US secretary of state to him around midnight, confirming the USS Tennessee's primary target was in all likelihood New York, and that they expected hostilities to start in five or six hours.

'I can't imagine they left their entire east coast defenceless!' Rebecca exclaimed. 'Why don't they send in a couple of bomber aeroplanes?'

M sighed and told her, 'My sources informed me Naval Command deliberately omitted to send word to the Air Force.'

'Why, for heaven's sake?' Rebecca asked.

'Naval Command convinced politicians to invest in dreadnoughts, rather than in military aviation. The Navy doesn't want Congress to know that aerial bombardments can put modern-day battleships out of action. A couple of months ago, they tried to bury test results that demonstrated this very fact. Aeroplanes are far cheaper than battleships. Another successful aerial intervention might lead to even deeper budget cuts for the Navy, they fear.'

Rebecca rolled her eyes in disgust.

'And what about coastal guns?' Professor Lagergren asked.

'The Coast Artillery suffered significantly during the Great War. After the Americans decided to join the war effort, they withdrew several of their heavy guns to ship them over for use in Europe. Ever since, their seacoast defence has been a shambles,' M answered. 'This means New York is defenceless against our nemesis, which puts a great burden of responsibility on our shoulders.'

M looked portentously at Wheeling and Lagergren.

'We need to find a way to thwart the Dream Whisperer, and we need to find it within the next five hours! Tell me, have you made any progress to that end?'

Wheeling met M's piercing stare without wincing. The visit to the Sarkomand monastery had given him much food for thought. It had fundamentally challenged his ideas about the Dreamlands' true nature. The Dream Whisperer was a far more fearsome opponent than he initially surmised. But he'd be damned before he acknowledged that to the likes of M.

'My strategy still needs a bit of work,' he replied in a noncommittal voice. 'I'd like some privacy to put the finishing touches to it, in co-operation with Professor Lagergren. Is there an empty office in the building we might use for that purpose?'

M was fuming. Still, he refrained from reacting to the warlock's insolence and guided both men to an empty meeting room at the end of the corridor.

As the door closed behind M's back, Lagergren asked, 'By Jove, please, tell me you do have a plan, Wheeling, and that it isn't all bluster! How much time do you need to come up with anything useful?'

'Calm down, Professor,' Wheeling replied. 'We'll get there in time.'

He took a sheaf of paper and a pencil.

'Let's break the problem down into its components,' he said. 'I need to design a sigil that can — at the very least — break the link between Fleming and the Dream Whisperer. Preferably, it should also prevent our enemy from re-entering our reality for a while.'

Lagergren nodded. So far, nothing new there.

'You know how it works,' Wheeling went on. 'My sigils consist of a sort of shorthand combination of words and symbols that are both meaningful to me and relate to the spell I want to cast. In this case, I'm convinced the spell's effectiveness will be enhanced if I can work with words written in the Outer Gods' script. I won't need everything — I'll sort it out as I go. For starters, I require the Dream Whisperer's true name, the Sarkomand monastery's location, and maybe some description of what was happening there — like the black void we were forced into, the human sacrifices, the Yellow High-Priest, things like that. Can you help me with that?'

Lagergren put his leather briefcase on the table and took a stack of pictures out. They were part of his friend Ove Eliassen's legacy and showed the bas-reliefs and texts found in the interior of the Sleepers' cradles. After meeting the Qohl'Hotl, Lagergren had studied the pictures again and made a start on translating the texts. He selected fifteen of them and spread them out on the table.

'They all mention the Dream Whisperer's true name,' he commented, pointing at one of the pictures. 'Here it is. Carter warned us not to speak it aloud, so I won't — you know how it sounds. And each time, that name is followed by the phrase *"shogg'ihn Leng lw'nafh'sh im'hosaat n'syha'h"*. It functions as an epithet that defines the essence of our adversary. It translates more or less like "eternally enthroned in Dreamlands' benighted Leng". Is that helpful?'

'Excellent,' Wheeling said while he was eagerly copying the name and the epithet in the Outer God's script on a paper.

The complex spidery signs that vaguely resembled Mayan hieroglyphs made him shudder.

'Anything else that might be helpful?' Wheeling asked when he had finished.

'I haven't had time to translate much of the texts on the photographs,' the professor said. 'Still, I have the impression the Dream Whisperer is only ever mentioned in litanies that sum up the Outer Gods' names — never as an entity actively participating in the conquest of new worlds or fighting against other species. He seems to be present everywhere but in a strangely passive way. I can't say I really understand it.'

'I saw you were studying the decorations on the walls inside the Sarkomand monastery,' Wheeling reminded him. 'Anything useful there?'

'Now that you mention it,' Lagergren mused. 'Behind the Yellow High-Priest, there was this inscription that stuck in my mind.'

The professor took Wheeling's pencil and wrote a series of glyphs on the paper.

'It says "*ch'b'thnk ngorr'e shugg ebumna ch'nglui*". It reads like an instruction. "Enter the pit that changes body and mind on Earth." I remember it because it wasn't what I'd expected.'

'What do you mean?'

'It looked like a slaughterhouse in there. The priests and the Men of Leng were murdering the faithful. I didn't experience it as a *transformative* ritual, but the glyphs behind the High-Priest told a different story. I thought, at the time, that was brutally cynical. Now, I'm not so certain anymore.'

Wheeling looked baffled and didn't know what to reply. Lagergren sensed his reflections had shaken his friend to the core.

'Anything the matter?'

'No, no, I think I can work with that. I need some time to take it in, give it its place, you know,' Wheeling answered without looking Lagergren in the eye. 'Oh and something else: Did you get the item we talked about? I forgot to ask before we made our trip to the Dreamlands.'

Lagergren chuckled, 'Yes, I got it all right. It's amazing how many doors one can open, simply by mentioning Lord Holmes's name. I never expected it to be so easy.'

'Show me,' Wheeling asked. 'I need to see it.'

44

New York Bight

Friday, 15 April 1921

When the first two Dreadnought-class battleships, the USS Wyoming and the USS Arkansas, left Norfolk harbour in pursuit of the USS Tennessee, they were lagging more than five hours behind their prey. Naval Command recalled all shore leave and hoped to man another ship before midnight. Two more submarines left Groton one hour and a half after the first three. Observer aeroplanes confirmed the target was heading from the New York Bight into the Lower Bay. Technically, Lower Manhattan was already within firing range of the ship's largest guns. Admiral Wilson and his staff were expecting a message confirming the onset of the city's bombardment any moment. There was nothing they could do to ward off the attack. The only strategy open to them was to seal off the Lower Bay and prevent the USS Tennessee from sailing back into the open sea. If their battleships and submarines could approach the Lower Bay, the rogue vessel would have lost its superior gun-range advantage. Only then, the pursuing ships stood a decent chance of sinking it.

Four forts had long defended the access to New York from the sea, but several guns were removed for use overseas during the Great War. In the years after the war, additional guns were withdrawn from service. Fort Hancock on Sandy Hook was put in caretaker status. Fort Hamilton in Brooklyn was entirely stripped of its guns and relegated to the second line of coast defences. The same was true for Fort Wadsworth on Staten Island. The only fort that could have threatened the USS Tennessee was Fort Tilden on the Rockaway Peninsula in Queens. Unfortunately, it was undergoing drastic renovations to accommodate the new and powerful 16-inch guns that were to become New York's first line of defence. These would, however, only become operational three years later. New York was defenceless, as M had predicted.

The submarines USS S-1, S-2, and S-3, coming in from the east, were eight miles south of Long Beach as the USS Tennessee entered the Lower Bay. They made the entire journey on the surface at their maximum speed of fifteen knots. For the last half hour, Commander Lewis had been fruitlessly looking for their target from the S-3's conning tower. Then he noticed a dark shape in the fading light on the southern horizon. At first, he hoped that, contrary to expectations, an unannounced US battleship might have sailed to the rescue. In the next few minutes, that hope was dashed. The contour of the quickly approaching shape was nothing like a ship's. Lewis was startled by the nearing object's speed. He estimated it must be over fifty knots, which was more than double the maximum speed of any battleship known to him. The thing wasn't heading towards them. It was aiming for a location that'd put it squarely between the submarines and the Lower Bay, cutting off their access to the basin. Lewis decided to break the self-imposed radio silence to warn the captains of the two other submarines. Lieutenant Commanders Berrien and Quigley emerged from their respective conning towers. They were just in time to see the object positioning itself at the tip of the Rockaway Peninsula, a mile south of Rockaway Point.

What happened next dumbfounded them. A massive upper body rose from the water until it towered three hundred feet above the waves. The Bight's depth at that location was one hundred and thirty feet. That put the creature's size — because it was now clear beyond a shadow of a doubt that it was a living being — almost in the same range as that of a Dreadnought-class battleship. The semi-darkness obscured many of the monster's features. Its seven eyes, glowing balefully in its huge head, were unmistakable, though. It threw its head back and produced a chilling, deep howl. Lewis, who was a passionate diver, likened it to the whale songs he'd heard first hand, although this sound was far more ominous. As the colossus continued its wailing, they could see its ghastly, circular maw with rows upon rows of sharp teeth. Its muzzle was surrounded by a teeming mass of differently sized tentacles — the longest measured well over eighty feet. The skippers had all heard tall stories about a Kraken-like being. It was said to haunt the Caribbean and had supposedly pulled many a ship into a watery grave, but this creature was far beyond their wildest imagination. The Cthulhu waved about its scaly arms with their gigantic claws, repeatedly hitting the sea surface like an aggressive alpha-male gorilla marking its territory.

Commander Lewis ordered Lieutenant Commander Berrien to submerge. The S-2 and the S-3 stood their ground at the surface, loaded their four bow torpedo tubes, and manned the deck guns. The S-1 began its stealth manoeuvre at a thirty-feet depth. The submarine made a southward circumventing move. This tactic could bring the S-1 to the Lower Bay, well beyond the threatening monster's reach, as its sister ships were attacking the enemy with all they had. After a five-minute standoff, Commander Lewis ordered the simultaneous launch of four torpedoes. While the 21-inch projectiles were speeding towards the creature, both deck guns opened fire. The flashes of the bullet impacts on the Cthulhu's torso lit up in the darkness. The behemoth didn't even appear to notice the hits. The four torpedoes reached their target within seconds of one another. The near-simultaneous explosions impacted the beast's lower abdomen and upper legs without inflicting any damage whatsoever. The Cthulhu righted itself to its full length and gave another threatening howl before it left its position. Lewis expected it to charge straight at the two stationary submarines. Instead, it turned south towards the submerged S-1.

In five bounds it reached the vessel and kicked the submarine with its left leg, before smashing it with both claws. The S-1 crew was defenceless against the frenzied attack. As several hull plates cracked under the beast's hammering blows, seawater began to leak in. Soon, the ship became ungovernable. The rudders no longer responded; several ballast tanks were punctured. The moment the monster brought its foot down on the submarine and ground it deep into the Bight's muddy bottom, the game was over. The Cthulhu trampled on the ship until its entire structure collapsed. The S-1's interior flooded in seconds.

The S-2 and S-3 used the opportunity to forge straight ahead towards the Lower Bay. Both skippers hoped they'd be able to launch a few torpedoes at the USS Tennessee before their nemesis caught up with them again. It was an idle hope. The Cthulhu instantly initiated the chase. Being far swifter than the submarines, it was upon them in an instant. The monster came at them sideways and hammered the defenceless ships with both claws. It ripped the hull plates from the vessels' keels and tore the conning towers from their decks. It was over in a matter of minutes.

The Dream Whisperer, who was observing the massacre through the Cthulhu's eyes, enjoyed every moment of it. His servant creature would faithfully guard the access to the Lower Bay, allowing him to savour New York's destruction to the fullest extent. He could have bombarded the city an hour ago, but he preferred to get up close to have an excellent visual of his work's destructive impact. The Dream Whisperer planned to squeeze the USS Tennessee through the Verrazano Narrows, which separated the Lower and Upper Bays. Then the battleship would steam past the useless Wadsworth and Hamilton Forts towards Manhattan Island. It would cruise north until it reached a position halfway between Ellis Island and Governors Island. Then the Dream Whisperer intended to turn the ship ninety degrees and relish the mounting fear in the helpless city. Until the early 1820s, the West Battery had been New York's last — and never used — line of defence. Its old cannons were, however, long gone. As soon as the USS Tennessee's starboard side faced Battery Park, it would open fire with all of its twenty-six big guns, unchallenged. It would level the proud skyscrapers in Lower Manhattan first and then work its way up north.

The Dream Whisperer's only regret was that the office buildings were empty. He imagined he would have been tickled pink watching desperate office workers jumping out of thirtieth-story windows of burning high-rises. He made a note to himself to schedule the attack on Boston during working hours.

45

M's Office, London

Saturday, 16 April 1921

'I'm ready,' Wheeling announced, entering M's office without knocking and with an apologetic Lagergren in tow, who was carrying a small wooden crate.

Lagergren put the crate on the floor while Wheeling unrolled a sheet of paper on M's desk. He had covered it with an intricate design in four colours of ink. As M studied it, he could discern parts in Roman script; other elements consisted of Elfish and Hebrew characters, and Outer Gods glyphs. Wheeling had elegantly woven them together into a round, complex occult sign that seemed partly inspired by Sumerian star charts and partly by cabbalistic interpretations of King Solomon's Seals. M had to admit it looked impressive.

He faced Wheeling without letting his admiration show.

'What's next, Wheeling?' M asked. 'Did you already cast the spell?'

'Can't do that from here, mate,' Wheeling smirked. 'The only way for it to have any effect at all is to cast it in the Dreamlands.'

He turned around to Rebecca and Lagergren, telling them, 'And before you can ask: No, you can't come with me this time. I've got to do it all by myself.'

Wheeling took the paper from M's desk and sat himself down in one of the armchairs in the room. He committed the sigil to memory one last time before closing his eyes, sat back, and went into a deep sleep almost immediately.

When Wheeling opened his eyes, he stood in the rain outside the inn where they'd met Carter on the previous visit to the Dreamlands. At the far end of the street, he saw a black-galley merchant waddling around the corner. Wheeling felt the urge to rush after him and run him through with his rapier but thought better of it. After some hesitation, he pushed open the tavern's door and walked to the back room, where, once again, Carter was waiting for him.

'Why didn't you tell us what was going on in Sarkomand?' Wheeling asked without wasting time on civilities.

Carter stared at the flat beer in his tankard, not looking up.

'Good day to you too, my friend,' he replied.

Wheeling felt torn between slapping Carter in the face or walking out again. The respect he'd always felt for this seasoned dream traveller was all but shattered. Yes, Carter had warned them repeatedly not to continue their journey to Sarkomand. But he should have told them the plain truth, instead of dropping mysterious hints and vague admonitions. Carter had been living in the Dreamlands for ages: If one man knew the true nature of this place, it was he.

'I now understand the Dreamlands aren't what I'd always thought them to be,' Wheeling told his silent friend.

'And what did you think the Dreamlands were?' Carter almost whispered.

Wheeling took a deep breath. The question was insulting. He remembered many a night the two of them sitting together, chewing the fat, drinking, and philosophising how the Dreamlands were the deepest, most secret, and most beautiful level of creation.

'You know damn well what I thought,' he said. 'I believed the Dreamlands were our collective subconscious, a place where experienced travellers and practitioners of the occult arts can purposefully effect changes that ripple back to the conscious realm and influence it.'

'But you no longer think that's the truth?' Carter inquired.

'Hell, no! I've realised the Dream Whisperer and the Dreamlands are one and the same. He's the terrifying void at the core of it all, isn't he? He acts as a vast repository of humankind's psyche, which he can manipulate at will. He sifts through our memories, our desires, our ambitions, our hopes, our regrets, our beliefs, our weaknesses, and uses that information to transform us to serve *his* designs. My dream city of Anhur-Lud, your Kingdom of Ilek-Vad, and your friend Kuranes' Celephaïs are nothing but barnacles on the skin of a monstrous deep-sea creature. They're not what this place is all about, are they? They're frivolous distractions, whose only purpose is to beguile naive visitors! Fancy facades that hide the ugly truth!'

Wheeling sat down at the other side of the table to finish his rant while Carter kept his embarrassed silence.

'The pilgrims we met in Inganok and Sarkomand weren't a presage of people about to lose their lives due to catastrophes in our reality, were they? No, they were *materia prima* — raw material about to be transformed into the Dream Whisperer's agents of chaos on Earth. The monastery in Sarkomand is the crucible where he forges his armies, isn't it?'

An awkward silence hung over the room before Carter pushed his tankard away and dared to look Wheeling in the eye.

'I was a fool,' he confessed. 'For years I've been travelling in the Dreamlands without realising what they were. I came here for kicks, for the kind of adventures my drab life on Earth lacked. It didn't occur to me to look for this place's deeper nature. I became so addicted to the adventurer's life that my existence on Earth became insupportable to me. Only when I took up permanent residence here, I was confronted with harsh reality. At first, I thought a cancer was eating my beloved Dreamlands. A cancer I could fight; a disease I could overcome. I thought dark forces were merely nibbling at the edges of my new homeworld. Before long, I had to admit this pestilence is the true core of the Dreamlands. All I could do not to lose my mind was to go on pretending everything would be all right and fight off the Dream Whisperer's inroads, at least in my own Ilek-Vad.'

'Tell me, Carter, what happens with those poor souls we saw? Do they all transform into subhuman servants, like the ones Janus discovered in the New Orleans and Innsmouth cults or at the Sleepers' cradles?'

'It's not as straightforward as that,' Carter replied. 'This place isn't the collective subconscious of all sentient life on Earth. There's nothing "collective" about it. The Dreamlands is where Nyarlathotep accesses, scrutinises, and manipulates every individual subconscious as if in a gigantic lab or factory. The Dream Whisperer, as you call him, takes the easy road. He looks for flaws, for subliminal buttons he can push to send his targets over the edge. The transformation is usually only a little nudge, a slight amplification of something that was already there in the first place. I've seen it happen so many times. Acquaintances whose convictions and behaviour gradually became more extreme until there was no way one could have a reasonable conversation with them anymore. Chaos has many different agents, Wheeling. Radical political ideologies, extremist religious beliefs, unfettered racism, social discrimination and snobbery, deeply embedded misogyny and sexual intolerance, selfish greed, paranoid conspiracy theories. The list goes on and on. Each one of them helps to create hell on Earth. Each one of them is a string to the Dream Whisperer's bow.'

'Well, *I* for one refuse to sit idly by and let him have his way,' Wheeling announced.

'I told you before. You can't fight chaos. It can only become stronger,' Carter murmured.

'The least I can do is throw a spanner in the works. Come, follow me.'

Wheeling stood up and climbed the inn's staircase that led to the rooms on the first and second floors.

'I never understood why you took up residence here,' Carter groused. 'You could have dreamt up a palace or a castle, and reigned over Anhur-Lud like a true king.'

'I can't stand bigwigs where I come from. I certainly wasn't going to turn into one myself over here,' Wheeling snapped back as he unlocked his door.

The room was sparsely furnished with a bed, a washstand, a table, and two chairs. Everything looked worn and tattered. There were papers all over the floor; the place hadn't seen a cleaning rag in ages.

'Welcome to my chambers,' he invited Carter in with a mocking, grandiose bow.

Wheeling lit a few candles, took the paper with the sigil from his coat pocket, unfolded it carefully, and put it on the table. Here in the Dreamlands, the interwoven characters and signs took on a life of their own. They shimmered with raw power, exuding a subtle glow that outshone the feeble candlelight. Then Wheeling took a seat and motioned Carter to do likewise.

'What does it do?' Carter asked.

He wasn't an initiate in the occult sciences and looked at the convoluted scribbles with barely concealed awe.

'It's a pair of scissors,' Wheeling declared. 'It's high time to cut the umbilical cord.'

46

All over the place

Friday & Saturday, 15 & 16 April 1921

After Wheeling went into a deep sleep, M's eye caught the crate Lagergren had brought in. He looked at the Swedish professor with raised eyebrows, upon which Lagergren put the box on M's desk. It was marked 'Property of the British Museum' in stencilled letters.

'What's this?' M asked.

As Lagergren mumbled a barely coherent explanation, M turned paler and paler. In all of the years she'd been working for him, Rebecca had never seen M closer to apoplexy.

'You've used my name to obtain *what* from the British Museum?' he cried out.

'An oil lamp,' Lagergren squeaked. 'A twelfth-century, Khorasan oil lamp, to be more precise.'

He sincerely regretted he'd been carried away by Wheeling's whimsical idea. He should never have contacted Sir Frederic Kenyon, director of the British Museum, with this silly demand.

The mentioning of Lord Holmes — one of the twenty-five members of the museum's Board of Trustees and the only one appointed by the Crown — had made the director unusually compliant. Lagergren was led to the museum's gigantic storerooms and picked the prettiest lamp he could find. It happened to be a zoomorphic, bronze oil lamp, which had a four-legged, elephantine body, a duck-billed snout with two cute camel ears, and a serpent for a tail. A lid with a small desert lioness on top of it covered the round opening in the elephant's back. It was simply irresistible.

The USS Tennessee had reached the midway point between Ellis and Governors Island, less than a mile off Battery Park, the most southern tip of Manhattan Island. It was making a slow ninety-degree port-side turn. Soon, all of its guns would be pointing at the scintillating metropolis.

The Dream Whisperer, standing on the bow deck, was disappointed. He'd expected the streets to be teeming by now with panicking people trying to escape the rat trap they were caught in, but the city was strangely oblivious to the thirty-two-thousand-ton steel juggernaut. It dawned on him that nobody had warned the population of New York at all. He grinned broadly. That was why he loved working with humans. There were no moral depths their politicians wouldn't plumb. President Harding had preferred not to go public with his plight, hoping some *deus ex machina* would make everything right before anybody noticed what was going on. Well, that was a bet the president would regret real soon.

The Dream Whisperer walked back to the upper deck's conning tower. The fun was about to begin.

Carter was mesmerised by Wheeling's unrushed, solemn hand gestures. The mage had his eyes closed and was humming a single, low note that seemed to come from his bowels. With each hand movement, he lifted a part of the sigil from the paper until it hung glowing over the table.

Element after element drifted upwards and found its place in a construct hovering in the room's stale air. The pieces that earlier formed an elegant two-dimensional design on the paper fitted neatly into a *Merkabah* or stellated octahedron that somehow appeared to have more than three dimensions. Whenever Wheeling slotted a new element into the puzzle, the hyper-geometric, star-shaped crystal's aura intensified until its luminescence became blinding, and Carter had to shield his eyes.

The perpetual sacrificial ceremony at the Sarkomand monastery was still going full tilt. Streams of new converts flowed inexorably towards the gaping pit under the all-seeing eye of the Yellow High-Priest. The smell of fresh blood rushing from the six altars into the arabesque-like grooves in the floor filled the air, which was already pregnant with the persistent drumming and shrieking flute-sounds.

Fleming's semi-transparent likeness floated above the priest in a womb-like cocoon. Its umbilical cord penetrated the back of the throne, feeding into the priest's body. Formless, glowing shapes incessantly travelled up and down the cord.

The final piece, a complex Elfish word that defined Fleming's dual identity as both human and elf, found its way into the mystical construct, which was now radiating an almost unbearable white heat.

Carter held his eyes firmly closed and was gasping for air. Wheeling's humming grew even deeper and louder. Somehow, he managed to sound like a Tibetan horn. Wheeling produced a profound, gut-churning wail that made the room shimmer and pulse.

'Why do we need a bloody antique oil lamp? Tell me, Professor; I'd really like to know,' M kept insisting to an ever more uncomfortable Lagergren.

As he was attempting to answer M's question, Rebecca interfered, 'Look at Wheeling! Do you think something might be wrong?'

Wheeling was shaking all over and perspiring blood. Reddish tears flowed from his eyes. When Rebecca checked his pulse, his heart was racing at over two hundred beats per minute. Wheeling's body temperature was sky-high. His low moan made the tea-cups on the table jingle. Beneath closed eyelids, they saw his pupils gyrating wildly.

A sharp pain where the umbilical cord was joined to his body made the Yellow High-Priest yowl.

Immediately, the infernal music stopped. The priests at the sacrificial altars froze in mid-motion. The pilgrim stream destined for the void coagulated. All eyes were directed at the High-Priest floating above the pit. His hideous shrieks filled the room.

The tube linking him to the womb containing Fleming's astral image darkened. Indentations appeared at different locations, preventing the free flow of the glowing shapes. The shapes themselves grew dim, shrunk, and died as the umbilical twisted and shrivelled. With each twirl of the cord, the High-Priest's screams intensified. Hairline fissures were appearing in the monastery's walls.

As he intended to open the door to the conning tower to give the order to fire at the city's skyline, Fleming fell retching to his knees.

The Dream Whisperer didn't know what was happening. This comfortable body he'd always found so easy to command was wrenching itself free from his grasp. Something was sucking him out of his fleshy envelope. It was a painful process as if all of his innards were slowly torn from his living body by an experienced medieval henchman. He'd never undergone such a cruel sensation before. He tried to hold on to Fleming's body but to no avail. He felt his grip weakening; he was inescapably drawn into sinister emptiness.

How was this possible? He was the Dark Void! He was the Crawling Chaos!

The umbilical cord was almost entirely desiccated. It looked brittle and dead. A few more twists and turns, and it would snap.

The Yellow High-Priest's veil was torn. His face was nothing but an obsidian chasm with two feverish, red eyes. He was sitting on his knees on the floating throne's platform, tearing at his garb. His screaming had stopped. He was twitching in eerie silence while the rest of the room was congealed in time.

One more contortion and the cord broke with a dry crack. The womb containing Fleming's image popped out of existence.

Where the hell was he?

Fleming was on his hands and knees on a steel-bolted floor; an icy wind cut right through his flimsy clothes. Every part of his body felt bruised and mauled. His eyes were tearing up; his vision blurred. Fleming swallowed back bile. When he tried to move his right hand to his face, it felt as if he'd forgotten how to use his muscles. He possessed memories that didn't appear to be his own — images imposing themselves on his mind's eye.

This body felt awkward, borrowed from somebody else without the instruction manual. Every single insignificant movement took incredible effort. Fleming's lungs were hurting. They felt like leathery, crackled bellows in a smithy that hadn't seen a live forge in ages. He tried to look up. Unrelated impressions coalesced in a dizzying turmoil. Gravity's pull was unconquerable, and Fleming fell over. Snot dripped from his nose in his mouth. His stomach was empty; nausea made him dry-heave.

The link was gone! The stable presence that had accompanied it ever since its awakening had disappeared without a trace. The voice in its head — the one that used to tell it what to do and think — wasn't there anymore.

The Cthulhu looked around helplessly. It was completely dark, but that was no issue. Its vision picked up wavelengths far beyond both infrared and ultraviolet. It turned around, where it had last sensed the presence of its master, in the Upper Bay.

The creature waded in a northerly direction, leaving the Lower Bay via the Verrazano Narrows to investigate.

'Did I do it? Did I get it right?' Wheeling screamed, eyes wide open, pupils dilated as if he'd taken a *peyote* overdose.

Rebecca was dabbing his brow with a damp, cool towel when he jumped up. His forehead narrowly missed her chin.

'I think I got it!' he announced excitedly. 'Did you notice anything special about the oil lamp?'

M glowered at him.

'What exactly did you do, Wheeling? And what about the oil lamp?' he asked.

Utter darkness. The Dream Whisperer was constrained, chained up in a miserable, lightless dungeon. His possession of Fleming had abruptly ended, against his own volition. He'd been unable to fight the separation, and that infuriated him beyond words.

He was the Crawling Chaos! *Nothing* could hold him back. He didn't understand. Where was he now? Why was he sightless? Why wasn't he free to roam the Earth in search of another human to possess? Why did he feel completely isolated? Why had he lost contact with his core being?

460

The Dream Whisperer tried to push against the boundaries that held him captive, to no avail. He raged and shouted. The darkness absorbed all sounds without replying, not even with an echo.

Dagon sensed a wave of unrest circling the globe. His Deep Ones felt disoriented. Matters were worse among the disciples onshore and were likely to deteriorate further in the future. His sway over them was slipping; the first heresies were already arising.

Something bad had occurred. The Dream Whisperer's presence on Earth was gone, his influence eclipsed. Dagon had little sympathy for the fickle Outer God but had to admit he was in Nyarlathotep's debt. His amphibian army had swollen to unprecedented numbers. Dagon knew he had the transformations the Dark God accomplished in the Dreamlands to thank for it.

He needed to find out what had happened.

Slowly, ever so slowly, Fleming grew accustomed again to his physique. Last years' memories were sketchy. He knew he'd been tricked and invaded by the Dream Whisperer, who'd pushed him rudely aside in his body. He'd felt like a quadriplegic, imprisoned in a frame over which he had no control at all. He'd seen, heard, and remembered things, though, enough to connect the dots.

He was on a ship. Why was he on a ship? The Tesla gun. It was a failure. Insufficient range. Think, Fleming, think! They were about to reduce New York to ashes. Or had that already happened? Fleming got to his feet — achingly slow, retching. The guns were silent. There was no cordite smell in the air.

There was hope still. Fleming looked past the conning tower and saw the city lights: Everything was calm.

The Yellow High-Priest got up.

Only the goat-men were still running around in total panic inside the monastery. There was no trace of the pilgrims anymore. The pit had vanished. The walls were cracked and crumbled in some places.

The Dream Whisperer's access to the human subconscious was blocked. The source had dried up. There were no more minds to trawl and subvert. This realm had become barren; it had lost its reason to exist.

What had happened? The connection to Fleming had withered. How could that be? Why wasn't his Earth avatar connecting with another sentient being? He always used to have a solid link with his presence on Earth. He'd seen through his captives' eyes, heard with their ears, felt, smelt, tasted. Now: nothing — complete sensory deprivation. Somebody had slammed a door in his face; Nyarlathotep felt weakened.

He shed his tattered garb and showed his true essence. The Men of Leng screamed, their minds gone in an instant.

Captain Leigh blinked. He recognised the skyline on starboard.

His last recollection was that he was boarding his vessel to test the new guns. He noticed the other officers in the room were also out of sorts. They looked about them uncertainly, asking themselves the same questions he was struggling with.

What were they doing here, in the Upper Bay, a mile from the tip of Battery Park? Leigh realised he needed to issue a comforting message to his crew, but what was he to say?

'Captain?' he heard one of his officers — Boreman, if he remembered well — say. 'Sir, incoming on port side, Sir.'

The door swung open, and a man stumbled in. Commander Fleming. God, the man looked a fright. No sea legs at all, that one. The water was dead calm.

'Sir? I've never seen anything like that, Sir!' Boreman almost shouted, panic making him slur his speech.

Leigh looked in the direction Boreman was pointing. An unspeakable monster was wading in their direction, coming from the south.

Wheeling was on the verge of fainting, his energy spent.

After his first frenetic outburst, he'd sagged back on M's couch. Rebecca had poured him a glass of water but couldn't make him drink. Lagergren checked Wheeling's pulse and was reassured the heart rate had come down to more normal levels. The fever was gradually ebbing away.

M was an impatient onlooker, pacing the room. He felt entirely out of the loop — a feeling new to him. Was New York saved? Had Fleming been freed of his parasite? He wanted to grab Wheeling by the shoulders and shake the fellow until he provided him with a comprehensive situation report.

There it was: The ship it came looking for, sitting silently in the water, much bigger than the ones it came to trash. In the psychic link it shared with the Dream Whisperer until recently, the Cthulhu had seen the vessel. But there was no trace of its master now.

A blind rage welled up inside it. It felt abandoned, purposeless, alone. Then it saw movement on the ship. Turrets were turning; the gun barrels aimed in its direction. The Cthulhu recalled memories it shared with a long-dead, short-lived sibling. A mountain, a white, icy landscape, and a grey, choppy sea. And a ship almost identical to this one. Noise, light flashes, smoke. Fire raining down on its sibling, tearing it apart.

The Cthulhu howled at the stars.

A galvanised Captain Leigh was shouting in his speaking tube. He ordered to turn the gun turrets to the port side and provided the gunners with their target's co-ordinates.

The Cthulhu's scream was bloodcurdling. The crew felt the ship quivering like a toy.

To Fleming, everything appeared to be happening in a haze. The frantic activity in the conning tower, the crew scrambling to their positions, the sound of the gun turrets turning. The nausea he'd felt since his awakening prevented him from thinking clearly.

The officers, focused on their impending engagement with the monster, ignored him. Feeling superfluous, he stepped outside again and closed the door behind him. Fleming walked down to the port-side superstructure deckhouse, where the anti-aircraft armament and a Tesla gun were situated. The batteries weren't manned; the captain planned to use only his biggest guns on this adversary from hell.

Fleming could clearly see the Cthulhu standing in the moonlight, bellowing in the night.

The gun blasts were deafening; all of the USS Tennessee's twenty-six big guns were blazing. Hurriedly, Fleming had to cover up his ears with his hands to protect his eardrums against the racket.

After a ten-minute bombardment, the captain ordered a ceasefire. It took a while for the smoke to clear and to ascertain the damage done. When visibility was restored, the sight was disheartening. The Cthulhu was standing where it had been before the shelling. It emitted a faint, reddish glow but was otherwise unharmed. Whether the shells had bounced off the monster or the target had absorbed their kinetic energy was unclear. The bottom line was that the vessel's heaviest ordnance had no effect whatsoever on the creature. The Cthulhu started ambling towards the ship.

The USS Tennessee had no way of escape.

Admiral Wilson was having a bad day.

The president and the US secretary of state had been chewing his ear off after he had to report the theft of the Navy's most modern battleship to them. Ever since, they'd been on the phone every thirty minutes. The last time they called, Wilson had to tell them communication with all three submarines in pursuit of the rogue battleship had been lost, and they had to be presumed destroyed.

This time, he had better news. New York hadn't been bombarded, and the USS Tennessee's crew had apparently returned to their senses. Captain Leigh had called him to confirm his ship was back under his command. The other news, however, was less uplifting.

'What do you mean, the USS Tennessee has been letting loose with all barrels in the Upper Bay? Has the captain lost his mind?' President Harding was yelling. 'Do they absolutely want to make a spectacle of themselves? Half of New York is watching the show from Battery Park by now! Please, tell me how do we explain this mess to the press, Admiral? Don't these people know the meaning of the word "discretion"?'

'Mister President, they are under attack by a gigantic sea monster,' Wilson cut in. 'If they don't stop it, it will destroy them, and there's no telling what the creature will do to New York next.'

The Cthulhu was two thousand feet away from the ship. It was uttering a threatening, lowing noise that drowned out all other sounds.

The captain desperately ordered another salvo. The target's proximity allowed them to observe how the shells appeared to vanish before hitting the monster. There was no explosion, no flash, not even the dull thud one would expect from a dud shell bouncing off its target. The only

465

perceivable change to the nearing enemy was an increase of its reddish glow.

As the distance between the USS Tennessee and its attacker decreased, the crew fell prey to hellish hallucinations that prevented them from functioning any further. In the blink of an eye, pandemonium broke out. Sailors were screaming with blind fear. They tore at their hair and clothes, rolling over the floor, on and beyond the threshold of madness. The visions overwhelming their minds were unbearably horrific. The officer standing next to Captain Leigh collapsed to the floor and tore his eyes from their sockets with an insane shriek. Shipmates stumbled around drunkenly, beating their heads bloody against gun casemates and bulkheads. Others got into vicious fights with one another or lay snivelling on the floor in a pool of their excreta.

Fleming recognised the symptoms all too well. The teams sent out to destroy the Sleepers' cradles had extensively documented them.

To his surprise, he felt more or less immune against the horrific psychic onslaught. Whether that was due to being a half-breed human and elf or to his long-time possession by the Dream Whisperer, he didn't know — and frankly, he didn't give a damn. Fleming was the only person on board who was reasonably sound of mind. He had to focus.

Why was the Dream Whisperer on this ship? They were testing the full-scale version of the Tesla gun. That was it. How had the Dream Whisperer sold the Tesla gun to the US secretary of state? As a weapon of mass destruction? No, it had been more specific than that. Fleming was racking his brain. Why did his memories have to be so confused? He saw Tesla in his rubber suit and then his hand in a rubber glove, a handful of dust spilling between his fingers. Dust. Destroyed Cthulhu tissue!

Fleming ran towards the Tesla-gun station and plumped himself behind the control board. He tried to make sense of the levers and buttons. The red one was for shooting; that was for sure. There! The master switch. Fleming flipped it and heard the gun spinning up. The targeting system was luckily self-evident. He swung the gun in the Cthulhu's direction. It was only eight hundred feet away. He aimed for the middle of the chest and hit the red button.

A blinding blue flash crackled. When Fleming opened his eyes again, he saw the Cthulhu still standing. It had stopped wading. The monster had a gaping hole in its chest, which was expanding like wildfire. Fleming could hear a sizzling sound while a foul smell filled the air. He aimed again and fired once more. This time, he took the Cthulhu's head clean off. It exploded in an avalanche of chewed-up tentacles and splatters of green goo. Then the disintegrating monster keeled over backwards and disappeared beneath the waves.

As M was fretfully waiting for Wheeling to regain consciousness, his secretary walked in with another telegram. Fearing the worst, M grabbed the message from the man's hands.

There were only two words: THREAT CONTAINED. M sighed with relief, even if he remained uncertain about Fleming's fate. New York was safe; no doubt more details would follow later.

The mood in the room immediately lightened. Rebecca cried and laughed at the same time. Lagergren hopped around, shouting happily. M poured everybody a drink, and they toasted the successful ending of what might have turned out to be one of the worst bloodbaths in human history.

When Wheeling awoke from his slumber, M enthusiastically shook his hands, all animosity between them momentarily forgotten.

'It appears you've done well, young man, very well indeed,' he congratulated him.

Wheeling smiled self-consciously.

'I knew it; I knew it,' he exulted.

'But, still,' M continued with an earnest frown, 'I want to know about the oil lamp.'

47

Edinburgh Castle, Edinburgh

Thursday, 28 April 1921

M was standing in the Crown Square of Edinburgh Castle with Rebecca and Lagergren. It was a grey day, and a very Scottish rain was pouring down. They'd visited the castle's most remote recesses to hand over the Persian oil lamp Lagergren had abstracted from the British Museum. That the professor had done it using *his* name still didn't sit well with M.

They had locked the lamp away in the castle's most remote vault. M entrusted its surveillance to the illustrious First Battalion The Royal Scots, which belonged to the British Army's oldest infantry regiment. The guards were all battle-hardened veterans who'd served during the Great War in such diverse places as the Dardanelles, Arras, the Somme, Egypt, and Palestine. M took the Regiment's commanding officer, Sir Edward Altham Altham — a scion of an ancient landed family and distinguished war hero — into his confidence and informed him of the gravity of his new responsibility.

When Wheeling regained consciousness after his latest exploits in the Dreamlands, he explained what he'd aimed to achieve with his complex spell. He intended to cut off the Dream Whisperer's access to our reality. Their opponent's core being was the Dreamlands. Nyarlathotep ensured the connection with our reality through his parasitic avatar on Earth. The avatar had no material body of his own and relied on the possession of physical beings to further his schemes. The link between the avatar and the Dream Whisperer consisted of the umbilical cord Wheeling had observed in the Sarkomand monastery. The cord was an information highway. It allowed the Dream Whisperer, in his Yellow High-Priest form, not only to have access to all of the possessed individual's senses and to communicate with his avatar. It was also the point of entry to the subconscious of all living beings on Earth. The umbilical cord's destruction served both the purpose of freeing Fleming from his possessor and obstructing the Dream Whisperer's access to the human subconscious. To prevent the avatar from re-establishing this connection and invading another host on Earth, Wheeling had to restrict the avatar's freedom of movement. He needed to erect a mystical wall between the avatar and both Earth and the Dreamlands. In his spell, Wheeling defined the coordinates of a magical space that'd serve as the avatar's confinement. Then he used a physical container to envelop that magical space.

More simply put: He'd locked up the avatar in Lagergren's twelfth-century oil lamp. It didn't *need* to be an oil lamp. Any physical vessel could have done the trick. The container walls didn't hold the Dream Whisperer captive: Wheeling had achieved that by limiting the magical space defined in the spell. That magical space, however, also required physical coordinates, and that was why the mage needed some kind of box.

'And I thought to myself: If we're going to imprison a genie, why don't we put him in an oil lamp like in the tales of *Thousand and One Nights*?' Wheeling concluded, beaming like a happy child. 'You know, like in Aladdin's lamp? Just for the hell of it? Admit it's kind of funny? Right?'

'So the Dream Whisperer's earthly presence is locked up inside this lamp?' M asked sceptically.

'Well, technically, *within the magical space*, but, yes, he's in the lamp,' Wheeling agreed.

'What prevents the Dream Whisperer from creating *another* avatar and starting the whole game anew?' Rebecca challenged him.

'I'm not sure,' Wheeling admitted. 'That's why I've not only confined the avatar, but I also destroyed the bridge — I mean, the umbilical cord. It'll buy us some time, I suppose. I never said it was a *permanent* solution, though. Honestly speaking, I was surprised to see the Dream Whisperer had only one active avatar. Lagergren told me about all the guises in which he suspects the Dream Whisperer has roamed Earth. I'm certain there must have been periods when he maintained multiple concurrent presences in our reality.'

Lagergren agreed. The information on the Outer Gods he could now read, thanks to the Qohl'Hotl, confirmed the Dream Whisperer could indeed simultaneously appear in many different personalities.

'The only explanation I have to offer,' Lagergren said, 'and, mind you, it's a tentative one, is that the Dream Whisperer has been levelling the playing field to make his games more interesting to him. I believe he increased both the stakes and his probability to fail. Do you remember Ove's last letter, Lord Holmes? He'd come to the same conclusion. A game is no fun if the outcome is already established from the outset. With the Dream Whisperer, it's all about the excitement of the game. Reducing his presence on Earth to a single avatar may be part of his intention to make the game as challenging as possible for him.'

'Can your spell be broken?' M asked Wheeling.

'Sure, every spell can be broken,' the magus replied. '*You* probably don't notice it, but *I* can see the oil lamp's aura. All of the initiated can read an aura. In this case, it contains information about the spell's nature and might offer clues about how to undo my enchantment. Still, I can tell you: It'll take a hell of a wizard to make heads or tails of that. I've designed the sigil the spell is based on myself; I haven't copied this from any book. It's a form of encryption if you want. They'll have to break the code first, and frankly — without intending to brag — I don't expect anyone to succeed in that anytime soon. I'm the only one who holds the key.'

'Then we'll have to take appropriate measures to ensure nobody will cast an eye on the lamp's "aura". We'll have to put it somewhere safe,' M concluded.

After some reflection, M decided on Edinburgh Castle. He selected that location because it was a stronghold with labyrinthine vaults deep underground, the access to which was easy to defend. M had ulterior motives for this choice as well. He wanted to keep the artefact far away both from the capital and Janus's headquarters in Glasgow. The latter had been compromised by the Dream Whisperer's escape from captivity, and M wouldn't dream of exposing London to attacks from their enemy's acolytes.

'Let's hope we can keep it safe here,' M said, opening his umbrella as the downpour turned into an actual deluge.

On their walk to the castle esplanade where his automobile was parked, M accosted Lagergren.

'Dear friend,' he said. 'You haven't yet told me how you happened to choose that specific oil lamp. Would you care to enlighten me, if you forgive the poor pun?'

Lagergren smiled shyly and said, 'It was the prettiest of the lot — I especially liked the duckbill and the ears — and it had the benefit of being Khorasan. That's a region in north-eastern Persia, but you knew that, I'm sure. Well, of course, you did. I mean, I didn't want to — '

472

M looked at the stammering scholar without understanding and asked, 'Why on Earth would you choose a *Persian* lamp as a reference to a tale from the *Arabian Nights*, Professor?'

Lagergren permitted himself a small, nervous chuckle.

'Don't tell your Arab friends, but the Arabian Nights were originally *Persian* tales. The *Hezār Afsān* was a collection of stories enjoyed by the Sassanid kings, a Persian dynasty that disappeared in the seventh century.'

'Is that so, Professor? Interesting. I didn't know that. Remind me to introduce you to some *djinns* I know. I think you'd quite enjoy that,' M suggested.

Lagergren cautiously kept his silence, uncertain whether this was a friendly proposal or a threat of retribution for misusing M's name with the director of the British Museum.

48

British Janus HQ, Glasgow

Wednesday, 25 May 1921

It took M substantial diplomatic efforts to obtain Fleming's release from a classified American high-security jail for individuals deemed to be a danger to the nation. For weeks, the Americans kept him in an isolation cell he'd only left for lengthy interrogations. The accusations against him filled eight folders. If the Americans had their way, they would have brought Fleming before a secret military court, sentenced him, and then thrown away the key.

President Harding wanted to make Fleming pay dearly for the humiliating press conference he had to endure about the USS Tennessee's presence and actions in New York's Upper Bay. With great effort, his staff covered up the loss of the aeroplanes and submarines, as well as the Cthulhu's existence. They ascribed the rogue battleship's actions to an official Navy exercise, vetted by Naval Command and the War Department, purposed to test the effectiveness of the nation's coastal defences. The president promised he'd bring the test's conclusions before Congress, and that, if necessary, he'd allocate additional budgets to accelerate the transformation and rearmament of coastal forts such as Fort Tilden. The fallen sailors' relatives received generous compensation packages in exchange for their silence. They all had to sign nondisclosure agreements that forbade them to speak to the press. Two over-zealous reporters, who didn't buy the government's ex-planations, were jailed — one for tax fraud and one for in-fringing the prohibition laws. Newly commissioned S-class submarines were assigned the hull numbers of the sunk vessels. A Navy diver team scoured the Upper Bay's floor in search for the Cthulhu's remains but came up empty-handed.

As Rebecca first walked into Fleming's office, the evening of his return to Britain, she had difficulties hiding her distress. Fleming appeared emaciated and hollow-eyed, a far cry from the self-confident leader she'd grown used to. He was filling a cardboard box on his desk with a few books and documents. A twelve-inch-high statuette of a crouching Cthulhu in dark stone was waiting next to it. They looked at each other and then hugged. It was their most intimate moment ever. Rebecca suspected there had been instants when Fleming had more than mere friendly feelings for her, but her inclinations and his troubled his-tory had always stood in the way of their relationship be-coming anything more than a professional one, laced with mutual respect and camaraderie.

'So good to have you back, Fleming,' Rebecca whis-pered, wiping away her tears. 'I can't imagine how it's been for you, all this time.'

'Well, to be honest with you, neither can I,' Fleming replied with downcast eyes, avoiding her gaze. 'Most of it is a blur. I recall enough to make it painful. Lying to all of you and, worst of all, killing Ove — he made sure I remembered that all right, the son-of-a-bitch.'

Rebecca was unsure about how to proceed. If Flem-ing was ready to pour his heart out, she was sure he'd come to her. Now, however, wasn't that time. She sensed a tur-moil of emotions raging inside him. It was all too recent, too raw to have a healing conversation about what he'd gone through. She imagined he remembered much more than he let on. The burden of his guilt was visibly crushing him.

'What are you doing?' she asked.

'As you can see,' Fleming said, pointing at the box. 'I'm packing my things.'

'What on Earth for?'

'I'm done here, Rebecca. I can't be part of Janus anymore. I'm not even sure whether I'd want to be.'

'Why?'

'After everything that's happened, the Americans don't trust me anymore. They need a scapegoat, and if I was in *their* shoes, I wouldn't be sure either whether I was still to be considered trustworthy.'

'What are you saying, Fleming? You're so unfair to yourself!'

'I've been the Dream Whisperer for three and a half years, Rebecca!' Fleming argued. 'Even now he's gone, I feel his lingering presence inside of me. This possession has changed me to the core. How could it not? I don't know whether I'll ever be entirely myself again. I feel so sullied — it's as if his filthy mind is all over me.'

Fleming shuddered with disgust. Having been a vessel for the most evil being known to man for years filled him with self-loathing. Rebecca took him by the arm.

'That's the trauma speaking, Fleming. You have to give it time. Get help to get over it; heal your wounds; learn to love yourself again. Find somebody to talk to. You know I'm there for you if you need me. It wouldn't be normal if you didn't feel shattered and upset after what you've gone through, but that doesn't mean you've become a bad or even a different person.'

Fleming shrugged, unconvinced.

'Anyway, what happened won't only be the end of me as Janus's leader,' he said. 'Janus itself won't survive the Dream Whisperer's deceptions. The Americans are in a

477

vindictive mood. They're convinced this could never have happened to them if they'd been in charge all along.'

'That's such nonsense, and you know it!' Rebecca spat. 'M was right to propose an international co-operation. We'll be so much less effective if we have to face the Dream Whisperer individually. He doesn't respect borders; pitting nations against one another is what he does best. Haven't they learnt anything from the Great War?'

'President Harding isn't President Wilson, Rebecca. Wilson, however flawed, was a visionary man. His successor wants to go back to an idyllic past that's never existed in the first place. His voters care only about their own back yard, not about the rest of the world. It'll take another world conflict to ripen the minds on international co-operation — if there's still a world left afterwards.'

'M trusts you,' Rebecca said. 'He moved heaven and Earth to get you back.'

'I know. I'm grateful to M, but he's skilled enough as a politician to know I'm hopelessly tainted, no longer an asset of any value,' Fleming pointed out. 'He'll move on as well. I know I would. M is meeting with the Americans and French today in London about Janus's future. I'm expecting a phone call any minute.'

'What are your plans? The secret service has been your entire life for so many years.'

'I don't know,' Fleming said. 'Being a gentleman farmer didn't work out so well when I tried it the last time. I need some more time to figure out what to do with my life. In the past, I could talk these kinds of things through with my grandmother, but she's left for good. I'm on my own now.'

He was so damned lonely. Although the secret service wasn't his first career choice, he'd given it all he had. In return, it helped him to forget what he could have had with his wife and daughter. Leaving Janus made him miserable. During the sea voyage home, Fleming hardly left his cabin.

Mingling with other people and the conversations turning to the inevitable 'Hey, and what do you do for a living?' were more than he could take right now. It felt as if his identity had been stripped away a second time. He picked up the Cthulhu statue to put it in the box.

'What's that ugly thing?' Rebecca asked with disgust.

'A souvenir. It represents a Cthulhu. A team raiding a cult in the New Orleans swamps brought it back with them. It's got nothing on the real thing, I can tell you.'

'Are you sure you want to take it with you?'

Before Fleming could answer, the phone on his desk rang.

'London calling, Sir,' he heard the operator say before patching through.

M came immediately to the point, sounding strangely upbeat.

'The Americans were intractable, as was to be expected,' he announced. 'They were adamant they wanted to leave Janus and take care of things at their end themselves. They wanted us to pay for their lost aeroplanes and submarines, but I've dissuaded them from taking that line of argument any further. It ended with pledges nobody will adhere to — of keeping one another informed, ad hoc collaborations if and when required, and so on, and so forth. It'll all be put to writ and then duly ignored.'

'What about the French?' Fleming asked, looking at Rebecca.

'Business as usual. They take a far more relaxed view of events,' M answered. 'The French prime minister, our good friend Aristide Briand, who's also in charge of external affairs, already contacted me earlier to confirm his continued support of our project. Please, inform Doctor Mumm when you see her because this concerns her directly.'

'She's standing here with me, M; she'll be glad to hear it.'

'What about *you*?' Rebecca mouthed.

'The French were also highly appreciative of your past performance,' M continued as if he'd read Rebecca's mind. 'They agreed to you leading Janus for the foreseeable future and asked me to welcome you back on their behalf. By the way, the Americans intended to claim the name Janus; so we had to tell them to go stuff themselves — in more diplomatic wordings, naturally. We'll speak later. I have some things I need to clear off my plate here. See you soon.'

Fleming stood dumbfounded for a while after M hung up the phone.

'What?' Rebecca wanted to know.

'They want me to stay on,' he said in astonishment.

49

Gilbert Place, Bloomsbury, London

Monday, 5 June 1921

Although M had baulked at putting Wheeling on Janus's payroll, he'd been uncommonly generous. The fee he paid him was enough to cover the artist's rent and living expenses for the next fourteen months. That was a luxury Wheeling hadn't experienced since his demobilisation two years ago. Encouraged by the sales of the book he published earlier that year, Wheeling was dreaming about publishing a periodical to popularise his mystical ideas. He was held in sufficiently high esteem in London's esoteric circles to find several eager contributors to this project. The people he contacted all reacted enthusiastically, and he'd already written two articles himself.

His most recent experiences in the Dreamlands had provided him with radically new insights. Wheeling planned to use them in a new book that was sure to cause a stir among the initiated and give his former friend Aleister Crowley a run for his money. As a teaser, he wrote a six-page essay on the subversion of the subconscious by occult forces. He told Lagergren about his intentions. Although the professor advised against any such publication, Wheeling — who was aspiring to a role of recognised spiritual mentorship in the esoteric community — went ahead nevertheless. He phrased his narrative in the typical abstruse language only accessible to the cognoscenti and distributed the essay through dozens of small specialist bookshops. To Wheeling's delight, it was selling like hotcakes. After four weeks, the text was already well into its third printing and had attracted several favourable reviews in hermetic magazines.

The future was looking bright — except for his art, which didn't sell. Wheeling was a brilliant draughtsman, yet his symbolist drawings and mysterious paintings of angels and demons were hopelessly outmoded. They were a throwback belonging to *fin-de-siècle* aesthetics, unfit for a world catapulted into modernity by the horrors of war. The few collectors still willing and able to spend money on art looked elsewhere. Consequently, there wasn't a single art gallery interested in showing his work. That forced Wheeling to exhibit in local pubs where his most exquisite drawings sold for a pittance. It was humiliating. Among drinking buddies, and after a few pints, Wheeling was given to self-pitying rants. He railed against all hacks who had the ear of incompetent critics nowadays and made life impossible for authentic artists like him. The drunkards surrounding him wholeheartedly agreed, drank another pint, and then ignored his griping like any snobbish art critic would have done.

Gilbert Place was a narrow street at a stone's throw from the British Museum. Wheeling's single-room flat was a small, rickety affair, which lacked the large north-facing windows every decent artist's studio ought to have. He used to draw and paint by artificial light — if and when he could afford to pay the electricity bill. The funds provided to him by M allowed the artist to look for an alternative to his untidy hovel. Lately, Wheeling often walked the streets of Clerkenwell and Southwark with that specific purpose in mind. In his eagerness to find a new dwelling, he failed to observe several individuals consistently followed him around. Lagergren had been right in his attempt to dissuade Wheeling from publishing a text that all too clearly relied on his recent experiences in the Dreamlands. Even if Wheeling refrained from mentioning any of the Dream Whisperer's sobriquets in the essay, his obscure references were well understood. At least, they were by a few members of his readership who also happened to belong to a secret East London Dagon cult. Word had gotten around.

At first, only a single person shadowed Wheeling. After a few days, reinforcement arrived, and a team of six began to monitor his activities. They tried to behave as inconspicuously as possible, although their habit of partially covering their faces with scarves must have looked odd to any casual observer. The late spring was unusually warm and sunny, with temperatures in the low eighties. Their leader was a sturdy, muscular fellow. He wore a flat cap with a stiff brim, which obscured his eyes, and simple working-class clothes in dull colours. The man always turned up his coat lapels to hide his throat and most of the lower half of his face. Whenever possible, he walked on the shady side of the street. He had large, unnaturally round eyes, an almost non-existing nose with two slanted breathing slits above a wide, lipless mouth, and a receding chin. His skin appeared iridescent and scaly. To avoid attracting attention, he kept his webbed hands in his pockets at all times. The same was true of three other team members; the remaining two seemed to be regular humans. They spoke Ugaritic mixed with even more ancient Mesopotamian dialects.

That night, when Wheeling arrived at his home — more than slightly inebriated — a hansom cab was waiting in his street. He didn't pay it any attention, drunkenly fumbling with his key. Inserting the key in the lock, he noticed the door had been ajar all the time. Wheeling cursed his careless co-occupants and staggered up the dark stairs to his dismal garret. Arriving in his room, he tried to switch on the light, to no avail. In the gloom, Wheeling saw that the single bulb hanging from a wire from the ceiling had been shattered. Glass splintered under his feet. He picked up a strong iodine scent before a club hit him in the back of the head. Everything went black. Two men wrapped him in a worn tarpaulin; a third walked up the stairs to verify whether everything went according to plan. In absolute silence, they carried the tarp down the stairs. A fourth individual was waiting for them in the otherwise empty street and held open the horse-drawn cab's door. With some difficulty, they squeezed their load inside. One man entered the cab to sit next to Wheeling, another climbed on the sprung seat behind the vehicle, and they rode off into the night. The two others walked away in opposite directions.

The hansom rattled in the direction of the Thames. It reached the quays near Blackfriars Bridge twenty minutes later. An old, paddle-wheeled steam tug was waiting for it. Two men helped unload Wheeling from the cab and carried him on board. A few minutes later, the boat left the quay, steadily chuffing towards the river's estuary.

50

Edinburgh Castle, Edinburgh

Monday, 12 June 1921

Rebecca hadn't expected to be back in Edinburgh so soon. She was standing with Fleming in the castle's outer ward. The bright afternoon sun and the clear blue sky belied the dark circumstances that precipitated their visit.

That morning, M had called Fleming around ten.

'Bad news, I'm afraid,' he announced, coming straight to the point. 'I need you to catch the first train to Edinburgh. I received a call from Sir Edward Altham Altham to inform me that the guard at the castle was overpowered last night and that the receptacle with the Dream Whisperer is gone.'

Fleming cursed in Elfish, something he only did when deeply distressed.

'That's the second time the Dream Whisperer has escaped on my watch! What happened exactly?' he asked after calming down a bit.

'This has nothing to do with you, Fleming. The Lieutenant Colonel is waiting for you. He'll debrief you upon your arrival, but it's bad. Apparently, the guards were swamped by large numbers of fish-men during the night. There are few survivors.'

'How many casualties?'

'Of the three platoons present at Edinburgh Castle, there are three survivors,' M said. 'I want you to question them as soon as possible. Take Doctor Mumm along as well if you please.'

'Why?'

'Four assailants were left dead. One was taken prisoner and is still alive, albeit in a critical condition. The wounded one is cared for in the castle's former hospital building, as are the injured guards. I thought Doctor Mumm could perform an autopsy on the fish-men's corpses. Maybe it could teach us a few things about their provenance.'

'Wheeling told us they wouldn't be able to break the spell without his help. When they find out, he'll be their next target,' Fleming warned.

'I had the same thought,' M agreed. 'This morning, I sent over a couple of secret agents to his Bloomsbury studio. Wheeling wasn't there. They found traces of a struggle. The light bulb in his room was shattered. A heavy load was dragged towards the door and down the staircase. Mister Wheeling wasn't exactly diligent in the cleaning department; the marks in the dust told an unmistakable tale. Webbed hand- and footprints completed the picture.'

'When did that happen?' Fleming asked, sounding concerned.

'His housemates weren't clear on the subject. They didn't hear or see anything suspicious. None of them had much contact with Wheeling. They thought he was a bit of an odd duck — can you imagine that? The other tenants hadn't seen Wheeling in at least a week; that much was obvious.'

'The fish-men found out about Edinburgh through him,' Fleming concluded.

'Yes, it would appear so,' M said. 'It's my fault. I should have put him on our payroll. He would have been easier to control and censor. No doubt that pamphlet he published became his undoing.'

'What do you propose, M?'

'Send over Professor Lagergren. I'll scour the occult publishers and bookstores in London with him. We'll try to find out if Wheeling's latest publication attracted some unusual attention.'

Lieutenant Colonel Sir Edward Altham Altham was embarrassed by the entire affair. He received his visitors in the castle's Governor's House and introduced his aide, Captain Stuart Craig, a ramrod-straight bear of a man in his late thirties.

'Captain Craig is in charge of the incident's investigation. He'll answer all your questions. Needless to say, what happened is a black mark on the regiment's reputation. We'll give you our full co-operation. Let me know if you need me.'

Captain Craig first took them to the square in front of the new barracks.

'The main group of attackers came from the south side,' he indicated with his arm. 'They approached the Castle Rock via Johnston Terrace and scaled the basalt rock from there like lizards without using ropes or any other climbing gear. They scrambled over the defences nearest to the south-eastern side of the barracks. The intruders then made their way to the great hall on their right and descended into the casemates. From there, they reached the subterranean chambers where we kept the *Object*.'

He walked back to the Governor's House in the direction of the hospital and continued his description of the attack.

'A second group ascended the western wall and entered the castle right behind the hospital building. A third group attacked via the north; they came in through the stables and the portcullis gate.'

'How many attackers were there?' Fleming asked.

'We estimate their numbers between one hundred and fifty and two hundred,' their guide replied. 'They overwhelmed the guards, knifed them or slit their throats. The surprise was complete. Nobody expected hostiles to scale the rock walls so quietly and in such numbers. We hadn't considered the face of Castle Rock to be a realistic route for such a massive attack. The cliffs are over two hundred and fifty feet high and sheer to boot. Only one guard detail offered some resistance. By then, the attackers were already in retreat after they'd secured the *Object*, and the battle was a lost cause.'

'The fish-men didn't carry any firearms?' Fleming wanted to know.

'They used knives and short swords. Singularly effective in a stealth attack,' the captain confirmed.

'They must have come in from the sea,' Fleming observed. 'That means they had to travel overland for at least two miles to reach their target. It surprises me they could move in such numbers without anybody noticing them.'

'They probably travelled in small units, taking different routes,' Craig reasoned. 'And it was the middle of the night. Not many people walk the streets at three o'clock here in Edinburgh. This isn't London, you know. We haven't found any trace of a boat that could have brought them to our harbour or beaches.'

'No, it's safe to assume they swam,' Fleming concluded.

'Do you want to interview the surviving guards?' the captain asked.

'No, let them rest,' Fleming declined. 'You gave us an excellent report, Captain; there's not much to add, I suppose. We'd like to see the fish-men, though. One of them is alive, I understood. I want to interrogate him.'

Captain Craig looked contrite.

'I'm sorry to say, he passed away two hours before you arrived,' he said sheepishly.

'That's a shame,' Fleming sighed, feeling more and more the entire trip was a terrible waste of time. 'Did you at least extract some information from him?'

'I'm afraid not,' Craig admitted. 'We tried, but we had the impression he didn't even speak English. What he said before he croaked sounded like gibberish to all of us.'

'All right,' Rebecca, who'd been silent the entire time, butted in. 'I'd like to see the bodies anyway, perhaps perform an autopsy. Is that possible?'

'Most certainly, Madam,' the officer complied, and he led them inside the near-empty hospital.

The five bodies were laid out on gurneys in a cool basement room. They differed slightly in size and girth but otherwise looked alike. They were naked but for leather belts and cross-straps, with sheaths for knives and short swords strapped to their legs or backs. Their skin had soft scales, coloured light green fading into blue, except for the chest and abdomen, which were a pale yellow. They all had gills in the neck. One had two slanted slits where the nose would have been, four of them had no such openings. The hands and feet were disproportionally large, all of them webbed. The tips of the nailless fingers and toes were broad and intensely ridged. Over the entire spine's length, they sported long dorsal fins that continued to the back of their heads. They were extraordinarily muscular. That and the significant layers of fat beneath the epidermis made them look much bulkier than the average human. Four of them showed fatal bullet-wounds; the fifth had sustained a deep and broad gash to the abdomen — probably from a bayonet — and bruises to the face.

'They roughed him up before we arrived,' Rebecca observed.

'Too late to do anything about that now,' Fleming said. 'Are you going to cut one of them open?'

'Might as well do it since I'm here anyway,' Rebecca said. 'Mind you, don't expect any precise clues about Wheeling's whereabouts.'

Before leaving the room, Fleming took several pictures of the bodies with his small camera. Rebecca opened her leather doctor's bag and retrieved a surgeon's gown and a box of scalpels and surgical saws.

When she performed a Y-section, she established the absence of a sternum. The ribs were attached to the spine, and the half-open ribcage also partially covered the intestines in the lower abdomen. The specimen had no lungs. Instead, a voluminous swim bladder sat hugged against the spine. It indicated that these beings used their gills in the sea to extract oxygen from the water, while they relied on cutaneous respiration on land. Stomach, kidney and liver were all high up in the chest. To Rebecca's surprise, the fish-man had two hearts — one on each side of the swim bladder — where the diaphragm would be situated if he was human. The gonads and penis were fully retracted inside the body; on the outside, Rebecca couldn't observe any distinguishable sexual marks. The layer of fat on the torso, abdomen, and back was a little over two inches thick. After she'd removed the top of the skull with a bone saw, Rebecca extracted the brain. Its size and weight were identical to a human one. In the throat, she found, as expected, vocal cords similar to humans'. Digging around in the skull, she also located two air sacks along the temples, as in dolphins. She knew dolphins made sounds by passing air through these sacks, allowing them to communicate underwater. She assumed fish-men did likewise.

'Well, what have you learnt?' Fleming, who'd gone for a walk outside, asked.

'They're as smart as we are and a whole lot more difficult to kill,' Rebecca answered. 'Given the thickness of the layers of fat and their bone structure's density, I'd think they can live even in arctic seas and at great depths. Where that leaves us regarding Wheeling's location: I haven't got the foggiest.'

51

London

Wednesday, 14 June 1921

Lagergren arrived in London the previous evening. Wheeling's disappearance affected him profoundly. Somehow, he felt responsible. He'd involved Wheeling in Janus's affairs by extolling his magical competencies to M. Although Wheeling had proven himself to be a masterful warlock, he was also wildly over-opinionated — a loose cannon, impervious to good advice. During the long train ride, Lagergren cursed himself for not talking to Fleming or M about Wheeling's publishing intentions. Dealing with other people's irrational behaviour had never been his strong suit. Lagergren loved peace and tranquillity, and he kept himself as far away as possible from interpersonal conflicts. With Wheeling, he knew he should have stood his ground more forcefully, but it wasn't in his character to do so. In his late thirties, Lagergren had even stopped having romantic relationships after discovering they all foundered anyway because of his inability to cope with his partners' tiresome emotions. The professor was a loner at heart, nowhere happier than sitting among his books. At least, *they* didn't require any cajoling or stern talking to from his part. He dreaded meeting with M alone. The man was so bloody intimidating. Lagergren was terrified to slip up in his boss's presence, and his apprehensions somehow always led him to put his foot in his mouth.

Lagergren supped with M in the latter's private gentlemen's club, Boodle's in Saint James Street, where they made plans for the next day. When Conan Doyle first included Mycroft Holmes in the telling of his brother's adventures and described him as a quasi-permanent resident of this club, M had strongly objected. For privacy reasons, he didn't want to see his club's name mentioned in these stories. The prospect that journalists and Sherlock Holmes devotees would besiege Boodle's was unbearable for him. The author grudgingly complied and invented the fictitious Diogenes Club, of which Mycroft Holmes was one of the founding members. M chuckled at the silly notion that he'd have invested time and means in such a trivial undertaking. London was positively teeming with clubs. Why would anyone — let alone a misanthropist like himself — want to add yet another one to the list?

Both Lagergren and M were familiar with London's most prominent antique booksellers specialised in the occult. They agreed to narrow their search to bookshops that also offered more current titles on the subject. In the end, they identified six such stores. M also wanted a word with the management of Pymander Press, the publisher of Wheeling's latest essay.

Pymander Press was housed in an unassuming early-eighteenth-century building in Pitfield Street in Shoreditch. M's Rolls Royce turned quite a few eyes when it stopped in front of the humble storefront. The owner, Evander Densmore, was a rotund, middle-aged man, who smelt of cheap cigars. He said he knew Wheeling by reputation from before the war.

'His first books were self-published. Heady stuff, densely written, not easy reads, but somehow they did find an audience. After Wheeling came back from the war, he published a new book at Moreland Press. It sold well —

relatively speaking, mind you: We're not talking about print runs of thousands in *this* market. I'm not sure whether it had to do with the content — because that was as obscure as ever — or rather with the erotic artwork that went with it. Adepts of the occult are only human too,' Densmore declared and winked.

'How did he find *you* to publish his pamphlet?' M asked.

'I approached Wheeling myself several months ago to let him know I might be interested if he wanted to publish another book. Wheeling got back to me recently,' Densmore replied. 'He was mightily agitated. Apparently, the man had an epiphany and wanted to turn it into a new book. He told me he had some groundbreaking ideas about the relationship between the conscious and the subconscious in magic. Half of the time, I wasn't sure what the chap was going on about. So I told him it sounded exciting and all, but that I'd like to test the waters before committing myself to publish a book.'

'You proposed he float some of his ideas in a shorter text, to see whether there was a sufficient market for it,' Lagergren interrupted, filling in the blanks. 'Publishing a six-pager doesn't represent much of a financial risk to you. But it would tell you whether the publication of a full-scale book made commercial sense.'

'Exactly,' Densmore agreed. 'As it happened, I had to reprint the thing twice in just a couple of weeks. It's a runaway success.'

'How did you distribute the essay?' M asked.

'The first run was limited to London occult bookshops only,' Densmore recalled. 'The second and third runs went as far afield as Plymouth, Southampton, Leeds, Manchester, Northampton, and Liverpool. Some forty shops in all.'

'Could you give us a list?' M inquired.

'Why would you be interested in that, gentlemen?' the publisher asked. 'Is there something going on I should know about?'

'Mister Wheeling has disappeared,' M informed him. 'One of the hypotheses is it might have something to do with your publication. Did you receive any letters from readers? People wanting to get in touch with the author, for instance?'

'Why, yes, a few,' Densmore acknowledged. 'It's not up to me to disclose an author's address; that'd be unethical. I put all the letters in an envelope and sent them to Wheeling. If he wanted to get in touch with the writers of those letters, that was entirely up to him.'

'You didn't keep the addresses of those letters' authors?' M asked.

'No, none of my business,' Densmore said.

'Any names that rang a bell?' M insisted.

'No, not really. All of the letters were sent from London, as far as I can remember,' Densmore pondered. 'Oh, yes, and one letter had a letterhead representing a figure from an Assyrian bas-relief — like the ones on display at the British Museum if you see what I mean.'

Densmore's mention of the British Museum triggered Lagergren's curiosity.

'What did that figure look like precisely?' he asked.

'They all look the same to me, Mister. Muscular, big square beard, represented in profile, looking to the right,' Densmore said.

'Any — how should I say it? — "fishy attributes"?' Lagergren prodded.

'No, no, he had two feet, no fishtail or fins I can remember,' the publisher answered, kneading his chin.

'And on his head, maybe?'

Densmore rubbed his eyes and pinched the bridge of his nose, trying to recall the image in detail.

'You may be right,' he said hesitatingly. 'He had this weird headgear, similar to a — what do you call it? Assyrian hat or helmet? It was in the shape of a fish head looking up. Gills in the helmet's front, eyes at the back, lips on top. And then a veil or a mantle made of fish skin attached to the helmet's back.'

'Thank you, that may be very helpful indeed,' Lagergren thanked him.

Back in the car with Denmore's list of booksellers, M asked, 'A Mesopotamian fish-god?'

'Yes, no doubt about it,' Lagergren confirmed. 'Dagon. He's represented in some of the bas-reliefs found at the Sleepers' cradles. I also saw him on the walls of the Sarkomand monastery. Dagon belongs to one of the extraterrestrial species that landed on Earth as a consequence of the Outer Gods' breakthrough. He quickly realised on which side his toast was buttered and submitted to them early on.'

'He could be in liege with the Dream Whisperer,' M agreed. 'How does this help us, I wonder? Could you pass me the booksellers' list, please?'

M noted with satisfaction that all six shops they'd marked for a visit last night were indeed on Denmore's list.

'If this lead directs us towards a Middle Eastern deity cult, I'd put *this* shop here at the top of our search list,' M declared, pointing at '*The Marduk Prophesy*', a bookseller near Covent Garden.

'And why not this one?' Lagergren questioned, indicating '*Azag's Lair*', a Kensington bookshop near the bottom of the list. 'Azag is also a Sumerian mythological being and distinctly more evil than Marduk. The sight of him made rivers boil. Definitely more likely to be on the Dream Whisperer's side, I'd say, don't you think?'

'I wasn't so much guided by the shop's name,' M replied with a tight smile. 'A lot of these booksellers derive their names from Egyptian or Middle Eastern mythological figures. I was more thinking of the shop owner in question. He's been on our watch list since forever.'

'Another god, like Deere?' Lagergren assumed.

'And he's reasonably well disposed towards us. He happened to be thick as thieves with our venerable predecessor Doctor Dee.'

'That's a while ago.'

'Blink of an eye for his sort,' M grunted and gave his driver instructions.

The man behind the counter of '*The Marduk Prophesy*' looked like an ascetic octogenarian. He had a full head of grey hair and a carefully cultivated square beard.

'Can I be of assistance, gentlemen?' he welcomed M and Lagergren with a generous smile; his teeth were perfect and blindingly white.

M introduced himself and his companion.

'Ha, monster hunters,' the bookseller said; the smile was still on his lips, but his eyes had grown cold. 'It's more than a century ago since I had the pleasure of receiving somebody of your ilk.'

'I know. That would have been Theobald Fleming when he was dealing with an Asakku-induced epidemic in Mayfair — bankers and businessmen dying from brain fever caused by demonic possession,' M confirmed, pointedly ignoring the pejorative 'ilk' in the bookseller's observation.

'That's a crude oversimplification of what happened, your Lordship,' the old man riposted icily. 'Humans have the habit of demonising beings not belonging to their race and expect to pull off whatever sort of trickery without paying the price for it. The Asakku aren't demons, but they're no pushovers either. Those men died for a reason, Lord Holmes, and Mister Fleming's intervention was regrettable and disproportionate. I feel contrite about having helped him achieving his ends. He fooled me. That won't happen again.'

'So much for being *"reasonably well disposed towards us"*,' Lagergren whispered in M's ear.

'Be that as it may, Nabu,' M said, trying to avoid getting involved in an argument that would have led him nowhere. 'In this case, there's no room for such opposing opinions. Deep Ones have abducted a colleague of ours. We know they are devoted to an old acquaintance of yours. Dagon.'

The bookseller froze hearing the name and became even more cautious.

'I have no quarrel with Dagon,' he muttered. 'He must have had his reasons.'

'Dagon is honouring an age-old alliance with the Outer Gods,' M confirmed. 'More specifically, he's in liege with the Dream Whisperer. And that happens to be the one Outer God with a long history of intentionally causing harm to both humans and other species.'

The man M called Nabu kept his eyes fixed on his counter, avoiding his visitors' stares.

'I believe Dagon has always been more well-disposed towards the Dream Whisperer than you have,' M continued. 'At least, we've never encountered *your* effigy in a submissive posture, kneeling like a slave to the Outer Gods.'

'The urge to wield great power is fundamentally alien to me. As a consequence, striking uneasy alliances isn't something I'm inclined to do,' Nabu replied. 'Knowledge and wisdom — one needs both to be a decent person — are what I've always aspired to, not leading worshippers or kin into battle. A life in the shadows of greater beings has suited me best all these years. Dagon, however, is a true leader. He's never accepted the dominance of humankind as the finality of life on Earth. Dagon will ally himself with anybody who shares that vision or helps him realise it.

What has any of this to do with the disappearance of your man?'

M explained their tribulations with the Dream Whisperer and the latter's capture thanks to Wheeling's intervention. Nabu listened attentively without interrupting.

'Somebody sent a letter to Wheeling's publisher asking for his address,' M concluded his narrative. 'The letterhead contained a representation of Dagon. Do you have any knowledge of a cult devoted to Dagon in London?'

'Londoners are avid amateurs of the esoteric. You can't expect me to keep track of every silly occult church, temple, or society in the city, can you?' the god said, lightly dismissing the suggestion.

'They are *your* customers, *your* livelihood,' Lagergren pointed out. 'Undoubtedly, you must have an in-depth knowledge of these communities? Even more so if they're devoted to someone belonging to the same pantheon as you and your father?'

'What are your intentions exactly?' Nabu wanted to know.

'We want to prevent Dagon from using our colleague to free the Dream Whisperer and allow him back into our reality,' M replied. 'We need to know where Wheeling's captors have taken him. Members of the Dagon cult may have been instrumental in his abduction. We need to speak to them.'

'You may already be too late,' Nabu suggested. 'Dagon is unusually persuasive. Your colleague may already have told him everything he desires to know.'

Neither M nor Lagergren dignified that with a response. Nabu looked at both of them, shrugged, and smiled.

'You might find this instructive,' he said, taking a magazine out from under the counter.

'"*Pathways to the Divine*",' M read. 'What about it?'

'I recommend you consult page nine.'

As M was about to take the magazine and leave the store, Nabu firmly put his hand down on the publication.

'That'll be one shilling, gentlemen. As you said, this is my livelihood. I can't make a living if I'm giving everything away for free, now can I?'

52

HMP Pentonville, Islington, London

Thursday, 15 June 1921

'Do you know where you are?' M asked the trembling fifty-year-old sitting in front of him in his pyjamas on an uncomfortable milking stool.

The man had been carried into the bare room, wearing a cloth sack over his head. Over an hour ago, a secret services team had roughly lifted him off his bed in his posh Belgravia home at 3 a.m., blindfolded him, and thrown him into a large horse-drawn carriage. During the ride, they'd beaten up their captive without asking any questions. The unfortunate was bleeding from his mouth and had a deep cut above his right eye. The eye was swollen, and it was turning a purplish shade of blue. He had at least two cracked ribs and several bruises on his arms and legs. The wretch fearfully eyed the two large men in civilian clothes flanking M, who menacingly held large rubber truncheons.

'You are His Majesty's guest at Pentonville Prison,' M went on, without waiting for an answer. 'Nobody knows you're here. You won't be allowed the assistance of a lawyer, and you won't be brought before a court of justice. I'm your judge, jury, and executioner. Do you understand that?'

The terrified man nodded.

'Down this hall,' M continued, pointing to the left, 'is the prison's execution chamber. A gallows is waiting there for you if you don't co-operate. Am I making myself clear?'

Another horror-struck nod.

The prisoner was the author of an article on page nine in the January issue of the esoteric magazine *Pathways to the Divine*. He'd signed his name as Baronet Thomas James Havisham of Reeves, Supreme Knight Commander of the Order of Dagon. M had never met him before. Baronets were rarely considered noblemen in Britain, and they certainly weren't peers. Baronet Havisham of Reeves wasn't entitled to a seat in the House of Lords. His title was more a hereditary knighthood, bestowed initially on an ancestor of Havisham's for helping to uncover the Rye House Plot of 1683 — a plan to assassinate King Charles II and his Catholic brother James, Duke of York. The title had made it easy to trace the author and find out where he lived.

'You're a traitor to your race,' M continued. 'You're guilty of actively participating in a secret organisation that aims to overthrow man's domination of Earth to the benefit of a fiendish marine creature and its aquatic cohorts.'

It wasn't a question, nor an invitation to hear the defendant's views on the matter. It was a blunt, irrefutable statement.

'The only thing that can save you from the gallows is a full confession concerning the recent abduction of a man called Morris Selman Wheeling. I want to know where we can find him.'

The baronet wearily shook his head.

'That man is beyond salvation,' he croaked.

M gave his henchmen a slight nod, and they moved towards the prisoner with raised batons.

'No, please, don't hit me anymore!' the man shrieked. 'I'll tell you everything I know, but it's too late to save the wizard!'

The aides looked sideways at M, who signalled them to desist.

'I'm listening.'

'The Order of Dagon is a church of influential people, created eight centuries ago,' Havisham began. 'My father was a member, and so was my grandfather, and his father before him. Church activities are limited to monthly ritual ceremonies in the fish-god's honour, held at our secret temple in the East End.'

'And all you do is sing and pray? That sounds pretty innocent. I find that hard to believe. Are you sure there's nothing more to your little reunions?' M smirked.

'We also financially support a small hybrid community living near Great Wakering in Essex,' Havisham admitted.

'What's a "*hybrid community*"?' M asked.

'A group of people who are transforming into aquatic beings,' the baronet explained. 'As hybrids reach a particular stage in their development, they leave their existence on land behind and go live in the seas.

'What are they up to in Great Wakering?'

'Nothing much,' Havisham answered. 'Their odd appearance prevents them from being hired by anyone. Hybrids can't make a normal living onshore. A few survive as fishermen or farmers, but most lead destitute, isolated lives. Their transformation into Deep Ones comes as a deliverance to them. Most hybrids resent humans for their heartless treatment.'

'Go on.'

'A few weeks ago, a few Deep Ones visited us in our temple.'

'Deep Ones can survive on dry land?' M asked, the raid on Edinburgh Castle fresh on his mind.

'Yes. They need to keep moist but can exist outside the seas.'

'Do they often come to your temple?'

'No, no, not at all,' the prisoner denied. 'Their visit was highly unusual.'

'Continue.'

'They told us a friend of Dagon's had been harmed by a powerful spell and then asked to keep an eye out for London sorcerers who might have visited the Dreamlands recently.'

'How did you find Wheeling?'

'We put out feelers in the city's occult communities and soon learnt about a recent pamphlet causing a sensation among would-be enchanters,' Havisham said. 'I went to buy it in a specialised bookshop and tried to obtain the author's address through his publisher. I pretended that I wanted to offer the writer a lucrative speaking opportunity at my club. The publisher must have passed my letter on because Wheeling himself wrote back, giving me his address.'

'The man is an even bigger fool than I thought,' M groaned. 'Where is he now?'

'The Deep Ones took him and put him on a tug boat on the Thames. That's the last I saw of him.'

'Where is he now?' M repeated.

'I don't know,' the prisoner hastily replied. 'The Deep Ones told me he'd be taken to see Dagon.'

'What'll happen to him?'

'No doubt Dagon will force him to undo his spell.'

'And then?'

The prisoner remained silent for a while, and M signalled his thugs again. They beat the prisoner on his arms, legs, and back until he cried out for fear of his life.

'What happens if Wheeling breaks the spell?' M impassively repeated his question. 'Speak. We can do this all night and the rest of the day.'

'They... they'll sacrifice him!' Havisham blurted out.

'When and where will they perform the sacrifice?'

It took another ferocious beating before the prisoner would speak again.

'Whalsay!' he yelled in pain. 'They'll take him to Whalsay! He'll be their summer solstice sacrifice!'

'Whalsay in the Shetland Islands?' M asked for confirmation.

'Yes, yes! Whalsay!' the baronet wailed. 'It's a sacred place for them! There's been a hybrid community on the island since the dawn of man! Please, that's all I know; please, please, don't hurt me anymore!'

M stood up and cast a last, indifferent look at the pitiful individual on the floor.

'Send a clean-up crew to Great Wakering, and I want a list of the names and addresses of all his church members,' he said to his two henchmen.

'What do we do with him afterwards, My Lord?' one of them inquired.

'Let him rot in jail,' M answered and left the room.

53

HMS Hood, Shetland Islands

Sunday, 18 June 1921

Historically, the British fleet's main naval enemies were Spain, France, and the Netherlands, which explained the large concentration of its naval bases near the English Channel. That picture changed at the beginning of the century when the Germans built their own high seas fleet that aimed to challenge Britain's naval superiority. Sir John Jellicoe, Admiral of the Grand Fleet and later First Sea Lord, understood that the British needed one or several important northern naval bases to keep the German fleet bottled up in the Baltic. Accordingly, Scapa Flow in the Orkneys was chosen as the main base for the Grand Fleet. During the first year of the war, the British reinforced their base to protect it from U-Boot attacks. The strategy paid off. The British fleet's superiority in the North Sea was so overwhelming that, after the Battle of Jutland in May 1916, the *Kaiserliche Marine* played no role of significance anymore in the war. While, since the end of the war, Grand Fleet Command had reassigned several battleships from the Atlantic to the Mediterranean, the Atlantic Fleet's flagship — the HMS Hood — was still moored in Scapa Flow when M called the First Lord of the Admiralty, Baron Arthur Lee of Fareham, for assistance. They agreed to send the HMS Hood and three hundred heavily armed Royal Marines from Scapa Flow to the nearby Shetland Islands under Fleming's command.

Consequently, Fleming, Doctor Mumm, and Professor Lagergren all flew to Lyness, on the island Hoy — the British naval base in the Orkneys — on Saturday and boarded the HMS Hood on Sunday morning. The ship was an Admiral-class battlecruiser, which had been commissioned as recently as the previous year. It was the largest, fastest, and most powerful battlecruiser of its day. The journey from Scapa Flow to Whalsay took four hours.

Fleming and his two colleagues briefed the ship's captain, Geoffrey Mackworth, and the commanding officer of the assigned Royal Marines, Major Derwyn Rees, on a need-to-know basis during dinner the previous evening. For the occasion, Fleming donned his military uniform, something Rebecca had seen him do but rarely. The captain and major were understandably sceptical at first, but they came around after Fleming showed them pictures of the five dead fish-men in Edinburgh Castle.

'The attack on Edinburgh Castle was carried out by maybe as many as two hundred of these fish-men,' Fleming pointed out. 'The Whalsay solstice festival we're planning to crash is a major event for them. It stands to reason they'll attend it in even larger numbers. In their thousands, possibly. That's why we need the battlecruiser's firepower as back-up for our ground troops.'

'Whalsay is about eight square miles,' Major Rees remarked. 'Do you know the specific location where this summer solstice ceremony will take place?'

Fleming had to admit he didn't have a clue yet.

'I think we can safely exclude the island's interior. I can't imagine all the fish-people making an inland trek,' he surmised. 'Whalsay has a coastline of approximately sixteen miles. We have three days to narrow the search down. This year's summer solstice takes place on 22 June.'

'I did a quick search in the literature available to me,' Lagergren said. 'There are indications Druids held ceremonies on the north-eastern part of the island in Neolithic times. The Shetland Islands hold a treasure trove of sites from that period, but archaeologists have until now neglected Whalsay. I could find no information about digs on the island, nor on specific local legends for that matter.'

'I'd like to point out Whalsay has several inland lochs, some of which may be connected to the sea through underground channels,' Rebecca added. 'I wouldn't exclude these lochs from the outset as possible locations for the ritual.'

'I propose we send a landing party to Symbister, on the south-western coast,' Fleming suggested. 'It's the island's main settlement where all the fishermen live. If this solstice festival is an age-old recurring event, they could probably give us some pointers.'

'Who's to say the Symbister fishers aren't hybrids themselves or in league with the Deep Ones? Can we even trust them?' the major asked.

'We'll know soon enough. Hybrids can hardly pass for ordinary humans,' Fleming told him.

Captain Mackworth drained the last drop of his whisky and said, 'You sure are rolling out the big guns on this one. Are you certain this is worth it? In the last war, hundreds of thousands of our men perished; generals sacrificed the lives of thousands to gain only a couple of yards on the battlefield. Now we're going all out to save *one* individual? What am I missing in this picture? Why is he so valuable?'

Fleming looked the captain in the eye and told him, 'I understand your misgivings, Captain, and I can't give you a full answer since we're dealing with highly classified material here. All I can tell you is that this man is the only person who has been able to neutralise an important threat to

511

our nation. The precious knowledge inside his head more than warrants this show of strength.'

After the meeting, Rebecca found Fleming staring at the sea in the twilight. Across the water was the small island of Fara. To the north were the even tinier islands of Rysa and Cava and the Gutter Sound. At the end of the war, a large part of the surrendered German fleet had been interned here — seventy-four ships in total: battleships, cruisers, and destroyers. While the Paris Peace Conference negotiated over the ships' fate, their crews were forced to remain on board in shameful conditions because the British refused to intern them ashore. Right before the signing of the Peace Treaty, *Konteradmiral* Ludwig von Reuter gave the order to scuttle the fleet to prevent the ships from being re-distributed to Allied navies. All but one of the sixteen largest ships were sunk, together with five light cruisers and thirty-two destroyers. The other vessels either remained afloat or were tugged nearer to the shore to beach them. The wrecks were resting beneath the waves, a hazard to navigation. Some of the battleships had their upper works sticking out above the water as rusting witnesses of the wasteful event. Others were lying capsized in shallower waters, waiting to be scrapped.

'Penny for your thoughts,' Rebecca said.

'This is what the end times must look like,' Fleming answered without looking at her. 'Nature reclaiming its ground; seagulls circling over empty seas. All of man's accomplishments disintegrating, consumed by time.'

'You should get out more,' Rebecca told him. 'Europe is rebuilding itself. Soon, this will all be a thing of a distant past we'll hopefully have learnt some important lessons from.'

'My grandmother told me humankind was the most inquisitive sentient species she knew, and the one most eager to expand its knowledge. She also said our nature prevents us from learning the lessons that truly matter,' Fleming mused. 'We forever continue to make the same mistakes. We always find reasons to hate and go to war, and we're becoming increasingly efficient at slaughtering one another.'

He made a sweeping arm gesture at the wreck-filled waters.

'Do you actually believe this was "the war to end all wars"? That from now on, we'll live in peace, love, and understanding? You know, when that German rear-admiral decided to scuttle all these ships, there was a public outrage. How dare he commit such a treasonous act! Some press articles even demanded Von Reuter be shot! The French and Italians were so eager to acquire a part of this fleet to strengthen their navies. You can imagine their bitter disappointment. M, on the other hand, wasn't disappointed at all. *He* intended this fleet to be scuttled right from the outset of the Peace Treaty negotiations because he wants Britain to remain the unchallenged ruler of the waves. Strengthening other nations' fleets doesn't mesh well with that ambition. In M's mind, all alliances are temporary. Every nation is a potential enemy that needs to be checked before it can pose a vital threat to Albion. Self-interest, suspicion, duplicity, and ruthlessness are the cornerstones of all government policies. The lofty goal to build a better world together is just one of those fancy ideas politicians like to flaunt to attract flattering newspaper headlines. In reality, that ambition ranks extremely low on their priority lists. I'm betting good money the next conflict is already in the making.'

'You sound like Wheeling,' Rebecca said.

'Then Wheeling isn't as stupid as M tries to make him appear.'

'And here you are, a high-ranking British civil servant, a soldier even.'

'Make no mistake; I'll do whatever is expected of me,' Fleming assured her.

He'd taken Rebecca by the shoulders and looked her in the eyes.

'Do you realise what'll happen on Whalsay?'

'We'll try to free our friend and colleague Wheeling, who's saved you from the Dream Whisperer at great personal risk, and we hope to prevent that fiend from reincarnating once more and wreaking havoc on humanity!' she responded fiercely.

Fleming took his hands off her and gazed at his shoe tips.

'Yes, true, but it'll also be a horrific massacre,' he predicted. 'We're confronting enemies armed with knives and swords, and we'll fire at them with heavy trench machineguns and bombard the crap out of them with 15-inch shells. Over the years, we haven't honestly tried to understand their motives or reason with them. Now, we're going to kill them, and all that blood will be on my hands.'

He reflected in silence about the time the Dream Whisperer had possessed him.

'In the States,' Fleming continued after a while, 'the Dream Whisperer helped the American secret services to uproot entire hybrid villages and put them in camps as if they were dangerous animals. The authorities separated small children from their parents. Medical doctors cruelly experimented on the captives. The suffering we caused them is indescribable. And we only did that because they're somewhat different from us. They're intelligent beings, just like us. Maybe they're the Dream Whisperer's pawns, but ask yourself what's the cause and what's the effect? Would they be so hostile towards humans if we hadn't rejected them from our society first? There must be a way to coexist without all the violence and hatred, or am I too naive?'

'Would you let them sacrifice Wheeling in a couple of days in the hope to *maybe* have a good heart-to-heart with them later?' Rebecca challenged him.

'You know I won't do that,' Fleming replied, annoyed at her barb. 'But you should realise that what's about to happen on Whalsay will make it *impossible* to start up a dialogue in the years to come. Too much blood. It's a no-win situation for us. The only one who stands to profit is — as always — the Dream Whisperer.'

That conversation still played in her mind when Rebecca first saw the humpbacked contours of Whalsay on the horizon. Fleming had changed since his return; that much was true. The experience with the Dream Whisperer hadn't made him a tainted or evil person, contrary to what he feared himself. What was happening had far deeper roots. The seeds of doubt Fleming's elfish grandmother had sown in his youth were now germinating. More and more, Rebecca saw Fleming struggling with his identity and with the question whether his blind allegiance to humanity's cause, to the exclusion of any other, was justifiable at all times. If unchecked, these budding hesitations, she feared, might grow into an inextricable tangle of uneasiness and insecurity that soon might paralyse Fleming entirely. She decided to have a more profound discussion with him once all this was behind them.

The HMS Hood moored at the mouth of Symbister Bay. Fleming set out with a crew of twelve Royal Marines in a motorised pinnace for the harbour. The battlecruiser turned a few of its 5-inch guns towards Symbister, to provide cover if necessary. When they alighted, a few fishermen were having an agitated discussion on the quay, pointing at the huge warship blocking the exit to the sea from their bay. Fleming introduced himself and started a friendly chat with them. Hearing he wanted to know about the presence of fish-men and their rituals on the island, the fishers fell silent, furtively glanced at one another, and hurried away.

'Well, they don't look like fish-men to me,' Major Rees told Fleming, 'but friendly, they most certainly aren't. Do you want me to round up a few for you and make them sing?'

'What do you fellers want?' a fisher who was mending nets on the quay called out before Fleming could answer.

He looked in his late sixties to Fleming, although it was hard to tell. Lifelong exposure to sun, wind, and the briny sea had tanned and grooved his skin prematurely. The straggly, grey beard and missing half his teeth didn't make him look any younger either. Fleming walked over to the man.

'Did you hear what I was talking about?' Fleming asked the old-timer, already knowing he had.

'Heard you were saying something about the two-legged sea-critters.'

His accent was so thick Fleming had difficulties understanding him.

'Have you seen any, Mister — '

'Tait, Garthe Tait.'

'Nice to meet you, Garthe. I'm Fleming.'

They shook hands. The other fishermen had all disappeared.

'You won't get anything out of them,' Tait told Fleming.

'And why's that, Garthe?'

'They stand to lose too much. They need to make a living for their families. Can't do that if your boat is sunk.'

'Don't you need to make a living as well?'

The man shrugged.

'There isn't much they haven't already taken from me,' he said. 'Lost my four boys. My wife died of the Spanish flu three years ago. If they drown me, it would come as a relief. I'm not that keen on living anymore.'

'They killed your sons?'

'Everybody around here pays them tribute to be allowed to fish in these waters.'

'What do they want? It can't be money, can it now?'

'No, part of the catch. Saves them the effort of hunting for food themselves. You don't pay up, they sink your boat. That's how they murdered my sons. I always refused to be blackmailed. Still paid the price, though. A terrible price at that.'

'I'm sorry to hear that, Garthe. You want to get back at these creatures?'

The man looked at Fleming dubiously.

'You're thinking about blowing them out of the water with your tin toy over there, aren't you?' he asked. 'Won't work; I can tell you that right now. There's far too many of them. I'd bet tomorrow's catch they'll sink your ship as well.'

'How many of them are there?'

Tait made a helpless gesture.

'Hundreds, thousands maybe. I don't know. As many as they need. Never counted them. They've been here forever.'

'How about catching them *out* of the water?' Fleming suggested.

'What do you mean?'

'They come on land to celebrate, don't they?'

The fisherman shuddered and stared down at his nets again.

'Don't they?' Fleming repeated.

Tait nodded reluctantly, avoiding eye contact.

'Yes, that they do,' he admitted. 'Every full moon. We can hear their unholy noise as far as Symbister.'

'Full moon? That's in two days,' Fleming noted, disappointed.

This would reduce the time they had to prepare for the confrontation even more.

'Nah, they make two exceptions, at both solstices. Then they skip their full moon rituals in favour of something even wilder. Folks here whisper about human sacrifices. I don't know; always kept myself as far away as possible from their beastly jamborees. Getting too close to them isn't healthy.'

'Where do these celebrations take place?'

'Loch of Huxter, about a mile to the east,' Tait said, pointing his thumb over his shoulder.

So Rebecca was right, Fleming thought. The fishmen didn't feast on the Whalsay shoreline but the banks of one of the inland lochs.

'Would you mind taking us there? It would save us a lot of time,' Fleming asked.

'Sure I mind. It's a nasty place, but I'll do it anyway,' Tait answered with a wry grin.

54

North Sea bottom

Sunday, 18 June 1921

Unsurprisingly, the Outer Gods' breakthrough into our universe swept along large numbers of marine species. Until then, the most advanced life forms in the Ordovician seas consisted of brachiopods, snails, clams, and the occasional cephalopod. However, the fierce Darwinian struggle for life between the countless competing alien organisms instantly turned the oceans red. Dagon had been quick to seize on the importance of an alliance with the Outer Gods. In a time Azathoth was still of sound mind — before he sank away in his current vacuous, slumbering existence among the stars of his home universe — Dagon submitted to him and prospered greatly as a consequence. The fish-god wiped out many of his competitors in the subsequent wars. The smartest among them looked elsewhere in their search of blue oceans where the competition was less ferocious. They left Earth via the cracks that led to other universes. The Bermuda Triangle was a favourite exit point for them.

Even so, Dagon had difficulties maintaining his dominance of the seas. During the last stage of the Devonian, the monstrous fish that had evolved in the Earth's seas refused to be commanded by the self-proclaimed ruler of the waves and significantly thinned out his armies. When the Outer Gods decided to leave the planet somewhere in the late Cretaceous, aggressive sea reptiles posed another threat to Dagon's hegemony. Fortunately, the ensuing struggle between the Dream Whisperer and the Qohl'Hotl led to a mass extinction that dealt a deathblow to the fish-god's reptilian competitors. Ever since, life had become much easier for Dagon and his kin. Even the advent of man had initially been beneficial to him. This new species showed itself all too willing to believe in higher powers and pay tribute to the sea god. He appeared — under many different names — as an influential deity in the teeming number of religions sprouting from the human craving for supernatural protection. Dagon welcomed humanity's adulation. He even selected specimens among his worshippers to breed a new type of aquatic being that could serve him as a fiercely loyal warrior class. Dagon set up secret cults all over the world with that aim. The alliance with the Dream Whisperer served both partners' purposes well. With the Outer God's help, humans flocked to Dagon's cult in great numbers. They increased his army of Deep Ones at a fast rate, whereas the Dream Whisperer substantially widened his ranks of devoted protectors of Sleepers' cradles. Humanity's emergence thrilled the Dream Whisperer. He saw these newcomers as an inexhaustible source of entertainment. Humans were violent and gullible to a fault, easily to be coaxed into all kinds of mischief.

Dagon followed the Dream Whisperer's antics with an amused eye. Lately, he'd been alarmed, though, by the exponential increase in the new species' numbers and its worrying technological developments. Modern steamships were loud and drowned out Dagon's long-distance communication with his marine subjects. Mega-cities grew on formerly pristine seashores and dumped their waste by the ton in his environment. The fishing industry's increasing efficiency was another cause for concern. Abundant fish schools disappeared everywhere at unsettling rates. In the last decades, Dagon identified humans as a threat to his survival. They were a disease that was rapidly destroying Earth's delicate environmental balance. In Dagon's opinion, the species needed to be either severely culled or even wiped out entirely. He'd applauded the Dream Whisperer's game that pushed humans into a carnage on an unprecedented scale. As far as he was concerned, that war should have been a mere prelude to the Outer Gods' return. His masters would reshape Earth according to their needs once more, without regard for man's existence. That would have solved Dagon's problems in one fell swoop.

At first, he'd been dismayed realising the Dream Whisperer had no intention whatsoever to bring back his fellow gods. His initial reaction had been to convince his ally to do what was expected of him. Lately, Dagon had given the matter some more serious thought. A nagging doubt crept in. He wasn't so sure anymore his alliance with the Outer Gods would or could be renewed upon their return if Azathoth were no longer in *compos mentis*. How could he ever hope to talk sense into a mindless god? Maybe it was indeed better to keep the gate closed to the Outer Gods for as long as possible. However, Dagon didn't want that initiative to be put at *his* door if worse came to worst. It had to remain the Dream Whisperer's responsibility entirely.

That raised the question of what Dagon was to do with his fickle, captive accomplice. The fish-god had been staring at the damned oil lamp for days, trying to make up his mind. If he left the Dream Whisperer locked up in the lamp, the Outer Gods might end up holding *him* responsible for their failure to return to Earth. On the other hand, Dagon doubted he could count on the Dream Whisperer to annihilate humankind. Humans were too great a source of diversion to him to be killed off without further ado. No doubt he'd keep on toying with them — tormenting them while also keeping them alive for future amusement. The second option seemed to be the lesser of two evils. In no way did Dagon intend to be on the receiving end of the Outer Gods' collective wrath.

Twenty miles northeast of the Shetland Islands, the sunken ruins of a long-forgotten, nameless civilisation sat at the bottom of the sea. While entirely overgrown with sea life, the remaining delicately sculpted walls, arches, and towers were a testimony to the refined culture that'd produced this underwater city. In the sprawling market place, Dagon's followers had erected a throne for him, on which he spent the previous days sulking and brooding, surrounded by cronies and guards. The quaint, zoomorphic oil lamp with its peculiar content stood in front of him, untouched. None of his subjects had any notion of how to break the complex spell. His agents had brought the author of the spell to him a week and a half ago. Dagon had tortured Wheeling to have him divulge what had precisely happened to the Dream Whisperer and then to reveal the lamp's whereabouts. Wheeling's tolerance for pain was infinitesimal. Dagon had wondered many times since how this weakling could ever have posed such a threat to the most powerful being on Earth.

Wheeling was naked and hung suspended in an air bubble a couple of feet above the market square. Most of the time, he was unconscious, blissfully unaware of his surroundings. The sorcerer was severely weakened by a lack of food and drink, even if Dagon saw to it that his prisoner didn't waste away entirely. Depending on his verdict, Wheeling was essential to the Dream Whisperer's liberation.

He didn't want to admit it even to himself, but Dagon had made his decision already a week ago. There were three full days left until the summer solstice festival. Having the released Dream Whisperer around all that time, in immaterial form and champing at the bit for revenge, was a prospect the fish-god wholeheartedly loathed. Therefore, he planned to free the Outer God's avatar only hours before the ceremony. The imprisonment had already lasted for a month. A few additional days wouldn't make that much of a difference, Dagon decided.

55

Whalsay, Shetland Islands

Monday, 19 June 1921

Tait was as good as his word. He led Fleming and his men to the Loch of Huxter. Huxter was a tiny, derelict crofter's village north of the loch. Its few remaining farmhouses left standing were roofless ruins. There were several traces of foundations of even earlier buildings closer to the water, indicating the spot had been inhabited for many centuries before going to waste. The Royal Marines searched the ruins but found no signs of life. The loch was L-shaped. It measured half a mile from west to east and was about half as wide. Low, grassy hills surrounded the body of water. There wasn't a tree or shrub in sight that could provide them with some cover.

Fleming walked with Tait to the lake's north bank, pointed across the water at an islet on the other side, and asked his guide, 'What's that over there? It looks like an old ruin.'

The fisherman nodded.

'Sure, that's the Huxter Fort,' he said. 'Dates back to prehistoric times, I reckon. There's also a causeway linking the islet to the bank. I'm not going to that side of the loch, though. This is as far as you'll get me.'

The next day, Fleming took Lagergren and Rebecca to visit the spot while the Royal Marines were disembarking in the harbour and unloading their gear. They walked along the fifty-foot-long causeway to reach the islet, where they found the dilapidated remains of a gate and a wide circular wall a couple of feet high. The fort had a one-hundred-foot diameter. On the farthest side, there was a gap in the wall. A large, horizontal, rectangular slab was hanging half over the water. It immediately caught Lagergren's eye, and he walked over to investigate it. When Rebecca joined him, they stood both speechless.

'What did you find?' Fleming asked from the other end of the fort.

Rebecca pointed at the grey stone. There could be no doubt it was a sacrificial altar. In its surface, several sinuous gutters were visible, designed to guide the sacrifices' blood into the Loch's water. Unlike the other stones at the site, no moss was growing on the slab, despite its unfathomable age.

'It's — it's an exact copy of the altar the red priests pinned me down on at the Sarkomand monastery,' Rebecca said with some difficulty.

'This may superficially look like the remnants of an iron age fort or dun,' Lagergren commented. 'But this altar shows the site's origins are far more ancient. I don't think we have to look much further for the place where the fishmen intend to sacrifice Wheeling. The lack of moss on the stone indicates it's still in use. I'm sure the dark brown stuff in the gutters is dried blood.'

Fleming stepped on the altar and looked over the edge into the dark water.

'No doubt you're right, Professor,' he agreed. 'The question troubling me is: For whom or what is all that blood intended? What antediluvian evil is lurking at the bottom of this loch?'

Back in the harbour, Fleming informed Major Rees of their find. Rees had set up provisional headquarters in Symbister House, the Georgian residence built by the Bruce family, who were the island's lairds since the sixteenth century. The major unfolded a large-scale topographical map on his desk.

'The logical thing to do would be to dig a seven-hundred-foot-long trench parallel to the loch's south bank at a distance of four hundred feet from the water,' he said, pointing at the map. 'We'd benefit from the elevation provided to us by the hillside and have a clear shot at anything clambering out of the water. I'd position a Vickers machine gun every one hundred feet. That should provide us with sufficient firing power. We camouflage the lot with nets, which will allow us to wait until most of them are onshore before we start mowing 'em down.'

'I'm sure you're right,' Fleming approved, 'but I'm concerned we'll be sitting with our backs turned to the island's eastern shore. The shoreline is only half a mile away. Instead of climbing out of the loch, they could attack us from behind, coming from the sea. They'd easily storm down the hill and overwhelm us.'

'I see your point,' the major agreed. 'Then we need to dig a second trench on top of the hill behind the first trench. We'll set up the machine guns in such a way that they can fire down the hill in support of our troops below and in the direction of the shore, in case the enemy tries to attack us from behind. We have plenty of gear; I can spare another four or five guns to guard the hilltop.'

'That's a lot of digging to be done. Better start as soon as possible,' Fleming recommended. 'I'm not sure how deep one can burrow here before hitting basalt; it's not as if we're dealing with soft clay like in Flanders.'

'We'll get on it right away, Commander,' Rees promised. 'Many hands make light work; there's three hundred of us. Don't worry. We'll get the job done in time.'

Onboard of the HMS Hood, Fleming briefed the captain and shared his main concerns.

'We have no idea of precise enemy numbers,' he began. 'There may be hundreds or even many thousands of them. Even if they're coming at us from two directions, the Vickers guns should be able to do an awful lot of damage before they reach our lines of defence. However, I wouldn't exclude a scenario where they keep on coming, wave after wave until they overwhelm us. In that case, we'll need your big guns to cut off their access to the battlefield. We'll have a radio unit that can give your crew detailed instructions. In case the radio breaks down, we'll also have colour-coded flares.'

The captain showed Fleming a large-scale map of the island and the surrounding sea, with a transparent grid overlay. Every square in the grid had been attributed an identifying code.

'All you have to do is to radio us the grid codes you want us to bombard,' he assured. 'Once we'll have finished digging the trenches, we'll add those to the map as well, to avoid bombarding our troops.'

'We assume the enemy troops will exclusively consist of amphibious men like I've shown you in the Edinburgh pictures,' Fleming continued. 'Hopefully, that's the case. My gut feeling tells me we might be in for a surprise. Something might be living in that lake — something old and monstrous. The instant we see something like that popping up, we'll need you to react immediately.'

'Same drill,' Mackworth replied. 'You radio us the coordinates; we blast the thing to kingdom come.'

Fleming wished he could share the captain's quiet confidence. He couldn't help remembering his almost-fatal encounter with the full-grown Cthulhu in New York's Upper Bay. He hoped all awakened Cthulhus had been destroyed in the meantime. Even then, there was no telling what their adversary might have up his sleeve.

'Finally, we need to assume the enemy is well aware of the HMS Hood's presence near the island. A ship this size cannot have gone unnoticed,' Fleming shared his third concern.

'Do you seriously believe they'd attack a *battle-cruiser*?' the captain asked incredulously.

'I believe we need to prepare for the eventuality,' Fleming insisted.

'Assuming these fish-men would be able to board the ship, what could they do?' Mackworth said with a smirk. 'We don't need any hands on deck to fire our guns. The loading process is fully mechanised; aiming and firing the guns is done in the control room. The conning tower is plated with 11-inch steel. The barbettes and turrets have even thicker plating. All our upper-deck structures are impervious to whatever force any attacker might muster. We can seal off all below-deck quarters. Their only way in would be the funnels, which would land them directly in the boilers.'

'Nevertheless, I advise you to arm all crew members with handguns and knives. Just in case.' Fleming maintained.

'All right, if you think that's necessary, I'll pass on the message,' the captain conceded.

That evening, Rebecca found Fleming pacing up and down the ship's upper deck, hands on his back.

'Something is bothering you?' she asked.

He was startled finding her in his path. At the same time, he appeared glad to be torn away from his black thoughts.

'No, as a matter of fact, all preparations are progressing according to plan,' he replied blandly.

'So everything is stellar,' she concluded. 'That's why you're looking so morose?'

Fleming had to laugh. Rebecca saw right through him, always had. He was surprised she'd been fooled for so long by the Dream Whisperer.

'Rees and Mackworth are confident they've got everything under control,' he explained. 'If I know one thing about a battle, it's this: All control goes out of the window once the fighting begins. I've been trying to think about what can go wrong, working out alternative scenarios and what our response should be in each case, but there's precious little to go on.'

'What's your worst fear?'

'Take your pick. That we'll be faced not with thousands of fish-men but hundreds of thousands. That they have another invulnerable monster waiting for us or maybe even a couple of them. That the Dream Whisperer has already acquired a new host, forgets about fair play or restraint, and blasts us with all he's got out of sheer malice.'

Then he added, 'That the Dream Whisperer hasn't yet found another host and chooses to possess me again on the battlefield.'

Rebecca hugged him.

'Don't let that monster intimidate you,' she said. 'We bested him once; we'll do so again.'

56

North Sea bottom

Wednesday, 21 June 1921

Dagon's legions gathered from all European seas — from the Barents Sea and the Baltic in the north to the Mediterranean and the Black Sea in the south — to attend the Whalsay solstice festival. He mustered his troops with quiet satisfaction. They were a mix of amphibious Deep Ones and other weird and wonderful creatures from the abyss. Many-legged, crab-like brutes waving terrifying claws, squirming, eyeless worms whose large maws were filled with dagger-like teeth, strangely shaped, spike-headed fish, and repellent, blob-like beings made of transparent jelly, with a multitude of mouths, eyes, and wriggling feelers, which slowly crawled over the sea bottom.

Only the Deep Ones could stay for extended periods onshore, but he had many thousands of them. Soon, they'd leave their watery refuges and swarm the proud seaports built by man. The days of humanity's hegemony were numbered. His kind would no longer be shunned or have to hide their true nature for fear of persecution. They'd claim what was rightfully theirs and slaughter their oppressors — with or without the Dream Whisperer's support. After Dagon set the latter free, he'd be so deep in the sea god's debt that he wouldn't dare to oppose his bold plans. At least, that was what Dagon hoped against his better instincts. He knew the Dream Whisperer was poor at showing either gratitude or respect. If Dagon hadn't feared the possibility of the Outer Gods returning without the Dream Whisperer's assistance, he would have been sorely tempted to leave his partner stuck in his ludicrous oil lamp. As it stood, the Dream Whisperer's deliverance was near. Midnight approached; soon, the summer solstice would be upon them.

Dagon lifted his arm. Immediately, all warriors assembled around the former market place focused their attention on him. He left his throne, picked up the lamp, and swam in the direction of the air bubble that held Wheeling captive. As the man saw him approaching, he fearfully tried to claw his way out of the air pocket. What did the fool hope to achieve? If the bubble collapsed, the water pressure would instantly squash him like a bug. Dagon made another arm movement. The air bubble shifted towards the altar and then descended until it formed a hemisphere with the stone table at its centre. Wheeling found himself sprawled on the ornate slab as Dagon entered his space.

The sea god didn't waste time on formalities. He wanted to get this over and done with without further delay.

'You know what I want,' Dagon told Wheeling, pointing at the oil lamp. 'Break the spell.'

The close presence of the hideous sea creature paralysed Wheeling. The overpowering stench of rotting seaweed made him retch. Dagon watched him through deepset, glowing eyes, his mouth with its horrific rows of needle-thin teeth half-open.

'I — I won't!' Wheeling cried. 'You can't make me!'

Dagon laughed heartily and put a long-nailed claw on Wheeling's breast, right above his heart. He exerted minimal pressure, and the nail broke the tender skin. Wheeling gulped in panic.

'Sure I can,' the sea creature softly spoke. 'We both know that, don't we?'

He increased the pressure, digging his nail deeper into Wheeling's flesh, and then tearing it slowly sideways through the pectoral muscle. The warlock shrieked in pain, thrashing with arms and legs.

'What'll you do to me?' Wheeling asked, weeping.

'You'll die,' the fish-god answered pleasantly. 'The manner of your death, however, depends entirely on you. One merciful blow with an obsidian knife, delivering you from all pain in the blink of an eye, if you decide to humour me. Or a prolonged, painful death, lasting many, many days, if you don't. Flaying comes to mind. Gouging your eyes out. Cutting off all of your extremities, one by one, preferably with a dull saw. Jolts of lightning, perhaps.'

As he spoke those last words, electric sparks jumped off the deity's skin and travelled over his victim's entire body. Wheeling shrieked and convulsed on the altar.

'You don't want to get under my skin,' Dagon added. 'I'm so much better at getting under yours.'

He tore his nail further across the man's chest.

Wheeling cried out in agony. He feared he wouldn't last much longer. He'd already given them the oil lamp's location after far less coercion. Wheeling couldn't tolerate pain. He'd lived through the horrors of war. He'd been shot at, bombarded, gassed, starved, exhausted, frozen with cold, drenched to the bone, up to his knees in mud for days, but he'd never been wounded — not even a scratch. In deepest despair, he'd considered taking his rifle and shooting a bullet through his foot to escape front-line duties. The prospect of pain always withheld him from executing this plan. He realised what it would mean if he gave in. The Dream Whisperer would have access to this world again. He'd be able to rake about in people's subconscious again, turning them into his mindless tools for inflicting chaos and destruction on Earth. Wheeling would be responsible for new waves of world conflicts, for the deaths of untold numbers of people. He didn't want that on his conscience. He would *not* give in!

Dagon dug his nail even deeper, scratching a rib, shredding Wheeling's flesh further until he reached the right nipple.

'St-o-o-o-o-p! Please, stop! I'll do whatever you want!' the painter howled.

Dagon pulled his nail from Wheeling's flesh and licked off the blood.

'Good,' he said. 'Very sensible. Now, make haste.'

'It — it would be easier if you allowed me to do it from the Dreamlands,' Wheeling feebly argued.

'Ah, what a pity. I thought we had an understanding,' Dagon replied, digging his nail back into his captive's flesh. 'You'll do it from right here. There's no getting away from me, understand? Maybe you considered leaving your body behind and taking up permanent residence in the Dreamlands, like some of your friends? No deal.'

'Aaaah — aaah, no, it — it would be easier, that's all,' the warlock whimpered. 'I wouldn't want to live in the Dreamlands anymore. Please, stop hurting me. Please. I'll do it from here, please!'

'I know you will,' Dagon confirmed. 'Use your imagination.'

'I — I shall! Could you please take your nail out of my chest?' Wheeling groaned. 'So hard to concentrate — the pain — '

Dagon obliged.

Wheeling took a deep breath. He had to calm down and concentrate.

'Use your imagination,' Dagon said, and that was what he'd have to do. Without going to the Dreamlands, he had to imagine he was sitting in his room at the inn. He had to visualise the *Merkabah* hovering over the table, shining its blinding light, and then, one by one, remove the parts of the sigil he had inserted earlier on. It was a delicate procedure. The sequence had to be exactly right. Unwittingly, he made the hand movements simulating the removal of the objects from the magical hyper-geometrical form.

The *Merkabah* was the closest Wheeling had ever come to witnessing the existence of a Divine presence. It was both the sapphire throne of the Supreme Being, the four elements of reality, and a representation of the seven heavens. It allowed the mystical pilgrim to make his journey towards the Divine under the guidance of what he'd call angels for lack of a better word, and to draw down the assistance of the Divine to Earth. It was an infinite memory palace of all things in the Universe, the key to encompassing insight into the true nature of the Cosmos and the forces behind it.

As Wheeling, in his mind, removed the sigil's elements from the cosmic shape, the aura surrounding the oil lamp began to shift and change until it disappeared.

In that instant, the Dream Whisperer felt as if the shackles fell off his astral body. Light chased the darkness that'd been encapsulating him for what felt like forever. A power flux flooded through his ethereal limbs. Like a cicada nymph climbing out of its constraining burrow, he regained the surface. Freedom at last.

The Dream Whisperer's presence on Earth was no more than an insubstantial spirit, a ghostly presence fluttering at the visible spectrum's edges. His first instinct was to possess the nearest human being to get in touch with the physical environment again. Wheeling's exhausted and bleeding frame was the first that entered into his field of vision, and he avidly approached this defenceless harbour.

'This one isn't for you, Dream Whisperer,' Dagon said, swatting him away. 'He's mine. In a couple of hours, he'll be sacrificed.'

The insubstantial shape shimmered and frantically darted from one side to another.

'Who are you to deny me my prey, vile snot-eel?' Dagon heard his partner shriek inside his head.

The fish-god, standing his ground, calmly let the Dream Whisperer's temper tantrum wash over him. After the Outer God had simmered down a little, Dagon informed him of what had happened. How a mere mortal had tricked an infinitely powerful being. How that god had lost everything he had, both in the earthly domain and in the Dreamlands.

'You lost that game, godling,' he couldn't resist rubbing it in. 'You're in my debt big time. So give it a rest. You'll be patient now and avoid aggravating me with your petty fits. We'll first celebrate this festival in honour of an old friend of mine. Afterwards, you can do whatever you like. Am I clear?'

Dagon felt the Dream Whisperer's howling rage and wounded pride bouncing around in his head. Then only an indignant silence remained.

57

Whalsay, Shetland Islands

Thursday, 22 June 1921

The short night set in without much conviction. The sun kept waiting in the aisle, eager for an encore. Twilight rather than total darkness cast its shadows over the island. Major Rees' men had finalised their preparations well in time. The three hundred Royal Marines were waiting in two trenches — one near the bottom of the hill nearest to the Loch of Huxter's south bank and one on the hilltop. Rees had deployed Vickers machine guns over the entire lengths of both trenches, and camouflage nets obscured the troops' presence. Fleming had taken up position in the lower ditch right across the fort's causeway. Circumstances allowing it, he'd lead a group of Marines to the fort to rescue Wheeling from the altar. All would depend on the number of adversaries surrounding the islet. Several sharpshooters positioned themselves in the lower trench to take out immediate threats to Wheeling's life, if necessary. Radio units were in place in both trenches and had been tested; communication with the HMS Hood was functioning as expected.

Rees eyed Fleming's outfit with some surprise. Fleming had donned a tight-fitting, hooded, quilted coverall in an unfamiliar material, which adapted its colours to its surroundings. Underneath, he wore a full-body armour in light chainmail. He carried two slightly curved swords in sheaths on his back and two long daggers strapped to his legs. Embedded in the knuckles of his leather gloves, were four sharp metal talons. His boot tips and heels had similar features. It was the standard elf warrior battle dress. Fleming had added two holsters with Colt Automatic .32 handguns and carried several spare magazines in a bandoleer slung over his shoulder and in his belt.

'Everything is quiet,' Rees said. 'When do you expect them to show up?'

'Astronomically, summer solstice begins this year at around half past midnight,' Fleming replied. 'As it's a celebration of light, I expect festivities to commence at dawn. Sunrise is at a couple of minutes past three. We'll see.'

On the HMS Hood, the sailors had sealed off all entries to below-deck quarters from the upper deck, as agreed. Captain Mackworth and his officers were observing the island through their binoculars from the cruiser's conning tower. The ship pointed all of its eight 15-inch guns at the island; four of them were aimed at the Loch of Huxter. The remainder targeted the strip of land between the hill and the eastern shoreline behind it. All was calm — no detectable traces of movement on the island and no unwelcome guests climbing on board of the ship. So far, so good.

Rebecca and Lagergren remained in their below-deck officer cabins. The captain had provided them with sidearms as well. As there were no portholes, they felt cut off from the rest of the world. Rebecca had argued she wanted to observe the rescue mission from the conning tower or the bridge, but the captain had been unyielding.

Half an hour before sunrise, the Loch of Huxter emitted a soft, white light, which gradually became brighter and brighter until the small lake shone like a beacon. The men had to shield their eyes as the luminosity intensified. Whalsay was a birds' paradise. It held large colonies of breeding kittiwakes, raingooses, arctic skuas, and many other smaller species, which customarily greeted the expected arrival of dawn with a deafening cacophony of calls. As the light first appeared below the loch's surface, all bird noise stopped, and an unnatural silence descended over the island. The absence of sound struck an ancestral fear in the hearts of the hardened Marines. It felt as if they'd been transported into a hard vacuum. The hush prevented them from thinking or even breathing. Several struggled with bouts of nausea. They fell to their knees as they were gagging noiselessly.

'The radio is dead,' the operator whispered, breaking the spell.

Soldiers breathed again, blinking against the light. Only with great difficulty, Rees and Fleming observed that, on the north bank, a procession was stepping out of the water at a solemn pace.

'Damn it! We're on the wrong side of the loch,' Rees cursed.

'Wait for it. They'll come round to this side,' Fleming assured him. 'Never mind. It'll allow us to assess their numbers.'

The first group bore torches that shone with an incandescent light. Next came trumpeters, flute players, and drummers. They brutally rent the veil of quietude with their discordant racket.

'How do they light torches underwater?' the major wondered.

'Greek fire probably,' Fleming supposed, 'or magnesium. Who knows?'

Behind the musicians, three Deep Ones marched with elaborate gold headdresses and breastplates. Fleming supposed they must be the priests who'd perform the sacrifice. His intuition was vindicated when he noticed six amphibians following the priests. They were bearing a gold-ornamented litter on which a man was lying. The blazing torches were casting capricious shadows, making it difficult to distinguish the features of the man on the stretcher. Nevertheless, Fleming had the conviction it was Wheeling. The rest of the cortège consisted of Deep Ones, armed with long spears and swords. Some of them were wearing gold helmets; most went bare-headed; about a third were carrying torches.

As Fleming had predicted, they marched along the north bank towards the east. Then they made their way around the Loch in the direction of the islet with the altar. Only when the first torchbearers reached the causeway, the last Deep Ones in the procession stepped on land. Fleming estimated between two thousand five hundred and three thousand individuals were participating in the event. The torchbearers walked down the causeway and positioned themselves in a circle along the inside of the fort's walls. The musicians formed an honour guard on both sides of the path, before the priests and the bearers with the sacrificial victim ceremoniously strode past them. The priests walked up to the altar, kneeled, and then turned around. They stood immobile, with raised arms, in front of the rectangular stone. Wheeling was lying on a bed of kelp on the bier supported by the six bearers. The remaining participants settled themselves on the Loch's bank in equal numbers left and right of the causeway, facing the water.

After everybody had found their place, the sun rose from behind the horizon. The trumpeters greeted the daybreak with an ear-splitting blast. Then there was silence. One priest, standing between the altar and the bier, intoned a high-pitched chant. Then the two others joined in, weaving a mesmerising and complex call-and-response pattern. As soon as the priests had ended their hymn, the crowd shouted in one voice, '*Y'hah!*'

The drummers on the causeway lifted their arms high above their heads and then began a menacing drum roll. The bearers put down Wheeling's stretcher, lifted him off his kelp bed, and laid him on the altar. Fleming could now see the captive's arms and legs were trussed. The three priests chanted again and danced with slow moves; the middle one was waving a black stone knife in the air.

'Do you have a clear line of sight?' Fleming asked one of the sharpshooters.

The man confirmed he had.

Fleming and Rees exchanged a glance, and the major ordered, 'Take out the three priests now!'

Three rifle shots cracked almost simultaneously, and the priests' heads exploded in fireworks of blood.

Before the bystanders could react, a green flash appeared over the hill. It was the agreed colour code for approaching hordes from the eastern seashore. The thundering sound of the HMS Hood's big guns rolled over the island in quick response, and machine guns rattled from the top of the hill.

'Shoot at will!' Rees ordered the machine gunners in the lower ditch as they heard the first explosions from the plain beyond the hill.

The Deep Ones turned to face the attackers' trench and ran in their direction. The Vickers machine guns mowed them down. Even though the amphibians outnumbered their opponents by a factor ten, their spears and swords were no match for the Royal Marines' far more sophisticated weaponry.

Fleming tried to keep track of several things at the same time: the wave of attackers racing at them, the events in the fort, and also the hill behind him because he expected to see another army of Deep Ones storming over the top. Deciding the machine guns had cleared him a sufficient path to the causeway, Fleming jumped out of the trench with his team of Royal Marines. He ran ahead of them, brandishing both Colts, shooting left and right at assailants coming at him with drawn swords. A Marine to the left of him keeled over with a spear through his throat; the rest reached the causeway unscathed. Fleming kept a Colt in his left hand and used the right one to wield a sword, as he was now facing bloody hand-to-hand combat to reach the fort's inner sanctum.

The HMS Hood kept bombarding the plain behind the hill. Royal Marines' Lieutenant Wilbur Rayden had fired the green flash seeing thousands upon thousands of Deep Ones running ashore in his direction. He knew his men could decimate the enemies before they reached the trench. Even then, the Deep Ones were numerous enough to overrun the Marines' defences and hurtle themselves at their positions on the loch-side of the hill. The explosions routed some of the attackers while others kept advancing under cover of the smoke clouds produced by the shelling. There was no way of telling precisely how many Deep Ones were still moving up the hill. The machine gunners were firing blindly into the dense wall of smoke. Rayden ordered his men to prepare for hand-to-hand combat.

'Intruder alert!' Captain Mackworth announced in his speaking tube. 'The enemy has boarded the ship.'

Through the conning tower's narrow slits, he'd seen the first Deep Ones clambering on board. His second-in-command shot the first two with his handgun. After that, the attackers kept out of the conning tower's line of sight. They must have scaled the ship's sheer steel hull without the help of grapple lines, confirming the analysis of their attack on Edinburgh Castle.

Four of the big guns kept launching shells at the island's east side. The tremendous noise of the blasts and the smoke were a perfect cover for the ship's invaders, who dropped a greyish object the size of a chicken egg through one of the conning tower's viewing slits. The egg burst hitting the ground, and a cloud of acrid, white smoke filled the inside of the conning tower. The officers broke out the gas masks Captain Mackworth had borrowed from the Royal Marines on Fleming's advice. Fleming had been running all kinds of emergency scenarios in his head. One of them was that the intruders would use chemical warfare against the HMS Hood's crew. The Royal Marines didn't have enough gas masks for all fourteen hundred sailors, but the officers in the conning tower all had one.

The Deep Ones found the ventilation grilles in the upper deck, unscrewed them, and rolled white phosphorus grenades into the vents. The smoke spread fast through the below-deck quarters, forcing crew members to the upper deck where their assailants were waiting for them. Fleming had provided Rebecca and Lagergren with gasmasks as well, which allowed them to sit out the attack in their quarters, their doors safely barricaded. The shipmates came out in the open, guns blazing. Many were cut down instantly while others were able to force their way to the forecastle and shelter decks. After vicious knife fights, the sailors gained control of several machine guns they could use against their assailants.

In all the fumes and confusion, Mackworth saw a blue flash light up over the island. That was the convened signal for shelling the loch itself. The cloud of smoke covering the isle prevented the captain to ascertain the battle situation on Whalsay. He could only assume the operation was going sideways. Otherwise, the troops would never choose to run the risk of being hit by friendly fire. The lake was so close to the lower trench that a stray shell might just as well plough into the Marines' line of defence, causing untold casualties. Mackworth shouted the order to bombard the loch in his speaking tube.

Fleming and his commando team were experiencing fierce opposition on the causeway. The musicians had dumped their instruments and attacked them with swords. Fleming shot several of them before putting his gun away and unsheathing his second sword. To his team's surprise, he vaulted over his nearest enemies' heads and landed somewhere between the fourth and fifth row, his swords a deadly whirr of steel. Remembering his opponents had two hearts, Fleming mainly went for the head and jugular. The Deep Ones were formidable fighters, but he was quicker, more agile. In a few seconds, he'd cut down six of them. Helped by the confusion Fleming had created, the Royal Marines pushed back the amphibians' first rows whereas he kept pressuring them from behind. The lack of space hindered the Deep Ones' movements, making them easier targets. Upon reaching the islet, Fleming avoided the narrow gate. Instead, he moved to the left intending to jump over the fort's low, ramshackle wall. Several torchbearers stood on the crumbling stones, barring his way. As his blade sliced through his first adversary's legs, toppling him off the wall, Fleming saw something huge rising from the Loch's surface.

If Rebecca had been present, she could have told him the creature resembled one of the largest echinoderms known to man. It looked exactly like a *Labidiaster Annulatus*, a horrifying starfish thriving in Antarctic waters. She'd have pointed out that it's one of the rare species of benthopelagic starfish, which means the animal doesn't merely sit on the sea bottom to hunt its prey but goes after swimming meals as well. It's known to reach a diameter of up to two feet and has over forty long, flexible rays seeded with *pedicellariae*, jaw-shaped pinchers used to trap its food. Only, this cousin of the *Labidiaster* family had a diameter of three hundred feet, and its *pedicellariae* were the size of bear traps. It was millions of years old and had lived in the Loch of Huxter from an early age. Its gigantic size prevented it from regaining the open sea via the narrow underground channels linking the Loch with the ocean.

Maybe it could reach the sea over land, but, somehow, it had never been keen to do so. The loch was teeming with brown trout, amply sufficient to sustain it. The Deep Ones made monthly sacrifices to the monstrous starfish, consisting of both fish and captured fishers who'd been so foolish to trawl these waters without paying tribute. Its solar shape convinced Dagon the creature was a fitting idol for the solstice festivals he was so fond of organising. The noise of the machine guns and the tremors caused by the bombardment had lured the animal to the surface.

As the starfish climbed on land, water sloshed over the islet, washing Wheeling clean off the altar. Both the amphibian warriors and Marines had difficulties keeping their balance in the swirling flood. Several flexible rays darted across the fort, their *pedicellariae* making snapping, metallic noises and picking off several Marines. Each time an arm caught its prey, it was lifted high into the air, the ray curving back to the animal's mouth on top of its central disk, and gobbled up in an instant. Fleming escaped two grabbing attempts by swiftly rolling towards the shelter of the fort's low walls. At the third try, he somersaulted over the sweeping starfish arm and cut off its tip with one of his swords. The Marines were desperately firing at the starfish with their handguns, and several Vickers machine guns from the lower trench took aim at the sea creature — all without visible result. That was the moment Major Rees decided to fire the blue flare.

The first shells fell short of their target, but the fifth and sixth hit the starfish's side that was still in the water, severing multiple arms. The seventh shell hit the animal's central disk. Although at first, the damage seemed minor, the monster thrashed about wildly, sweeping down the fort's remaining walls and hitting several Marines and fish-men with flying rubble. Fleming escaped the rain of stones and killed three more adversaries in the ensuing confusion. One ray came thundering down, missing Wheeling by a few feet but crushing another Marine. Fleming hacked furiously at the wriggling arm, only inflicting a couple of deep gashes that healed almost instantly. The HMS Hood continued its bombardment. One of the shells landed dangerously close to the lower trench, blowing up dozens of attacking fish-men. The starfish sustained several more hits before it retreated into the loch.

The lower-trench machine guns had dispatched the enemy army on the loch's banks. Only in and around the fort, intense fighting continued. Major Rees had sent in another forty soldiers to decide the battle. Then it became clear that the top trench was being overrun. Hundreds of armed Deep Ones stormed down the hill. The Marines turned a couple of machine guns around in time to stop the first wave of attackers dead in their tracks. Their initiative bought some time to direct even more firepower at the hillside. While the machine-gun fire was deadly effective and exacted a high toll on the enemy, wave after wave of fish-men kept stampeding down the slope. Soon, the Marines were engaged in savage hand-to-hand combat with the Deep Ones in the trench.

Four large amphibians had cornered Fleming; his back was to the wall next to the fort's gate. Fleming had received a massive blow to his left shoulder. Only the tough elfish chainmail underneath his battledress had prevented his arm from being sliced clean off. He'd lost one of his swords and drew a dagger instead. He parried several thrusts from his adversaries before piercing the upper arm of one of them with his knife. Fleming then had to let go of the short blade, rolled over the ground, slashing at another opponent's legs, and shoved his sword upwards into a third's abdomen. He blocked a blow from the remaining enemy with his left arm and hit him in the face with a right hook. The talons in his glove tore away half of the Deep

One's face. Fleming finished him off by thrusting his second dagger deep into the gilled throat. He collected both his swords and dagger and killed the fish-men he'd wounded in the arm and legs before staggering towards Wheeling.

The reinforcements sent over by Rees were finishing off the remaining resistance. They had cleared the fort's inside of all hostiles. The fighting in the lower trench was savage, but the defence held. The Marines done fighting on the banks of the loch ran back to assist their comrades at the foot of the hill.

Notwithstanding heavy casualties, the HMS Hood's crew gradually regained the upper hand in the fight on the ship's decks. They were no match for the Deep Ones in the hand-to-hand combats, yet capturing several 4-inch machine guns provided them with unassailable positions and resulted in significant enemy losses. The battlecruiser kept blindly bombarding both the lake and the plains behind the hill. Impenetrable smoke clouds covered a major part of the island.

In his cabin, Lagergren listened to the hectic battle sounds on the upper deck, sitting as if petrified on his bunk. His breathing was laboured. The gas mask stifled him, and he felt dizzy. He'd never been a man of action. Even standing in one of his Alma Mater's classrooms, facing maybe a dozen of students, had always felt like an ordeal. He took after his father, Gerthorn Lagergren, a scion of a wealthy family and a gifted poet in his own right. Gerthorn crafted the most exquisite Swedish translation ever of the Old Norse Poetic Edda but had always been too shy to show it to any publisher. His father's well-stocked library had been Lagergren's childhood paradise. It was a place that allowed him to dream, safely away from reality's daily cruelties and disappointments.

Eliassen's invitation to help him out with research work for the Swedish secret service had procured Lagergren immense joy. It involved long, solitary hours devoted to ferreting out facts from obscure manuscripts and occult tomes. However, accepting M's proposal to join Janus had been a dire mistake. M exuded a form of raw power and ruthlessness Lagergren felt unsettling. Although being with M always felt like an ordeal, Lagergren had to admit that the couple of field trips he'd made in the man's company had been more instructive than what he could ever have gleaned from his grimoires. The new knowledge he'd acquired working for Janus was a mixed blessing, however. The information shared by the Qohl'Hotl and the translation of the Outer Gods' glyphs prevented him from sleeping at night. Lagergren yearned to be back among his books in peaceful Gothenburg.

As Fleming wanted to check on Wheeling, who was lying face down next to the sacrificial stone, he saw a shimmering shape hovering between him and the artist.

'Fleming! What a nice surprise!' a familiar voice sounded in his head, giving him an instant migraine. 'You created quite a carnage among my good friend Dagon's soldiers. I like that, I truly do. It'll cut that miserable upstart back to size, and maybe, just maybe, it'll help to redeem yourself for the mess you left behind in the States. I'm surprised M let you stay on after that failure.'

'What do you want, Dream Whisperer?' Fleming gasped. 'You lost this battle; nothing is going to change that.'

'This was never *my* fight, you blockhead,' the sneering voice answered. 'I don't pit any troops of mine against your kind. Why should I? Humans are always eager enough to kill one another. We played a good game, you and I. I've never been closer to defeat, I must admit. I enjoyed the thrill, but we've reached the end now. You lost; your downfall was inevitable. I'm retaking possession of your body, and then I'll think of a nasty way to die for you.'

The spectral presence closed the gap separating it from Fleming. Fleming felt the hatred radiating from his adversary.

'How about letting you perish in the flames of your beautiful Glasgow office?' the voice in his head continued. 'That'd be fitting, wouldn't it? Then you can die in the same manner as that stupid bitch you married and that horrid, mewling spawn of yours. Perhaps I'll first let you kill that lovely Rebecca. You could never get under her skirts, could you? I can arrange that for you. Wouldn't you like that? I'm sure she can scream beautifully as well. And now I'll have you slice to ribbons that bleeding piece of excrement behind me. The bugger thought he was so clever he could imprison me forever in an oil lamp, didn't he? I'll see to it that his death is slow and painful.'

What could Fleming do? He'd been in precisely the same position, more than three years ago, in the basement of his Glasgow headquarters. Fleming felt powerless. This fiend was intimately familiar with him, knowing perfectly well how to hurt him. His words cut through him like so many knives. Fleming expected to be shoved aside in his body again, and he didn't doubt the Dream Whisperer would make sure that he consciously experienced every remaining instant of his miserable life.

'Yes, you got that right,' the mirthful voice in his head commented.

The diaphanous spectre slowly drifted towards Fleming, savouring his distress, its vaporous tendrils reaching out to its victim.

'Ready or not, here I come!' it giggled.

And then: Nothing happened. The ghostly appearance flew twice right through Fleming without connecting to his body at all. Fleming felt a detonation of blinding hatred and fury in his mind. The agony was excruciating; his head seemed to explode. A glacial current traversed his spine affecting every nerve ending. Surprisingly, he remained who he was, in full command of his body. As the pain ebbed away, Fleming was alone once more, sitting down among his enemies' corpses.

Wheeling was laying in a pool of blood. As Fleming turned him over, he saw the bleeding gash across the man's chest, the one inflicted on him by Dagon, and a deep cut to his forehead caused by falling off the altar. He also discovered to his dismay that, during the fight, Wheeling's abdomen had been torn open. His guts were spilling from his belly. Wheeling had lost so much blood he was barely conscious. Nevertheless, there was a faint smile on his lips when he looked up at Fleming.

'I got him good, the bastard,' he said in a whisper.

'Yes, you sure have,' Fleming answered soothingly.

'I was forced to set him free, you understand,' Wheeling pleaded remorsefully.

'Don't worry, I get it,' Fleming tried to set him at ease; he wasn't about to judge the man, knowing full well the extent of their enemies' cruelty.

'I had to undo the spell,' Wheeling continued with difficulty, 'but there were many aspects to the enchantment. I unpicked them one by one, leaving one in place — '

'Making sure the liberated Dream Whisperer couldn't possess another human being,' Fleming completed his sentence.

'Yes,' Wheeling agreed triumphantly. 'Yes, he can't interact with the physical world anymore — for the moment, at least. I'm sure he'll find a way, though.'

'You did great,' Fleming assured him. 'I owe you an enormous debt of gratitude, my friend.'

'I was a vain fool,' Wheeling confessed. 'Publishing that pamphlet. Stupid. Blinded by my ambition.'

'They would have found you anyway, it doesn't make a difference,' Fleming tried to comfort him.

As he uttered these last words, Fleming realised he was speaking to a dead man.

As he was closing the deceased's eyes, Fleming heard a high-pitched sound, well beyond human hearing range. He walked to the fort's gate to check whether the battle was still raging on and saw the remaining Deep Ones had abandoned the fight and were running away from the trench. Some ran back up the hill; others hurried towards the loch and jumped in the water. He counted no more than fifty enemy survivors. The bank was strewn with corpses, as was the stretch between the bank and the lower trench, and the hillside as well. He marched to the lower trench. The soil was soppy with blood and stuck to his boots. The ditch offered a grim spectacle of entangled dead Marines and amphibians. Fifteen men were still standing; they looked blankly at one another, totally exhausted. Rees was propped up against the trench wall. The major had sustained several injuries. He was bleeding from wounds to the head, right shoulder, and left leg but would survive.

'What happened?' Rees asked.

'I heard a whistle calling them back,' Fleming answered. 'They dropped everything and retreated at once.'

'How is your mate?'

'Dead.'

'Damn.'

Fleming took Rees' flare gun and fired a white flare. The bombardment stopped instantly.

'Do me a favour?' Rees asked.

'What?'

'I can't walk. Could you have a look at our boys in the trench up on the hill?'

Fleming nodded and trudged up the slope, knowing he was in for an ugly sight. When he reached the top, he found five Marines alive, all of them grievously wounded. He tried to tie off their worst injuries, aware that for at least two medical help would arrive too late.

The plain behind the hill looked like a lunar landscape. There wasn't a blade of grass left; the terrain was pockmarked with hundreds of craters. Thousands of bodies covered the flatland, from the foot of the hill all the way to the beach. It was Flanders' Fields all over again. Fleming fell retching to his knees.

When the machine guns stopped their rattle, Rebecca held her breath, anticipating that the fighting would recommence the next instant. As the silence endured, she cautiously lifted her gas mask and went to listen at her cabin's door. Rebecca couldn't hear a sound. She waited for another five minutes and then opened her door, Webley in hand. The corridor was empty. She knocked on Lagergren's door; there was no response. On the upper deck, the view was sickening, with mangled corpses everywhere. The captain and his officers had left the conning tower and were taking stock of the damage.

'I sincerely hope it was worth it,' Mackworth told her as he saw her pale, drawn face.

She couldn't meet his eyes. What on Earth could be worth a bloodbath like this? She looked at the island. It was shrouded in smoke. She imagined the situation was probably even worse over there. Why else would they've called for the ship's assistance?

'The radio is working again, Sir,' she heard a sailor tell the captain, who walked back to the conning tower.

Around noon, the medics had tended to most of the wounded on the ship. Two hundred and sixty-four sailors were dead, another one hundred and seventy-eight had been injured. The captain estimated eight hundred fishmen had fallen, the majority mown down by the ship's machine guns. A medical team set off to the island in a launch.

Lagergren still failed to show himself, and Rebecca became anxious for him. The captain sent down a couple of men with a cutting torch to his cabin. When they opened the door, Rebecca saw Lagergren sitting upright on the edge of his bed, wearing his gas mask. With a gasp of relief, she ran into the cabin and grabbed her colleague by the shoulders, telling him everything was all right. The professor fell over sideways on the bed. He'd suffered a heart attack during the fighting and died.

In the evening, Fleming and the other survivors returned to the ship. Only fifty-nine Royal Marines had survived the battle. Seventeen were in critical condition. After contacting the marine base at Scapa Flow, they decided to bury the fallen in the cemetery of Lyness. Estimations of the number of enemy casualties on the island ranged between ten and twelve thousand. Enormous flocks of sea birds had descended on the battlefield to feast on the Deep Ones' corpses. Fleming informed M of the outcome by telegram from the base in Lyness and he immediately sent his congratulations in return.

When Fleming met Rebecca, he was still in his blood-encrusted battledress, his face smeared with gore and dirt. He was worn out, hollow-eyed, and despondent. While grieving for Lagergren and Wheeling, Rebecca was happy to see him. They held each other tight.

'How are you?' she asked when they'd let go.

'Alive,' he answered with a shrug. 'That's about as much as one can hope for in this horror.'

'Wheeling and Lagergren had no such luck,' she commented.

Fleming shook his head.

'How could I've been so stupid to bring you and the old man along?' he sighed.

'We both wanted to be here. We wouldn't have missed it for all the gold in the world,' Rebecca reminded him. 'This is *not* on you.'

'Wheeling did great, though,' Fleming said and told Rebecca how the wizard had tricked the Dream Whisperer.

'What does that mean for us?' Rebecca wondered.

'As far as I can tell, it means the Dreamlands are operational again. Our enemy has regained his access to the human subconscious, but he can't physically interfere in our world. No more possessions, no cataclysms, no hands-on interventions,' Fleming pondered. 'He can still do plenty of damage from the Dreamlands, though, messing with people's minds. Anyway, Wheeling crippled him badly, no doubt about that.'

'That's wonderful news. I never thought we stood any chance at all against that monster. Did you?' Rebecca asked.

'No, I still have difficulties believing it,' Fleming confessed. 'Wheeling warned me it's probably only a reprieve, but I'll take what I can get.'

'How about Dagon?'

'I haven't seen him on the battlefield. He's apparently the type of general who safely stays far away from the front line. He lost more than ten thousand soldiers today. That must give him at least some pause for thought if he had any invasion plans. We showed him humans aren't helpless kittens.'

Fleming rubbed his tired eyes.

'Still, all those deaths — ,' he sighed. 'It sickens me to think about them. If we had dealt differently with all the other sentient species on our planet, we might have achieved a form of harmony that benefited everyone already ages ago. My grandmother used to call humans short-sighted egotists. This carnage is where that attitude has brought us — a mindless waste of lives. Blood calling for still more blood.'

'What I've seen of these other races in the past few years doesn't impress me either,' Rebecca countered. 'It's not as if *they*'re all enlightened altruists, are they? You said it yourself when you were telling me about the efforts your father undertook in India to reach a better understanding between humans and the *Devas* and *Asuras*. What did you call some of the local gods? Blowhards, wasn't it? You know what I think?'

'Enlighten me.'

'The principles of the theory of evolution apply to every species,' she pointed out. 'To survive, they all have to be adaptive, opportunistic, ruthless, and effective in the short term. These characteristics remain part of their make-up — however far they evolve. They'll always keep carrying around the equivalent of our reptilian brain. We can try to cover up our nature with thick layers of nurture and culture, but, deep down inside us all, without exception, the selfish beast keeps lurking, ready to lash out.'

58

Beyond the Mountains of Madness, Antarctica

Monday, 18 July 1921

The Antarctic truly was the last continent unex-plored by man. There'd been a frantic race to the geo-graphic South Pole right before the war. The Norwegian Roald Amundsen had won that competition, but neither he nor his competitors had unlocked the white continent's deepest secrets. The Dream Whisperer estimated it would take another ten to fifteen years before aeroplanes became sufficiently robust to cope with the terrible weather condi-tions in the Antarctic. When they did, humankind would be in for a surprise. The mainland contained mountain ranges that dwarfed the Himalayas, and that wasn't all. The most intrepid explorers would, sooner or later, find out that the oldest civilisation on Earth had once lived in these inhos-pitable climes. It had left behind a sprawling mega-polis, well-ensconced on an almost inaccessible plateau guarded by the forbidding Mountains of Madness. The Dream Whis-perer let himself be inspired by this barren land creating his plateau of Leng in the Dreamlands. These antediluvian beings preceded the Outer Gods' arrival by half a billion years. They were the real architects of life on Earth. The conflict between the two races had been fierce. The Elder Things weren't able to withstand the onslaughts of the

Outer Gods' dogs of war — mostly Cthulhu-like beings, specially designed for battle. Their society was even then already in decline. It was a showcase of how self-aware tools created by advanced bio-technology could destroy civilisation itself. Their vast, alien-looking city, with its bizarrely shaped buildings, was nothing but a ruin now. Its once-mighty occupants — the few of them who were left — were reduced to an almost feral state.

After the Outer Gods had defeated their rivals and annihilated the remains of the Elder Things' culture, they built a citadel on the mountains towering over the wasteland. Their peaks easily surpassed the Mountains of Madness in height. That was the Dream Whisperer's destination. Even in his immaterial form, it had taken him weeks to reach this unwelcoming place. The Outer Gods' ultimate stronghold was firmly entrenched in non-Euclidean space. It consisted of four weirdly intersecting, flat-topped pyramids that changed shape depending on the angle from which one looked at them. These central buildings were surrounded by a high, circular rampart, made of dark, plutonic rock. The sheer defensive wall, which reached far into the clouds, had no gates nor openings of any other kind. It hermetically sealed off the fortress.

The spectre ascended in the freezing air and entered one of the pyramids. At the centre of its great hall stood, encapsulated in rows of transparent containers, several types of creatures. They comprised three categories. First, there were octopus-like relatives of the Cthulhus in several shapes and forms. The largest one was the size of a fledgling Cthulhu. The smallest one, a spider-legged monstrosity with many tentacles, was no bigger than a border collie. The second type consisted of arthropod-like beings that varied from heavily armoured crustaceans to slender insect-like creatures with multitudes of feelers and other specialised appendages. The third one was a catch-all category that included dozens of nightmarish species that had nothing in common with anything living on Earth and were as thus almost indescribable. All of them were prototypes of artificial life created by the Outer Gods, each one serving a specific purpose. Their translucent vats could be transported into incomprehensibly complex bio-incubators, where their content could be 'read' and duplicated at will.

Upon entering the second hall, the Dream Whisperer heard the clicking of what sounded like hundreds of hefty, steel needles on the flagstone floor. The creature turning the corner belonged to the arthropod-like category of beings he'd observed in the previous hall. It was a twenty-five-foot-long myriapod. Its upright front-end resembled a praying mantis, whose multi-faceted eyes instantly took in the entire room without having to focus on any specific object inside it. From the upper-body, some thirty highly specialised appendages were waving. The lower ones were razor-sharp claws that could dismember a whale in minutes, the higher ones dainty instruments, designed for the most delicate tasks imaginable. The Swiss-knife millipede-mantis stopped a couple of feet away from the Dream Whisperer's ghostly avatar.

'Sli'ha'ni,' the creature greeted its visitor in a metallic voice.

'Greetings, Ulq'Ylleh,' the Dream Whisperer responded in the same language, projecting his thoughts to his host.

'Ulq'Ylleh' signified 'writer' and, in a broader sense, 'archivist' and 'recorder'. It was an artificial life form created by the Outer Gods. Unlike the dull-witted Cthulhus, it was a highly intelligent creature, single-mindedly devoted to its masters. The Dream Whisperer knew its loyalty wasn't to him but to those higher in rank that'd left the planet. It would be impossible to outwit this guardian of the keep. The Dream Whisperer braced himself for what was to come.

'It's recorded that the stars were aligned, yet the Gate was *not* opened. Our Lords won't be well pleased,' Ulq'Ylleh began matter-of-factly.

'Our Lords are forever dreaming, Ulq'Ylleh. Time means nothing to them,' was the Dream Whisperer's disingenuous reply.

'The lives of many Cthulhus were wasted in your half-hearted attempts to fulfil the task bestowed upon you,' was the next accusation.

'More Cthulhus have been destroyed over the aeons by the sheer forces of nature,' the wraith countered. 'There are plenty of them left to help me fulfil my brief at another opportunity. Anyway, you can always make more of them here.'

'A human reduced you to a phantom-like status. You've been defeated by the weakest of the weak. Even if your intentions were ever sincere, you are, by any definition, an abject failure,' the incriminations went on.

The Dream Whisperer was surprised by the extent of the guardian's knowledge. How closely had Ulq'Ylleh followed his antics?

'The once-weak humans grow stronger and smarter every day,' he repeated the argument he'd used earlier with Dagon. 'Soon, they'll discover your dwelling place and bomb it out of existence. They need to be destroyed before they definitively close the Gate to our Lords. *I* am the only one who can stem this tide. Help me or prepare to be washed away.'

The Dream Whisperer desperately tried to steer the conversation to his advantage. The threat against the citadel was a long shot, he knew. Human technology was centuries away from being able to endanger this age-old fortress. Still, it was worth a try. To Ulq'Ylleh, millennia were a mere heartbeat. It was the arthropod's mission to keep the stronghold safe until the Outer Gods' return. If it identified a threat against this shrine, however remote it might be, the guardian would be remiss in its duties not to act upon it.

'Bold words coming from one who failed so miserably at a much easier task,' his interlocutor mocked him.

'Humans will find an answer to whatever challenge we throw at them, but they are their own worst enemy. As they grow stronger, their capacity for self-destruction also increases. I'll set them at each other's throats, and they'll rip themselves to pieces.' the Outer God argued.

'What do you need from me, silver-tongued spectre?'

'I need you to let me drink at Yog-Sothoth's Source to restore my powers.'

Ulq'Ylleh waited a long time before replying. The Dream Whisperer heard its appendages clicking while it was thinking over his request.

'Very well, Dream Whisperer. You know the consequences. The Source will restore you only once, and there's always a price to be paid. Always.'

'Thank you, Ulq'Ylleh, you won't regret this.'

'I know no regret, but *you* might learn yet.'

The millipede guided him to another room, deeper in the building. It was a round hall. The walls were covered with opaque glass, shaped into innumerable different-sized globes. Behind the glass was a light source that varied in intensity, causing the orbs to take on a life of their own. In the middle of the floor was a circular basin, with what appeared to be crystal-clear water. The arthropod curled itself around the pool and intoned a chanted prayer:

'Yog-Sothoth,
Guardian of the Gate,
All-Knowing, All-Seeing, All-Understanding,
Your servant, who holds the Key to the Gate,
humbly asks Your support to restore his strength.

Please, permit him to drink from Your Source.'

Ulq'Ylleh repeated the prayer over and over until the water became effervescent. Then the archivist retired to the next room and left the Dream Whisperer alone.

The wraith waited at the bubbling pool's edge and then reluctantly glided in. Inside the viscous liquid, the Dream Whisperer felt surrounded by the illusion of ghostly globes, which opened and closed like so many eyes. Yog-Sothoth was a being who existed outside time and space, infinitely powerful, omniscient. If Ulq'Ylleh had given him a hard time, the Dream Whisperer knew the real test was still to come. As the orbs were swirling around him, he sensed a new presence. An instant later, a message was carved in his mind, as with a red-hot sculpting knife:

> *'I am the Gate.*
> *I am Past, Present and Future, All in One*
> *I am the All-Seeing Eyes of the Gods*
> *The-One-Who-Cannot-Be-Deceived.'*

Although technically, the Dream Whisperer was a ghost, nothing could have convinced him he was incorporeal. The pain he'd experienced while being pried loose from Fleming's body was in no way comparable with the agony he was going through at this instant. The fluid held him like a glove made of molten lava.

> *'You have proven yourself unworthy.*
> *You are the lowest of the low.*
> *There is no place for you anymore in Our ranks.'*

The fist in the glove was crushing his brittle, imaginary bones. The searing heat peeled the bubbling skin off his virtual body. His eyes were boiling in his skull. He wanted to scream, but his tongue seemed to have melted in his throat.

'You are hereby stripped of all honours and responsibilities.
You are the Key no longer.
You are banished from Our Race.
When the Gate opens – and open It will, without your intercession –
You shall be the first to be devoured by My Spouse Shub-Niggurath.
You shall be held captive in a single instant of eternal torture.'

The horror was unsurpassable. The notion that this was only a foretaste of perpetual punishment was ripping his sanity to shreds. Never had he felt as puny as in this instant. All the Dream Whisperer wanted was the pain to stop. His mind was a total throbbing blank.

'Now, begone.
Live out the remainder of your time until Our return.'

Suddenly the agony subsided. The voice had gone silent; the eyeballs had disappeared, and the Dream Whisperer was drifting alone in the cool liquid. Leaving the pool, he noticed his ectoplasm's contours were more crisply defined. He'd been restored to his previous powers.

Ulq'Ylleh was waiting for him at the rim of the basin.
'Do you still believe it was worth it, Dream Whisperer?' the arthropod asked.
The Dream Whisperer ignored the guardian's dripping sarcasm.
'Certainly,' he answered as if it was a foolish question to ask and drifted towards the exit without further acknowledging Ulq'Ylleh's presence.

The confrontation in the pool had made him realise he'd never have escaped Yog-Sothoth's attention anyway. Now at least, he could have himself some more fun in the years left to him. And that could be a very long while, since his kind counted time in aeons. He'd been in tight spots before. He'd find a way to wriggle out of this one as well. In the meantime, he wouldn't make it any easier on his tormentor to return without his help. He looked back at the forbidding citadel on the mountain.

His next step would be to call a piece of space detritus from the heavens, he decided. Destroying the citadel and the alien city below was the logical thing to do. He had no use for the Outer Gods' stronghold anymore. As far as he was concerned, it had served its purpose. However, he didn't want to allow Ulq'Ylleh the opportunity to churn out five new Cthulhus behind his back and have them open the gates for his vengeful kin. All he had to do was wait until a suitable comet or meteoroid swung by close enough to Earth. Then he'd give it a little nudge to help it come crashing down with surgical precision. He knew the drill. He'd done it before. Only, he'd have to be careful this time not to select a rock sizeable enough to wipe out all trace of life on Earth. Humans were so entertaining. It would be a shame to let all that potential go to waste.

Epilogue

The news about the Whalsay massacre spread fast in the alien marine communities. Dagon had been a much-feared tyrant, and other ocean dwellers looked at him with distrust because of his ambitious nature. Events on Whalsay demonstrated two facts to his competitors. Firstly, Dagon had built a vast army to implement his world-domination schemes. Secondly, humans were perfectly capable of withstanding and even defeating Dagon's horde. This realisation fundamentally changed the way several aquatic species perceived humankind almost overnight. They remained convinced humans were obnoxious upstarts whose interests were far from aligned with theirs. Still, if these arrivistes could put a halt to Dagon's hunger for power, they were worth talking to, was the general reasoning. A few species decided to choose the lesser of two evils and reached out to Fleming to come to an understanding.

Manann made the first move. During the Iron Age, the Celts worshipped Manann as a sea deity. His traditional power base was the Irish Sea, although his influence reached as far as Scotland, the Outer Hebrides, and the Orkneys. Dagon's bellicose activities in his back-yard convinced Manann to contact Fleming. After a few discrete meetings, they agreed Manann would monitor Dagon's efforts to rebuild his troops. In exchange, Fleming promised to help with harsh retaliation if need be.

M and Fleming celebrated the new pact at M's club. It was the first such agreement the British had concluded in many a year, and they expected several others would follow soon. The two men were savouring an excellent Warre & Co's 1868 vintage port, accompanied by a beautifully ripened Stilton cheese, after a satisfying supper.

'*Divide et impera* is a strategy that has served Britain well for a long time, and we'll also benefit from it in this particular situation,' M lectured. 'Instead of trying to fight one's enemies on all fronts, it's much better to let them focus their attention on one another. Skilfully balancing the powers that be in such a way that none of them ever have the clear upper hand will keep our adversaries on their toes. They'll forever remain suspicious of one another while we can do as we please. Britain will always support the weaker rivals to tip the scales against the more powerful, helping to establish a fragile equilibrium. If we can conclude a few more treaties with Dagon's other foes, it will check his expansion designs. We'll prevent him from reconstituting an army that might become strong enough to invade our cities and trample our civilisation underfoot.'

'I'm afraid, M, this evening isn't all about good news,' Fleming told his boss, reaching into his vest pocket. 'Yesterday, I found this in my mail.'

He handed M a postcard. It showed a painting of a vast hall with a sumptuously decorated barrel-vaulted ceiling. The place was filled with happy, beer-drinking people, sitting at long, broad tables.

'*München, Hofbräuhaus am Platzl, Festsaal,*' M deciphered the tiny letters at the bottom of the card, before flipping it over.

On the back, he read on:

My dear Fleming,

As we have shared so much lately, I write you this little note to let you know all is well with me. I have fully recovered from my brief indisposition during our last meeting. Also, I am thrilled to tell you I have recently tied the knot with the most delightful creature. The future looks bright!

With great affection,

DW

In Munich, a physically unimpressive individual stepped on the beer hall's podium in the *Hofbräuhaus.* He sported a Charlie Chaplin moustache and parted his dark hair to the left. The man adjusted his tie and gave a sharp tug at his brown shirt with a red-black-and-white armband before addressing a meeting of the *Nationalsozialistische Deutsche Arbeiterspartei* or NSDAP. A crowd of two thousand — many of them hostile to the speaker — filled the room. Knowing full well the evening would inevitably end in violence, he'd warned his SA-henchmen that tonight would test their mettle. He looked defiantly at the crowd and then launched into an hour-and-a-half-long speech. There was a slight red flicker in his eyes, which was only discernible from the first rows in the audience.

Printed in Poland
by Amazon Fulfillment
Poland Sp. z o.o., Wrocław

61986079R00334